The Moonlight Pegasus

SECOND EDITION

C. A. Sabol
&
C. S. Johnson

THE MOONLIGHT PEGASUS

For anyone who has a special dream.

Also dedicated with much affection to the Rhodes family:
Jeff, Kelly, Douglas, Gretta, and Carson. Especially Jeff, who
gave me constant encouragement through his words, dreams
through his songs, and fatherly love throughout our time
together. I love you. I thank God so much for you all.

For the second edition, I would like to add Evan onto the
previous list, as well as my own special son and daughter. My
mother in particular is also worthy of a special thanks. Time
has passed, and my appreciation for families has grown, as
mine been my support system, a comfort and refuge in times
of trouble. I can only hope I will carry on the legacy I have
been given.

THE MOONLIGHT PEGASUS

To Get *Awakening* (A Special Christmas Episode of The *Starlight Chronicles*) as a bonus for picking up this book,

Click Here

Or Download It At:
https://www.csjohnson.me/awakening

THE MOONLIGHT PEGASUS

AUTHOR'S NOTE ON THE 2016 SECOND EDITION

Dear Reader,

It seems as though a lifetime has passed since I set about writing this work, back when I was struggling in high school and working two jobs. I remember those cold nights, where I would work on this manuscript in the front seat of my car in the parking lot of one job, my computer pressed up against the steering wheel and my feet sore from my hard shoes. Watching my breath warm the windshield against the winter months. Waiting for inspiration to strike as the clock counted down on my break time.

Maybe it is because I remember it so well that it seems hard to believe that nearly ten years have passed since its publication, originally by Publish America (Now American Star Books) in 2007. But here I am, having graduated high school as well as college and graduate school, now married with children in a new town and almost a nearly new life.

There have been some things that haven't changed, however, despite all that did happen.

The presence and realness of God is still there, as is the battle inside me. Some days I struggle with how far he seems, and other days he is still so real I feel like I could wake up and see him, standing over my bed, his hand on my brow, as a peaceful, loving father keeping watch over me.

The Moonlight Pegasus was inspired by a number of things, as these things usually are. At fifteen, when I began writing this, I was in love with the idea of warfare, having no real experience with it. And I was—am—in love with the idea of falling in love, finding the arms outstretched and ready to catch me as soon as I let go of fear. I was also in love with

TV more than I'd like to admit as an adult, and reading, which I will gladly boast of. Reading through this again, I can still see many of my favorite things in here, which have a special nod in this work. Of course, "Footprints" remains in its special place, right at the beginning, but there are others, as well.

Part of the reason I have kept my C. A. Sabol name as the author of this work is a nod in itself; the girl who wrote this has grown up and found the world much less to her liking than she'd ever thought in some cases, and much more pleasantly surprising in others. I think my younger self would be if not proud, at least understanding to some of my choices, and very happy with the results of others. She would have been relieved on many levels to find someone who loved her enough to want to marry her. (You might see some of that desperation reflected in some of my characters.) The movement from innocent faith to virtuous faith, the change from being an idealist to a failed idealist and moving onto a redeemed idealist, is a battle where simple several choices, over and over and over again, have made all the difference.

It was nothing to hope for a bright future as a child; it is painstakingly intentional now that I am an adult.

But with new experiences, there have been several good ones as well as troublesome. Getting my degree, working in the public and private sectors, writing more, getting married and starting a family, and moving—several, several times moving—have all taught me my hope is not unwarranted. I think of Paul's words: "Though sorrow may last for a night, joy comes with the morning."

While this book might seem to be from a lifetime ago, I know the time that has passed is really nothing in eternity.

THE MOONLIGHT PEGASUS

It is my hope that you will enjoy Selene's journey with her friends and faith as I did—as one who grows up and finds the things that truly matter were always there. I also hope you will hang onto till the very end for a sample chapter of my newer work, *Slumbering* (Book 1 of The Starlight Chronicles), where you'll see some of that growing I did, going from C. A. Sabol to C. S. Johnson. I also hope you'll check out some of my other, more recent work. While I am grateful to *The Moonlight Pegasus* for allowing me to have my first adventure in the world of publishing, I am glad and grateful for the growth in writing and experience I have obtained since then. I'd love to keep up and keep writing for you, my dear reader.

Until We Meet Again,

C. A. Sabol Johnson

One night a man had a dream …

~ From "Footprints"

THE MOONLIGHT PEGASUS

***

Prologue
***

There had been a time, once long ago, when all dreams had been beautiful.

The One above looked down from his eternal sitting at his creation, his most beloved dream, below. The planet Sapphira hung in a small corner of the universe, its sea swept lands home to a small population of humans. The shining blue of the waters reflected the light of the bright sun into the far reaches of the surrounding space.

This one who had dreamed all of this for good now saw that the evil he had tried to expel many millennia ago was slowly beginning to take over the Sapphiran sands.

Though this one has many names, to his world he was known as the Guardian of Dreams. His heart was heavy and sad; his crystal eyes were a clear reflection of his thoughts as he saw his world begin to die. He had known that this day would come. He had known that it had only been a matter of time before his world would fall prey to the Dark Plague.

Watching Sapphira fall into the looming darkness, the Guardian of Dreams saw his own kingdom grow apart from the darkened world below. He looked around to see that the lushness of his home, known as the Guardian's Kingdom, Crystallon, had almost seemed to dim, as though the very poison of his beloved Sapphira had managed to pierce through. But he knew that it was not so; the people of Sapphira had begun rejecting the light, creating a deep chasm between the spotlessness of Crystallon and the impurity of Sapphira.

1

THE MOONLGIHT PEGASUS

The sickness spreading on the land below was one that took root easily in human hearts. The Plague multiplied without struggle, surrounding and dividing love's pure light between the humans of the world. Encompassing all those gifted with the Guardian's love in a shell of darkness, the light that radiated from the bright sun below scattered, binding only in small portions to each of the people below. Sapphira's glittering landscape, her crystal oceans and desert lands, speckled with dots of green foliage and rocky terrain, grew dull and dreary with the onslaught of the Plague's shadow.

It was similar to watching the stars come out at the end of a bright, happy day. No one would want to see the end of such a day. The approaching night would be long.

The light of dreams below dimmed and turned black as the darkness knifed throughout the land.

The Guardian's heart wrenched as the dreams steadily faded, growing dark. He knew that the world below could not hear him, could not be with him, without knowing the light. He also knew that he could not let Crystallon be contaminated with the Plague. Though he knew that there would come once again the light of day, the Guardian despaired at the thought of losing his children. The people of Sapphira could not accept this evil sickness, if they were to join him one day in his kingdom. But they could so quickly succumb to the Plague into giving up their light for the thought of power. The Guardian thought about it.

But now was not the time. There was one way to dispel the darkness. There was only one way to save his people. With the Light of Hope would all the dreariness be consumed. And only would the Light go forth into the world when the night was at its blackest, at its most impervious point.

The Guardian looked down. There would be those he blessed with a joyous glow, who would keep the light hidden in their hearts. From them would come the one who would give the Light of Hope an entrance into the world of night.

There would be a fulfillment of time in the world of man, and the Guardian would make it so; but for now, he watched as his world fell into the hands of the traitor.

"Obsidian," he murmured to himself. "What have you done?"

3

THE MOONLGIHT PEGASUS

***
Chapter 1
The Beginning of the End
***

It had been a tradition, for as far back as human minds could remember, for the Kings of Sapphira to live and rule in the palace of Diamond City. It was a tradition so deeply rooted in time, nobody really wanted to dig it up. So it was here in Diamond City that the royal family resided.

The city was named for the sparkling waterfall that flowed out of the stream located at the highest point of the city. Legend said that when the Desert people had first seen the magnificent landscape, it looked just like a diamond; the sunlight reflected off the water, creating a dazzling pathway, flowing down straight into the present Gemstone Oasis. And it was at night that Shira, one of the two small moons that encircled the world, would cast a silver glow on the entire area.

Despite the several thousands of years since the habitation of the planet by man, the city failed to reflect the complete advancement of current times. Looking around, there was nothing too special about the city, except for the palace. There were no skyscrapers, no soaring towers; instead, there were hovels for houses, stone buildings, and streets inlaid with patterns of old-style bricks. Citizens often remarked how the abundance of trees and plant life in the city caused an unwanted variety of vectors and insects to settle around, but not one of them could stand the thought of tearing down the trees or uprooting the flowers to put in a multi-dimensional skyscraper complex. Sapphira at heart was a world of water and sands; there was only one large landmass, simply called the Continent, on the whole planet, and a variety of islands that sprawled all around. From space, the tiny, sand-covered isles looked like small necklace chains throughout the seemingly endless oceans and seas. And it was only in Diamond City that, located on a high plateau and several slanting hills, the earth could reach high enough in the atmosphere to support plant growth as lushly as it managed. The large green leaves provided shade in the almost constant desert land, the many blooming flowers adding a sweet scent to the courtyards throughout the city, and the monsoon phenomenon that occurred every sixth season drew many of the Desert people to the city every year.

It was on the highest area of the city's plateau that the Palace of Diamond City sat. This area, located in the very heart of the city, was often referred to as the Table. The Table was an appropriate name for the plateau, many people thought, because the palace looked like a twinkling centerpiece. The palace was more a large building, made out of a strong granite mineral that shimmered a deep red in the noon sunlight; there were four towers, reaching high into the air. The keep was extensive, and the building also had many additional wings and courtyards, where study and entertainment could take place. The castle was old, and thought to be built by the ancients. It had sunk into the scenery as naturally as though it had sprouted from a planted seed, at harmony with the nature all around it. There were even special vines with tiny moonflowers growing up around the four towers of the castle. At night, when it was dark, the flowers shone brilliantly with an inner luminescence, adding an eerie, yet magical glow to the castle. The palace's unique design had been silently set as the standard for which all buildings around it in the city were to be measured.

The rooms of the palace were elegantly made. Seeing the foliage as a rarity, the kings of olden days had filled the palace with many plants, not just in the greenhouses but all around. Many eloquent features of the rooms were also attributed to the golden lining, the extensive woodworking, and the many exquisite paintings and chandeliers. Out of all these rooms, however, the most grand was that of the Throne Room.

The Throne Room was based just atop the waterfall; the muffled sound of running water was constantly pouring in through the high, arched windows, especially during the monsoon season. The floor, reaching two hundred yards in length, was interrupted every so often with a tree root sticking up, adding to the charm of the room. The floor was made of smooth, blended green and blue sapphire marble, resembling a large, calm pool of water. There were ornate decorations hanging from the ceiling, and sculptures placed wistfully around the room. However, these things were nothing compared to the main focus of the room, which happened to be the throne itself.

There was a very old tree that had grown up in the middle of the river. Those who had built the palace had been just as afraid as modern citizens to cut down a tree, so they had merely built the palace around it. The branches of the tree seemed to add support to the ceiling, and several stray limbs provided excellent hanging structures during a festival or a celebration. Sometimes the branches, if they received enough light from the large windows, out of them blossomed small, pink flowers. But it was the very trunk of the tree that caught the eye and held it. At the base of the trunk, it was there was the magnificent throne seat had been made. Some generations ago, having seen the tree as a symbol of power, strength, and endurance, the king at the time had ordered that a throne be carved out of the willowy trunk. Eight large, stately white columns, made out of the smoothest marble

THE MOONLGIHT PEGASUS

stone stood proud and tall, outlining the splendor of the area in front of the throne.

It was here on this throne that the present King of Sapphira, King Lukiahs, presently sat. He was a man of many years, and his body was deteriorating more and more as the days and months went by. His silver hair, once colored brilliant ebony, had turned almost white over the long years. Though he sat on his comfy, well-cushioned throne, his back was aching, and despite all the treatments and pills, his skin was full of wrinkles. He had been a strong ruler in his day, his eyes full of fire and his sword held with steady hands. But lately, the once shining green eyes had grown listless and weary; the complexion of his skin, typically luminous as all royalty was, had faded to the point that when the public saw him, he had to be painted in a thin coat of moonflower chemicals to match up to his reputation. His weak wrinkled hands were shaking all the time, and he felt his body grow tired and susceptible to the eventual coming of his final twilight years. Today, he had been dressed in his most decorated robes, adding an illusion of power and strength that no longer could be produced involuntarily.

But it was not this that he was sad at. He felt tired now, but he knew he could not sleep. He had been having a strange dream of late, and he could not rest without knowing what it could possibly mean. King Lukiahs was not one to be foolish, despite his age. And he was worried.

He'd heard the rumors of the rebellion. He'd heard them all. He'd heard about how the people off of the Continent were unhappy and unsatisfied with his rule. He'd heard about the spies that had been sent to the palace. He'd heard all of the stories of the Islanders attacking the Desert people and pilfering their villages. He'd even seen some locals at the

THE MOONLGIHT PEGASUS

Gemstone Oasis fighting about it at the Waning Moonshine, a popular bar and hangout for the middle class people of Diamond City. His biggest fear, besides becoming the first King in history to be killed by an army of rebels, was that his dream, or rather his nightmare, might have something to do with it.

There was a soft sound at the end of the room. King Lukiahs looked up to see his most trusted advisor, the high priest Jerommien, making his way over to him.

"Your Majesty," Jerommien greeted hastily, "I bring word of both good news and bad news to you today."

"Jerommien, we are friends," the King responded. "You are my most trusted advisor. We can do away with the formalities here."

Despite the burden of bad news, the high priest smiled slightly. "All right, we'll do things your way, Your Maj—I mean, Lukiahs."

"Naturally." The king and Jerommien both laughed. Of course things would be done according to the king's preference, no matter how outlandish or untraditional it was. The king hated to use formalities with his friends, so they did not use them. It was as simple as that.

When the laughter died away, the amusement left the priest's face as he said, "I have a report from Major General Rosemont. He says that the forces of the Rebels have grown in recent weeks and are potentially a threat to you and your family."

The king sighed. "So, this is a threat now. Those islanders should be grateful for all I've done for them. Free passages across the seas, less taxes, and all that technology given to them … why are they so intent on being difficult about this?" With saying this, his eyes seemed to grow even more tired, and his skin grew duller, almost like a normal human now.

"I'm sorry, Luke. There are so many unusual people out there. But on the brighter side, I do have some good news for you."

"That's a relief," the king muttered, his voice dripping with scorn. He straightened up in his seat, not without some difficulty, and sighed. "Tell me what it is."

Jerommien's eyes glittered in anticipation. He knew the king would be pleased with this information. "Your Majesty, we have found another man who has claimed to be able to interpret your dream."

The King threw back his head and laughed, a cruel undertone clearly coming through. "Really, do not bother me with such nonsense today, Jerommien. I am already upset enough. What makes you think that this man will be any different from the last forty men that tried to tell me about my dream? Did you find him on some physic hotline or something? Or did you find another cult running around my planet that has a specialty on this sort of thing?"

"No, My Liege, I did not. You know as well as I have that I have been making secret inquires, and those who have failed to give you a satisfactory explanation for your dream are all imprisoned until you are fully, and correctly, informed. He came walking normally as you please up to the castle doors, the doors that enter into my wing, and said that he had been

THE MOONLGIHT PEGASUS

sent here by the Guardian himself to interpret your dream, and he could prove it."

"Oh, no! Do you not know that there are spies in this castle? No doubt everyone's heard about me by now!" the king wailed. He stood up, rather suddenly for a man of his age, and slammed his fist angrily onto his throne's arm. "I will not see him, do you hear? The last thing I need is for some rebel spy telling me that I'm going senile, and that it's time for the monarchy to either end or be passed along to Prince Dorian, though he's only eight years old!"

"Luke, I think you should see him," Jerommien spoke up a little shakily. He was not used to defying the king's wishes too often. He was not even used to the King disagreeing with him. "He told me that you would say exactly that, even before you said it. I told him he was crazy for even thinking that you, at your age, and one of your quiet temperaments, would go into a rage such as that. But I see now he was right. I have a feeling he was telling the truth."

"Ha! An unlikely tale!" but the King's voice faltered slightly, betraying his shock and sudden case of doubt. The King did trust his priest. Jerommien had been with him since his father the previous king had died, and Jerommien had always given sound advice. Why would he falter now? There was little but time to be lost in hearing this man out.

They were both quiet for a long moment before the king let out a deep sigh.

"Sir?" Jerommien took a cautious step toward his king. He knew that the king was not himself when he was angry. Jerommien knew he had to tread lightly here.

The King rubbed his temples in exasperation. "Fine, I'll see him. But, Jerommien, if he tells me that I'm overexerting myself and worried about the coming of war on my planet, like all the others, I'm going to hang every one of those so-called dream interpreters in my prison and I will personally see to it that you are exiled to a faraway island for a good number of days."

The high priest grinned. They both knew that the King was only half-serious. Jerommien had never once been punished for anything. The king had always valued his advice and most of the time carried it through, unlike his threats.

"I'll send him up, Your Majesty," Jerommien said, bowing and hurriedly walking to the fetch the man waiting in the priest's office.

"I won't tell you again, Jerommien, it's Lukiahs!" the King yelled after his friend.

He watched as the high priest left the room. Another sigh escaped him as he sat down once again in his throne. He grinned ruefully. It seemed lately all he did was sigh.

A moment later, a viewscreen appeared out of the right armrest of the throne, and the lovely face of his young wife, the Queen, appeared.

"Your Majesty," she whispered in reverence to her husband. This was not the same Queen who had given birth to his only child and son, Prince Dorian. Queen Kaena was a relatively new addition to his household, his second wife.

The King smiled warmly at her, even though he was stressed out. "Yes, my dear?" he responded. "Everything okay?"

"Oh, yes, everything is quite lovely," the queen assured him, a smile beginning to show just slightly on her face. "I wanted to make sure that you were feeling okay. You did promise me earlier that you would accompany me for a stroll in the new gardens today."

He gave her a blank look. "Oh, I did?" the king asked, a little surprised. "I'm terribly sorry, Kaena, I'm in a meeting right now. Once I am finished with this one, I will come and join you. How is that?"

Her eyes dropped and her smile faded. She was young yet, only about twenty-one years old. They'd been married for only a short while. King Lukiahs had been coerced into marrying once again at the word of his persistent advisors. They had warned him of only having one heir to his throne. Prince Dorian was a strong child, the King knew, but Dorian also, like most boys his age, tended to be somewhat reckless. And that was dangerous. So the king had agreed, and the councilors, instead of picking an older, more experienced woman to marry him, had chosen Kaena, a young woman with no notion of the world and no will of her own. She was so timid and delicate in her appearance as well as her manner. How she carried herself often caused him to think that she would break into millions of pieces if she fell over.

"Kaena?" the king asked. "Are you well?" The king, though he did not feel great love for his new wife, he shared some level of small affection for Kaena, and did not wish to see her upset or sick. He also did not want the council members breathing down his neck at his wife's poor health.

Her eyes met his once again. King Lukiahs would often remark that Kaena had the most beautiful eyes he'd ever seen, a golden brown color that enchanted in him thoughts of gold-speckled leaves in the Resting season. "I am fine, My Liege. Thank you for asking. I will await you in the Luxury Garden Hallway." She bowed once more, and then the viewscreen flickered and died.

He frowned at the thought of his new wife just then. She was a nice commodity around here, but she could be entirely depressing and uninteresting sometimes, he thought. Well, maybe she still was not accustomed to being here. She had only just arrived a couple of months ago.

His thoughts turned away from his wife all at once as the door to the throne room once again opened, and the king saw that Jerommien had returned with an unfamiliar face in tow. King Lukiahs saw this man, following along behind the over eager Jerommien with footsteps of steady patience.

The man was old, like himself, but Lukiahs got the feeling that this man was no one to take lightly due to age. The evidence of a hard, though blessed, life shown on his dark face, as though an extra light was shining on him. He wore the robes of a common man, long and simply cut, and a dark green in color. He had a long, white beard drizzled with gray, and his eyes were buried beneath thick, full, striking white eyebrows. He wore no hat to hide his balding head, and his hands seemed to hold onto each other as he made his way to the King. Everything about him seemed humble, but at the same time, he seemed to exude an unnaturally high amount of wisdom and confidence in himself.

"Your Majesty," his voice rumbled deeply as he bowed low. "I am honored to meet you."

"Rise," King Lukiahs waved him off. As the man rose from his bowing position, the king continued with the formal preceding. "I am King Lukiahs, son of King Gammias. I welcome you into my home."

The man bowed once again. "I am known to many as the Prophet Haiasi. I have been told from a reliable source, Your Majesty, about your troubled dream. I have come by his command to your aid."

"Really? Who is it that has sent you?" the King asked, a little interested in who it was that had leaked out the information. He doubted that this man, this Haiasi, would tell him who it was that had sent him, not wanting to appear to be a fraud, but the King prided himself on the ability to tell when men were lying. Ninety-nine times out of a hundred, it was easy for Lukiahs to see through a lie.

"I have been sent by the Guardian of Dreams, sir."

"Preposterous," the King scoffed, though he could not detect a trace of deceit in the man's tone. "I do not believe it."

Haiasi looked away. "I know you do not, Sir, and that is precisely why I have been sent to tell you of your dream."

His words had struck a chord in the King. The resounding notes sang a tremor of doom throughout his mind. King Lukiahs had kept the family tradition of having the priests around, but he himself had long ago given up in believing in the power of dreams. What were dreams but illusions of reality? What good would they do for someone like him, who was king over the entire world?

The Prophet Haiasi stood before him with a look of patience on his aged face. There was a mien to his features, suggesting that he knew along which lines the king was thinking. "Tell me about your dream, sir. I will interpret it for you."

Normally, at the thought of doom, King Lukiahs would've sent this joker away and dismissed him without a thought. But seeing the eager look on Jerommien's face, the King decided that he would listen to this Haiasi, and then send him away as quickly as possible. It was after all, the diplomatic thing to do.

"Well," the king began, somewhat slowly, "I have been having this dream of late, and I think it is trying to tell me something. In this dream, I am standing on the coast, and I see this black wave forming in the distance in the ocean … but the unusual thing is, the darkness of it seems to be pouring from the sky, almost from a box. It rises up very high, and blocks out all the grayness of the sun. I can hear in the distance a horse, but I cannot see it. I can only see the wave blocking out the sun. And that's when I hear a different noise. It sounds like crying. And that's when blood begins to run out from the sun, and run with the waves. I see myself reach down and taste the water, and I can actually taste the saltiness of tears. After that, everything fades as a bright incredible light, golden and nearly blinding, begins to shine. There are two shadows in it, one of a boy and the other a girl. They are holding onto each other. Then the girl suddenly turns away, and almost disappears into the light before she grabs a hold of the boy. Then the light shines, much brighter than the sun, blocking them out, and the last thing that I can remember is thinking that I have died."

The prophet nodded. "I have seen this dream as well. You were right in assuming that the red liquid was blood. A lot of blood, indeed … " his voice trailed off. "King Lukiahs, son of Gammias, there is to be a prophecy made today. One of your offspring shall be born at the hands of night's shadows. At that time, there will be much blood shed indeed, and many tears will be cried. The end of our time of sickness is approaching. We shall be cleansed when the Spirit brings forth the one who will save us and lock away the darkness with his blood." Haiasi looked intently at the king as he continued. "When a pure princess marries, peace will be restored to this kingdom at last."

"What?" the King looked at this man as though he was speaking a foreign language. "I do not believe this."

At this, Haiasi's voice grew strong and full of anger. "You have turned away from your roots, King Lukiahs. You will suffer the penalty. The sickness in you has grown over the years. When all your inner light fades into nothing, the passing of the crown will occur."

Even Jerommien looked at Haiasi with disbelief. "What do you mean, 'inner light'? I don't understand."

Haiasi's eyes turned to focus on the high priest. "I know you do not. But it would be like explaining to a child what it cannot grasp; I myself do not always understand. But I have faith that I shall know one day."

Jerommien and the King still looked dumbstruck at his words. "A 'passing of the crown'?" the King asked. "It doesn't mean that I shall be overthrown, does it? And what's this about a child? I am too old to have a child. I have been tested by the best medical doctors on this entire planet, and it has been proved that I have no longer the capabilities to reproduce."

"You do not have the capabilities to see past yourself, either," the Prophet shook his head sadly. "Your world is all about you. You can no longer see the light, nor can you spread it. You will gather up your glow that is left and hold tightly to it, but eventually you will suffocate it in your grasp and kill it."

The King was angry now. "You have some nerve, saying these things to the King of this entire planet!"

"You forget that I have been called here by the one who has made this entire planet!" Haiasi's voice echoed throughout the room, followed by a moment of deafening silence. His eyes softened as he saw the startled look on the faces of Jerommien and the King. His voice quieted as he continued. "A dream once dreamt cannot be undreamt. And a dream once corrupted cannot be saved until the dream once again knows purity, just as a crooked line cannot be called crocked unless there is an idea of a straight line."

"What's this about lines now?" the King looked from Haiasi to Jerommien and back to Haiasi in utter confusion.

Haiasi sighed. The King was not following him at all. "You have been warned, King Lukiahs. Mark my words, by the end of today, you will know who is in control of your destiny!" At this, the King felt his anger and impatience get the better of his judgment at last.

"Get out! Get out now!" King Lukiahs threw himself out of his chair and pointed angrily at the door. "I demand that you leave at once, Prophet! Do not think of coming back here. You will only come back at my biding, and I can guarantee that will never happen!"

Haiasi bowed once more, and then turned to leave. His steps were still slow and full of patience. Lukiahs kept his gaze on Haiasi's plain figure until he was at last out of the room.

When the prophet was at last gone, the King slumped lazily back into his throne, exhausted from the confrontation. Wearily, he held out his hand towards his priest. "Jerommien," his voice whispered. "Get me the moonshine, would you? The strong kind." When Jerommien looked hesitant at this, the King glared at him and yelled, "The Moonshine! Now!"

Before the king could sentence him for a punishment, the high priest went and got out the hidden moonshine out of the cabinet in one of the throne room's hollow sculptures.

Moonshine was the most popular form of drinking throughout Sapphira. The strong drink not only caused the body to produce a feeling of relaxation and merriment, it also was able to seduce the mind into thinking about nothing at all, and often heavy drinkers would comment on the hallucinations that the drink stirred in the mind. The scenes would blur over the eyes and play on the mind's large viewscreen, almost like an alternating reality. The liquid was a slivery array of many minerals, unique to Sapphiran islands. There were a variety of colorings, flavorings and additions that could be made to the Moonshine in order to spice it up, but they all reflected a lustrous radiance, thus justifying the name Moonshine.

"Here you are, Majesty," Jerommien said, reluctantly offering the decanter of Tropical Moonshine to his friend.

"Fine, fine," Lukiahs waved him off as he took a long sip from the decanter. The glowing liquid burned down his throat and clouded his mind from what had just occurred, the flow of it down his throat almost whispering assurance to him. "Did you ever hear such ridiculous nonsense? Imagine me, a father, again, at my age. I am well past that at this point in my life."

"Yes, sir, ridiculous. I am sure he was not sane in his mind."

After a few more careful sips, the King laughed. "I guess I ought to see about which island I want to send you away to after you kill all my prisoners," he said between laughs.

"Oh, come on, Luke, don't jest with me," Jerommien rolled his eyes. "It has been a disappointing, exasperating day. And you still have to meet with your wife, remember? Actually, you are rather late for your tour of the new gardens, are you not? You were supposed to meet her earlier."

The King laughed. "I forgot about her," he admitted. "I'll have to tell her about the 'Prophet' and his little joke. She'll like that, I'm sure."

"Er … Luke, that's a bit heavy for her to absorb, don't you think? She might not like that there is supposedly a lot of blood and tears to be shed. She might cry."

Lukiahs sighed. Then he looked up at his friend once more. "I am a king. Right, Jerommien?"

"Of course, Your Highness," the high priest agreed.

"I am a king, and yet I still cannot demand that my new wife get a sense of humor!" Lukiahs stood up and threw down his strong moonshine bottle, the glass cracking against the marble floor at the impact. "What good is it to be the king, if you cannot decide how things should be around this trash heap?"

"Kaena seems to be warming up, sir, she really is. It's just that, well, you know that she had been supposed to marry an Islander before the council intervened. She is most likely trying hard to think of a way in which she can please you as much as you have pleased her in saving her from marrying a dirty, uncouth islander. And let's face it, Sire, that is a hard thing to think of."

The King seemed satisfied with this explanation and sighed. "I guess you're right, Jerommien. I cannot only blame myself for this. I am just too nice sometimes."

Jerommien clapped his arm around the king's shoulders in a brief, brother-like action. "That is absolutely right, Your Highness." He started to walk with the King out to the garden halls when he added, "Speaking of being too nice, sir, you aren't really going to send me away to an island, right?"

The King laughed all the way down the hall.

***

THE MOONLGIHT PEGASUS

Queen Kaena looked down the hall as she heard the familiar steps of her husband coming. His elderly, grandfather-like steps, so different from her own vigorous and able pace, stuck out in their slow pattern. She rolled her eyes in annoyance and disgust.

She had been from the realms of Diamond City, and had been born into a well-bred family of the middle class. Her long, blond hair was combed back for the day, held up in an elaborate and ornate headdress, with many braids and some silken flowers here and there. Her royal robes were of the finest, softest material, encrusted with gemstones and fine, gold-threaded material. On her feet were the daintiest of expensive fur bed slippers; they were hidden from questioning eyes by the large expounding layers of her gown she was under. She stood there, next to the entrance to the Luxury Garden Hall, waiting for her husband to show up. Kaena was grateful that for the first time since she had arrived at this Palace that she had been able to get her handmaidens to leave her to herself while she waited. Currently, they were all out about the town until the noontime meal. Once a job was granted at the Palace, trips to the city were only twice a month for those in such a prestigious position. It was only when a worker got married that he or she could move out of the castle; it was either that or when a worker was fired that they were let out of the palace. The handmaidens were much more than willing to accept a free lunchtime from the new queen.

Kaena thought as she waited, her eyes staring far off into the distance as she allowed her mind to wander. She thought about her family, and how she missed them. Royalty, especially the women, were often considered by the councilors to be 'in danger' outside of the castle, although this was a friendly world. There were few people would want to cause trouble here, Kaena thought. It was unfortunate that she knew some of the ones who did.

Having been a part of the middle class all her life, her family had taken her and her brothers and sisters every year to the sand swept beaches of the Jewel Island, located in the South Seas. It was there that she had met her one true love, the Islander, Ammos. She'd been his friend for years, until her family, kind and sympathetic to her love, had agreed that she could marry him if she was truly in love.

So the engagement had been announced at the end of the past summer at last. Ammos and Kaena had been deeply in love, and the celebrations had gone on until well into the early mornings as they celebrated. When she left that time, she had been his promised wife.

Until the king and his councilors had decided she would be perfect for the new Queen.

Despite the title, the house, the fine clothes and gifts and parties and servants, Kaena only wanted the one thing she did not have—love. Her parents had begged her to go at the King's command. She had eventually agreed, but reluctantly. She could never see her beloved Ammos again. Once the engagement had been broken off, he had wed another girl from the island, and they'd already had a child together. From what Kaena's spies had told her, another child was on the way, along with a rebellion.

She had heard news of the Rebellion all right. Try as the king might, he could not keep her locked away from the world forever. She had been planning to run away, but this plan had been ruined by the news she had received today.

Her worst fears had been confirmed; she was stuck here, playing Queen for the rest of her life.

Her thoughts would have lingered on her misfortune had King Lukiahs had not appeared just then, with Jerommien holding him up. She disregarded this action, though it was untraditional for the King to be so close to his advisors. Kaena curtsied for her husband and nodded to the High priest. "Your Majesty," she welcomed him gracefully. "I have been waiting for you. Shall I take your arm as we look through the gardens?"

The King looked at her with fondness in his eyes. "Yes, you may," he agreed as he dismissed Jerommien and took hold of her extended arm. "Queen Kaena, might I say that you look as ravishing as a blooming orchidia today?"

"Thank you, Your Highness," Kaena whispered uncaringly in response, as was her usual custom. She knew he did not mean it. He had not cared for the idea of a wife in general, just as she had not wanted to become his, and she— along with the rest of the court elite—knew it. Regardless, it was her duty now to carry through with this charade of a life, this imitation of a marriage. She reached out and took his arm, tucking hers around his. Together, they walked through the door into the new Gardens.

The Luxury Hall Gardens had been the Great Hall Gardens the previous year. This year, they had been redesigned to give the Queen a hobby, a miniature job to oversee as she began to grow adapted to the Palace life. Lukiahs had seen it as an opportunity for the Queen to make her own mark on his Palace. This was supposed to be the premiere tour for him, before it was opened up to the public a few weeks later on the King and Queen's first year anniversary.

The ceiling was opened up, windows placed in certain areas to illuminate the darkened hall. They walked in silence for a while until Kaena spoke up. "Do you like what I have done to the gardens, Your Majesty?"

"What?" the king asked, jumping slightly. He had not really been attentive. He was getting sleepy, and the scent of the wonderful flowers all around him was not helping him to pay any attention or even to stay awake. He was half-ready to fall over fast asleep at this point.

"I asked you what you thought of the gardens, Your Highness," the Queen replied without changing her tone or expression.

"Oh. Right. Um … I think it's very beautiful, Queen Kaena. You are truly a master of gardening, it looks like." He then slumped back into his world of apathy.

"I have to confess, Sire, that I did not bring you in here to merely talk about the garden," Kaena said slowly. She was hoping to get his attention.

"Oh. Right. Um … that's nice of you, Kaena," the King said. "Say, is that a bench? Well, how about a break here, love?"

"Sure, all right."

When the King was sitting down, Kaena could not hold her news in any more. "My Liege, I am with child."

"Oh. Right. Um … " His eyes had been glazed over until the impact of her words had sunk in. His eyes grew clearer than ever, as wide as ever, and he nearly shot out of his seat. Then he smiled and chuckled, as though he alone understood his joke. "I'm sorry, Kaena. I thought you just said you were with child. What a funny old man am I? I'm sorry, what did you just say?"

Kaena's striking eyes held no joy as they found his. "I am with child, Your Highness. We are going to have a baby."

"No," the King said. "No, we are not, and I do not appreciate this joke of yours, Kaena. It is not funny at all. Not at all, do you hear me?" His sentence ended with him shouting, nearly sending Kaena into a crying fit.

"I'm sorry," she whispered as her eyes began to water. "But it's the truth!"

"Liar! Liar! You cannot be telling the truth!" Lukiahs looked wildly around and around, his disbelief melting away as he tried to comprehend this. That blasted prophet, that annoying old man, he had been right! Haiasi had been right! His hands flew up to his ears, and the King crouched over, trying to block out the sound of his crying wife. "This cannot be!" he yelled, turning away from his young, pregnant wife, and running away.

***

As much as King Lukiahs did not want to believe it, it was true. Queen Kaena had been plotting to leave, but she had found out only days before her exodus into the real world once again that she was carrying the King's child.

25

After nine months, the queen had grown big with child. But she was also very, very sickly.

Having calmed down a bit, and having more than enough moonshine, the King had come to accept this. He assumed that the prophet had simply heard about the Queen being pregnant, along with the exact details of his dream, from some spy who was in the castle. He'd torn Diamond City apart, sending his guards to carefully comb the area, looking for the spies who had betrayed his secrets and his wife's to the prophet. In the end, he could find no one. So, he had Haiasi captured and detained within the prison until further notice.

On the day before the birth, King Lukiahs sneaked down to the prison. The King looked around as quietly as he could. He had never before been down to the prisons. They were bleak and gloomy, and very unwelcoming. The small rectangular windows were cut with an array of cloudy glass, the walls adorned with small fire lanterns. The shadows, little as they were, were cast onto walls of a deep gray. He had to make a mental note to congratulate the designer of the prison. They had a point to get across, and that point was that no one would want to be in here. And their point was met very effectively.

He was just starting to shiver and to think about leaving when a voice called to him.

"So, Your Highness, you have come to visit?"

It was he, the one who called himself a prophet. So, Haiasi was apparently never surprised. He had the appearance of a man who had been expecting King Lukiahs all along. This idea made King Lukiahs think that maybe this was neither the time nor the place to start letting paranoia settle in. Besides, royalty such as him never made this type of a trip unless there was a special reason. And the King had an exceptional reason indeed - he had come down to gloat to Haiasi, of course.

The King would allow himself to admit, at last, that his nerves had been rattled by this strange man's words. But he had now, in his hand, all the proof he'd needed to establish this so-called prophet as a false one.

"Hello, there," the King smiled. "I trust you are enjoying your residence here with us?"

"This is not my lodge, but I find it quite suitable for the time being. Congratulations, My Liege. I hear that you have a child on the way soon."

"Yes. Well, I must congratulate you, as well, for finding that out," the King replied. "I must get you to tell me one of these days how you managed to get that information from the queen, but that can wait."

"Oh, I see," Haiasi said with a knowing look. "You still take me for a fraud."

"Of course I do," Lukiahs said. "You told me that, well enough, but I'll have you know that after you came, I agreed to see no others pretending to know what my dream was about. I have gotten plenty of good, needed rest these days, with no dreams to harp upon my nerves. Also, I can even tell you that the rebellion has been losing ground swiftly. There are so few left against me. And as for the matter of my child … " The King paused here, and held out the weekly weather report out to Haiasi. Haiasi took hold of the paper, and read it with mild interest.

Haiasi read the paper, and then handed it back to the king. "Very interesting sir, but I was hoping to see the City Chronicles, not the News Line."

"It's not the newspaper, idiot! It's the weather report. You told me that my offspring would be born of night's shadow! Ha! Can you not see that the day report is going to be sunny and clear! And I'll have you know—in case your little spies had not thought to tell you this—that the child is thought to be arriving in the middle of the day tomorrow. There is not a drop in your bucket of hope that can prove you right on any terms!"

Haiasi looked disinterested still. "Who are you trying to convince, Your Highness - me, or yourself? I do not need to see the weather or know the times to know that the Guardian will work all things out according to his will." His gaze turned from one of sureness to that of a very tired, very sympathetic man. "Your Majesty, I beg you, quit fighting this battle. Reason and logic are often lucid—it is your emotions that you are struggling against. Why are you so afraid to embrace what is clear?"

"I'm not afraid … And tomorrow, I'm going to embrace the clear, sunny day!" the King laughed all the way out of the prison. He had won this battle. He was sure of it this time.

***

"Augh! Ooooh! Ooooh!" Queen Kaena's face broke into a horrific scream as the baby made its way out of her body. It was one of the only times that she raised her voice. Even all through her pregnancy, she had been as meek as a lamb. But it was a different story now. Her brow was covered in sweat, and her body ached all over. She did not care, she did not care, she thought. All she wanted was this baby out of her body, and *now*. "Ow! Ouch!"

There was tremor after tremor ripping through her body. The doctor's room was supposed to create a sense of calm, but the queen for the large part had only been disturbed and concerned with the large windows open. The last thing she needed was for the entire city, indeed the entire world, to know that she was in the process of giving birth to the King's baby.

And to top it all off, the sun was shining right in her face. Queen Kaena was not very happy at the moment.

The contraction slowed, but another one was coming soon enough. She breathed deeply, in and out very fast, wishing very hard that it was over.

It was then that the sky suddenly started to grow darker.

Queen Kaena looked over at the windows briefly, silently thanking whomever it was for shutting the blinds. She was surprised to see that the sunlight had just faded, and there were no clouds in the sky. "What is going on? Why's the sun getting darker?" she yelled, completely confused and no doubt overwhelmed.

"I don't know Your Highness, but we have more pressing issues at the moment," a handmaiden named Enricée hurried over and held onto the queen's shaking hand. "It's going to be alright, I promise you."

The queen felt no desire at all to bring a child belonging to the King into this world. Kaena felt completely alone, and depressed at the thought of not having a child that she felt she could not love. She wanted to have a child that belonged to her, and someone she loved. She had not seen the King throughout her pregnancy at all. It had been this morning when she'd seen him for the first time, looking happier than ever. It looked like he had come to terms with having another baby. She turned and watched out the window, screaming and yelling every so often, as the sun slowly disappeared.

"Is there an eclipse today?" She yelled half in wonder, half in pain, as she watched the gray sun disappeared completely behind a Sapphiran Moon, though she did not know which one it was at the moment. It was dark now, dark throughout the whole world. "Hurry! Get this kid out of me now, please!" she yelled more loudly as the pain increased.

"I'm sorry, My Lady, but it looks like you are going to have to push once more," the doctor said as she moved to help catch the baby. She had completely ignored the Queen's question. "Are you ready?"

"No!" Kaena screamed as she pushed out one more time. She took a long breath, and then cried out, "Ammos!" and then slumped over, fainting, as at last the baby was completely free of the womb.

A tiny baby, seven pounds, four ounces, lay in the hands of the Queen's doctor. "It is a girl!" the doctor smiled happily. She held onto the tiny newborn with cradled arms, and then said without looking away from the child, "Someone, go and tell His Majesty that he has a daughter." At her command, a warden hurried off, running with joyous steps towards the Throne Room.

All the doctors and nurses came around to look at the newborn. She was beautiful. Already she had a curly bunch of dark hair on top of her head. She didn't make a sound as she wriggled around in the doctor's arms.

For a long moment, the alarm signaling the critical condition of the queen went unnoticed.

When the Doctor finally put the new baby down, she heard the beeping noise of the failing heart rate alarm and turned with shock towards the Queen. "No!" she yelled. "Crew! All hands available to secure the Queen!"

Everyone rushed around, someone hurrying to get a pair of electric shockers. The doctor quickly injected a syringe filled with rejuvenating nutrients into the Queen's body, but it was too late. The heart rate plummeted. She had lost the desire to live.

The heart rate monitor flat lined. Queen Kaena died; she was gone, as though a thief in the shadows had taken her.

The doctor slumped down, pulling off her bloody gloves. The handmaidens started to slowly weep louder and louder. Enricée took hold of the queen's hand once more, holding on as the warmth dispersed from the queen's lifeless body. It was a long while before anyone noticed that the sun had returned to its normal gray illumination.

***

The King was in the throne room when the eclipse happened. He was calmly awaiting the arrival of his new born when he'd begun to notice the eclipse. Lukiahs felt his stomach turn, his eyes bulge, his throat constrict as he saw the sun disappear behind Sapphira's moon. "No!" he cried. "No! No, this cannot be!"

He stormed to the royal bedroom, refusing to see his new daughter or attend his wife's funeral. He did not come out of his room for days. Those days turned into weeks, and after that, only Jerommien and a few of his chamber men would be allowed into the King's room, Jerommien to advise and the chamber men to clean up all the moonshine stains.

As for the baby girl, she was left to the queen's handmaidens, and then just to a maid or two to be taken care of. No one had even given her a name yet. It had been decided that if the King did not name her, then it would be left up to Prince Dorian, her half-brother.

News of the death of the Queen reached the ears of the people first. The birth of a new baby seemed too happy for the people to celebrate just then, with the death of the baby's mother happening just after. It also reached the news that the King was indisposed, and the councilors were beginning to plan Prince Dorian's coronation ceremony. For the citizens of Sapphira, it seemed that dark times were upon them.

***

It was a week after the Princess' birth that Prince Dorian, now nine years old, walked into his half-sister's room with silent footsteps. The nurse who had been placed in charge of her was fast asleep; all the while, the baby was wide awake in her little bed, no one even noticing.

Prince Dorian was tall for his age, just reaching four and three-quarters feet at age nine. His hair was black as night,

THE MOONLGIHT PEGASUS

and his eyes were a golden-speckled green. His face was still young, but his eyes showed an intelligence that was not to be taken lightly. He knew of many things, and thanks to his father he had seen the world for what it was; it was dark with pain, and full of corruption.

Dorian made his way towards the Princess without making a sound. His black hair curled gently over his brow as his gaze focused on the Princess' crib. He peered over the side of the crib and looked for the first time at his new sibling. The tiny baby girl looked up at him, her eyes wide and innocent. Her skin was bright, even for a royal. She glowed with a shiny, almost diamond-like glimmer. Her hair, a little ruffle of dark blond hair, stayed flat on her head as he reached down and felt the softness of it. Her eyes were mystifyingly dark blue, with a touch of purple around the iris. She was really pretty, for a baby, Dorian thought.

"Hi … " he began softly. "You're my new sister, you know. And I'm your big brother, little girl. Your mommy's gone, just like mine is. I don't know why Father won't come to see you, but until then, I'm going to be the big brother and take charge of you."

Careful as possible, he reached down and pulled her up out of the crib. He, as an afterthought, put his finger to his lips and shushed her, but she just laughed a little baby laugh, and then quieted down as though she had understood him, but still thought he was funny.

Dorian smiled at her. "Let's go to my room," he said, "And I'll show you my soldiers and all my toys."

After Dorian sneaked out of the room, he shut the door quietly and looked around. He didn't want anyone to realize that he'd been the one to take his sister. "That's going to make them shape up a bit," he said. He smiled down at his sibling and said, "That's the trick to these people. Get them to worry about themselves and their jobs, and they'll shape up. I remember I used to ride big horses when 'no one' was looking, and that's when they all rushed out and took care of me."

The baby laughed again at his story, although Dorian was certain she didn't understand. He started to walk down the hall to his room. "What about you? You've never worried these guys enough, and I hear you were born while the moon was blocking out the sunlight." Dorian smiled again.

He reached his room and put her down on the floor in the middle of the room, laying her down and grabbing her one of his blankets from his bed. He sat down next to her and took her hands in his, playing with her tiny fingers and marveling that someone had told him that he'd been as small as she had been once. "You're so tiny," he said at last. "I guess the first order of business here is to introduce myself. I'm your big brother, Dorian."

She sputtered and giggled, blowing a spit bubble and then smiling. Her eyes then found his, and he looked closer at him. Her eyes ... they reminded him of the moon on a starry night. "You know ... you're going to need a name around here. And since Father's not going to even see you, I guess it's my job to name you, huh?"

She looked from side to side, her gaze taking in everything. The baby seemed not to notice Dorian's words.

"I think your name should be something pretty and not too long, and not too short," Dorian said. "Hmm ... " he

THE MOONLGIHT PEGASUS

thought about it for a while, and then he made his decision. "What do you think of Selene?"

The Princess happily giggled and smiled, spitting out another bubble. Dorian decided to take this as a yes. "Good. Selene it is."

***

King Lukiahs was more than old and sick by the time he agreed to come out of his room; he was deadly ill. Selene had just turned a month old. The Rebel forces from the Isles were once again destroying cities on the main Continent. What had made him come out of his room was the news from his only remaining General that the Islander forces were heading for Diamond City, and that those blasted rebels had managed to get within fifteen miles of the city. He had also heard that the Rebel leader, some dirty Islander named Ammos, was calling for the death of King Lukiahs.

"I can't believe it's been four weeks since the King went into his room," a maid whispered as she passed Dorian's room. "The poor children. They have no mother, and a mad father. How sad."

"Yeah. Did you hear Ammos' forces are gaining land against the King's soldiers? The Royal soldiers are just giving up, surrendering. They're sick of having a King who will not fight with them, or at least tell them how to fight."

"What I don't get is why the soldiers can't see that he's grieving for his wife?" the first maid responded.

"Are you kidding me? Everyone practically knows that King Lukiahs never loved his second wife. I feel so bad for

Queen Kaena. She was just a pawn in selfish gain to her family and the council. She knew that the King didn't love her. Did you hear that all her family received a nice chunk of the royal treasury because she died?"

A third maid joined the conversation. "Yeah, really. How comforting can that be to her family? They never even really got to see her that much—what was it, once or twice since she'd come here?"

The first maid chimed in again. "She was always so depressing and quiet. She'd fallen in love with that Islander, you know. Ammos. He's leading the troops now, calling for the death of the person that killed his love, you know, the King. Totally sweet, I think. Personally, though, he has a wife and kids now. I don't think he should be doing this kind of thing."

The second maid shook her head. "Uh huh, I know. How tragic for all of them."

"I feel so bad for Dorian," the first maid admitted. "He's got to face this rebellion at such a young age, and with his sister to consider … that poor boy. He's never going to have a normal childhood. Such a shame, you know?"

"Yeah, I know."

"I agree, uh huh, uh huh."

"I see, yes."

Dorian rolled over in his big bed and tried to block out the maids and their whispered words. He knew what he had to do. He did not need to hear the whispers of doubt to know his duty.

He crawled out of bed and got dressed in his finest clothes. He called for a maid, although not one of the chatty ones outside his door, to take Selene for a while.

Dorian sneaked away from his chamber men, and then headed towards the throne room, where his father was rumored to be at the moment.

Indeed, that's where his half-drunk, half-awake father was.

"Father, I have come to talk with you," Dorian said. "I wanted to speak to you."

"Huh?" the old man was more inattentive than usual. "What? Who are you?"

Dorian flustered slightly, but squared his shoulders. "Father, I am your son, Prince Dorian. I want to talk to you about your daughter, Selene."

"Selene?"

"Yes. I have named her Selene, the baby, the Princess … Father, please!" Dorian cried out as his father grabbed a nearby decanter and drunk heavily from it. "There are people coming here, wanting to kill you!" He started to cry, something that he rarely did. "Don't you care at all?"

"Why should I care about this life?" his father asked. "My light, it's going! I have smothered it. I'm going to die soon anyway. Might as well be at the hands of my enemies, you know? Less painful, I think."

Dorian turned from his father. "How could you say a thing like that? I will not stand by here and watch you throw away your kingdom—our kingdom!"

In response, the King let out a large belch. "Okay," he muttered, and then falling asleep, began to breath loudly and slowly in a heavy, drunken stupor.

Dorian raced out of the room, and called for the high priest to attend to his father as he scheduled a meeting with the King's councilors. Dorian knew that it was his duty as the king's son to take control around here. His father was indeed mad.

***

A few days later, Dorian sat on his throne, shocked to the core at the letter he had just received. The last few days had been a silent blur to him. He had run from here to there, and had talked with this person and that person, but it was over now. The rebellion had ended. Thousands of soldiers and fighters had died, as well as two very significant catalysts in the whole war. His hands were having a hard time holding still as he read the letter he held.

To His High Royal Majesty,
King Dorian,

I write to you news of grave importance. Your father has passed on, as of the early morning light. He had suffered so much in these past weeks that he had become emotionally as well as bodily ill. He had taken an astonishing amount of Moonshine of late, and had killed his heart with it. The last words he said were, "I cannot see the light!" before his heart gave out and he dropped wordlessly into his bed. I send my deepest regrets for your loss, Your Highness. I have attended the late King for years, and I have never seen him in such a way. He is at peace now.

Word has traveled throughout the country of the King's death, apparently satisfying the Islander Rebels. They have agreed to cooperate, as long as there are some changes in the law regarding them. They are willing to send advisors and are deciding at this very moment just who those advisors will be. We shall be able to deal with them quite easily, Sire, and I know it will not be too much of an inconvenience on your behalf. They have also readily agreed to this, I am sorry to say, because of the death of their leader, Ammos. He has passed on himself, though by his own hand, leaving only a note in farewell. According to the letter, it seemed, life, without his love Kaena, as he so called her, had driven him to madness, just like the King your father. As a peculiar coincidence, the last words he said were also, "I cannot see the light!" Strange.

I shall return from my tour of the Islands with my reports in less than two weeks, just in time for your coronation ceremony.

Yours truly,
Your Humble Servant,
The High Priest of the Order of
The Guardian of Dreams in Crystallon,
Jerommien

Dorian put the letter aside and thought no more of his father. He had work to do.

***

A few days later, the new King looked down at his baby sister as she slept soundly in her crib. She was almost five weeks old to the day. Dorian smiled down at her, and felt relieved to know that this little girl was going to be his only family for a long time. He had felt that his father had appreciated neither him nor her enough. She was, after all, an innocent little baby in the midst of all this turmoil.

"So, Your Majesty, you are relieved that this war is over?"

Dorian turned to his newest advisor. Jerommien had been dismissed shortly after the official coronation ceremony, discharged of his duty because he had been labeled incapable and ineffective. Dorian had been tempted to add 'unnecessary' but he had restrained his unkind conduct. He was a king now, and he had to act like one if the council was going to let him keep the title. "Yes, I am, Haiasi. Blood is too much of an ugly thing to be around someone as young as I am. I'm concerned now with peace. What do you think about that?"

The old prophet looked at the child with twinkling eyes. "As far as peace goes, I have no doubt that you will be able to maintain it for a long time. After all, this planet is full of people who are more suited to peace than war. But I am afraid that there will be a time, Young Leader, when it will come about that you may have to fight. The day I first came here, a prophecy was made. It will be kept, according to the Guardian's plan."

"Tell me more about this prophecy," Dorian commanded, as he turned away from his sister's crib and headed out the door with his newest advisor.

Haiasi smiled. "I have to say, first, Your Majesty, that I am impressed by your devotion to your sister. Her Highness is most fortunate to have a brother like you."

"Thanks."

"Like all siblings, there will come a day when you have to let your protectiveness pass on to someone else, I must warn you."

"Selene has no one but me," the King said. "I doubt it."

Haiasi smiled ruefully. "There is a Guardian of Dreams, you know. He has made this world; this world is his dream. You would not let such a wonderful dream turn into a nightmare, would you, young King?"

Dorian shook his head. "I like good dreams," he said in a childish, misunderstood way. "I have such good dreams all the time."

"That's part a gift for those of us who are blessed," Haiasi agreed. "We must remember not to corrupt them. And for those of us who have been corrupted, we must repent or die in Obsidian's darkness."

***

Dorian continued to be King. His accession to the throne was not questioned, and the rebel activity, little that was left, was quieted down. The Princess Selene grew more and more each day, becoming a happy child who bounced around the palace with joyful steps. Haiasi continued to be the King's most trusted advisor and counselor, until his death seven years later.

Haiasi died when the princess was seven. His death had caused much pain to Dorian, who had come to love the old prophet like a father. King Dorian, barely a teenager at that time, would remember forever the day he had to say good-bye to his most faithful advisor.

***

Haiasi had been lying on his bed, with King Dorian standing nearby. The old prophet had smiled as the King had made his way closer to the side of the bed.

"Ah, young Majesty. I see you have come to see me off, then. Such a sad sight for one as young as you."

Dorian had grinned. "I left Selene outside."

"Your sister means so much to you, and it is obvious that you are not the only one that loves her so. She is special. When she was born, you remember, she was born under night's shadow ... and for that I'm sorry."

"Why? What have you to be sorry for, Haiasi? You have been a wonderful advisor to me these past years."

"I'm sorry, because I was part of the reason your father hated Selene. I told him that one of his offspring was to be born 'under night's shadow'. He hated her because he hated me, and he hated the truth." Haiasi's voice grew soft. "Please, King Dorian, don't hate the truth. It is light, you know. It can shine, the smallest spark illuminating the biggest darkness."

Dorian could feel the tightening of his throat as he tried to speak. Finally, he cleared his throat and said, "I have learned many things from you, Haiasi, and I will try to live up to your hopes."

"Watch over Selene. She's unique. There are tough times ahead, Dorian. I have seen them. She is the one who will help bring peace to the world. But she has a great burden. Her heart shall be a field of blood."

"She won't die, will she?" Dorian asked, alarmed.

"Some part of her will have to. But when she marries, the times of trial and war will be over. Peace will be restored, and you, along with the entire world, shall be cleansed. The sun will shine a great light once more."

"What do you mean? The sun has always shone," Dorian asked, apparently not able to comprehend what his advisor was saying.

"It has not always been so dull, you know," Haiasi said, his voice soft and weak. "There was once a time, once long ago, when all dreams had been beautiful."

"Haiasi?" Dorian took hold of the man's hand, only to pull back at the coldness that was in it.

"I can see … the light," the prophet murmured quietly, and then he was gone.

Dorian felt a pain in his heart as he turned and walked out of the room. He hid his face from his advisors and servants. With the passing of his dear friend from life to death, from dark to light, Dorian felt the sting of angry tears well up behind his eyes. What would he do now, with his friend gone? He wondered, how could such a thing happen, that his advisor would die and leave him all alone in the world, right when Haiasi was needed the most? Was the Guardian of Crystallon really looking after the world of

Sapphira? Dorian could not help feeling his doubts. Haiasi had been so sure, but now that he was gone, who was to put Dorian's doubts and fears to rest?

THE MOONLGIHT PEGASUS

***

Chapter 2
The Princess and the Protector
***

She was dreaming.

There she was, looking high above the world. It was all cloudy from this view, but she could not bring herself to care. There was sunlight, there was warmth … there was freedom. Absolute, and complete freedom; freedom from darkness, freedom from pain, freedom from the loneliness that kept itself hidden in the darkest corners of her mind—the whole world, at that moment, could both belong to her and have nothing to do with her. To take any part in it was her choice.

The light grew brighter, almost calling out to her. Her head rose to face it, to reflect the warm and welcoming glow. Then a voice below her called out. It was a familiar voice, one that she had known well. For the moment, she tried to ignore it, not wanting to divert her gaze from the light.

She could not look away; she knew this. But the voice from below grew louder and more persistent, and at last, she turned to face it. Instantly, the dream grew foggy, as the transition from night to day once again began to take place.

All she could feel in her heart as the sunlight awoke her that morning was the feeling of being in chains.

***

The Princess Selene woke up in her lavish comforts, her soft, cloud-like bed, in her lovely, polished home, with the smile she'd kept on her face throughout the whole night slowly diminishing. She sighed.

"Why is it," Selene murmured as she half-listened for the sound of her governess's footsteps coming up the long hallway, "that all good dreams are too short?" She silently decided that it must have been so in order that the world would not simply sleep their lives away. Still, she was sorry to say good-bye to such a pleasant night. She might have been the heir apparent to the crown, but she could not stand to face the thought of getting through her life without the gift of her beautiful dreams.

Almost reluctantly, Selene got out of bed and began to get ready for her day.

"Your Highness," a voice called from the door. "It is —"

"I know, I know," Selene broke in. "Time to get up … I'm coming, Aura."

The woman named Aura appeared at the doorway and smiled pleasantly. "Good to see you up, Your Highness." She was an older woman of the High Court, and also the elected governess to Selene. She had held the position for nearly the last fifteen years, since Selene's third birthday. "May I come in to discuss our agenda today?"

"All right." Selene had started to gather up her the necessities for her maid Chevée, who was in charge of dressing the Princess's hair.

"Thank you, Your Highness," Aura said graciously as she walked in, a small tilt of her head extended towards the Princess in a casual bow.

Selene sneaked a peek at her, silently wishing herself to be more like her Governess. Aura was tall, proud, and a well-known beauty in the Courts of Diamond Palace, despite her age of fifty. She still had perfect long hair framing her features, a curling shower of glossy burgundy. Her eyes were glass green, and her poise was perfect. There was not a hair on her head out of place or a wrinkle in her expensive, well-cut dress. After nearly fifteen years of having such a governess, Selene felt even less like a lady. And the feeling of being so awkward often intensified every time she watched Aura walk, sit, sip at her herbal water, eat, or basically do anything. Nearly everything that Aura did was perfectly genteel, tactful and serene. Selene felt some days, with her short hair, clumsy feet, and ever-present smile, she would be lucky if she survived Aura's tutelage at all.

However, there was one thing about Aura that Selene did not admire. Selene knew her governess loved to gossip excessively about the High Court members, or anyone else of interest. And for all of Aura's good manners, she disapproved of nearly everyone for one reason or another. The only person that Aura truly loved, as far as Selene could tell, was Aura herself. The governess carried herself with such pride, that even a display of modesty and humility was acted on with a glint of stubborn smugness.

"Well, Aura," Selene spoke up as she sat down at her bureau, "Tell me, what does Dorian wish for me to learn today?"

Aura looked down her nose at the Princess. "Such impertinence," she muttered, scowling. "You should not address His Majesty the King so informally, Your Highness. It is not proper."

"Aura," Selene cast a glance in her direction that plainly told the governess that she did not care and that she had heard this speech before. "You know that Dorian is my brother. I can call him whatever I want, so long as it is not treasonous."

Aura was probably the closest thing that Selene had to a mother. Maybe that was the problem with her, Selene thought. She was like a mother, and did everything that a mother should for her … everything except give her the true warmth of such a connection. Formality, Selene thought, should never come before family. Aura, on the other hand, practically denied that she even felt the tiniest drop of affection for Selene by her somewhat aloof manner.

"Really, Your Highness, His Majesty is to be revered, not ridiculed. And, for that matter, neither is your responsibility as Princess or his duty to be King."

Selene looked away. "I know." Her eyes almost seemed to lose their sparkle momentarily. Yes, it was her job to be Princess. Yes, she had to consider the choices and think of the repercussions of a bad decision, and yes, she had to believe every day that she was going to do the right thing for the people. She turned to look in the mirror and saw that Aura was looking at her with a peculiar face. That sent a jolt through Selene, telling her it was time to forget her thoughts and concentrate once more on the day ahead. After all, it was a very important day, she thought as she once again put on a small smile.

Aura took the hint and opened the leather-bound book she'd brought with her. As Selene's handmaiden Chevée arrived and began to style the Princess's hair into a curly setting, Aura began to announce the schedule.

"Let's see ... Ah! For the seventeenth day of the twelfth moon, Your Highness is due for her daily lesson in the schoolroom until midday. Then, Your Highness is supposed to get a quick meal, and then off to Your Highness' self-defense class, reminding Master Omni that Your Highness is to leave early due to the big Islander's Reception tonight. And Princess—" Aura's eyes stared intently into Selene's as she continued on—"You must remember that you are required to go to this one, as is it is now considered by His Majesty the King to be inexcusably mandatory."

She could've said it in two breaths without all the formal titles, Selene thought as she sighed. "It has been three years since that happened. Are you and my brother never going to let it go?"

Aura's hard gaze answered her question effectively. "Your presence is required."

Chevée put the finishing touches on Selene's short hair and took a step back from the Princess. "There. Now you are ready to begin the day, Your Highness."

Selene looked up at Chevée and grinned. "Not quite, Chevée. Thank you for doing my hair this morning. It looks quite lovely, I think. But there is one more thing I need before I can be completely prepared for this day." She turned to face her governess, her best pleading face at the ready. "Aura, do I have time to go and get Etoileon?" she asked.

Aura tried to hide her smile at the eager expression on the princess' face. She did not get very far. "Yes, you may go and pick him up from his training session, Your Highness. But please remember, your presence is required in the schoolroom with the other royal court children an hour and a half after breakfast."

Selene flashed her brilliant smile. "How could I forget?" she asked just a little too sweetly for Aura's comfort.

***

She watched him as he fought hard against another student in training as the last class finished up. They were using a number of weapons against each other today. Selene watched with a tingle of trepidation curling in her stomach as she saw the star-points, the many swords, the hyper blasters, the daggers, and the various other sinister looking devices hanging on the wall nearby.

Her worry began to disappear when she noticed the easy grace of the one she was watching, as he tangled with his friend with a single purpose on his mind—a determination to win. His feet were shuffling and quick, managing to steady the balance and keep his footing. He had sweat running down his forehead, and his shirt was sticking to his back. His name was Etoileon, and he was Selene's protector. He had been her protector for over two years now, ever since he had finally passed all of the King's tests for him.

He was rather tall, though short compared to his opponent. His short night-black hair flew out in all directions as he made counterattack after counterattack. No doubt, Selene thought with a tiny smile, his eyes were burning with a gray fury she knew all too well.

Ronal, his opponent, was a taller, more muscular looking young man with striking white-blond hair. Though he was strong, he had nothing against Etoileon when it came to speed or endurance. Their daggers whipped past each other, the star-points whizzed on by; the swords tangled, the blasters fired, but eventually, Ronal grew tired and slipped, thus leaving Etoileon to stand over him in victory a moment later.

A feeling of pride in her friend and protector's accomplishment welled up inside of her. Selene smiled and unclenched her now-white hands, which she could not even remember balling up. As the princess, she had been trained in self-defense; but she knew that she could not hold a candle to those who had been instructed in the Fighter's ways.

The life of being a Fighter was not easy, and Selene imagined it to be only harder while one lived in the Palace in Diamond City. There were over two hundred of them, all of them boys from the middle-class families that lived in the City. To be a Fighter meant to protect the royal household from any kind of danger. They were more like highly trained guards than special armed forces. Since Sapphira was rarely at war, the Fighters were kept mostly at the palace, though in times of war they would be spread out all over the globe. At the palace, they all had to wake up two hours before daybreak, getting dressed in their uniforms, often forsake breakfast, and exercise for hours. After that, the boys only had an hour to get washed, some food, and change into their Palace wear. Some of them would be on authorized duty after this training session. If they were not, the Fighters were required to help the maids, the stewards, the armory keepers, and all types of various other jobs that were strewn throughout the Palace walls. Often the Fighter squad got little

THE MOONLGIHT PEGASUS

or no quality time to themselves, although they did get to go into the city twice a month.

Etoileon had to have it the hardest among them, too. Nearly all the high-level students had applied for his position, to be her protector, and she was slightly worried that Dorian, who had put himself in charge of choosing, would overlook Etoileon in spite of her wishes. Selene was certain, even more so as she watched him now, that Dorian had made the right choice for her. Etoileon was well known for his skills on the Fighter's squad.

She watched as he headed over to Ronal now, and reached down his hand to help his friend up. Selene couldn't help but smile. Etoileon had grown so much in the short time she'd known him.

***

"Are you okay? You were all out on that battle back there." Etoileon had a shadow of a grin on his face that clearly told anyone looking on him that he had just won.

"I'm fine," Ronal replied gruffly. "Nothing a nice City steak-o-filet can't fix. You're buying, by the way."

"Yeah, we'll see about that," Etoileon replied, the intensity of his eyes disappearing as it was replaced with a laugh.

Ronal grinned, before his eyes caught sight of the figure at the top of the viewing glass on the next floor up. "The Princess is here," he said. "Wow. She sure looks lovely today."

Etoileon did not need to look up at Selene to know that she was beautiful today. Instead of looking in the direction of his friend's gaze, he instead frowned at his friend. "What's that supposed to mean?" he asked.

Ronal nearly jumped at the icy tone. "What's wrong with you, Etoileon? I mean, I know you're her main protector, but you don't have to get in my face because I think she's pretty."

Etoileon sometimes hated how his friend was right. He hated it even more that he had reacted in such a bad way. Now he was stuck listening to Ronal give him a lecture on how he took his job too seriously.

"Besides," Ronal was saying, "If you fought off everyone who thought she was cute, you would have half of the world killed, the other half waging war against you, and not a man would be left when you finished with them." He paused here for a moment and then added, "You'd have to kill yourself, too, 'cause I know you think she's pretty, too."

Etoileon caught the sarcasm and let it go. It wasn't his fault that he had reacted to Ronal's statement. He couldn't seem to help it, just like he couldn't help denying it a moment later. "No, I don't! Just drop it, okay Ronal? I thought you liked that city girl, that's all."

His friend shrugged, unconcerned. He'd made his point. "Speaking of which, Cyerra might be down there, and you know I love seeing her. Want to get that settled steak-o-filet this afternoon? I was thinking I'd go on a trip to the City anyway. The New moon's coming up soon and I want to use up this month's city trips before I lose them."

"Cyerra? Is she the one you 'can't stop thinking about'?" Etoileon inquired as they began to clean up the weapons that they had flung all over the room. The battle course was really too into using weapons, Etoileon thought, as he picked up four of the used battle blasters they'd throw away after using up all their ammunition. There was enough ammo strung around the room to fight off a small war effectively. And the Fighters in training had used nearly all of it. It was really a waste sometimes.

The grin on Ronal's face was all Etoileon needed to see to have his question answered. "The one and same," Ronal declared, dramatically sliding his sword once more into its scabbard. "She's trying to get a job here as a maid, you know. She's afraid with her boarding space being sold to another bar owner that she'll get kicked out. And if I help her to get her here, it'll be sweet paradise for me for a good while."

"So you've told her how you feel about her?"

Ronal nearly jumped a foot high. "Of course I have," he said. "In fact, I have several times. Let me tell you something, my friend, the minute you start telling a girl that you love her, if you miss even a day or two of telling her that, she'll start getting weird on you, and she'll cry and whine and sigh a lot. So if you ever find a girl in the city that you like, make sure she's the one before you say anything."

"Thanks, I'll keep that in mind," Etoileon smiled. He broke off in a moment of silence as he thought about how to phrase his next sentence. "Have you ever liked a girl and couldn't bring yourself to tell her how you felt?"

"Why? Having some problems with the ladies?" Ronal, having just been badly beaten by Etoileon, was rapidly gaining back his cheerfulness to hear of his friend's bad luck.

"No, there's no problem. I was just wondering." But in his voice, there was casualness all too smooth to have made his statement completely true.

"Right … sure … listen, pal, if you want my advice, the minute you find the cutest chick who'll say yes to you, go with it. When you're a little more advanced, things get a little easier when it comes to picking up the women. In fact, I'll see if Cyerra has a friend, how about that?"

"No, thanks," Etoileon just nodded and kept his head down so his friend wouldn't see him laughing. Ronal had always thought of himself as such a lady hunter, but it looked more like Ronal was a lady fisher. Always getting nothing from his bait, but the stories grew more and more unbelievable each time he talked about it.

Before Ronal left for his Reading Class, he turned back to Etoileon. "If you are going to tell a girl you like her, then get her flowers. They all go crazy over flowers."

"Hmmm … " Etoileon pondered the thought. It was a sensible idea; it was actually one of Ronal's few good ones. "Maybe I will."

He hurried to change and clean up, and when he was done, he walked out of the room and breathed in deeply. The air outside the dojo area was colder, and more refreshing.

"Etoileon!"

He smiled as he heard the voice call out. He did not have to turn around to see that Selene had come to pick him up once again. While it was sweet of her to think of him, Etoileon sincerely hoped that she didn't do it out of pity.

He turned on his heel and found himself face to face with the most charming face he'd ever seen. "Selene."

She smiled that irresistible smile of hers, and he felt a familiar pain in his heart. "That was wonderful," she praised his session. "You really are one of the best fighters I've seen."

He felt the color in his face start to rise. "It's nothing anyone couldn't have done with the right training," he dismissed. "How are you today, Princess? Did you have another good dream last night?"

"Yes, of course," she giggled. "I even think you were there."

"Then it must have been a good dream," he joked. He took his 'on-duty' stance, straightening up and standing at ready. "Let's be off, then, shall we?" He always walked with her down to the formal dining hall for breakfast. He loved it when she came and picked him up from class, so he could spend a couple more minutes alone with her, just talking. When he'd first arrived at the Palace, he'd only been able to see her for a few minutes once in a while. But now, as her Official Protector, he had the privilege of not only seeing her nearly all the time, but also watching over her, to keep her safe. Etoileon felt, in his own way, that Selene was like his own precious treasure.

And she was like a treasure, in some ways. She was the Princess, but that didn't mean as much to him as others.

Selene always was ready to smile, always ready to laugh, and she seemed to enjoy his company above the other students that attended the Palace Education center. Etoileon had first met Selene when she had been younger, only fifteen then. She'd been beautiful then, too, he'd thought. Some of the guys in the Fighters and the gentlemen in court would say that she was pretty, and some would even write her poetry or a love letter to her every now and then. Now at the age of eighteen, she was more captivating to him than ever. She was still shorter than he was, with her head barely reaching his shoulders. But she walked with a joyful step, and in her own nontraditional way, she was graceful at it. Her hair was short and today it was styled in a curled fashion; it was a look he felt didn't suit her as much as her hair when it was let free.

Tonight was a big night for both of them. The Islander's reception was tonight, and there was going to be a surge of new representation of the Islanders at the Palace. As much as Etoileon might have wanted to go to the city, he knew that there was no way that he could leave Selene to face all those gentlemen and elected Islanders alone. Since the princess was now eighteen, she was considered ready to marry. There would be a lot of offers from the Islanders, no doubt—there had always been a waiting list just to dance with her. Etoileon smiled as he imagined a whole group of isles going to war just to have Selene's hand in marriage. He even laughed a little, causing Selene to look over at him.

"What's so funny?" she asked. "It's not the hair, is it?"

"No, no," he shook his head. "It's just … I was thinking about the reception ball tonight. I was thinking about how all the Islanders were going to go to war with each other just to gain your hand in marriage."

THE MOONLGIHT PEGASUS

Selene laughed. "That would be funny," she admitted. "Though it would be a little disturbing, not to mention unlikely."

He grinned. "Well, I wouldn't be surprised if they did," he said. "You are eighteen now, right?"

Selene nodded, her face turning away from him.

"What?" He knew when something was wrong. "What is it?"

"Every day, Dorian gets letters in the mail concerning me, did you know?" her voice was soft. "They come from all over the world, asking how much longer he is going to hold off on getting me betrothed."

Etoileon felt a lump forming in his chest. In that moment, it felt so hard for his heart to beat. "What does the King say?" he asked slowly.

"That the decision is ultimately mine, and I am not ready."

"Oh." He was relieved. "Well, that's … not too bad."

Her head snapped around and her gaze was sorrowful as she looked at him. "I don't want it," she said. "I don't want marriage, or to live on some Island, no matter how pretty it is or not. If I'm alone … " she broke off, unable to say the words.

He didn't know what made him do it. He reached out, and touched her shoulder uncertainly, trying to offer her comfort. It was something that was frowned upon by the

High Social Courts. "It's okay, Selene. I'll go with you, if you want." He hesitated a moment and said, "Please don't be sad."

She wanted nothing more than for him to be with her. But she could never say it, never admit it to anyone or even let herself think of it, for fear of wishing for it too hard. She struggled to smile once more. "Okay. Let's talk about something undoubtedly more pleasant."

He smiled. "I agree." His hand dropped from her shoulder, and he once again resumed his position as her guard. "Did you know that the Lunar Storm Festival is supposed to happen later this week?"

"Really?" Her eyebrows rose in surprise. "That's a bit early for it this year. The Lunar Storms usually come right before the rainy monsoon season, which isn't supposed to come for another couple of weeks or so, I thought."

"Yeah … it's a rare phenomenon. Happens only once every couple of years, I hear. We'll have to catch it." I know she loves to star gaze, Etoileon thought, so that news should cheer her up quite a bit. If nothing else, it would give her something else to think of. A Lunar Storm was always something to be seen, and the festival at the palace never failed to entertain.

There were two Sapphiran moons, Shira and Kuro. Shira was big and round, covered with mountains of crystalline rock. The moon of Kuro was smaller, but while Shira managed to reflect the light of the sun to brighten the night, Kuro seemed to absorb the light onto its own glittering surface. Even though Kuro held steady an amber overcast on Sapphira, the majority of moonlight came from Shira. During the Lunar Storms, also widely known as the Moonbeam Festival, the gathering of the clouds over Diamond City and the angle of Kuro managed to shine enough light on Shira that the light was reflected and separated, almost like a prism effect. The rainbow of colors often varied due to the alignment of Shira, but it never failed to amaze the citizens. The colored effects on the sky lasted for only a couple of hours each day, until the rain clouds grew too thick to see through, and the monsoon season officially started. Legend said that when the Lunar Storms came earlier than usual, it was an ill omen. Science stated that it was due to unusually high tides.

"That's amazing," she said in an awed whisper. "I can't wait to see it! When's it happening this week, do you know?"

Etoileon noticed the deliberate change in the volume of her voice and was more than a little surprised to find that they had reached the doors to the Great Hall. He had not been paying much attention to their surroundings. Not a particularly good habit to make, he thought. I'll have to watch that. He felt a wave of disappointment. His time alone with her always seemed shorter than usual.

The Guards there opened the door and bowed gallantly as Selene made her way through with Etoileon now the customary two steps behind her.

He leaned forward after passing all the guards and whispered, "It's going to happen in two days' time ... Your Highness," his voice returned to normal as the King entered the room to the side of them. A flicker of fury sparked into his gray eyes as he momentarily locked gazes with Selene's brother. It was well known throughout the palace that King Dorian was not fond of Etoileon. The exact reason was unknown to Etoileon, and he did not like the King overly much himself. But still, the King was the King, and if Etoileon wanted to stay in the Palace, he had to abide by the rules (or at least most of them).

Dorian greeted him with his usual sneer, and then turned to face Selene. "Selene, don't you think you should find more useful ways to spend your time than waste your life on this Orphan Boy?"

Etoileon felt a small fluster of red on his cheeks. He was never quite sure why he still felt a sting when the King called him that. But it was Dorian's name for Etoileon, and it still managed to make Etoileon feel slighted. "Hey, Selene," Etoileon replied in scathing tones, "Don't you think that the King should have some better diplomacy in regards to his household?"

"Really, you two, stop it," Selene scolded. She never quite understood what it was about her brother and her friend. They had never quite got along, although she was certain in her mind that they respected each other.

"I'm just saying," Dorian said, "That I think you should—"

"Dorian!" Selene stood up from her chair and interrupted him. "Tell me, brother, whether or not you are going to be setting the example for me in this, or are you simply going to continue your little squabble with Etoileon?"

Dorian glared at Etoileon, who frowned back. But Selene's words stuck out, and managed to calm both of them down. "Selene, we have much to discuss," the king said. "Tonight is the Islander's Reception, as you well know. The

Council has advised me to pass some sort of agreement in regards to whom you are to marry."

There was a brief silence at the table. The servants ceased whispering to each other. All of the maids present shifted, their attention obviously captured. Even all the silverware seemed to stop clinking as all eyes and ears turned to the King's conversation.

"Oh." Selene began to grow increasingly occupied with her breakfast of Almonde muesli. "How interesting."

"Yes. I—are you listening to me?" He broke off in mid-sentence as she leaned forward over the table, completely intent on her food.

"Yes, of course I am listening," Selene assured him. And indeed she was. But she also feared the worst, and she did not want to be seen crying. There were people who went out into the city in the room. She did not want rumors of her instable emotions to raging throughout the city by noon.

"I was thinking also that you should be able to pick an Islander out yourself," he continued. "After all, I know that there has to be some connection between you and the one who you will marry."

"Yes, of course," Selene replied with the same stoic tone she'd used before.

"Curses, Selene! I want you to know right now that you are not the only one going through this," he interjected sharply. His fist slammed on the table, bringing Selene's eyes to meet her brother's. His teeth gritted together. "Right now, council is more than politely hinting that I am to be married

THE MOONLGIHT PEGASUS

as well. Having seen you safe to the age of eighteen, and the Islander's reception tonight, all of my councilors want me to get married, so that I may have a family."

"What's wrong with that?" Selene asked. "You are the King, brother. And well past the marrying age. You are nearing thirty. Men today usually marry at twenty."

"I am not yet thirty, for one thing; I am only twenty-seven. I am not sure I want to give up this life," he remarked. "I like being the King. I like having you to be my heir. I do not really care for the idea of another woman around here. I remember all too well what having your mother marry our father was like."

Selene was silent. No one ever talked about her mother—or at least, they never talked about her mother to her. No doubt stories of her mother were still reported throughout the High Courts every so often.

Etoileon felt his feet shift uncomfortably beneath him. He'd heard the stories that he would never tell Selene. Remembering the awful gossip, he could see why Dorian did not want the councilors to pick him a wife. The last time, they had done a lousy job, although the Queen had done her duty and Selene was here as a result of that.

"I do not know what to tell you, Dorian," Selene whispered softly. Her voice seemed to settle the anger within her brother's heart for the moment. "I am honored that you would have us to stay a family, but I cannot believe that you would so easily give up a chance to be happy with a wife, and maybe a family, of your own."

"I can't even think about it, Selene," he admitted, keeping his voice low, so only she could hear. "But what am I to do?"

"Yes. What are we to do?" she asked. She turned her attention back to her muesli and said nothing more. Well, she thought, the notion of marriage is certainly depressing in this family.

***

Chapter 3
Another Rebellion?

***

The Islander Reception was always one of the grandest
balls throughout the year. The entire Palace was cleaned
thoroughly, and then decorated almost to the point of gaudy.
The bell boys, the maids, and the cleaning staff ran around
hours before the guests starting arriving, polishing their silver
uniforms, cleaning off every surface in the Palace, setting up
the covered tables, the food, the drinks, the music …
everything had to be perfect.

All the different chefs from all over the world flocked to
the Palace at this time of year. Chefs from Capricious Isle,
from Sunset Island, from Jejuna, from Aril, from Kuna, from
the Crescents, all of the islands sent the finest example of
their cuisine for this international ball. It was well known that
the newspapers would promote any Island delicacies they
found appealing, and bash those they hated; the islands that
were well known for their food were particularly hoping to
gain worldwide acknowledgment once again. Besides keeping
the peace, the Islander Reception promoted international ties,
whether it was politics or pleasure.

The palace was strewn with lights, sweetly smelling
flowers placed in highly priced vases, ranging in all sizes and
set in all corners of the rooms. The ballroom had a clear floor
for dancing, and the throne room was dressed up as the main
reception room, where the all the varieties of food samples
were in place.

The large orchestra and the singers performing tonight all
arrived, their attendants in tow. All through his, Dorian's

handpicked planner was racing around telling everyone where to go, when they would be on, and what to do. This was considered to be the foremost reception of recent years; two of the royals were looking for spouses. The islands that married into the families, if it happened, could reap generations of benefits. Though the last Queen had been from the middle-class society of the Diamond City inhabitants, it was tradition that the marrying royal came from an island off the Continent. Something about being far away from the rousing life of city folk made islanders seem more pure, more favored among the courts, even though the city folk considered them more barbaric and uncivilized. Also, there was all that more gossip to go around. Everyone was eagerly waiting to see if any significant connections were going to be made tonight.

Ronal might have been anxious himself to go into the city, but he was looking for a way to sneak Cyerra into the Palace for the party.

He figured it would be no problem, seeing as how his family had been able to arrange for an invitation. Most of the High Court had been invited to attend, and he was from one of the most prominent middle-class families of the city. His bright blond hair was combed, his robes were in place, and he had enough currency with him to tempt Cyerra out of working tonight effectively.

She worked in a crystal shop, full of special, beautiful gems. There were many kinds of charms that were sold as well. There were good luck charms, love charms, friendship bracelets, promise necklace set, and even some helpful plant seeds that were sold here. Ronal had first seen Cyerra and had followed her into the store, thinking it would seem gallant of him to offer to buy her something she liked. He was a little surprised to find out that Cyerra was the assistant proprietor of the shop. She and her twin brother were Islanders who had been sent ashore to live with their aunt after their parents had both died years ago. Ronal had never met either her aunt or her brother—Cyerra's brother was nearly nineteen, but he'd gone back to their island home some months prior to Ronal's meeting with Cyerra. Ronal was more than a little relieved at that. Though he liked Cyerra a lot, he had a feeling that dealing with his own family's reaction to his relationship was going to be enough for him. He was certain his city-bred parents would never approve of an Islander for his choice of woman.

She sure was beautiful, though. Her hair was a vibrant violet black, with bangs that nearly covered her eyes. It was cut in the island style, long and straight with varying lengths, shorter in the front and longer in the back. Her eyebrows were delicately arched, adding elegance to her facial features, especially her smile. Her cheekbones were high, and angular, giving her a grown-up look for someone who was close to nineteen years old.

He walked into the shop just a couple of hours before the pre-premiere of the Reception. In recent years, it had become more like a fashion show and an awards ceremony, with broadcasters constantly following in the rich people and digging up the dirt on who was doing what now and who had babies on the way. Ronal was certainly glad to be out of that mess. For a few short hours, he was allowed to be in the city.

"Cyerra!" he called out. "Where are you?"

"Shhh!" Cyerra hushed him from the corner of the room. "I'm over here, and my aunt is asleep in the back. If you don't want to wake her up, be quiet!" her voice was a soft, harsh whisper, but her clear blue-gray eyes were affectionate as she caught his attention.

"Sorry," he whispered sheepishly. "I couldn't wait to see you. I wanted to invite you to come to the Palace tonight, for the reception."

Cyerra's eyes lit up, but the light in them faded as quickly as it had come. "Oh … that's so sweet of you, Ronal," she started. "But-"

"I know, you're working tonight," he said. "That's why I'm willing to buy your store out for the night. I've got all the currency you and your aunt will want for just six hours tonight. What do you say to that?"

"Ronal, it's not the prospect of riches or the work," Cyerra whispered. "There's something else going on."

"Oh … oh!" Ronal's face turned a slight red of anger and embarrassment. "There's someone else you're waiting for?"

"No! Don't be silly," Cyerra brushed the thought aside. "My brother … he's … he hasn't been himself lately. Not since he's come back here. I'm worried about him."

"Your brother came back from his Island … today?" Ronal's voice was filled with uncertainty and almost a tingle of disbelief. Why would her brother come back now? It was the worst time for an Islander to come, especially one who was not invited to the reception. "Why?"

Cyerra sighed. He was certainly leaving her little room for ambiguity. She took his hand. "Come with me," she whispered, taking him to the back room and out the back door. She turned the corner around the alleyway, and beckoned him to follow her as she opened a small shed. The shed was connected to the main shop, supposed to be used for storage and other similar purposes. However, it had been cleaned out and fixed up, made up to be more of a meeting spot.

Once inside, she pulled a string, and a lantern came on.

"Look, I can't be too long in here, but there is something I feel I must tell you," she said, her voice suggesting that she was torn apart inside. "But you must promise me that you will not hate me or my family for this first."

"Okay," Ronal promised. "That's easy. I won't hate you. I could never." His hand squeezed hers relaxingly, reassuringly. "Tell me what's wrong."

"It's my brother, Aemon." Her voice broke as the tears welled up in her eyes. "He is angry at the Royals. He and some of the Islanders around here are using the reception as a cover to find more enemies of the monarchy—almost like a reconnaissance mission."

"Another Rebellion?"

Cyerra nodded. "He is intent on becoming the King, I'm afraid. After the last Rebellion, he feels that it is his destiny."

"What? Are you sure?" He took a hold of her gently and asked, "How bad is it? How bad is it? Does he have a lot of support?"

She began to have trouble breathing. In the dim light Ronal could just make out the barest glimpse of tears beginning to form in her eyes. "Yes, it looks quite bad," she muttered. "He has nearly one hundred small islands behind him, and his numbers are growing, though slowly, but with more joining every day. He has managed to convince the Island leaders that the entire Continent is taking over the islanders' resources and exploiting them, and how Diamond City is loaded with riches that the Islanders will never see for themselves because of the King's greed."

"What?"

"I know, it seems to us to be a lie. But the islands are not as rich as the Continent. They will only see the profits and fall into step quite easily behind the enemy."

Aemon had to be crazy, Ronal thought. But it looked like crazy was just what some of the Island leaders wanted. One hundred isles and growing behind him! Ronal couldn't believe such a thing was possible. He knew, from his strategy class, that even from fifty islands in the Sapphiran seas that the occurrence of war would involve legions and legions of the King's army, let alone a hundred or more! Even if the defenses had time to mobilize, the war would take thousands of lives.

"Cyerra," he said. "I know that I cannot ask you to spy for me. But I need your help."

She started to weep. "I would do anything to not go to war! I would do anything for my brother to let this go!" she cried. "And ... then there you are. I have only known you for a few short months, but I cannot help but feel I was meant to know you. I do not want you to die ... least of all, because of me."

Her words were touching, but he did not need to hear them now. His hands grasped her arms, trying to assert the seriousness of the situation. He knocked her off balance as he held onto her and willed her to think logically. "Then convince your brother I am a sap. Tell him that you can go with me to the Palace and check for suitable allies. I need you beside me tonight." Ronal's voice never faltered, never wavered. But he was worried for her, and for himself.

"Please, my friend, please! Try to understand. My brother is not a bad man," Cyerra started to try and regain her footing. "He is just angry, that he was deprived of a childhood. He grew up too fast. Aemon … " her voice trailed off and she sighed. She could hear her aunt moving around in the upstairs room. "We have to go back now. I cannot guarantee that he will let me come tonight. But I will try. If I can come, I will meet you there."

"Thank you," Ronal said. "That's all I'm going to ask of you for tonight." I've got to let Etoileon know about this, he thought. If anyone would know what to do, it would be him.

Cyerra put on a brave smile. "Really? No dance?" she teased him as she walked out of the shed, trying not to let anyone see that she had been crying.

***

The King silently groaned at the thought of having a meeting with the Heads of Council that day. Breakfast had been far from fun, when he had finally told Selene the news of the council's opinions. Even thinking about what those old men on the councils were going to tell him about what they thought he should be doing in order to help the prosperity of the world made his blood stir in anger. But he was comforted by the thought that the old men would be well into their spirits before too long. This was his last meeting before the reception.

On Sapphira, the Heads of Councils were also known as the Judges. They had been hand chosen by the Judges before them to replace them. The original generation of judges dated back to the first hundred years of the establishment of the monarchy.

He looked at the water clock in the middle of his study. From the look of it, he had no more time to delay; it was to leave for the meeting.

Dorian walked down the luxurious grand hallways of his home and marveled at how the decorations were coming for the party tonight. The wreaths of tree branches hung over and beside doorways, the world colors, appropriately blue (for the seas) and gold (for the land) were hung in plain and tasteful sight. He couldn't help but smile at all the effort that had been put into some of the outrageous designs; the guests were going to have plenty to talk about in those first awkward stages of starting a conversation.

Some of the really early guests were even coming, no doubt anxious to get off of their ships. Some islanders needed to spend over two weeks at sea in order to attend the Representatives' Ball. They would sneak ashore early, prepare for their grand entrances, and then once more sneak away to the welcoming blue carpet, where the television broadcasts, the newspaper journalists, and all the city people were anxiously awaiting them. It was almost like a contest, to see which island's representative would get the most airtime. The movie stars could have been put to shame by the off-hand attempts of some of these people to stay on the small screen,

Dorian thought. He grinned as he at last reached his destination.

"All bow to His Royal Majesty, King Dorian, son of Lukiahs!" the royal guard at the door announced. Dorian looked around to see that the surrounding men all greeted his arrival by giving him, remarkably, the same expression of quiet indifference. The king was just starting to think that he'd been late when the proceedings began, officially starting the meeting. Dorian kept his enjoyment to himself. After all these guys on the council were putting him through, he was a little more than glad the Council members had to bow down to him respectfully.

Dorian waved them off after a long moment. "All may rise."

Simultaneously, all of the men stood up straight from their bowed positions and after a moment of all of them trying to avoid rubbing their sore muscles and aching joints, everything was all ready for hours of discussion.

Dorian's chief councilor was a short, nervous looking man sitting to the right of him. Dorian couldn't help but feel a warm smile come to his face as he looked at this man; his name was Josiah, and he had been serving in the Council ever since Dorian had turned eighteen years old. Josiah had the heart of a child, and was Dorian's favorite in the Judges by far. Josiah alone was sympathetic and willing to listen to Dorian's thoughts on certain ideas. The tiny man's eyes twinkled with respect as he nodded, telling the King that the Heads of Council were ready for him to begin.

"Welcome, men," Dorian greeted. "It is good to see that you have not been delayed by all the partying, I must say."

A soft, almost inaudible chuckle sounded out among the ranks. There were a total of twelve men. Out of all of them, three of them had grinned, two had laughed, and the rest had no change of expression on their faces whatsoever. Dorian raised his eyebrow in speculation. You'd think that the men would be a bit more cheerful—they were given all the comforts of the Palace, and had nothing to do but once in a while gather for these silly meetings, he thought. "Anyway, to business."

"First order of Business," called out the speaker. His name was Gibberson, and he was a loud man, the only one with a full head of hair that was some other color than gray or white. His voice was only slightly softer as he looked at the king and continued. "Your Majesty, if you have not yet noticed, we have a new face with us today."

Dorian had not noticed the unfamiliar man sitting front and center in the boardroom. Now, looking on it, there was indeed a young man in the room, dressed in a simply cut black woven cloak. He sat directly across from the King's seat. He had to be young, Dorian thought. From his assessment, the king figured that this new arrival had to be only a few months older then Selene. But unlike his sister, this boy was completely solemn in his manner. Dorian was quite certain that he'd never seen such an intense face before at such a young age. The closest he could think of was that brat friend of Selene's, that orphan she'd dragged home. "Introduce yourself sir, if you please."

He stood up, barely coming to a short six feet in height. "I am Aemon, son of the late Ammos the Lost, of Jewel Island. I am the representative from my home island to the

City." He sat down once again, patiently waiting to be addressed by King Dorian.

Dorian raised his eyebrows in surprise. He knew who this was now all right. "I see. Welcome to Diamond City. Might I have a reason for your visit with my councilors this afternoon?"

Josiah spoke up. "Sir, we have been approached by Aemon –" he was cut off as Aemon once again stood up.

"I have come here to speak for myself and my people, and I would appreciate the chance to do so," Aemon interrupted him quite smoothly. "I have a proposition for you to carefully consider, Your Majesty." His voice and manners both lacked the full respectful formality that was due to the King and his advisors.

Dorian could guess where this was going. "You dare to mock the King?" he asked. "Either you have much bravery, sir, or little sense."

Aemon grinned. "I prefer to think that we are on even ground, Your Majesty."

"Really? Why's that, if you don't mind my asking?"

"I have come to get what I rightfully should have had long ago, and I warn you, I am willing to use whatever means necessary to accomplish my goals," he started out. "There is something I want from you."

"And that is ... ?" Dorian was starting to sense that something was terribly, terribly wrong here. It was a feeling he had not felt since before his father died. His fears were confirmed by the Aemon's response a moment later.

The smirk on Aemon's face grew. "How is your sister doing, now that she is eighteen?"

***

The time had just come for the reception to begin as Etoileon made his way up to the highest tower of the castle. He was late as far as the party was concerned, but he had a special reason for missing out on the pre-premiere and the beginning of formal announcements, and coming to this special room at the top of the high tower.

This was the place where he and Selene met each night they could both sneak away, often talking until the midnight hour. It had been their tradition to do this since they'd met, almost three years ago. This was where they laughed and talked together, and told each other all their secrets ... well, most of them at least.

Etoileon smiled as he pulled out his special gift for Selene—having taken Ronal's earlier advice, he had a tiny bouquet of deep red ekedlets, small minuscule flowers that smelled like sweet fruit. The ekedlets were tied together with a small yellow ribbon. He'd thought that the small gift would be perfect for her. It had taken him a while to get them, too. He was only allowed into the city, along with the other members of the Palace crew, only twice a month. Etoileon was lucky that he'd known the streets well enough to know where to go so he could get back in time to escort Selene down to the ballroom entrance.

The city was crowded for the opening of the reception. Etoileon had run into more than one person trying to reach his destination, Madame Flora's Shop. Though he had meant to hurry up, Etoileon slowed down to look around, amazed to see just how the streets had changed to him in so short a time.

He'd been raised on the streets, mostly all alone.

It had been a miracle that he had survived there, let alone to manage to get a job in the Diamond City Palace, considering a job at the palace was a highly coveted position in society. Middle class children often took jobs in the palace, using their connections to be introduced into the flashy world of riches and wealth. After a number of years, they were able to use their earned capital to be educated in the way of society. Using the skills they would acquire from training and teaching of their instructors and parents, the now young adults would be able to be placed in a position where it was likely for a marriage to be arranged or sought after.

Etoileon had none of this.

He had no parents, no real family, few allies … there were plenty of untrustworthy people, enemies, and dangers around every corner. All he had were survival skills, and the good fortune to happen to be in the right place at the right time. As Etoileon leaned back on the tower wall, he thought about the night that he'd met Selene. He did not get too lost in his memories. The Palace was beginning to feel more like home to him as time went on, and his memories of the darker times of his life were beginning to fade.

It was a moment later that the door opened and Selene walked into the Tower room as well.

"Etoileon," she greeted him, her eyes quickly losing their flicker of surprise and replacing it with an expression of warmth. "I did not think you would be up here this early."

"You are," he pointed out, a small smile forming on his face.

"Well," Selene blushed, "There was something I wanted to do before later."

"You mean before I came?" Etoileon asked. "What was it?"

"Well … " Her face had turned even redder, and she looked away as she reached behind her and pulled out a small bag. "I wanted to give this to you later, but I have no objections to giving it to you a little early."

Etoileon looked down at the bag she placed delicately in his hand. It had been carefully prepared for him, he could tell. The bag was all dressed up, tiny curls of ribbons surrounding the drawstrings of the sack, and made from cheerfully colored fabric.

Selene nodded. "Open it, Etoileon. It's for you."

Inside the bag, he found a small silver-framed photograph of Selene and him from a few years ago. It was when he had first undergone his training for the Fighter squad. Selene was sitting in front of him in the picture, while he was standing behind her. He could tell that his eyes had been focused on her; Etoileon figured that he must have missed the camera. His eyes examined the picture closely, running over Selene's face again and again.

"I don't remember this picture," he said slowly.

"It's from the time that you came storming out of the Fighter's training room, remember? You were not too happy, I recall. My memory of the reason has faded, but I remember thinking you needed me there," she said in a hushed voice. "I still come to watch, sometimes."

I still need you there, he thought. But he could not say that. So instead, he looked over at her intently, and said, "Thank you."

"So you like it?" Her smile seemed to brighten up the entire evening sky.

"Very much," he nodded. "That must've been the day that Master Norio told me in front of everyone that I had been poorly trained and it would be a miracle if I amounted to anything."

Selene's sad smile flitted to her lips. "Poor Master Norio. That has to be the most incorrect he's ever been."

"Just goes to show you that no one is always right," Etoileon shrugged. His eyes fell to the picture once more.

"Well … Happy Third Year Anniversary, Etoileon," she whispered. "That's what it's for. We met on this day, three years ago, remember?" She sincerely hoped he had remembered.

So that was why she had been so excited. His face curved into a smirk. "How could I forget? Actually, I was just thinking about it, if you want to know. Do you remember it?"

Selene grinned. "I remember it as though it were yesterday."

THE MOONLGIHT PEGASUS

***
Chapter 4
Memories
***

It had all began on that day, three years ago to the day.

The Princess Selene, under Dorian's careful guidance, managed to grow up in a short amount of time. She was constantly kept under watchful eyes, and it was thought that because of her that the world seemed to grow happier.

Dorian watched his sister as she played in the main hall's water fountain. She was fifteen, almost sixteen, years old, and she had never grown out of this habit.

She had never grown up to him, either. She still had the same angelic eyes, innocent look, and soft hair (though of course lots more of it) she had when he'd been nine years old and had picked her up for the first time. She had changed somewhat over the years, though. She was of average height for fifteen years, a couple inches short of five and a half feet. She was thinly built and, according to all of the boys that were employed as bellboys around the palace, the most charming girl that they had ever talked to or looked at. She was absolutely luminescent with the radiant light that seemed to shine from within her royal blood.

"You're going to get sick," he warned as he walked closer to her.

"Brother," Selene replied, while she was giggling hysterically. "You are incredibly too serious at times. Besides, if you would just let me have a tour around the city, I would not be so bored as to cause trouble."

"You know that this is not too much of a problem—after all the years you've been playing in this fountain, the staff is quite used to cleaning up after you," Dorian shook his head. "But the world out there is dangerous, Selene. It is no place for one as innocent and as carefree as you are. You know I cannot let you go out there. I have told you this before."

"And I have seldom listened to your speech, Dorian," she spoke as honestly as she did gracefully. She climbed out of the fountain, her feet and legs soaking wet. Her dress had absorbed a sizable amount of water while she had been playing, and not the once crisp, flawless white garment dragged across the floor, making wet, dirty smudges both on the gown and on the Palace floor. "Please, please, just once, for a couple of hours? I have finished all my studies and have read more books than the library can hold, I am certain of it. Please?"

Dorian shook his head. "I know you dream of freedom, but I cannot give in to you in this case. Please, sister, do find something else to occupy your thoughts."

Selene rolled her eyes, and then reached down into the fountain once more, scooped up some water, and tossed it playfully at her brother. "You are entirely too serious sometimes!" she exclaimed again, before laughing and then running away, so Dorian did not have time to retaliate.

＊

Selene had run to the high tower, the one that she secretly called hers. When she had been little, when she could not seem to find sleep, she had sneaked up to this highest tower of the Diamond City castle and gazed at the city below. She

82

was never allowed to go into the city, with the exception of a few parades and holidays. And even then, there had always been Dorian around, or at least a large number of guards. She'd never been completely free of those watching palace eyes. They'd made her feel guilty for even thinking of enjoying herself or looking around with interest while she was in the city.

She had always looked down there, and wishing for freedom from atop her palace; then she'd look up to the dull moon, and had wished to be free to fly there, to fly anywhere. From the tower, she could see the desert sands, the faraway villages where fires had burned in tiny specks, and lights could be seen for miles.

From her tower now, she could see the fading light of day as the gray sun began to drop behind the rest of the world.

The stars, seeming to shine more brightly than the moon, started to come out as she gazed across the world that was unfamiliar to her. A small bird came to land on the tower balcony next to her. The white bird cooed softly at the princess.

"I'm not unhappy," the princess said to the bird, smiling gently. "I like my life here, and I like my brother. But for once I wish I could see the world as you do." The bird jumped a bit closer to her as she added, "I bet there are days you wish you could be a fish." She laughed softly as she added, "It sure would make it easier for you to catch fish, I'll imagine." She held out her hand, and the bird jumped away from her, flying off into the nearby city.

"Well, Dorian said I should occupy my time with different thoughts," Selene thought aloud. "Thoughts of escape are different than thoughts of getting permission to visit the city." She smiled slightly. "Yes, I would say they are."

***

Dorian felt uneasy as he watched Selene throughout the next few days. She was unusually quiet by her standards. It was more than a little perturbing. He waved it off and let it go for the time being. His sister had always been somewhat unusual to him, and he had to plan meetings, organize campaigns for laws, look over the new staff at the castle, and organize his paperwork. He grinned. Whoever thought being a king was easy did not know what it was really like to be one.

Selene took advantage of the time she had to get ready. Her brother was planning a dinner party for the weekend. She knew it was for the newly elected Islander advisors. There was one of these parities every year, when the newest crowd of appointed representatives came to the Diamond City palace in order to present to the King concerns from each individual island. It would be six months later that the King would set out on his yearly 'Good Will Tour', visiting all the islands and inspecting the conditions there for himself. Dorian had promised to take Selene with him when she was married. She had complained good-naturally, saying it was unlikely that she would ever get married, seeing as how she was trapped within a prison disguised as a castle. Dorian had agreed to let her go at eighteen years if nothing else after that argument.

Selene hurried around her room, gathering things that she would need for her time outside the Castle. She wanted to be able to spend as much time as she could in the City. She'd rarely been off the Table her whole life, and the first time she was off of it alone she was going to celebrate by doing the thing that she'd most wanted to do—she wanted, most of all, to visit the Gemstone Oasis. It was the liveliest part of the city, and she'd always heard stories from the maids and workingmen in the castle about the Oasis when they'd thought she was paying them no mind.

It was not long before the day of the party arrived. Selene waltzed into the main office to the side of the throne room, where the servants had told her the King was.

"Dorian?" she called out. It was a surprising large room, complete with a library-sized collection of the King's most referenced and most favorite books.

"Over here, Selene," he responded, his voice drifting from the second layer of the room. There was a small staircase leading to a harbored room. It was the main room of the office, where Dorian had his filing cabinet, electronic devices, and latest projects.

"How's the engineering project going?" Selene asked as she looked into the smaller room. She knew that Dorian had a passion for creating new ideas for faster and better technology. He was studied under some of the best designers in the field of mechanics when he did not have any kingly duties.

Selene, personally, didn't know a viewscreen from a television.

Dorian looked up from his papers and nodded, a sure sign that he was on the verge of something big. "It's okay," he said in humble tone of voice.

"The representatives are going to be here soon, you know," Selene started out carefully. "It's almost mid-afternoon."

"I know," he replied absentmindedly. "I'll be ready soon."

"I wanted to ask a favor of you, Dorian."

"What is it? Do you need something?"

"No, no, I'm fine … well, maybe. Kind of. I was hoping that you would excuse me from the dinner celebration tonight."

Dorian looked up, his brows raised in a suspicious, almost untrusting manner. "Why? You know as Princess you have been born with the obligations to fulfill the traditions of the royal family."

"I know, I know, Dorian, but well … you see, there are going to be two full moons tonight, and I wanted to stargaze for a while in the High Tower. Besides," she said, moving on to her main point, "I'm getting close to the marrying age, and I don't want you to bond with one of the Islanders and marry me off to an old man who never stops talking about fishing or sail-hopping, or the war, or about himself –"

"I get it, Selene," Dorian interjected. "Okay, I'll let you out of the dinner tonight. Knowing how you are with some of the bellboys here, I'd say your reasoning is sound enough."

Selene blushed. "I do not flirt with any of them! I know that they are not the kind of boy for me. They all only see the title and the large house. Really, brother, you should not listen to them talk so. I have never even held hands with any one of them. I only treat them with the respect and the politeness that is merely due in regards to human dignity, I assure you."

"Oh, really?" Dorian said in teasing voice. "I'll have to keep that in mind next time I think about firing a couple of them."

Selene laughed, an infectious sound that Dorian found himself laughing with a moment later. "You are such a tease, Dorian. Thank you for letting me out of the dinner tonight. I appreciate it." She bowed deeply out of respect as she backed out of the room.

"Have fun," he called after her as she left.

Selene felt the guilt rise up in her as she thought about Dorian's kind words. He was such a nice brother. Selene would make sure that she would look up at the stars for a while before she took her leave of her home.

***

The night arrived, and Selene was watching it come from the top of her tower. She found Shira's glow as it met her full in the face. The other Sapphiran moon, Kuro, cast out a soft yellow tone to the world below. She would be free tonight. She could feel destiny coming toward her faster than ever for some reason.

She had taken the time to select her clothing. On the rare times she'd been able to leave the Palace, she had paid close attention to how the city folk dressed. They mostly stuck to simple outfits, unlike the royal family. Since Selene could hardly ask for a peasant girl's outfit, she'd decided to wear the most plain and simple outfit she owned. It was a simple white skirt and shirt design, the skirt with two simple layers for flounces and expensive burgundy trim and gold-laced embroidery, the design of many small tiny flowers on a background of dazzling, striking white. Not only did the white look plain, but also it managed to help her skin glow look less bright. The shirt was supposed to go with the skirt, but it was simple enough, only the velvet lines and three small flowers on the front. The rest of it was blank, and there were no sleeves to complicate the overall design of the outfit. Selene decided that she would have to borrow a walking robe to hide her shoes, which were considerable fancy for a city resident. The shoes were white with gold designs, and they were custom made just for her dainty feet.

Selene came down from her tower after about an hour of waiting for the dinner downstairs to escalate. She could hear from the top of the tower the violins and mandolins, and hear the ancient piano keys being skillfully manipulated to produce a melodious tune.

She peeped around the corner to see into the throne room, which was currently full of dressed up dancers, socializing and drinking businessmen, and lots of waiters serving little samples of the unique cuisine that Diamond City had to offer. Chez-haut, cheese wrapped around egg and ham slices, and expensive Filet-bet, steak sliced with thin bread and sprinkled with nuts, were among the more popular choices. Selene, who had a fondness for the Chez-haut, was tempted to sneak away with some, but she instead decided to stick with her original plan. If she were seen tonight, everything would be ruined.

Selene grabbed an old maid's walking robe as she made her way to the servant's entrance. She pulled up the hood, covering her face effectively. Her glow was even hidden to a surprisingly high degree.

She smiled as she reached the door. The sound of the waterfall nearby was louder than she ever heard it before. A bird whisked past her, and she smiled. It was time for her to spread her own wings.

She took her first step out of the Palace and couldn't resist taking another. She felt the darkness of night encase her as she walked away from the bright lights of the Table down the slanted streets off the plateau.

Selene, despite her disguise, could see the streets that she walked down without carrying a lantern. She felt like she stuck out like a bright light in a dark sea. Her skin was a milky white, and like all royals it cast out a glow. Now her skin seemed lighter than ever, as though it was a beckoning call for strangers' eyes. She walked down Calamity Street, known for its constant chaos. She walked past the many restaurants, where there were hundreds of men and women watching a television screen, laughing at a stage show, or throwing food at the performers in the stage show. A small restaurant had only a few people in it, with a center stage that looked like a poetry reading from outside.

Selene watched in amazement as she peeked over a fence and saw a flame dancer and a team of dancing wild men all performing amazing feats with the fire. I wonder what was so completely terrible about this world, Selene thought as she walked around.

There was an old woman who was standing on the street corner, holding a crystal in her hand. "Want to hear your fortune, sweetie?" her scratchy voice called out.

THE MOONLGIHT PEGASUS

"No thank you, ma'am," Selene smiled up at her. "But thank you for offering. Have a nice evening."

The old woman looked surprised and even smiled a little back at her. "You're welcome," the vender murmured. Selene wondered why it had seemed so odd that she would be kind to this businesswoman. It was true that more men were in business, but surely there were those women who needed more currency as well.

The princess made her way around a couple more streets, walking down "Isle Island", the small gathering of homes owned by those who had migrated to the city from the isles off the coast of the Continent. Here she made her first ever purchase—a string of beautiful pearlstones. It was not that expensive, and Selene thought it went well with her outfit.

"Thank you so much, sir," she politely said. "It's beautiful." She handed him her cash and put on the purchase, secretly pleased with her decision to come to town. She smiled and walked on. Gemstone Oasis was nearby. The excitement in her stomach bubbled up quietly.

Gemstone Oasis was the popular section of town. There were several shopping centers for clothes and even more bars for drinking, where moonshine was available from sun up to sun down. Selene had no desire to see this; she had heard stories of her late father drinking uncontrollably, and had vowed to stay off the stuff for as long as she could. Besides, she knew that she didn't have a lot of time here. And it was the water basin, at the end of the waterfall, which she longed to see most of all.

Having been raised her entire life on top of the waterfall, Selene had never seen firsthand the bottom of the waterfall. Even during those brief moments, at celebrations, openings of companies, and parades, she had never been allowed to wander off, even for the smallest glance, of the end of the waterfall. The mystery of what lay down there had been a burning question in her mind for years; Selene remembered when she was little, she used to think, before she'd ever climbed up to the High Tower, that the water simply fell off, and below was the end of the world. She'd never even imagined what a basin was. She did hear stories, though, time to time, of her trying to 'fly' out of the throne room into the waterfall from when she was little. Dorian sometimes teased her relentlessly of her adventurous nature.

She smiled as she neared the Oasis. She could hear the laughter, the sounds of dice being rolled. She could hardly wait to get there.

That was, until she heard someone scream. Looking around, in the dim light of the streets, she could see that the Gemstone Oasis had suddenly gone very dark.

The electricity must have gone out, Selene reasoned. It was nothing too, too scary. Surely it was nothing dangerous.

It happened every so often, that a dancing fool would manage to spill their moonshine on one of the area's generators. Those that were still sober usually sighed into their drinks and started to head on home, but those who were not merely laughed and cleared the way for the tavern owners to light the table lanterns.

Selene made her way cautiously to where she'd seen Gemstone Oasis sparkle only moments before. People all

91

around were walking past her, their obvious disappointment at the power outage evident. Selene stayed off to the side, letting the people saunter away from that part of town. Keeping her destination her main focus, she walked on past them, silent as a shadow.

Walking with slow steps, Selene left behind the city lights and had only the moonlight to light her way. It was her first time, she thought, to be in such a state. Then the clouds moved above, and the stars shined through once more. The moons even seemed to bring even more light to her surroundings, almost as though they were watching over her. A new wave of determination washed over her.

She hugged what little warmth her walking robe could offer close to her as she continued on, determined not to let the lack of lighting and power defer her to her destination. It looked to her that this was going to be one of the last times she would ever be able to explore the city on her own; she had best make the most of it, despite the problems she might run into.

It was then that she ran into the biggest problem of all. She was just looking over her shoulder to gaze back at an illuminated clock she'd recently walked past when she bumped into something—or rather, more accurately, someone.

"Hey! Watch where you're a-going!" A loud, booming voice rumbled down at her.

Selene instantly backed up, and lowered her head in apology. "I'm sorry," she started to say, backing up away from the boy, and tripping, falling backwards. Her eyes widened with sudden fear and confusion as she fell, and her hands clutched at her chest as though to keep it from beating out of her body. She felt the scream rise in her throat. Her eyes squeezed shut, bracing herself for hitting the hard, stony pathway.

The impact never came. A strong pair of arms reached out and broke her fall, inches away from the ground. The hood of her cloak flew back at the sudden, jerky stop.

She glanced up and found herself in the arms of a young man with short black hair, so dark night itself seemed to seep from it. In the pale moonlight, his eyes were gray, with speckles of silver. They held an inquiring look at the moment, as he met her eyes with his. Suddenly she could hear her heart racing. She was so surprised that she did not pay much attention as the boy who had caused her to fall sauntered over angrily.

"Hey! What do you think you're doing?!" he demanded. "Etoileon, this is my part of town!"

The gray eyes snapped up angrily at the boy's words. "Hey, Bubo, watch where you throw your weight around, would you?" Selene's rescuer sneered at the boy who had caused Selene to trip and fall. "You almost caused the Lady here a head injury." He easily lifted her and placed her on her feet, keeping her in his arms as he held her steady.

The boy called Bubo shrugged in an apathetic manner. "Call it however you see it. She's just a klutz, if you're askin' me … But hey, she's a pretty little thing, now that I can see her. Maybe she'll be wanting to have a little moonshine?" His eyes sparked with amusement, but the hopeful glimmer evaporated as Bubo caught the expression on his enemy's face.

THE MOONLGIHT PEGASUS

Selene's rescuer frowned. "Get out of here, Bubo. I'll have you dealt with later. It's people like you who give the streets a bad name. It's a good thing I have her now," he remarked, anger brewing in his eyes. "Or else I'd give you a sound whipping for saying that. I'm going to take care of her now … ."

Bubo saw the anger he'd caused in his adversary and shook briefly as he tried to discern whether or not this joker was telling the truth. When Bubo realized that he was in severe trouble, he hurried away, off into the darkened alleyways.

"Are you all right?" the stranger asked. His words were soft and kind, and Selene's eyes widened with sudden fear and confusion. Her hands gripped at her heart as she stood there for a moment, her searching eyes looking up to meet with his.

She watched as he turned to face her. He had a hard, but not unattractive face; it was a face that Selene imagined could be easily turned into a gentle smile. At the moment, he wore a face of concern mixed with the disappearing remains of battle. He was tall and lanky, and he had to be around her age—maybe a few months or even a couple of years older. He was dressed in simple dark green fighter's pants, with a sleeveless black shirt. The cloak he wore was black, with a couple of decorative symbols sewn on, but it looked faded and well worn. His black hair was unruly and stuck out in various places. Selene looked up at him to see that his eyes were blazing with a fire that was slowly reducing once more to a spark as he looked down at her.

She was shaking a little from the rush of adrenaline, but besides that she was basically fine. "Yes … I'm fine … " she whispered in what she hoped was a gracious and humble tone. She hurriedly pushed out of his arms and stood up, scrambling to appear to be the graceful young lady she'd been raised to be. "I did not mean to bother you, uh, sir, sorry for disturbing you."

"Etoileon." He had noticed her a while ago, heading toward the darkened Oasis before. He had not been able to recognize her. The palace robe she'd been wearing had made him look twice, and he knew as soon as his eyes fell onto her that there was going to be trouble. Maids and other palace workers were not a favorite of the Oasis nighttime regulars. Now that he'd been able to see her face up close, Etoileon was pretty sure that she would've had a lot of problems with the drunken men at the Oasis tonight. She was absolutely breathtaking.

Her hair curled at its ends, framing her face and setting it off at the same time. The wind had managed to dishevel it up a bit, but it looked all the more charming and appealing. He almost succumbed to the impulse to reach out and touch it. At the moment she was flustered and trying to pull herself together gracefully. She was no doubt somewhat ruffled from her close call with the ground. Despite her attempts to give the appearance of being grown up, she had to be younger than him. Her eyes were a deep, beautiful blue, like the sea on a clear night. But the thing about her that stuck out most in his mind was the feeling he'd had when he'd held her. He had felt almost certain that he was supposed to be there with her.

Selene, who had been watching the ground with a growing interesting, jerked her face up to look at his once more, her cheeks flushing a bright red at her eagerness. "Beg Pardon?" she asked.

"Etoileon. My name's Etoileon."

"Oh." Selene put on a small smile; it was her first since she had met him. "I see. Euh … " Why can't I think of anything to say? she thought as she hugged her arms to herself. She had never quite felt this way before. She was no longer afraid, and in fact she was beginning to forget the whole encounter with that Bubo or whatever his name was rapidly.

She looked shyly up at this gallant young man who had saved her. There was something about this boy …

"This is not a nice part of town," he said. "You shouldn't be here. When the power's back, all the other drunks, gamblers, and roughhousers are going to come back. You'd best go home now, miss … er … miss … " his sentence hung as he waited for her to give him her name.

"Selene." No time to be shy now, she thought.

"Really? I thought your name was Trouble for sure," he smiled lazily down at her.

What was he doing? He was never this nice to people he'd just met. Why did he want to make her laugh, make her smile? The questions running through his mind were left unanswered as her mouth curved into a warm smile and she began to relax. "Thank you for saving me, Etoileon. It was so nice and very admirable of you to intervene on my behalf."

"Bubo is not my favorite person," he admitted in an angry voice, but he scratched his head nervously and looked away, a sure sign that he was unaccustomed to praise and even more unnerved by how much he liked it. "I'm sorry that he had to cause you problems."

"Oh, it was an accident," she waved it off. She frowned all of a sudden. "That's too bad that you are not friends. I'm sure that you would be a great example for him to look up to," Selene said kindly. She felt bad for the Bubo person. He'd only been in the wrong place at the wrong time.

"Euh … right. Anyway, go home. Someone as naïve as you needs to be safe." Etoileon started to turn away when she reached out and took hold of his arm.

"Please," she said. "Please, I want to go and see the Oasis. Will you stay with me?" she looked up at him with her imploring and enigmatic eyes.

Etoileon felt his heart skip a beat. This girl was weird. But there was something about her that he couldn't ignore, something he couldn't quite identify … He did not hear himself say "Yes," or even see her smile brightly. The only things he could clearly remember later on were her unblinking, mesmeric eyes and the rapid beating of his heart as her hand took hold of his.

***

Selene was too excited about seeing the Waterfall basin she did not see that her new friend felt awkward.

"I have always wanted to visit this place," Selene confided in him. "It's been one of my most secret dreams for almost forever."

Etoileon was unused to this. His life was not all pretty and bubbly like this intriguing girl was. She seemed so aloof, so wonderfully separate from all the evil. She almost did seem to glow. He wondered if he should be worried.

"I haven't been to this part of the city before, you know. I'm glad I don't have to go here alone," Selene whispered to him. "Thanks for coming."

"Yeah, sure," he responded. "Look, the power is coming back on now."

Selene looked down on the scene before her and indeed saw that the lights were starting to flicker back on. It was completely dark and lifeless one moment; the next moment it was warm and welcoming, a beacon calling out through the waves of city life.

Selene could hear the growing intensity of the sound of the waterfall as it hit the waiting water below. She could soon feel the gentle spray of the mist as the wind blew caressingly on her face. Her ears suddenly perked up at a sound of a horse neighing in the distance.

"Did you hear that?" she asked.

"Hear what?"

"What do you mean, 'hear what'?" she giggled. "I'm talking about the horse. I heard one just now."

Etoileon shook his head. "There have been no horses around here. Not since before the rebellion fifteen years ago. The royal family outlawed them in the city because they feared that they would be used against them in battle."

"That's nonsense," Selene remarked. "I just heard one."

"If you say so," Etoileon shrugged. "But I didn't hear anything at all."

"Do you ever think that's because you don't want to hear it?" Selene asked, her gaze slanting over to meet his. "Sometimes I think people block out certain things that they just don't want to accept or know or hear about."

He shrugged. "I guess … " he looked up at the Gemstone Oasis as they reached just around the basin's bend. "This is it, Selene. Gemstone Oasis."

Selene's eyes filled with the array of lights flooding the area. There were more buildings and places than she'd imagined there would be. It was a wonderful, almost unbelievable sight as she looked around. "Wow!"

"This place has everything and everyone—drunks, idiots, and the usual people who make a town colorful—and it looks like we've got newcomers here tonight," Etoileon noticed, a slight look of surprise and interest on his face.

"What do you mean?" Selene asked.

Etoileon pointed over in the direction of the band of brightly dressed newcomers. "Those guys over there in the royal blue outfits, the ones with the emerald trim, see? They are part of the Royal Palace guards. I've rarely seen them here before in uniform. Don't get me wrong though, lots of them come here when they're off duty."

"Uh … Royal Palace guards?" Selene repeated uneasily. When her new friend nodded, she looked away and began to head over in a different direction, pulling Etoileon along with her.

"Hey! Where's the fire?" he asked as he trudged along after her.

"I just wanted … I just wanted to get a cone of ice cream, that's all," Selene hurriedly explained. "I think I see a stand over there." She pointed to a less active corner of the Oasis. "I've never been allowed to get any of the stuff before, and I'm dying to try it! Hey, can we take the tour up to the waterfall?"

"Sure," Etoileon agreed. He thought for a moment and then added, "If you'd like, I'll show you the secret perch you can sit on and see the whole basin oasis from the waterfall."

"Is it safe?" she asked. When he nodded, Selene's eyes went huge with excitement. "That sounds wonderful!" she agreed, her smile mile wide. She'd already forgotten about the troops that her brother had sent after her.

***

It was a few hours later when Selene sat up on a rocky precipice about a quarter of the way up from the Oasis, licking up her third cone of ice cream. It was absolutely the best night of her entire life, she thought. And it was all thanks to Etoileon.

He was eating his own cone of ice cream at a slower, controlled manner than the Princess was, and he was looking down at the Oasis water, his eyes glazing over as he stared out into space and got lost in his thoughts.

Selene smiled a tiny smile as she looked over her newest friend. He was so quiet, she thought. He had barely talked about anything on their whole adventure together, but Selene had not minded. He'd answered all her questions, and told her a couple of interesting facts she was sure she could not find in any textbook in the Palace. And she loved the sound of his name. Etoileon. Another smile flittered to her lips. It sounded like a name of an epic war hero or something.

He caught her glance as he was thrown out of his distant trance. "What?" he asked.

"Nothing," Selene blushed slightly. She knew it was rude to stare at another person, and she had no doubt been doing that for some time before he'd caught her. "I was just trying to imagine how you'd gotten the name Etoileon, that's all."

"I know it's a little unusual," he scratched his head nervously. "But I don't really know why it's my name either. My parents ... " He shrugged and let the sentence go.

A moment later, Selene tried once more to get him to talk to her. "Do you like your parents?" she asked. When he still said nothing, she continued on. "I don't remember mine. I've always sort of wondered what it would be like to have a real mom and dad."

"You don't have parents? Did they die?" he asked, slightly shocked to find out she was an orphan just like him.

She nodded. "A long time ago. My brother takes care of me now," Selene answered, looking up at the sky as she talked. "I'm glad I have him, but sometimes he gets distracted with work. In fact, he was paying me no heed tonight, and that's why I was able to get out. And I have to say, as much as I am glad to be here, I am disappointed in his abilities to pay close attention."

"Hmm … " He shrugged once more. His gaze turned away as he considered it as he ate his ice cream thoughtfully. Someone as pretty as this girl had no parents, just like him. It wasn't much of an encouraging similarity, but it was there. Looking over at her again, seeing her lost in her thoughts, he felt compelled to tell her the truth about him.

"I don't have any parents either," Etoileon admitted. The truth was, he had no memory of his real parents at all. For most of his life, the closest thing he'd had to a parent had been the old Shaman priestess who'd taken him in 'out of the goodness of her heart'. He almost laughed at the thought. All she'd wanted was a maid or a cheap cleaning service. It had taken Etoileon two weeks, when he was eleven, to figure out that she was out of her mind. He'd fled from her, to a new area of the city, and had scrounged around for years until he had at last been strong enough to carry on by himself. He was now nearly seventeen years old, and he'd learned many things in the last ten years. "I've lived in this part of town for some time now. When I'm eighteen, maybe I'll try and get a decent job at the docks or aboard some ship. I've always wanted to travel, see the world."

"I know exactly how you feel," she nodded. "I can't do anything like that, but my brother says he'll let me go when I'm eighteen." She smiled ruefully over at Etoileon. "You're so lucky that you only had a year to go. I have three … well, almost two and a half.”

“I wish I was old enough to sign up now,” Etoileon admitted. “Battling against corporations and trying to ship everything all over the world sounds a bit more civilized then fighting Bubo and his friends for space and dignity on the streets.”

Selene scooted a few inches closer to him. “It must be hard living alone,” her voice soft, like a whisper. Her ice cream lay forgotten a few feet away as she waited for his response.

“Sometimes,” he admitted. “But no one really wants to trust a street kid. You should know that. It’s a real shame, too. Not all of us around here are like the Demon Chasers.”

“Who are the Demon Chasers?” Selene asked. One could detect the ominous evil from the mere sound of the word.

“Have you ever heard of the stories of the Guardian and Obsidian?” he asked her. “A woman I once knew a long time ago told me about them.”

“I think I have. It was a long time ago, when I was younger, however. Is the Guardian you mean the one who watches over the world of Dreams?” she asked. “That’s the only Guardian I know.”

“Yeah, that’s him,” Etoileon confirmed. “And Obsidian was one of his helpers, before he turned away from his duties.”

"I thought he tried to take over the Guardian position," Selene said. "I've heard the tale about how he was imprisoned in the Four-point Celestial prison, between four of the brightest stars in the night sky." She looked up. "I was hardly told of the Demon Chasers. I was always told of the goodness of the Guardian and his love for all of us here on Sapphira."

"That's true enough. Anyway, the point is, when Obsidian was cast into the Celestial Prison, he vowed to get revenge on the Guardian. In order to do that, Obsidian had taken the Guardian's most precious dream and had poisoned it with a sickness." Etoileon held Selene's full attention now. "And that most beloved dream was Sapphira and its people."

"So the Demon Chasers are … ?" Selene shook her head in slight confusion. "Obsidian's helpers?"

Etoileon smiled warmly at her. "Yeah. The woman who told me was one of them, actually. She'd been a priestess for about forty years. She was probably one of his most devout followers. I hear that she constantly talked with him herself, and pulled off amazing feats of dark magic in his name. Many people came to see her about sicknesses and had them healed. But it was at outrageous prices. She had this one man give up his most treasured possession, a beautifully carved sword, in order that she could heal a broken ribcage. And I remember that there was another woman who had to give up her laughter so her boyfriend was saved from death."

"How awful to have seen what the darkness can do," Selene whispered. She thought a moment about her own past, with the prophecy that had been given at her birth in the Guardian's name, and her own special dreams. "I'm glad that I love the light too much to be afraid of shadows."

"It was a little ironic that her boyfriend was an entertainer, though," Etoileon added, almost as an afterthought.

"Etoileon," Selene cocked her head to the side and smiled in a curious way, "What if I was in danger? What would you give up to save me?"

"I don't know; give me an idea or two."

"Would you walk on hot acid coals?"

"Depends if I get to wear shoes or not," he smiled at her. "But since probably not for the shoes, I doubt it."

"Huh. Well, what about giving up something for life? Would you give up your most precious item for me to be safe?"

"I don't really have items that mean so much to me that it would be a burden to give them up for you," Etoileon decided after a moment's thought.

They sat on the perch overlooking the basin, Selene's eyes catching sight of more guards entering the bars and entertainment places below. The worry in her heart was growing. It was not like the guards to go into the City wearing their Palace uniforms. She almost jumped out of her seat when Etoileon spoke up and asked her a question.

"I'm sorry, what did you say?" she asked, forcing herself to turn her eyes away from the guards on the ground and focus completely on her friend.

"I asked if you think someone would agree to give up his life for yours, would he do it?"

Selene looked up at the White Moon Shira as she pondered the question. Her best friend in the whole world had to be Dorian … could she even call him her best friend? He was her brother, first of all. But nonetheless he was also the King. Hence, his life would have to be protected first of all no matter what the cost was. So she doubted that he would give up his life for her. "Well … I don't think I've ever heard of that," she admitted, taking the diplomatic way out of answering. "Do you mean that a person would take a punishment for me, or just die for me to get better?"

Etoileon shrugged. "I don't know," he said. "I guess both, in a way. Still, though, I can't imagine doing something like that for anyone. I mean, isn't life the most important thing you can give up? I just can't see it happening."

"Me either," she admitted softly. As much as everyone meant to her, she could not imagine placing a person's life, his entire life, up against her own life, her own entire life. It was just unheard of.

"But then again," Selene added a moment later, "I can't see a woman giving up her laughter for her husband or boyfriend or whatever it was to get well again, either." She laughed at the thought. It just sounded so silly, so unbelievable.

Etoileon looked over at her and laughed, too, his first true laugh in a long time. Selene was startled, however pleased, to hear his short laugh. She decided that she liked this boy a lot. He was so … familiar to her, in a way. Like she'd met him before somewhere.

She scooted over to him a bit more and took his hand in hers. He shrunk back a bit and then looked at her questioningly. "Etoileon … Etoileon, I just wanted you to know this has been the best day I've ever had. Thanks for sticking around," she smiled at him. "I've never had a friend like you before."

He didn't know how to respond to her tender gratitude. He was hardly used to it. So he just nodded and looked away, his face starting to turn a bright red.

After a few moments of a deafening silence, Etoileon spoke up. "Look," he said, his voice an awed hush. "You can see a lunar rainbow." His eyes were on the end of the waterfall, only a few yards away. The gentle mist splaying up from the water basin caught the light of the two moons and shimmered indeed, creating a darkened rainbow effect across the night.

Selene looked down and felt her eyes widen, and her world lose focus as her gaze held steady on the beautiful sight. The rainbow arched up, seeming to dance in the moonlight.

"Wow. It's so amazing," she whispered. "I've never even heard of a lunar rainbow before."

"It's quite a sight," Etoileon agreed. "I almost never see it when I come here. I guess two moons have to be up for there to be enough light for it. Every time I do see it, though, I'm always surprised. It always seems to look … I don't know … it's hard to explain."

Selene's eyes traveled back to Etoileon's. "Do you mean that it looks more beautiful than the last time you saw it?"

He shrugged. "Let's go back down there," he suggested, changing the subject. "I could use another ice cone."

"Sure," Selene agreed, a tiny smile starting to come to life on her face despite her concerns. "My treat."

Selene thought that maybe everything was going to be okay then. There were practically no Royal guards around now—still, just enough to make her nervous. So Selene put on a grin and ordered the two cones for her and Etoileon. Instead of climbing back up to the precipice, they decided to sit on a bench in front of the stand. It was right in the heart of the Gemstone Oasis, full of music and dancing. Selene couldn't resist staying to watch some of the local talent.

"Selene?" Etoileon came up to the bench. She felt the warm night air coming off of him as he sat down next to her. "Do you like this place so far?"

She nodded. "It's the first time I ever came here," she said. And I think that while it is vastly different from the Palace, it has a certain charm all to itself, she thought. "It was accurately named, I think."

It was a glorious night. The music was rustically lively, her ice cream was scrumptious, and she had made a new friend, not to mention she hadn't been caught. She looked up and saw the stars twinkle and the moons shine; it was as if there was nothing to worry about, as if the world was at peace. Selene sneaked a glance over at her new friend, and felt the breath in her body rush out. The moonlight reflected off of his face, causing Selene to appreciate for the first time how handsome he really was. She felt the color rise in her cheeks, but for the quick second she had, she let it go. Wow, she thought, Etoileon is really handsome … I wonder what he thinks of me? Then she turned away, as the rush of emotions that were inside her began fluttering away. The feelings were unfamiliar to her; suddenly she felt that there must be something different about Etoileon that had caused these strange feelings to arise in her. It was something exciting, but at the same time more than a little frightening.

She was just taking another bite of her chocolatti supreme ice cream cone when Etoileon nudged her shoulder. "Hey, look," he whispered. "The Royal Guards are about to go into action."

"What?" Selene jumped up. She turned to face Etoileon. "We have to get out of here!"

"No, it's okay, Selene, these guys are professionals," he tried to assure her. "They're going to get the people in trouble and drag them away. We shouldn't have a problem."

Her ice cream fell to the ground. The music stopped, and a fire shoot was thrown into the sky. Music and laughter was quickly replaced by screaming and worried whimpering. Selene felt her heart stop and her hands go numb.

"Please, let's go!" Selene begged Etoileon. She grabbed his hand and started pulling on him. He stood up, and attempted to begin trying to calm her down as she pleaded with him to get moving. He wondered what was wrong with her all of a sudden. Why was she afraid of the Palace guards?

Suddenly a guard came up and stood behind Selene. "Give it up, Your Highness." His voice was deep and carried a warning in its tone. Everyone around them were trying to scramble away, trying to hide in small corners to get the gossip, or screaming and yelling here and there; but Selene retained her Princess manner, standing perfectly tall and straight, not moving an inch. The slightest movement of her body caught Etoileon's attention—she'd tightened her grip on his hand.

A voice came over the local sound system. "Attention, attention every one: Put your hands up, and step away from the Princess. No body moves, nobody gets hurt!"

She felt her eyes fall to the ground as her body was paralyzed with indecision. Already she knew it was too late.

They'd found her.

***

Etoileon felt the shock of disbelief flood through his body as though he were suddenly standing under the icy waterfall. *What? This was the princess?*

This girl, this one who had, in the short hours they'd spent together, become one of his few friends? And those feelings ... those feelings that had stirred in him, the ones that he would deny even came at all, they were for the Princess of the Entire World?

Selene. When he'd first heard her name, and saw the walking palace robe, he'd assumed that her parents had named their child after the Princess in order to gain favor in court. But he'd been wrong, apparently.

Now, he found himself looking at the Princess, her back turned to him, his eyes wide with shock and confusion and uncertainly leaking throughout his whole body. "Selene?" his voice was a quiet whisper. His hands, he realized a moment later, were shaking slightly.

"Yes," she whispered back. She'd sensed the surprise in him and felt both happy and sad. Someone had become her friend without seeing the benefits of her title. But now, it looked like he was going to be unable to deal with the truth.

A royal guard came forth and broke the two apart. It was the commander, the leader of the search party. "Hands off the Princess, sir!" he announced to Etoileon. Two more royal guards came up behind Etoileon and began to hold him back, grabbing onto his shoulders. One of them nodded to their commander. "Who do you think you are, holding onto her like that? You have some nerve!" He turned to the Princess and bowed. "Your Highness, your presence has been demanded by the King."

"Commander," she started, unsure of which commander he was; she wished briefly that Dorian would make them wear nametags. She was about to continue when the guards holding Etoileon interrupted her words.

Or rather, the guards who had been holding Etoileon back had interrupted her. Etoileon, in a typical reaction from a child from the streets, had counterattacked in order to escape their clutches. He'd landed a roundhouse back kick off of the one, and had punched the other with the freed arm he'd gotten from the kick. Other guards came up, but Etoileon was well versed in how to defeat an enemy. He launched out several attacks, leaving Selene silent as she watched in horror as the guards tried to get him settled.

He propelled himself through the guards, looking for a way to get away from them, driven by the anger burning inside him. It wasn't that he was angry with these guards, but he was angry with himself, for not recognizing the Princess when he'd met her, and he was also angry for being held like a prisoner, as though he had done something wrong, when he'd in fact saved her from a bully and a fall. He had only tried to be nice to her. With the emotions raging through his blood, he punched here and there, lashing out his kicks with tremendous skill and precision. The guards advanced, also landing a few good shots to the boy and causing Etoileon to struggle on his way through the mass of them. The battle went on for a long, almost heartbreaking moment.

Finally, Selene squeezed her eyes shut and cried out, "Stop it! He is my friend! Stop it!" The guards, under her command, stopped fighting. Etoileon, breathing hard, sweat starting to appear on his forehead, remained still on the ground after Selene had called the guards to stop fighting.

Selene rushed to him and stood in front of him. "That's enough! I came here of my own free will, and this boy has nothing to do with me getting out of the Palace. Leave him out of this!"

She calmed down a bit and looked down at Etoileon. His breathing had returned to normal though he still looked like he wanted to fight. There was a stream of blood coming out from his shoulder. "Etoileon ... you're bleeding," she said softly, her eyes showing that she was concerned for him. "Come with me, please."

Etoileon had a good reason to say no. He couldn't, for one thing. He was a poor, young, street urchin, an orphan.

THE MOONLGIHT PEGASUS

This was the Princess of the World! "Sel—Your Highness, I must decline," he said back, standing up and looking her full in the face, maybe one last time. She would understand, and let him go. And that would be it. He was certain of it.

"No, you may not," Selene smiled back. Her smile faded as she continued. "But if you have no care for me at all, though I may be a Princess or a pauper, I would insist that you leave at once, and forget all about me. It is only then that you shall be free."

"I could never forget about you," Etoileon whispered without thinking.

Her expression softened, but then hardened a moment later as she caught sight of the royal guards around them. "Then we shall return to the Palace," Selene announced, turning her attention back to the guards. "Let us go." She straightened out her walking robe, and held her head up high, trying to regain some of her lost composure. It was not hard for one as well brought up as she.

The guards filed in two lines beside them, and Selene beckoned for Etoileon to follow her. Normally, she would have reached out and taken his hand, but she could not. Selene sighed. She already missed the warmth.

***

Dorian was waiting for her, not in a small, private receiving room, but in the large, empty Throne Room. There was still garbage thrown all over, gathering the corners of the floor, and everyone had been dismissed. Selene had a sinking feeling in the pit of her stomach that she'd been the reason for the early closing.

113

Dorian was sitting regally, with his arms on the rests of the wooden throne. His kingly robes were straight and unbending, as though to simulate his approach to this matter. But if this was true the look of his robes—aloof and uncaring—was nothing compared to the look of barely contained anger he wore on his face.

His eyes seemed to promise silently that punishment would not be averted, nor delayed. Dorian watched as his sister and his guards slowly made their way to the throne. Despite his anger, he also noticed that a young man was following Selene, freely, as if it was nothing to be in the house of the royal family. Dorian was suddenly very worried and overcome but a mixture of unwanted surprise and jealousy as he realized that Selene must be behind this kid's appearance, or at very least, she was responsible for him not being bound. Dorian tried to place this kid's face in his memory, trying to see if he recognized him to be a kitchen boy or a bellboy or something like that. But when he could not, and noticed the simple clothes the boy was wearing, he knew that he had come from the streets. What he did not know now from observations, the King was determined to find out.

The Commander, whose name turned out to be Commander Kef, bowed low before him, and then everyone else followed the suit, except for Selene and Etoileon, Selene because she did not have to, and Etoileon because he did not like the look of this King, or how he had demanded that his sister stay outside of the city. Also, Etoileon did not know how to bow in correct form. He did not want to make a fool of himself here.

THE MOONLGIHT PEGASUS

"Your Royal Highness," Commander Kef greeted him formally, "I have found your sister, Her Highness for you. She was at the Gemstone Oasis Plaza."

Dorian's eye flashed anger even more, but he brought it under control. He was already upset and insulted that the strange looking kid who had also been brought to the palace had not bowed to him. But this news, that his sister had disobeyed his commands, was at the very place that he'd been so set against, was just adding fuel to the fire. "I see," he said through gritted teeth. "Continue, Commander, if you will," he ordered.

"Yes, Your Majesty," the Commander complied. "Princess Selene was found with this young man. She claims he did not assist her out of the Palace, though I am not sure that is the entire truth here, Sire."

"Selene would not lie," Dorian assured him. "But then again, I did not think that she would sneak out, either," he added after a moment's thought.

"I'm sorry, Brother," Selene spoke up softly. "I will not ever do it again, I promise."

Dorian breathed in, trying to let go of his anger. "Do I have your word on that, Selene?" he asked gravely.

She looked up at him, her eyes full of sincerity. "Please, believe me, Dorian," she whispered earnestly. "I will not leave again, unless it is necessary."

Dorian nodded, satisfied with her promise. His eyes turned from hers to rest on the boy behind her. "Commander, step back, if you please. Guards, you are dismissed. Leave at once and resume your posts. You, Boy. Come forward." The guards saluted the King and left, turning on their heels and brushing past Etoileon as he made his way in front of Selene, who had stepped off to the side. She looked anxious for some reason.

Etoileon frowned at the King as he was called. Already he could sense that the King did not like him much. "Yes … Your Majesty?" Etoileon wondered what the King was going to do to him. Though so far the King seemed to be arrogant and insane, Etoileon fervently hoped that the monarch would be as gracious and as kind as he was rumored to be.

"You, boy, tell me your name, if you even have one," the King's tone rang with unspoken distain, and Etoileon knew at once that the King really did not like him and was not going to be as nice as Etoileon would have liked.

"My name is Etoileon," he answered, regardless.

"Etoileon? What kind of name is that?" Dorian scoffed. "What island are your parents from, Imbecile Island? Or don't you have any?"

"No, I don't have any," Etoileon answered through gritted teeth. He was getting angry himself. He hated it when people made fun of his name.

"Dorian, please stop!" Selene interjected. "That is not fair of you to judge him, or his parents for that matter. Please, Dorian, stop this. It is my fault he was brought here." She turned red, her cheeks flushing over in unspoken affections as she whispered, "He is my friend, Dorian."

Dorian saw the reaction his sister had and could not believe it. She liked this … this … this orphan boy! Out of all the suitors he'd shown her, or all the bellboys that were running around the palace, or … or any other boy she'd ever been in the presence of, this was the one that had become special to her. He groaned silently. He was not going to enjoy this at all.

"Selene, I do not approve of you being around this boy. Can't you see he's dangerous?" Dorian said. "The training he has received as a Fighter is proof enough!"

"Huh?" Obviously, Selene had missed the fighter insignia on his cloak. When Dorian pointed this out, Selene just shrugged. "I know he would not hurt me, Dorian … In fact, he protected me from some of the other people that were at the Oasis."

"He … protected you?" The words seemed to hang eerily in the air.

"Yes, he did," Selene smiled after a moment. She'd been waiting for Etoileon to say something for himself, but he had not. "And he made sure I did not cause any more trouble, which I did not until your guards stirred up the entire Oasis with their entrance."

Dorian just looked down at her and sighed. "Selene, you are dismissed. Go to your room, and remain there. You, Boy … Etoileon … you are to wait here. We will discuss your position here."

"You mean he can stay?" Selene's eyes were wide with happiness.

"What else can I do with him? Send him into the streets, to stir up trouble? Send him to jail, with no just reason to imprison him?" Dorian said exasperatedly. "Not to mention ensuring a deep wrath in your heart against myself? I would be most unwise to do so." He glanced at Selene and then said, "Go. Leave us. Now."

Selene bowed in thanks, and then caught Etoileon's eye. In that moment, he suddenly knew that he was going to be okay.

***

"Yeah, that was pretty much how it happened," Etoileon agreed with her. "I still remember thinking you were crazy for hearing a horse."

"It was possible!" Selene huffed jokingly. "I never did find out what happened after I left the throne room, though. What did Dorian say to you?"

"Well … he wasn't so bad," Etoileon admitted, "but it did take me a while to come to respect him—you should know that. I still have days where I know he does not like me." He saw the look of an oncoming denial on her face, and decided to continue before she could start.

***

When Selene disappeared from the throne room, Dorian stood up. "Good. She is gone. I have little resistance when it comes to her. There's something about her eyes, and her smile … you know? Yes, you undoubtedly know. I can tell that you've fallen under her spell."

118

THE MOONLGIHT PEGASUS

Etoileon saw the bait. He wasn't going to take it. King Dorian was looking for any excuse in the world to declare him unfit for Palace service. "I don't know what you mean, Sire," he said in blank tones.

Dorian frowned as he began to pace. "So, you're smarter than you look. How old are you … Etoileon, was it? I have the hardest times remembering the unimportant facts."

"Yes, it's Etoileon. I'm nearly seventeen years old."

"Well, then, I'm going to have to get you trained for the Palace work I have in mind for you. I think that you will do nicely to begin training to be the Princess' body guard."

Etoileon's eyes had been looking at the spotless, shimmering floor when he caught Dorian's words. "What? You're going to allow me to watch over her?" he asked. "But … why?"

"It seems that I share my father's flaw," Dorian muttered as he turned away. "I am sometimes entirely too nice."

Etoileon said nothing.

Dorian sat down once more in his throne. He'd worked out almost four hours that morning, and after all the hubbub that had occurred today, between the Island Representatives, Selene's secret adventure, and finding this joke of boy following her home like a lost pup, it was almost too much to stand up anymore.

He almost smiled, remembering how his father would drink. At that moment, Dorian understood his father better.

His attention focused once more on Etoileon. "I am no fool," he said. "You have been able to see what protecting Selene is like somewhat, I assume from her tales. I can no longer keep her safe from the world, though I have tried throughout these last fifteen years. You know the world. You can protect her from it much more effectively than I could. Within my palace, I cannot keep tabs on her any longer. As much as I hate it, you are most suited for such a purpose."

Etoileon looked down at the ground. He did not know what to say. Suddenly, it seemed like his whole life, the trials, the hard times, all of it had been to build him up for the tasks ahead. It had been mere hours since he'd met Selene. Already his life was changing in ways that he'd never expected, he'd never dared to even dream or speak aloud. "Thank you, Sire," he said softly, finding nothing to say.

"Let's get something straight here, though," Dorian said. "You are going to have to be educated, and trained for more battle skills, and you're going to have to prove yourself worthy of the task. And we're going to have to get you some new clothes and definitely a bath. And some medical attention, too." The king frowned down at him. "If you cannot hold out against the tests I have for you, I want you to know that you are even less of a man than I already think you are. Selene is going to be married in a few short years. Until her husband takes over, the position of protector stands."

Etoileon's eyes hardened. "Understood."

"Good." The King pressed a button off to the side of his throne. "Garth, please come and take our newest household member to his new quarters in the Training Quarter. Give him anything he needs, and call the maids to ready a room and bath for him, and the Tailor Morris to get some new clothes for him."

"Yes, Sire," the voice responded over the intercom.

The King turned back to Etoileon. "There. Garth will take you to your new room. Order some dinner, if you like. You must be hungry after all the excitement."

Etoileon shook his head, saying nothing more as Garth came in and took a hold of him, guiding him to his new room, to start his new life.

Before Etoileon left, Dorian yelled after to him once more. "Hey, Orphan Boy!" he called. "I don't like you that much."

Welcome home, Etoileon thought grimly as he left the Throne Room.

***

"I cannot believe that Dorian actually said that," Selene dismissed the possibility as easily as though it were dust in the air. "Of course he likes you."

"Believe me, he said it," Etoileon grinned. "At least he was being honest about it."

"Surely then, he was joking," she responded.

Etoileon sighed, letting it go. He was much more interested in other things. Things that included giving her his present.

"Here … I bought these for you," he offered. "I thought that they looked perfect."

Her eyes lit up at the gift he held. "Wow!" she held the flowers gracefully up to breathe in their fresh fragrance, her hands held in such a way as to cradle the tender buds. "They're wonderful!"

"I know it's not much … " he was about to tell her that he had not remembered their 'anniversary' but she interrupted him.

"Etoileon … " Her voice was softer now, more serious, more thoughtful. "I know that the gift is not important, no matter how small or grand. Remember when that leader from Bypass Isle offered me all those jewels and fine materials for me to accept his marriage proposal? After Dorian had to convince him I was still too young, he never sent me a message or anything. Point is, he cared little for me personally. It means so much to me, that you simply came." She was looking down, because she did not want him to see her eyes water as she came close to telling him just how important to her he was.

"Selene?" he was not sure if she wanted to go on or talk about something else. When she said nothing, he decided to ask her a question. "Do you remember when I came here for the first time?"

She managed to hold back the sentimental tears. "Yes, I do," she remarked. "It took me forever to sneak those notes into your room, you know that? I had to have Kadrianne sneak them in."

He grinned. "It was really nice of you. The notes made me feel better. After all, I was suddenly in a new, rich world, in unfamiliar territory." He had grown accustomed to the five-thirty wake-up calls for the training classes in the morning, education classes with Selene until noontime, and evening meals, the curfews, the sharing, the rough labor, and the constant social balls and parties. But when he'd first arrived, he'd been so unused to everything, so baffled by how much and what he had to learn and do, he had no clue where to start or what to think. All he could remember thinking was that he felt lonely. But that had all changed when he'd met with Selene in their tower.

***

At the beginning of his life at the palace, Etoileon could only see Selene during mealtimes, when her brother and the entire household were all around. She had always smiled at him, and tried to talk to him, but he could sense that her role as princess kept her from saying some of the things that she really wanted to say. She often slipped him notes under his room door, and had special treats arranged for him. The first night he'd seen his room, he'd found a note under his pillow from Selene, telling him everything was going to be okay, her brother was odd, and she'd help him out, and good night. He kept it safe for reasons unknown even to himself. More notes would follow the first.

The night came when Etoileon was just getting ready for bed when he lay down on his bed to find a note from Selene once again. He opened it up, expected to find a message about how she was and hoped he was, and how she heard he was doing good in class or something along those lines. Instead, it was a short message of a completely different nature.

123

E–

Come to the Highest Tower, top room.

-S
P.S. Do not get caught.

He sighed. It was close to curfew for those who were being trained. He smiled as he thought about how Selene was right in saying that he should not get caught. Etoileon did not like to take chances, especially after almost a month living here; he'd come to grow fond of having a room that was his, and the great food served every day, and new comfortable clothes, and the uniform. He especially enjoyed seeing Selene every day, even if only allowed for a few moments of quiet talking. She was his special friend. So, hands down, when it came to seeing her versus risking curfew, it was always going to be seeing her.

He made his way down the hallway, searching for the High Tower. He had one of the trainees show him around, but Etoileon had gotten along with him so well that they had talked more and Etoileon had not paid as much attention to where they were going in the palace.

After a few moments of searching, and even more moments of hiding behind curtains, dodging guards, and running around corners, Etoileon found it. He found the stairway to the highest tower. He took the steps two at a time, a happiness swelling in his heart at the thought of seeing Selene again in private. He had no idea why she was so important to him, and when he thought about it, he'd only had one real night of getting to know her, when they'd first met. But for some reason, she managed to creep into his mind every so often, or he'd hear her laughter down the hall, or here of her getting into mischief again, and he would wonder when he could talk to her again.

Now he had his chance. And he could not wait.

He opened the door to the tower and found Selene overlooking the balcony's edge. When she heard the door open, she turned around to face him.

She sure looks nice, Etoileon thought. Selene was wearing a white flounced skirt, with crimson patterns sewn in it around the edge, with a plain white silk shirt and a short button-down crimson sweater to match. She had her long crimson stockings tucked into her matching white slippers. It made him wish he'd put on something nicer than his training outfit.

"Etoileon," Selene smiled over at him. "I was wondering what was keeping you."

"I got confused," he admitted. "This is a big palace, after all."

"Yes, it is," she agreed. "I suppose that one advantage to living here is getting to know the territory well."

"I had a friend from Battle Class show me around," he said. "But we ended up talking more than looking around. His name was Ronal. It was nice. I can't remember a time when I had the luxury of living in such an honest place."

"Dorian says that the reason everyone's so nice around here is because of me and my light," she laughed. "He's always teasing me about how light my skin is."

Etoileon had never really been bothered by the fact that she did seem to light up a room all by herself. Except when other boys seemed drawn to look at Selene in a way that made him feel like he should hit them.

"I did not think that the outside world was so horrible. Are the streets really that bad?" she asked.

"Well," Etoileon remembered what Dorian had said. It was his duty to protect the princess from the outside world. "It's not as nice as it is here. There they may have lights and bright signs, but it's a world that lives in darkness a lot. I was lucky to see early on that the darkness was not something to befriend, but something to fight against. That was one of the reasons I took refuge near a Battle School. The manager allowed me to attend a class as long as I cleaned up and ran errands and the like for him."

"Is it wonderful to see how our lives seem to come full circle sometimes?" Selene murmured thoughtfully. "Hey, come over here and take a look."

Etoileon moved and stood a few feet away from her, overlooking the balcony. "Wow," he said. "That's a long drop."

"When I was little, I would toss something over the side, and see if it would break," she admitted. "It's silly now, but I was always a little reckless. I think Dorian taught me that."

"It's not a bad idea. From what I hear, you're so nice and kind to everyone that you can't be seen as mischievous, even by your brother."

"Yes, that's true," Selene agreed. Her dark blond hair caught the wind and began to dance with it. Her eyes looked away to Diamond City's horizon. "But I don't mean to be a troublemaker half the time, I really do not. True, I do sometimes get overly curious, and I talk way too much. But I have never really felt the overwhelming need to be bad."

"Why's that?" Etoileon asked, his eyes following her hair.

"When I was little, before Dorian was so busy and arrogant, he and I would go to bed each night only after one of the workers here would tell us a story. The story was simple enough, always about the Guardian and the light that he smiles down on us. I remember that I could never wait to go to sleep, with the stories still lingering. My dreams, after hearing the stories, were always … " She paused here, trying to find the right adjective. "Peaceful, I guess." She noticed the confused look on Etoileon's face and shrugged. "Or it's maybe because Dorian always encouraged me to be so difficult when I was young, I don't know," she confided. "But I think there's a reason for it I'm not supposed to understand. At least, not just yet."

"Oh."

They stood there in silence for a moment.

She spoke up once more, this time her voice was soft and full of uncertainty. "Um, Etoileon … you aren't mad at me because I didn't exactly tell you I was the Princess before, are you?"

"Huh?" He looked over at her in surprise. "Well … I have to say, I was shocked, and confused, but I was angrier with myself than you. I should have realized who you were the moment I saw your face. But I didn't. It happens, I guess."

"I'm sorry if I caused any pain," she whispered. "And I am sorry that you had to leave your home to come here."

"It's okay. I can still go off the Table once in a while," he said. "And I like being here a lot better anyway. This is much better than any job on the docks."

His words caused a smile to pop up on to her face, her worry disappearing as it was replaced by a sense of contentment once again. She glanced over at him. "I am glad that you're going to be put through the stages of testing soon, Etoileon. Dorian told me that I am going to get a new protector soon, and I knew he was talking about you. I could tell by the way he said it."

"What, with anger creeping into his voice, talking like he wanted to punch something?" He smiled.

"Well … yes, actually," Selene admitted, grinning. "I think he plays it up, personally, but I have noticed a bond between the two of you."

"A bond? More like a canyon," Etoileon objected.

"Admit it. You respect him, and not for being the King. It's a quality that I can see in you, because it's the same for me," she said softly.

He was surprised. She was a perceptive one, all right. "Okay. But don't tell him," Etoileon whispered back. Yes, Etoileon thought, he did respect the king, even if he didn't like him that much. Dorian was a good person, and he'd helped to raise Selene. Surely that meant that there was good in him, for it to be reflected in her.

She nodded. "Look over there," she pointed into the sky. "The moons certainly are beautiful tonight."

"Sure are."

"Oh, and there's the Four-point Celestial prison," Selene said, pointing at a star constellation. It was a series of four stars in the sky that made a crooked box, the night between them the darkest of the whole sky. "Look, the one point is flickering almost, you can see it."

Etoileon looked up and saw that she was right. "I've never seen a star look like that before," he said.

"I wonder what it could mean," Selene said. "That is one of the most famous constellations throughout all of Sapphiran history. There's an old Sapphiran Legend about it, telling about how it was the final resting place for all the bad rulers and people."

"It's something to think about, I guess. Oh, by the way, was there any particular reason why you summoned me here, Selene?"

She smiled. "No," she giggled. Her face grew serious then. "I missed you, that's all. I like it that you are around, and that you would risk being caught after curfew to come and talk to me for a while."

She just liked seeing him, she told herself. It was not because she dreamed of him, or because she hoped that he would hold her hand like they did while they were outside of the Castle walls, or that he would smile and laugh with her once more.

"That's good," Etoileon said, cutting through her daydreams. "I thought maybe something was wrong."

"No, noting like that," she promised. "People won't believe this, but sometimes it gets very lonely being a Princess. I used to wish I had a sister to play with, like Dorian did, or another brother even. Dorian's way too busy for me sometimes, and I know how much the maids and bellboys talk. I am no fool. They would usually betray confidences quicker than it takes to turn the corner. Besides my handmaidens, I have no one to really trust."

"I didn't know you thought about this kind of stuff," Etoileon admitted. "I'm used to thinking you're all smiles and happiness."

"People are usually thinking things nobody would expect," she smiled. "And I learned a long time ago that people were not reliable, especially when it comes to the truth."

"I can see why you would think that," he agreed. "People usually don't want to admit to certain things." I would never confess to thinking about you when I'm supposed to be working, he admitted silently.

"I'll tell you a secret if you tell me one," Selene proposed. "How about it?"

He thought about it. "Okay. You first."

"Which secret do you want to hear?"

"Um … how about the worst thing you've ever done?" Etoileon could not imagine anything that the Princess would have done that would be counted as horrifying. It was a small stepping stone of a secret, a foot in the door.

"Probably go out into the city," Selene answered. "I'm not allowed to, you know … "

He felt a little guilty standing there. He hadn't meant for her to feel bad. He could see the guilt written on her face as she looked away from him.

A moment later she spoke up once again. "I know what darkness is," she said. "And I've seen it. But I try not to do it myself. You know that ancient sickness? I think I'm trying to keep fighting it by finding things to smile about, to laugh at, to play with. I know it's there, waiting for me to slip up. But I give it a nice run before I fall."

Etoileon thought about it. "What happens if you do fall?"

"I have fallen," she replied quietly. "I'm trying to get back up. Think about it, Etoileon. Before you could fight, you wanted to be better. And you got the skills with hard work. I think it is the same with people."

"What do you mean?"

"We don't always want to do the work or follow the rules, so we give up. We give up, for silly reasons or fears, on being something better than we are right now. I think that it's just sad to give up. So I try to get better. And I try to set an example for others." She smiled for a moment. "I really hope that one day I … I don't know, exactly. But I know that there's almost like a secret wish hiding itself in my heart, and I want to know what it is."

He thought about her words for a moment. "I think that's pretty noble of you," he admitted. "Dorian's probably right in saying that you are the reason that everyone here is more pleasant. You don't hide the light from others. You try to reach out and embrace others with it."

Selene turned away. No one had ever said such a thing like that before about her. It was something she almost could not accept as a compliment. She could not remember a time when she had not been this way—she was just living her life, trying to follow her heart. She had thought it was that there was a specific reason that she was this intent on being good. But she could think of nothing that made sense. Nevertheless, she smiled. "Thank you." That was all she could think of to say.

"I'll tell a secret now if you want," Etoileon offered up, causing a smile to come to her face. It was obvious that she wanted to hear more about him.

"Okay. Tell me about your first clear memory."

He sat down. "Well, my parents died, or at least, I think they did. I can't really remember them that well. Nothing but distinct shadows can be made clear in my mind, truthfully."

Selene sat down across from him, arranging her skirts in a ladylike manner. "Distinct shadows? Hardly a memory."

"Well, When I was little, the first thing I remember seeing is a black moon," he said. "That's the first thing I can remember."

"A black moon?"

"Yes. It was a black moon. That's all I remember. I remember standing around near the oasis, looking up at a black moon, looking around for my parents. And they were nowhere to be found."

"Is that why you stayed near the Oasis? To see if they were alive still?" she asked softly.

"I guess. But I'm not real sure."

They looked up at the sky in a comfortable silence, aware that such silence was more intimate than words.

Etoileon was over an hour late for curfew that night. Before he left, Selene took hold of his shoulder. "Will you come here tomorrow?"

"Yes," he promised, before he stepped out into the hallway and disappeared from sight.

So it went on nearly every night, the two of them met in the High Tower. And that's how it was for three years to the day.

***

Yes, Selene thought, Memories are something to cherish. She looked down at all the people arriving, and saw to her disappointment that more than a few old-looking men were coming in from the city transports. Deciding to forget what she could worry about later, she turned her gaze to face Etoileon. He was almost twenty now. And he still managed to

133

have the same effect on her senses as he'd had three years ago. Time had gone by, but her understanding of this feeling had not yet been revealed.

They stayed up in the Tower for a few more moments, quietly enjoying each other's company, looking down at the arriving guests. It was soon after that that Selene sighed, looking into the beginning of the yellow-gray sunset.

"Look," she whispered. "It's almost time now." She sighed. "I have a busy night ahead."

"I know."

Suddenly, all of her boundaries were let down. She did not want to be alone on her pedestal. She wanted to be comforted, to share in the sorrow of seeing her time with Etoileon go. Selene leaned on his shoulder and closed her eyes, relaxing against him.

"Etoileon, why can't you protect me from this?" she whispered. "I have a strange feeling that something is going to happen tonight."

He did not respond. He was too much in shock from having the Princess leaning on his shoulder. A whisper in his head murmured, reminding him that he was just a child of the streets—maybe in royal attire, and fancy clothes, with a bunch of highly coordinated education and skills—but a child of the streets nonetheless.

***

Chapter 5
Two Guys, a Girl, and a Rebellion
***

Etoileon was practically glaring as the Representative from Kani Island danced with the Princess for the third time that evening. Etoileon felt the unpleasantly familiar feeling of jealousy creeping into the pit of his stomach. It had always been like this; he would watch over Selene at some banquet or some gala, and she would be looking into the eyes of some handsome stranger. He had to stand off to the side, and watch the one person in the whole world he wanted to be with twirl the night away in the arms of her endless list of dance partners. Deep inside his heart, he dreaded each dance she took more than the last. It meant that she was one dance closer to falling in love and leaving him to hold her wedding carriage door open as she and her husband stepped in.

But this time it was slightly different; she was of the age to get married now. Before, Etoileon could rely on Dorian to hold off the suitors. Now he was left to consider that any dancer could be Selene's future husband. The thought was more than a little irritating.

One of the maids, a young girl whose name he couldn't quite remember, sauntered over to him and stood next to him.

"Hey," she greeted him. "Some party, huh?"

His eyes remained on Selene's laughing smile as Kani Island guy swung her around in a twirl. Not wanting to be rude, he answered her with a simple, "Guess so."

135

"I see the Princess is busy for the moment," the maid whispered. "Do you want to sneak away for a while? Some of the other workers have their own little party going on."

"No."

The maid pouted her mouth and put her hand on his shoulder. "There's plenty of moonshine and cookies in the kitchen for the staff," she offered. "You can go get some and be back here in time for the next dance."

"No, thank you."

She scooted a little closer, and tried again. "Are you sure?"

"Yes. I am certain I do not want to eat. I ate earlier. Please, you are distracting me from my work. Find someone else to play with." He hadn't wanted to be rude, but she'd left him little choice in the matter.

The maid stalked away, apparently unused to having her offers turned down. Etoileon looked back at her and shook his head sadly. That girl could have only been sixteen years old. She should try to find someone her own age.

His complete focus turned once again to the Princess. She was more radiant than he'd ever seen her, he thought. Dressed in a ruffled, flounced gown the color of wild burgundy berries, she more than looked the part of a Princess. The gown was decorated with thousands of tiny ruby beads, each sewn on to highlight the deep tones in the dress's fabric and cut.

Everyone had been awaiting her arrival. It seemed like a sea of eyes had turned to throw the most deadly waves at her when she'd come down the main hall's staircase. Etoileon had taken the servants entrance down onto the ground floor to see her come in. It was like watching a lightning bolt light up the sky—striking, electrifying. Every cell in his body had tingled with a sense of enchantment as he watched her glide down the halls staircase.

The music began playing a medley that was off beat and loud, even making one as engrossed as Etoileon start to hum a line or drum a beat. Another dancer tapped on Selene's shoulder. Etoileon watched, prepared to see Selene start dancing into another man's arms, but then she held up her hands, bowed slightly, and walked away.

What is she up to? Etoileon thought. He was just thinking that he should see where she was going when she came up behind him, her arms straight and her eyes somewhat narrowed.

"And just who was that you were just talking to?" she asked, trying to sound interested rather than annoyed.

"I don't know, to be perfectly honest," he said. He shrugged. "One of the maids, I suppose. "Why aren't you dancing with that guy? It is his turn."

Selene looked away. "I … did not want to dance this time. My feet are tired."

"Oh." As much as it sounded reasonable, and most likely true, Etoileon wondered if it was the main reason she had left the dance floor. "What are you going to do now?"

"I don't know," Selene shrugged. "I am glad that you did not leave me here alone, though. I was worried for a moment there that you were going to leave with Seri."

"Seri?"

"That maid. I recognize her now. She's over there," Selene said, jerking her head in that direction. Her voice suddenly grew gentler. "You were not really going to leave me here, were you?"

He shook his head. "No. You know I couldn't do that to you. What if you got hurt or something? Selene … " Both of them looked away. There was a slight pink tint to their cheeks. Neither of them could say the words.

Finally, Selene peeked up once more at her friend and decided that she couldn't stay like this forever, much as she might have wanted to. She reached out and took his arm. "My feet are feeling much better," she said, her smile starting to come out once again. "Why don't you dance with me for once?"

Etoileon immediately felt the uncertainty. "But, Princess," he started to object. "It's not … it's hardly appropriate … " his voice trailed off as Selene pulled him onto the dance floor and took his hand in hers.

"Please, Etoileon, I know that they train you in dancing as well as fighting," Selene said with a knowing look. "Might as well put it to use, right?"

His eyes met hers, and that was his first mistake. If Etoileon should have learned anything by now about the Princess, one pleading look from her was enough to ensure she would have her way. No human could possibly resist those eyes.

"All right." He took a much better hold of her hand, and took a step closer to her.

Catching the beat of the music, he started to whisk her away.

The advanced level of his dancing skills was surprising to him most of all. He could find the tune, could remember the steps. In class it was always harder because the teacher was old and frail and she tended to spit in his eyes as she curtly instructed him to turn this way, or go that way. But something about having his choice of partners made dancing appealing. What he'd come to see as a burden and embarrassing was more pleasant and even fun. Holding onto the Princess, he felt a lightening of his heart and began to laugh. He guided her into a few easy steps, and then pulled her close to him, twirling her away. Soon she was smiling up at him, those eyes sparkling with her own laughter.

The music was blaring fast now. Around and around the ballroom they went, twirling this way, switching to a two-step that way. It wasn't long before Selene found herself laughing; she was having such a wonderful time.

What's going on here tonight? I must be crazy, she thought. This is so wonderful, I can't seem to stop smiling or laughing, and I don't want this dance to end.

The music was loud and fast and exciting. They were laughing so hard it was difficult to keep up their pace; they almost didn't realize what happened next.

It would be argued later who tripped over who, but in a whirl of burgundy red and black, Etoileon suddenly found himself off balance with Selene holding onto him. He stumbled back, completely lost his footing and hit the floor. Selene followed after him less than a second later. He reached forward and tried to stop her from falling, catching her … in his arms.

"Selene?" he asked. "Are you okay?" he was still smiling, trying not to laugh. Her laugh had been completely forgotten as she lay there, with her face in his chest, her ear pressed up against him so she could hear his heartbeat. Etoileon grew worried a second later. "Um, Selene?"

She had landed on his chest, and her arms folded up between them, trying to break her fall unsuccessfully. For a moment neither of them moved. Selene could smell him through his uniform, a warm, intoxicating scent that reminded her of the waterfall. He held onto her tightly, encasing her into a protective, almost comforting shell. She did not want to let go.

She grimaced at the thought of getting up, but she put on a smile and grinned up at him. "I'm okay," she said, scrambling to hurry and stand up. It was difficult with all the layers in her dress. She did not want to cause a scene. A hand extended out to her, and she took it, helping herself up off of the floor.

She brushed herself off and said, "Thanks, Etoileon. We'll have to work on that dance, I suppose."

"Ahem." Selene looked up to see that the man who had helped her up was not Etoileon in the least. She found herself blushing as she realized her mistake.

"Oh, excuse me, sir, I thought you were –" She stopped in mid-sentence, taken aback by surprise. This man was gorgeous. He had the most perfect black hair, with light blue eyes, just like the sky, with a twist of gray in them. And when he smiled at her, Selene could feel a sense of recognition wash over her.

"I know who you thought I was, dear Princess. Please pardon my intrusion, but I was under the impression that I had been promised this next dance."

"Huh?" Selene had barely noticed that there was indeed a new song playing now. "Oh." Remembering her protector, she noticed he had gone. "Please hold on for one second, Sir."

She turned and looked to see that Etoileon had gone. She looked around wildly for him, finding him a moment later at his usual post, watching over her once more. With the new man's arrival, their playtime had been brought to an effective halt. She was about to go to him, but he caught her gaze at that moment. Even from the space of a few yards, Selene caught the expression in his eyes. You have to do your duty. I have to do mine. Go.

She hesitated a moment before Aemon came up beside her. "Sorry about that," Selene apologized as she was led around the dance floor by this handsome young man. He was around Etoileon's age, but he seemed to have less of a sense of humor. Selene noticed that he shared Etoileon's hardened look, but that was all they seemed to have in common.

"It's okay, Your Highness. I understand. After causing that fall, I think that the gentleman should have apologized to you as well."

"Hmm? Oh, no, I was going to see if he –"

"Let us forget your rude dance partner for the moment, Princess. Allow me to introduce myself properly. I am Aemon, of Jewel Island, located in the Southeastern part of the Sapphiran seas. Might I say that you look ravishing as a flower in bloom tonight?"

"Thank you, Sir," Selene answered automatically. She'd had compliments thrown at her all night. She smiled up at him and politely said, "You look very nice yourself, Sir."

"Please, call me Aemon," he insisted. "I intend to get to know you very well in the next couple of waltzes, my dear Princess."

"But I have a full card tonight, Sir," Selene meekly reminded him. "I cannot forget about all the gentlemen who have been longing to dance with me since I was sixteen."

"Believe me, if I have my way, I will have been waiting much longer than any one of those gentlemen."

Selene was suddenly worried. She did not like his tone at all. That feeling she'd had earlier came rushing back to her, fueled now by a sense of dread. Something was wrong here. Her eyes narrowed slightly as she gave an interested half-smile. "What do you mean, Sir?"

"Please, call me Aemon," he repeated. "What I mean is that I shall be the one who you will be married to. As your future husband, I think it would be wise to start thinking about how this arrangement of ours is going to work."

Selene dropped his hands, and pulled away from him. "Excuse me?"

"I know, I know. You're so concerned that you won't like your home on the Island with me and my people, but I assure you, we're all looking forward to your arrival, Princess." He tried to take her in his arms, but she stepped back.

"Stop it! My brother the King has given the right for me to choose who it is I am going to marry," Selene informed him, anger creeping into her voice. "I think you should brush up a little bit on your manners before you see me again." She turned around, hurrying to find Etoileon.

She nearly ran into him. He'd come up behind her while Aemon had tried to dance with her.

"Excuse me," Etoileon said, stepping in front of the Princess. "Is there a problem here?" His eyes blazed with the anticipation of battle.

And he wasn't the only one who was preparing for a battle, either. The music stopped. The room hushed over in silence.

Aemon's eyes met Etoileon's with a hatred that startled the Princess even from where she was standing.

Dorian came into the room. "What is going on in here?" his voice thundered throughout the silent corners of the ballroom. As he made his way over to his sister and her guard, everyone else in the room bowed deeply in reverence to the King. Even Aemon went down on his knees. It was only Selene who remained completely upright before him. "Someone, tell me now."

Selene stepped forward. "This gentleman is trying to claim my hand in marriage, Brother." Her voice was soft and light, but Dorian could tell she was trying hard not to get upset. He turned and faced this man, who was bowed facing the ground.

"Rise, Sir," he commanded to Aemon. "What is your name? Tell me."

"I am Aemon," he lifted his head up to look up at the king. His voice, inflicted with deep, resounding tones, was completely different from the harsher voice he'd used in talking to Selene. "Of Jewel Island."

Dorian's eyes softened at once. "Oh, I see." He turned to Selene. "Sister, this is the man who has approached the council and me with an enticing offer for your hand. He has offered many treasures for you, as well as this court."

"No, thank you," Selene replied as graciously as she could. Her voice was light, and had no trace of condemnation, but Aemon felt her words hit him like a slap across the face. I've spent enough time with this gentleman to know that he is accustomed to buying into power, that he knows little of human decency and cannot be trusted with the title over me as 'husband'. No riches, no treasure is worth such a fate, she thought.

"Think it over, sister," Dorian urged her, this time his words more hard and carefully accentuated. "You might change your mind."

"Dorian!" Selene was wide-eyed with shock that he would take someone else's side on this.

"Leave Selene alone," Etoileon spoke up. "She said her piece, now let this matter drop."

Dorian looked as though he might have thrown Etoileon out of the castle for good after that, but instead, he turned on his heel. "Resume the music!" he commanded, heading towards his throne.

The music started up once again, and for the moment, the proposal was forgotten. Everyone got up and began to awkwardly dance once more, eventually lighting up and seeming to forget the matter entirely.

Aemon looked spitefully at Etoileon. "You might think that you're in charge of the Princess, but Selene will be mine."

He turned once again to the Princess, who had just been staring at her brother's retreating form with a look of disbelief on her face. "My lady," he started. "How about I give you two days to accept my proposal? Your guard here can't object to that."

"Ha! Etoileon is the best Fighter we've got here, and he is in charge of my safety," Selene huffed. "I do not think you could win against him if you tried." She put her arm through Etoileon's and added, "Please leave."

Aemon glared at her, but said nothing as he made his way out of the room.

"The nerve of that man!" Selene's voice had a surprisingly shaky sound to it.

"Selene?" Etoileon took a hold of her hands. They were shaking along with her voice. "I think you should take a break. Your hands are cold."

She looked up at him. "Why did Dorian take his side? Why? I don't understand this." Her voice was shaking even more as she voiced her unanswerable questions.

"Well, he did offer you a whole lot of treasure," Etoileon reasoned. "Maybe the Continent could use the funds, or something. I'm guessing it was the council's insistence that you consider his proposal."

"I would rather renounce my title," Selene assured him. She sighed. "I think you were right. I could use a little break after that. Let's go and do something else."

Etoileon nodded. "Okay. Shall I escort you to your chambers?"

"No, I have a better idea. Let's go to the Luxury Garden Hall," Selene suggested. "It has not been used in this kind of reception in years."

***

It was true that the Garden had not been used in years, but it had been kept up. Selene wandered through the door and headed down the arched hallways of the purple starlet flowers. Starlets, small flowers growing on vines, only bloomed during the night. The long bordered entrance way was a comfort to Selene's nerves. She was starting to settle now, her worry dispersing rapidly as the comforting surroundings of her mother's garden enclosed around her.

"Wow. I've never seen this place before," Etoileon's voice whispered through the darkened garden some distance behind her.

"I come here sometimes, when I feel alone," Selene admitted. "My mother died when I was born. I never knew her."

"Why would you want to come here when you feel alone then? Wouldn't that make it sadder?" He'd caught up to her and was talking softly now.

Selene smiled as she looked up at the starry night through the transparent skylights. "I guess you would think that, but it's not like that at all." Selene knelt down in the garden square and played with a few leafy plants. "I feel closer to her here somehow."

"Why's that?" He came and knelt beside her.

Selene slumped down, lying back on the soft earth. She rearranged her skirts in a lady-like fashion. "She was the one who designed this garden, you know. I hear some of the maids talk about how she was lonely, too. My father wasn't exactly what you'd call a hero or a great catch."

"Well, he was way older than her."

"Yes, but he loved Dorian's mother a whole lot. I could tell by his old photo discs. There are thousands of pictures of Dorian's mother, but there are only about five of my mother.

One of them was taken in this garden. She looked lonely in the photo."

"So when you feel lonely, you think of her being lonely, and feel better?" he asked, trying to understand her more clearly.

"Sure, I guess." Selene folded her arms behind her head in pillowing effect as she watched the rolling clouds above go by through the skylight. Etoileon came up beside her and lay down too, causing her to turn her face away as she blushed slightly.

"I feel lonely too sometimes," he admitted softly. "But I try not to let it bother me. When I'm lonely I think about the times when I'm not alone."

"But isn't that lonely? Doesn't that make you feel even more alone?" she asked.

"Not really," he tried to explain. "I think of some adventure we've had together, or remember Ronal's jokes, or think about people who have cared about me. Some of them might be gone, or not around, or –" he looked at her with a smile—"getting ready for a ball, but they all helped me in some way. It's kind of nice to think about how you'd be different if you had no memories, and grateful that you're who you are because of certain people."

A moment of silence allowed the profoundness of his words to wash over her. "I never knew you were so idealistic," Selene smiled up at him. "Etoileon ... I'm grateful for you."

The sincerity of her words echoed throughout the long silence that followed them. Etoileon did nothing to indicate that he even heard her. For long moments the two of them simply stayed there, looking out into the distance, allowing the silence to embrace them.

Etoileon caught sight of the bright moonlight in the skylight windows in the ceiling. He gave a tiny smile as he once again recalled the day that he'd met Selene. She'd proven to one of the best things he could ever have hoped for. He let go of his focus on the world and closed his eyes.

All at once, something took hold of his mind. It coaxed him to wander back to the day he'd awaken to remember nothing and no one, an old memory catching his full attention. The only sight filling his eyes was an eclipse, a black moon in front of a bright light. It was so real to him; Etoileon tried to call out to Selene to look, but his voice made no audible sound as the picture continued to hold steady in his mind's eye. He felt a sense of confusion, but it was strange, because he felt no tingle of fear, no heightened sense of dread.

Opening his eyes, he still saw the blackened moon and flinched; he was still watching only with his mind. He was sure that he was still awake. Etoileon took a consensus of his surroundings, and found that he was in the same place, in the same position. Before he could think on what could possibly be happening, he saw the moon grow bigger and bigger in his mind's vision, until he knew that he was lying on the grass in the palace garden, but he could not look away from this vision, this divine daydream.

THE MOONLGIHT PEGASUS

As he watched, there was a small sparkle near the edge of the black moon. A second later there was a sound, and Etoileon strained his ears to listen.

It sounded like a horse, he thought as the scene in front of him suddenly changed. The darkness passed away as the light ruptured from the area near the sparkle, the blackness of the moon disappearing as a bright, shimmering light suddenly filled his eyes. Etoileon brought his hands up to block his eyes from the powerful surge of light, and suddenly he found himself lying on the grass, his hands in front of his eyes shaking. He felt his heartbeat and knew that he had just had a vision from the beyond, but he did not know what it could possibly mean or why it had happened. Looking over at the princess, she was right where she'd been before. There was no evidence to suggest anything had happened to her, or that she'd seen anything of the vision he had.

He sat up. "Are you ready to go back to the ballroom?"

"Yes, I suppose I should go back there," Selene agreed. She picked a single bud, a small flower blossom. She handed it to him. "Thanks for making me feel better."

He took hold of the small bud and then reached out, tucking the small flower into her hair. "It's been a privilege." As he turned to head out of the garden, he thought about telling Selene what he had seen. Looking back at her as she shook out her skirts, he decided to wait awhile before he did. She had enough troubles of her own to worry about for the moment. She might even think that he was crazy, or that he was losing it.

Despite the kind remarks, Selene felt alone. Who could she tell, that she wanted nothing more than to be with this kind boy, this one who had been her best friend, this boy who she felt feelings for that she did not even understand? She could barely even admit it to herself. How could she tell Dorian that not for all the treasures in the world, all the gold in the earth, would she marry any of the islander representatives? She would not, because they were not the right one for her, and they were not meant for her. They were not this boy.

***

Ronal looked down at the note in his hand and read it again, this time with a full glass of moonshine in his other hand. He wasn't in the best of spirits, despite the happy party and the smiling guests.

Cyerra had not been able to come tonight. She could not convince her brother to allow her to be put in such a vulnerable position. For Ronal's sake, she had managed to smuggle to him a note, explaining everything to him.

Dearest Ronal,

Please understand and forgive me for not coming tonight. Not only must I see to the business and Auntie here, but also my brother Aemon has refused to let me near the palace. He is worried for my safety, you see. You must forgive him. Please believe me when I say he is not a bad person, only misguided. Try to come and see me soon.

Yours,
Cyerra

The note was hurriedly written and barely readable. But Ronal knew that she'd been as polite as she could, and had tried to excuse her brother's behavior to him. Ronal thought

151

considering her brother was planning a rebellion, she was too good for him to have as a sister.

He would go to see her soon, he vowed.

***

Selene returned to the ballroom, only to find that most of the people had migrated into the dining rooms in order to get their drinks and their food. The evening was more than half over at least, Selene thought gratefully as she found a nice section of the wall to lean against. She did not want to be here much longer.

Etoileon was not far from her, watching over her as usual. They'd been too close all night long; he could not get close to her without causing more whispers to stir, more eyes to narrow. She watched and sighed, longing for Dorian to excuse her to her rooms for the night.

"Excuse me, ma'am, is this space of wall taken?" the last person Selene wanted to deal with had shown up quickly enough, that was for sure.

"Aemon, please," she started.

"I want to apologize, My Lady," he interjected. "I wanted to humbly ask for your forgiveness and another chance to convince you that I am worthy of your hand and title."

"You can have my forgiveness. Take it with my pleasure. But as far as I am concerned, you do not have to be worthy of my hand or my title," she responded. "You have to be worthy of me."

Aemon shot her a confused look. "Princess, I think that maybe you should have all your facts straightened out before you make up your mind. I am the Representative from Jewel Island, the youngest ever elected. I am almost nineteen years old, you know."

"Really? From the way you act, I would've guessed ten," Etoileon's hardened voice came up from behind him. His eyes flickered over to meet Selene's once again. "Is there a problem, here, Princess?"

Another voice came up. "No, there is no problem." Etoileon looked behind him to see Garth, the King's head of personnel. He cleared his throat in a presumptuous manner, and nodded to Etoileon. "You. The King requests your presence immediately. Your Highness, will you excuse us?"

Selene looked like she had been hit in the stomach. But she smiled brightly, seeing no alternative. "That's fine."

Etoileon didn't have any time to object as he was practically dragged away by Garth, who, at seven foot one and thirty-four years old, easily managed to take him into one of the rooms off the side of the ballroom.

"What's going on?" Etoileon asked, his fists clenched and anger written all over his face. "Why are you doing this? Don't you realize that Selene is in trouble?"

"We're all in trouble, Etoileon." The King sat in his office chair, his hand wrapped around a rare glass of moonshine.

"What is this? What's going on?" He noticed the glass, and the worry began to creep up into his spine.

"Guards." The King raised his head. "Leave us."

The guards positioned at the door looked at each other, and then left quietly, quite sure that the King was still stable enough to make clear decisions—or at least clear enough to punish them if they disobeyed him.

When Dorian and Etoileon were alone, with only Garth for company, the King pulled out another bottle of moonshine from his desk drawer. Glancing at Etoileon, he grinned. "Don't tell Selene," he said. "She'll be heartbroken if she finds out that I seem to act more like our father than she would wish."

Etoileon said nothing about the moonshine. He had other issues on his mind. "Why are you letting that Islander call the shots when it comes to Selene?"

"He's requested her hand, Etoileon," Dorian replied, pouring out some more moonshine. "And he has a good reason for me to accept his proposal."

"What?" Etoileon felt numb as the stark truth of the matter hit him. Selene could end up married to that guy. A shower of chills seemed to pour over him as his despair mounted.

"Yeah, I know what you're thinking. He's not my first choice either, but I have to say … this fits the prophecy pretty well."

"What are you talking about?" Etoileon forgot his boundaries once more. He stood up and slammed his fist onto the table. In his fury, he didn't even feel the reverberations of pain that jolted up his arm, nor did he realize that he'd made a dent in the piece of furniture. "She can't marry him!"

"Control your temper!" Dorian shot back. "There was a prophecy, long ago, that the Princess would be married, and then a time of peace would come to the whole world. Don't you get it, you brat? You can't stop this. I can't either. Only Selene can, and I will not have you repeating any of this to her, or I'll fire you straight out, and throw you back out on the streets where you belong."

"Why? Why can't you get her out of this?"

"Why?" Dorian's face was nearly purple from anger. "I'll tell you why. It's because of Aemon. He's a nut, completely insane. He's dead set on becoming the next king of the world, and he's told me that Selene has until the day of Moonbeam Festival to accept his marriage proposal. If she doesn't, so he can legally claim the right to the throne after me, he's going to handle this the old fashioned way by rebelling, and killing us all—including Selene and myself."

"He can't do that!"

"What do you mean, he can't!" Dorian shouted. He slumped down in his chair. His voice lowered. "Look … I've never liked you that much. But there have been rumors overseas for the past couple of months about this guy. He's the son of Ammos, the last leader of the previous Rebellion."

Etoileon's eyes widened slightly at the coincidence. "You mean … he's intent on revenge, because the rebel cause ended up driving his father to kill himself?"

"Of course," Dorian nodded. The moonshine was beginning to take a stronger hold on him. "That's how these guys work. We're trying to handle the situation here as best as we can." Before Etoileon could say or do anything, Dorian leaned forward and met his gaze intently. "Look. I saw you tonight. I've seen you since you've come here. And I know my sister much better than anyone I know. She would not ever choose herself over anyone else. But you … you're not just anyone else to her. I can see by the way you talk to her, the way you look at her, the way that you guard her. I want you to lay off your duties as her Protector until the beginning of the Lunar Storms. If she says no to Aemon, of her own free will, we're going to have a war on our hands once again."

"And if she says yes?" Etoileon could barely make the words form on his lips.

"Then I guess you'll be out of a job." Dorian sighed. "What a horrible mess this is. You will go to your rooms, then. And you are not allowed out of your wing until the festival night of the Lunar Storms. Garth here will personally be monitoring your rooms." Garth straightened up at the King's words.

Etoileon saw no way around it. He was sunk.

***

Selene was ready to leave almost as soon as Aemon started talking about himself. She was finding it hard to keep on looking like she was paying attention to him; it was more tiring than she'd realized.

"Yeah, that's right, I was the best strategist in the whole class," he was saying as Selene nodded. Her eyes darted to

THE MOONLGIHT PEGASUS

find a clock as a sense of desperation seemed to be slowly taking a hold of her. She sincerely hoped that Etoileon was going to come back soon. She did not like this. Although Aemon was a much more amiable fellow now that Etoileon was gone from view, he was still trying to impress her and it was not working.

"So, I quickly rose in rank due to my education," Aemon continued. "I have a sister who lives in the city, along with my aunt. I used to have another brother, but he died or something when my father came to the Continent to fight in the rebellion."

"That's nice," Selene muttered. She brightened up as an idea struck her. "Would you excuse me, Aemon?"

"Why?"

"I have to freshen up a bit," Selene responded, turning on her enigmatic eyes and humble smile.

"Oh. I suppose. But before you go, I would just like to apologize, once more, for my rudeness earlier." His eyes lowered, the first meek thing he'd done all night. Selene decided she was probably being a bit too hard on him, if he cared somewhat about how she viewed him. "I was actually quite jealous of your Protector, and I could not seem to get a grip on my emotions."

Selene turned red. If Aemon had noticed the unusual closeness between her and Etoileon, no doubt others had as well. "That happens all the time, I'm sure," Selene tried to bow out gracefully, but he wouldn't let her.

"Please, Princess, will you at least consider my marriage offer? Jewel Island is so beautiful, and you would love it there, I'm sure."

"Look," Selene lost her smile. "Aemon. You seem to be a nice boy, despite your earlier impression. But I really must insist that you stop asking me. I'll consider it, but I can assure that there is little that would change my mind. Though I am of age to marry, I was not really planning on it to be anytime soon."

Aemon met her gaze intently. "Tell me your final answer on the day of the Moonbeam Festival. I'll be staying at a local hotel, and there is a meeting I have with the King. But at least consider it. Oh, and one more thing. Will you join me for lunch tomorrow?"

There's nothing to consider about marriage, she thought. She did not want to have lunch with him, but if it would get him out of her hair, she was willing to allow it. They could eat here, in the main dining hall or something. But she nodded. "Fine. I'll see you here for lunch tomorrow. Good night, Sir."

She hurried off before he could get her to talk with him anymore. She figured that if she was of age to get married, and her brother had entrusted her to make that decision, she was more than able to determine for herself when she could leave the reception.

***
Chapter 6
The Darkness Takes Hold
***

"What do you think you are doing?" Aura scuttled about the room the following night. "Your Highness, His Majesty the King has ordered you to stay away from that boy! You can't go see him! What if he's more ill than the King let on?"

Selene glared at her governess. "But Etoileon's always been there for me! Why can't I be there for him now, when he may need me?"

"Your Highness, the King said –"

"I don't care! I want to see my friend!" Selene declared. "I've had a long day, Aura. Please do not deny me this one request."

Aura's mouth pinched in an indecisive manner. The Princess was an excellent one to play on a person's emotions. But Aura knew that the King would fire her, or worse, if she allowed the Princess to walk out of the room at this late hour. And eventually, her logic won her over, despite her feelings.

"I'm sorry, Selene, but you cannot see that boy," Aura said, her voice icy with scorn. "Not until the King says so. Besides, you saw him yesterday. Half of the High Court was buzzing with tales of you two on the dance floor. What a preposterous idea. You know that you cannot do things like that with a silly orphan."

"And why not?" Selene asked. "Are we all not people in this world?"

The old governess sighed. "Your Highness," she began. "There is a little thing in this world called currency, might I remind you. And a person cannot be considered worthy of human company if he has nothing but a little. Enough of this, I tire from our argument. Tell me about your lunch with that nice Aemon fellow."

The Princess sighed. Maybe Etoileon was so sick that it was better for him to be under watch by Dorian. It was nice to see her brother take such an interest in her friend's health. The King had come after the reception, just in time to stop her from leaving her room to go up to the tower, and told her himself that she was not to go and see Etoileon, because he was ill suited to see her. Selene had asked all sorts of questions, such as whether Etoileon was going to be all right or not, but Dorian shook his head and said nothing about it. The only thing besides that he said was that Yana, one of her favorite handmaidens, was to act as her chaperone for the next couple of days, and Aemon would be coming for dinner as his special guest for a while. Selene had groaned inwardly. Of all times for her friend to get sick!

She slumped down on the bed, trying to think of a polite answer to Aura's question. It was the least she could do after being so impertinent. "It was okay," Selene admitted. "He was much more polite and friendly since I only had a handmaiden with me today. He even gave Yana some funds to buy herself a gift in the city. She liked that, I'm sure."

"Did you go to the city with him?"

"No, of course not. We had a picnic lunch in one of the Garden Halls," Selene said. "The flowers were in bloom, but the scent of all those flowers overpowered the taste of the

THE MOONLGIHT PEGASUS

food. I felt like I was eating grass or fleur buds all throughout the meal."

"Did you talk about anything interesting?" Aura inched a bit closer to her. "Tell me all about it, dear."

"It was a nice day, and the open courtyard Garden Hall was lovely," Selene recalled. "I was having a pleasant daydream when Aemon interrupted me." She looked over at Aura. "You know, Aemon's not that bad of a guy. But I wish he wasn't so mean towards Etoileon."

"Dear, dear, you must understand," Aura explained gently. "When Aemon first became a representative, he'd lived on the Continent nearly all his life. Jewel Island is one of the bigger isles out in the Sapphiran seas. He had grown up under his aunt's care, because his parents had both died shortly after he was born. No doubt when he sees you treat that Fighter of yours with such high respect and care, he is outraged because he was not treated like that, not until he had gained political power."

"I knew he was jealous," Selene admitted. "He even told me. But I guess I never understood why exactly. Maybe tomorrow I'll try to be more of a friend to him."

"With patience comes understanding, and with understanding comes patience," Aura pursed her lips together in thoughtful consideration. "That sounds like a good idea—a really, really good idea. When is he coming over tomorrow?"

"Dorian says he'll be here all day tomorrow." Selene looked up at Aura. "Do you think Etoileon will be better by then?"

Aura's grin disappeared. "Your Highness, let me be honest with you for a moment. I think … I think it would be best if you did not hang around that boy so much. After all, you are to be married soon, and he can't keep having such a large place in your life. Not to mention you are the Princess. You must stop seeing him as your friend and begin to accept him more as a servant to you."

Selene frowned. "I hope that your moment of honesty has passed, Aura."

"Ah, yes, it is hard for the young to accept their destinies," the governess quipped. "So you do have a bit of your mother in you."

Selene's head whipped around. "What was that about my mother?"

The ruffled look on Aura's face said it all—she wanted nothing to do with that particular subject. But there was no avoiding the subject now that she'd let it slip. "I said you have some of your mother in you, that's all."

"So you remember her?"

"Who can forget the last generations of rulers?" Aura said crisply. "They were very good politically, but, and I hope you don't take this the wrong way, Your Highness, but they were also very troubled emotionally. You might not believe it, or want to believe it, but Queen Kaena wanted nothing more than to be free of this life, too, just as you. And look what would've happened to her if she had not been here. She would've been married to an Islander, bringing shame down on her entire family."

That would not have been so bad, Selene thought, if they were in love.

"You should remember her and be grateful for your life here, as a Princess. Do you have any idea how lucky you are?"

"Good night, Aura," Selene said calmly. She looked over her shoulder at the surprised woman and smiled. "I'm tired now. I'm going to go to sleep."

Her governess frowned down her nose at her. "As you wish, Your Highness."

Selene waited until the door was closed completely to get off of her bed and look out of her window. She looked up at the High Tower, her tower. She sighed sadly. It looked like she would not be able to get up there tonight. Somehow the idea of going without her closest friend made her feel sad.

Her thoughts turned to Aemon as she looked up at the night. She sincerely hoped he wouldn't try to propose to her again. Something in her heart told her that she could not survive being married to him.

***

It was early in the morning when he gave up trying to get back to his troubled dreams. Sleeping was pointless, Etoileon thought, if it did not bring rest. However, staying awake wasn't a much more anticipating option either, though, when he thought about it.

Etoileon banged on the main door to his room, taking a break from pacing around all over the cerulean carpet. He'd been trapped in there for almost a day, and he'd had enough of this.

He turned and slumped on his bed, longing for the tower's majestic overlook of the city. It was true that there had been a rebellion in the past. Pulling out the book from his desk drawers, he flipped through the pages to find the article he'd read about the war. It was his history book, one that he'd been reading from the library. He had looked up the rebellion of the past as he'd been held in his room. Now he flipped through the pages, searching and looking for anything that could distract him from his thoughts. It was true that the rebellion had been a horrible chapter in Sapphiran history. Etoileon could not remember anything about that period of time personally, but he'd heard plenty of horrifying stories about the short but devastating conflict.

Seeing nothing of particular interest, he got up restlessly and went to stand by the window once more. Looking over the skyline of Diamond City, seeing all the green trees and the sands closer to the outskirts of town, he could hardly imagine it. He could not ever see it really happening. This city was known for its beauty. War could get ugly. The two of them just did not mix in his mind, as sure as the idea of Selene marrying Aemon did not make sense.

Etoileon felt his heart ache at the thought of her marrying someone. He'd come to the heart of his problems, admitting it silently to himself. Etoileon smiled ruefully as he realized that he had allowed himself to grow much closer to her than he had originally intended.

Being a child of the city streets, he should've known better than to let his dreams get in the way of reality. Selene was a princess. True, she didn't always act like it, but there was a line between what princesses could do and what a princess would never do. And if Etoileon knew anything, he knew that Selene would never … he couldn't even bring himself to think it! Why was that so hard for him to come to terms with? He should be happy for her. He should be glad that she was going to marry that Aemon guy by the sound of it, and bring complete peace to the land, like the Prophecy said she was supposed to.

He looked over at his window once again, and saw that the dawn was just peeking over the horizon. Etoileon had let the night pass, unable to find any solution to his problems. Sighing, he slumped down on the window seat and pressed his head against the cool glass. With nothing left to do, he prayed that he would be able to handle the future.

***

Selene was walking extra slow to the breakfast dining hall as her eyes looked up to the ribbons lining the arched ceiling that morning. The Palace was still decorated for the Representatives. There were always a bundle of them who stuck around the city for a few days, even weeks, after to observe and draw up reports to send back to their homes. Thinking about the representatives, Selene was relieved that Aemon was going to go home today. He'd told her yesterday that he was going to leave right after the Lunar Storms appeared that day. He was even going to leave sooner than that because he was going to have lunch at his relatives' house prior to that.

She'd made a promise to be more of a friend to him last night. And she figured that after their time together was over, she would formally and graciously send him on his way, with a traditional handkerchief salute from atop her tower. There were lots of large ships from the various islands around this time. Few had left port yet, since high tide was coming later that afternoon.

It was so unusual for her to be alone on her walk here that she found it difficult to even want to get to breakfast. She slowed down. Part of her was hoping Etoileon was better today and was just running late, and that he would eventually come running around the corner, that small half-smirk on his face. She'd give anything if he would come and tease her about how she couldn't wait for him.

Selene recalled what Etoileon had told her in the garden two days before; when he was alone, he thought about the times he wasn't. She decided to give it a try.

She thought of how he would laugh at her stories on the way to the dining hall for breakfast each morning. She was able to recall how he would carry himself respectfully in her presence, even when she was sure no one was watching them. He always seemed afraid to let himself get too close to her. Selene had thought it was endearing; now that she had a moment to think about it, she was a little more than curious as to exactly why he did that.

She had just reached the door when she heard the running footsteps behind her. The doors opened wide as a voice called out to her.

"Your Highness! Don't go in there, please, they're –"

Selene turned to face the caller. She saw that it was Etoileon's friend, Ronal. His face was red and he was breathing hard. No doubt he'd run all from wherever he'd been. When she looked at him, he stopped running and tried to catch his breath. Selene was about to go over and see if he was all right, or if anything was wrong, when Dorian's voice called to her.

"Princess. Get in here now."

She was caught. To any one of the onlookers, it was clear that she was hesitating. She could feel her heart start to be faster as she tried to weigh her choices. Dorian never called her Princess. She knew she should listen to her brother's command, but what if Ronal was in trouble? Or what if he was trying to keep her out of some?

"Selene, now!" Dorian called. "We have a surprise for you!"

"Your Majesty, do you think you should tell her?" one of the servants asked in a somewhat low voice.

"Yeah, don't tell her!" another all too familiar voice said. "I will."

Selene could feel her skin crawl. Her hands clenched and unclenched themselves as she took a step in the doorway, as slowly as she could. She could hear Ronal behind her, trying to hurry along after her.

"Selene." Aemon came and stepped up in front of her, bowing in a grandly manner. "I have been awaiting you for some time now. Please. Won't you join us for breakfast?" He held out his hand to her, and Selene suddenly could not seem to do anything at that moment but look at it.

Aemon tried again. "Come on, the eggs are going to get cold," he urged her once more. Offering his hand out even further for her to take, he looked at her intently, and (for him) kindly. Selene's eyes traveled from his hand to his eyes and back again, as though to silently ask him what this was all about. He seemed to get her question, because a moment later he answered her.

"Selene," he said, getting down on his knees before her. "Please, don't say anything," he said, quickly intervening as she was about to indeed say something. "I want you to know that I would greatly appreciate this one chance to say what I feel in my heart."

She said nothing. Half of her was in shock.

"I know we have not always gotten along as perfectly as you would like," he began. "But I cannot help it sometimes. I saw you, and in that moment I knew that I must be yours, and you be mine. I saw you, like a dream, descend down the stairs merely two days ago, and I know I must become your husband. I am young, yet, I know, but that is precisely why we are so good together. Do you want some old man for a husband? Do you want some older man who doesn't understand you or the ways of your generation? I am the representative of one of the most beautiful and bountiful islands in the entire world. I have power, and wealth, and the skill to handle both much more than an aging leader. Do you want a husband that cannot possibly hope to give you as much as I can? I am sure you don't. We can rule forever, on your throne, side by side until death. I care so much for you, words cannot say how happy I would be if you would just say the one little word that I want to hear." He quieted down here, apparently waiting for her to speak.

Selene was about to speak when a loud crashing sound broke through the room. She looked over to see that Ronal had come bursting through the room. His chest was heaving, his breathing labored, as he looked at her. "Princess, stop, do not accept him!"

"Guards," Dorian snapped his fingers once and three guards from the behind, all of them trying their best to silence him. Ronal tried to fight them off, but he was too tired from all the running he'd done to get very far. Selene was just about to ask him what was wrong when Aemon cleared his throat.

"Well, Princess," he asked, "What do you say?"

Selene turned and looked back at Ronal briefly before she sighed quietly to herself. It looked like she was going to have to deal with Aemon and her brother before she could help Ronal. Her family, she thought, picked the most inconvenient times to be a problem.

She looked up at Aemon's hardened blue-gray eyes. Her hand, which had been at her side, rose up, like she was going to reach out and take his hand.

For a moment, Aemon's eyes glittered with what looked like success, but her hand found its way to her heart, not to his hand.

"Please," she said in her softened tone, "Please, forgive me for what I am about to say. That was a very touching speech, and I'm sure that any girl in the world would love to hear it." Her eyes lowered away from his as she continued. "But I cannot accept you, Aemon, as nice as you can be, or as young, as rich, as powerful you are. Despite all that you've tried, or may try, you can never give me the one thing I need."

"Selene," Dorian said, "Think about this carefully. Aemon can give you a comfortable home, a place to call your own. He could even give you an island, all the food you love, a family, wealth, what else do you need?"

"Love." Her voice was barely over a whisper as the tears in her eyes began to cloud her vision. "I have a comfortable home here, and my very own place within it. I can eat what's here. And I have you for my family, Dorian. But I need love - love in a different way from all the ways I've ever known. Friendship … family … those things I have, and I know … but … " her voice trailed off, as she looked even further away from Aemon's angry eyes.

"Your Highness!" Ronal finally managed to break out of the guards. The Princess had distracted everyone in the room as she'd given her answer, allowing for him to wriggle free. He pointed at Aemon. "It was all a trick! He doesn't care about you at all—he was planning to marry you in order to become King!"

"You! Fighter! Be silent, or else!" Dorian jumped out of his seat.

"Ask him! I doubt he'll deny it himself!" Ronal had apparently decided against Dorian's warning.

Selene shot a glance at Aemon. Her eyes were wide with shock, and her hand rushed up to cover her opened mouth. "What?"

"He's the leader of a rogue league of islands who want to overthrow the monarchy!" Ronal said angrily, still continuing to fight off with some of the guards while pointing at Aemon. He leapt into the air and slammed into a guard's chest, effectively throwing the guard and the guards behind him into a wall.

"Oh my … " Selene felt the air rush out of her lungs as she tried to take in this news. Shock trembled down her body. Her gaze was wide with shock and her body seemed to move in limp manner as complete realization dawned on her. The implications of everything started to fall together. "I knew you didn't love me," she finally said, looking over at Aemon. "But … why? Why be so deceitful about it?"

"Selene?" Dorian took a step closer to her. "Are you feeling well?"

"And you knew … " Selene's gaze turned away from Aemon and found Dorian. "You knew … and you were going to let this happen?"

There was no accusing tone in her voice, but still the guilt managed to worm its way into Dorian's heart. "No, no, of course not!" the King took a step back. "I wanted to give him a fair chance to get you to like him, Selene, that was all. The Judges Council all agreed to the plan."

"Princess," Aemon spoke up. "I cannot believe that you are so surprised. Please, tell me you are not this naïve. Surely you must know the great advantages that Dorian has as long as he has you to barter away."

"Enough," she whispered softly. "Enough of this. I am no child, not any longer. I wish that the people around here would start treating me as more of a human than as a Princess." She looked up at him. "I know as a princess I am supposed to do my duty, and leave my heart for the people.

But … ” Her voice trailed off as she found that she could not finish her sentence.

“I knew it!” Aemon yelled, his patience broken. He marched over to her, and stood menacingly over her. “I knew it! You and that so-called protector of yours!”

“Hey!” The princess was torn out from her thoughts as his hands lashed out and gripped her wrists, pulling her to face him. He was taller than she was, and he seemed to loom over her menacingly.

He looked her square in the eye. “Tell me you do not love him!” he demanded.

She pulled back, away from him. “You’re hurting me!” she tried to wriggle out of his grasp, but only succeeded in making him angrier.

“Aemon! Let her go!” Dorian thundered, his own anger starting to boil. When Aemon continued his hold on to the Princess, the king nodded to the guards.

As the guards took hold of their sword hilts, Aemon continued to glare at Selene. “Tell me you don’t love him!” When she just stared up at him with a pained look, he jerked his hands off of her. His hand whipped around and planted a slap right across her face.

She stumbled back, falling onto the floor in front of him, tears springing to her eyes as the shock faded away and the stinging sensation took a hold of her senses. She had never been hit, not once in her life, until just now. The palace guards surrounded her fallen figure, drawing their weapons.

"How dare you!" the King roared, coming to stand by his sister. "Get out! Get out I say! You are no longer a member of my court. No one treats the Princess with such vulgarity and disrespect."

Aemon refused to show his fear or regret, if indeed he had any at all. He just looked with pity down at the Princess as she remained on the floor in front of him. It looked like for a long moment that he would stay.

Selene hesitated slightly before addressing him. "Aemon, I cannot accept you. I will not. Please take your men and leave immediately. You came for me, and I will not go. Therefore you have no more business to attend to. Good-bye."

He looked over at Dorian as all the Palace guards suddenly drew their swords and held their tight defense around the Princess. She was still looking intently at him from her sprawled position on the ground. "Farewell, Your Majesties. I will see be seeing you again, mark my words."

He did not bow, but simply turned on his heel and walked out the doors. Silence descended upon the room. Feeling slightly better, Selene started to move to get up. A hand reached out for help, and she took it. Looking up, she saw that the hand belonged to Ronal. She gave him an approving smile. "Thanks," she whispered, giving his hand a friendly squeeze and letting go.

"Your Highness, are you hurt?" Ronal asked.

"No, it is not that bad," Selene assured him. "It was more a shock than anything." She turned to face Dorian.

He was looking past her, at the lieutenant guard. "Officer Crowell!" he called. When the guard turned and saluted to him, Dorian sighed. "Call the troops to ready. War is on the way."

"Yes, Sire!" The lieutenant responded. He saluted once more, and then walked out of the room.

"Dorian?" Selene's voice was full of uncertainty. "What do you mean, war? Surely you don't think that Aemon would be so … rash?"

The King sighed. "He's threatened to rebel. If you did not marry him, he would take over the monarchy the 'old-fashioned way' as he so diplomatically put it."

"But … why? Why would he do such a thing?"

"He wants to be King, what else?" Dorian sighed. "Please, Selene. Do not bother me at the moment. I have to call in the diplomats. I have to see just who is on our side."

Selene watched as the guards left the room. How strange, she thought, that just ten minutes ago breakfast had been on everyone's mind. She sat down at the table, her head falling into her hands.

Ronal stayed behind as the guards all shuffled out of the room after the King. He shuffled over to her and said, "It's going to be okay, Your Highness. Don't worry about anything."

"How I can I not?" she whispered before looking up at him with a curious glance. Remembering his part in the breakfast quarrel, she asked, "How in the world did you manage to find all that out, Ronal?"

He shrugged. "I have a couple of dependable contacts in the City," he said. "Between what they've said and what I've figured from Etoileon, it wasn't hard to see that this Aemon guy is bent on retribution all right."

"What? Etoileon? He knew about this?"

"I guess so … I thought that was why he was out of the way." Ronal's face turned an unpleasant shade of scarlet. "I wasn't going to say anything, until I learned that Aemon's ship was heading out today, and it was all prepared to take you with them. One of the crew at the palace port told me about it. Etoileon would have killed me if I had done nothing to warn you. I know he's been sick."

Selene smiled at him. "Thank you, Ronal. I am very grateful for your concern. In return, I'll have it arranged for you to go into the city whenever you like. How does that sound to you?"

Ronal's face lit up with smile, and then it suddenly turned to a more thoughtful look. "Well, that is generous of you, Your Highness. But I was wondering, instead of that, could you possibly consider hiring a new maid? I have a friend in the city who would love to work here at the Palace."

"A woman?" Selene asked. "Oh. I see. You like her." A small, almost teasing smile flitted up to her face.

Ronal grinned. "Sure do."

"Well, that sounds fine to me," Selene agreed. "It would be nice to get some new handmaidens anyway. I'll get Dorian to find me some more. Tell your friend to come tomorrow at dawn. We'll find her a nice uniform and put her to work."

"A handmaiden?" Ronal's grin grew even wider. "That would be great! She'd love that! Thank you so much, Princess!"

"Good, it's settled then. I'm going to take breakfast in my room, I think," Selene murmured as she exited the room swiftly, determined not to think of how Etoileon had known about the rebel threat.

Ronal was no doubt surprised by the abrupt manner in which the princess excused herself. Had he not been so preoccupied with his own good fortune, he might've caught the hint of tears in the Princess's eyes.

***

Etoileon was grateful that the evening had come at last. He'd been pacing his floor for nearly the past two days. And when he was tired from pacing, he'd tried, without much success, to get some rest. All he could think about as he shut his eyelids was Selene, as she danced with him, Selene laughing at one of his stories, Selene as she was trying to escape that rotten man.

He'd been hoping with all of his being that Selene would not be conned into marrying that Aemon person from Jewel Island. Even if it was a good match for the princess, he did not want her to leave.

Right now, he was hoping that he would be allowed to go to his training session at least. Etoileon needed anything—anything at all—to get his mind off of his problems.

There was a knock at the door, and Etoileon looked over from the window just in time to see Garth come in.

"I have brought word from the King," Garth said. "The Representative from Jewel Island is away now. You are free to leave your room. He highly recommends that you head to the Fighters' training room, for their afternoon classes."

"Where's Selene?" Etoileon asked. "Is … Is she … is she going to be married?"

"His Majesty has informed me that you and the other Fighters are to suit up for extra training tonight," Garth replied. "War is upon us."

Etoileon had been holding his breath up until that point. When he released it, all of it flew out in a rush. He was relieved. He was about to ask what happened when the full impact of Garth's words hit him. War was coming.

Etoileon had thought about going up to the High Tower to see if Selene would come, but he'd decided against it now. It was much too early in the evening for Selene to come anyway, despite the anticipation of the Lunar Storms. The festival would start at sundown, and he would meet up with her before that, he thought. Besides, he thought, I should really head for the training section of the palace; after all, if there was a war on the way, I had best start preparing for it.

***

Etoileon had missed training the past two days. He was surprised to find how much he'd missed it, how he enjoyed practicing and refining his skills. He was not surprised to find out that he was hoping that Selene would come and get him.

"Hey," Ronal greeted him. "Are you feeling better, Etoileon?"

Etoileon turned around at the sound of his friend's voice. "Ronal," he nodded, "Glad to see that you missed me." Etoileon lowered his voice and said, "I wasn't sick."

"Oh … Oh! I see," Ronal smirked. He couldn't resist teasing his friend a bit. "Been out practicing your social skills, or punished for something? Tell me all about it."

Etoileon made sure no one could hear him as he told Ronal the whole story. "The King made a deal with that psycho Aemon representative. His Majesty told him that if he could convince Selene to marry him the right way, he would allow him to have her." He filled in Ronal with all the details that he'd been able to get from the King.

"I know," Ronal said back. "I was told. I thought that it had something to do with your timely sickness."

"What? How? You were there when Dorian ordered me to stay away from Selene?"

"Huh? That's what happened? His Majesty can be so –" Ronal broke off, noticing the impatient look on his friend's face. "Oh, right … well, I only found out that Aemon is Cyerra's twin. He was planning to take over the crown any way he could, and he saw Selene as his quickest route, I suppose. Actually, until I heard he was willing to wage a war, I thought it wouldn't be that bad a match. Then he hit her."

"He hit her? He hit Selene?" Etoileon suddenly felt as though someone had punched him in the stomach.

"Yeah. As soon as I heard about what he was planning on doing, and realized he was playing on her emotions, I hurried to warn her about him. With you out, I knew you would kill me if I didn't."

"You're right about that," Etoileon agreed, a small smile on his face at the joke. It quickly faded back into a frown. "But he hit her?" There was no getting past it.

"Yeah. There was this whole incident at breakfast," Ronal replied as he grabbed his practicing gear from his personal Fighter cabinet. "You should've been there. He was all 'I'll love you forever' and 'we'll rule together until death parts us' and all this other really emotional bull. Selene turned him down, and then he started yelling about how she loves you, and –"

"What? She said she loved me?" Etoileon felt something stir inside his heart.

"No, no. She didn't say anything like that at all. He was convinced that she did, though, and kept nagging her about it. It was a little scary. Selene just kind of stood there. She didn't seem to know what to do after that."

"I see." Etoileon felt his heart sink. So she hadn't said that she loved him. It was nothing he shouldn't expect. He cleared his throat. "What happened after that?"

"He slapped her and then the King finally broke him away from her, telling Aemon to get out of the Palace, and that he was removed from being a representative."

"That's good."

"Yeah, I'll say. I'd come to warn Selene just before, but I thought she'd come down to the Fighter's room first, so I was running to catch her. Hey, and guess what? Because I did warn her though, I managed to get Cyerra a job as a handmaiden here."

"That's good," Etoileon said once more, thinking more about how he was going to make this up to Selene. She'd been away from him for two days, and she'd been hit and used as a political gambling piece. He could not just stand by and let this happen again. He smirked despite his anger; he'd said it before, that girl was trouble. And this was just the first official marriage proposal, too, now that she was of age. He sincerely hoped that this wasn't how it was going to be until the King finally married her off to someone. "That should make you happy."

"You bet," Ronal agreed. "Anyway, we're going to get in trouble if we don't start warming up soon. Let's go." He'd noticed the look on the Master's face as he had been talking to Etoileon.

"Sure." Etoileon followed his friend out of Fighter's storage room and into the practice dojo.

They warmed up quickly enough, before they were once again ordered to fight for practice. This time, Etoileon was partnered up with another Fighter student, a twenty-two year old named Trion.

Trion smiled viciously at Etoileon. "Ready to fight, Orphan Boy?" he asked. Etoileon grimaced slightly. The King's nickname for him was always used to taunt him, but it was a surprise that Trion was being this antagonistic today. Trion was an advanced Fighter like Etoileon, and was usually on good terms with him - despite losing before to Etoileon as the Princess's protector. He was of medium build, with friendly light blue eyes and dark brown hair.

"Ready," Etoileon nodded stoically as they prepared for battle. He had found out long ago that showing any pain or care in reaction to taunting helped no one, least of all himself. In fact, if he ignored it, usually the opponent would get more easily distracted and worried, leaving Etoileon an opening to attack them more effectively.

Trion and Etoileon stood three meters apart. They circled each other, like birds around their prey. Their eyes took into account all the subtlest of movements, looking for an opportune moment to strike.

Etoileon was just about to settle back into a waiting stance when Trion smirked and stood back in a neutral position. "Huh?" Etoileon gave him a questioning look. "What're you doing?"

Trion raised an eyebrow. "If I told you, it wouldn't be a real fight then," he sneered. "I was just thinking about how your face is going to look when I beat you."

"Daydreaming is dangerous when you're fighting," Etoileon warned, moving his arms up a bit higher in order to block his face more effectively. He was losing his patience.

Trion's face contorted in anger. "Well, then, let's get this over with then," he muttered, and then jabbed out hard to the left, then the right, faked left, went back to the right. Etoileon blocked him, and lashed out with a kick. His leg met with nothing but air.

Trion jumped and somersaulted, landing on Etoileon's far left. An outside crescent kick whirled around, landing on its target. Etoileon was knocked to the ground as the kick sent him flying back. Trion grinned and moved in for more. Etoileon rolled backwards, curling back up to his feet. All of his thoughts drained out of his mind as the determination to win replaced all concerns. His feet shuffled, his fists came out fighting. He slashed out, Trion blocking and dodging at every angle. "Give it up, you can't beat me," Trion boasted.

Etoileon said nothing, only smiling a moment later when he landed a nice punch to Trion's face.

Trion stepped back, and Etoileon attacked. One roundabout kick and a trip later, Trion was on his knees, struggling to get up. Etoileon was just about to land the finishing blow to Trion when his adversary rolled away and tumbled off to the side, Etoileon's fist only managing to brush slightly by.

Etoileon felt the sweat run down his face as he backed up a step and took another ready stance. Trion followed his lead. Both of them were breathing harder now. Etoileon could feel his heart pounding in his chest.

Trion relaxed again. "I see your fighting skills have worsened since we last met," he called out. "You're such a scared, helpless little orphan boy, aren't you? I bet you

THE MOONLGIHT PEGASUS

cheated to get the role of the Princess's protector—maybe she even felt sympathetic enough to help you cheat."

Something in Etoileon snapped. It was one thing to tease him, call him names. But it was another matter entirely to bring the Princess into the mix. He action was swift, his retribution hard and fast. Before Etoileon could think to consider what he was doing, his arms blocked all of Trion's movements as he charged forward. He nearly tackled Trion, lashing out in hard, quick punches. Trion ducked and tried to block, but there was a rage in Etoileon that even he didn't seem to understand completely. He didn't even realize while he was punching Trion's face that his rage had nothing to do with Trion's remarks and everything to do with losing Selene.

A moment later, Etoileon felt his body being pulled out. He could tell that someone had taken hold of him and pulled him off his opponent. Etoileon stopped fighting and looked up to see that the Master Fighter, their teacher, Master Norio, had taken a hold of Etoileon by the scruff of his neck. "Etoileon. I think it is clear that you have won."

"Oh." Sweat ran into his eyes. He could feel his shirt sticking to his back. There was blood on his fists. On the floor in front of him, Trion was trying to stop his nose from bleeding and his right eye was swelling up.

Etoileon felt the guilt in him start to rise. "Sorry," he said. "I guess I got carried away."

Master Norio grimaced. He pulled Etoileon aside, and said with a frown on his wrinkled face, "Don't try it again, Etoileon. Trion may have said something you do not agree with, but hurting him in retaliation to a remark will not change his mind. There are other battles that matter much more than this one, battles of the heart. This behavior is really unworthy of a true Fighter. Now, you're dismissed."

"Master, I'm so sorry," Etoileon tried again. He was reaching out for an explanation, but he didn't know what had happened to his loss of control. Something had snapped inside of him. "I … I don't know what happened."

"You are both dismissed," Master Norio said turning to face both of the boys, this time with much more emphasis on his words. His hard hazel eyes glared down at his students as his hands folded and he walked away.

For an old man, Etoileon thought, he was pretty tough. Etoileon reached down and offered his hand to his opponent. "Sorry," Etoileon apologized. "I didn't mean to hurt you."

Trion glared at him, making his face look even more twisted because of his black eye and swollen nose. He reached out and knocked Etoileon's hand out of the way. "I don't need your pity," he sneered, getting up and heading for the showers. "I'll win the next time, mark my words."

Etoileon hung back a moment as Trion left. He was usually much nicer, he thought. "Wonder what happened to him?" He shook his head, trying to clear his mind. He was finished for the morning it looked like. He had the rest of the time to himself.

Checking the clock on the wall outside of the gymnasium, he saw that it was just about time for the Lunar Storms to begin. The palace that evening, was preparing to hold their traditional Moonbeam Sky Show Festival. If he hurried, he could make it to the High Tower just in time to see it. He pulled on his fighter cloak and headed off.

***

It is common knowledge that the moment that a person tries not to think about something, thinking about anything else becomes impossible. Selene was just thinking this as she miserably slumped about in her room. Usually by now she was changing into a different outfit by now to go down to lunch. But for the moment she just stayed in her royal bed; the covers were tossed here and there, almost all on the floor, as she lay there, curled up in a ball.

She'd been like that since she'd come back from breakfast. The only break she'd taken was to scribble a note quickly down to Dorian, asking for him to allow her to take on a couple more handmaidens. Chevée had taken it down to the King for her. Selene had decided that she did not want to see him for a while.

She did not want to see Etoileon either. She did not want to see him, because the moment she did, she knew her heart would break. She would demand him to tell her why he'd just stood back from letting this intruder try and take over her life. Sometimes what we want to know, Selene thought, is not worth giving up what we already think. Sometimes.

Chevée returned, bowing her head. "I have delivered your message, Your Highness," she said. "His Majesty told me to tell you that some additional handmaidens for you were fine with him. He also would like to see you at dinner tonight and respectfully requested that you be there."

"Tell him I'm not coming tonight, Chevée," she answered. "Tell him I would like to go to sleep a bit earlier tonight." She sat up as an afterthought, adding, "With my highest respects, of course."

Chevée stood a moment in silence before she nodded. "Yes, Your Highness."

When she was gone, Selene rolled over and looked at the door, a loud sigh escaping her. Her fists balled up and placed themselves on her forehead, as though they were trying to pound out some of her anxiety. Maybe all this will look better later, she thought, closing her eyes.

"Please," she whispered, as she did not know who would listen to her. "Please … Help me."

A moment later, she sighed once more, and decided to get out of her room. Her eyes looked all around, and landed on the window. From her room, she had a perfect view of the courtyard, covered this time of day with servants and the many gardeners. Looking up into the glare of the fading sunlight, the princess decided she would take a visit to her tower. Selene forced a small smile. She wanted to see the sky show, anyway. It would be in perfect view from the High Tower. Since she'd just sent Chevée to get her out of the festival dinner, she had time to herself. Selene crawled out from her covers. After quickly changing into a simple white dress and making sure that her servants were otherwise occupied, she quietly sneaked out of her room.

***

Etoileon dashed up the stairs. He was no longer thinking about what he'd done in the practice room. All he was thinking about now was that he was going to see Selene again. He hadn't been away from her more than a day in a long time, and in his mind he realized how much he'd come to depend on her kindness. There was a smile on his face as he rounded the last circle of steps and came to the door. With Trion and the others like him, it was good to see a friendly face.

He paused a moment, to catch his breath, and then opened the door. His first step inside had him looking around for Selene.

"Selene?" He couldn't find her. "Huh … " She must not be up here yet, Etoileon thought as disappointment began to come over him. He shrugged it off. Surely she would be here soon. She would not want to miss the sunset and the start of the Lunar Storms, no matter what had happened earlier. He walked over to the edge of the balcony and saw, looking into the far reaches of the horizon, there were crowds of people who had settled in the desert outskirts of the city, all in hopes of getting a picturesque view of the phenomenon.

He placed his hands on the balcony's edge and slumped over, looking at the scenery of the city below. Etoileon saw that there were more than a few ships leaving port and heading back in the direction of their respective homes. He recalled the time when Selene had told him that Dorian would take her on a Goodwill Trip to the other islands when she was married. He wondered if she would be by the time the next trip would come around in six months, or even if there would be another tour at all. Catching sight of the sunset light on the ocean water, he smiled as the simple beauty stole the rest of his thoughts away for a while. With the war starting, such moments were to be more treasured for their rarity.

That was how Selene found him. His head resting in his folded hands, leaning heavily onto the granite stone. For a moment she looked at him with shaking hands. She had not wanted to see him today. What a foolish wish, she thought. It was hardly a possibility. As long as she'd known Etoileon, he'd been there to watch the city scenes with her. She sighed and tried to swallow the lump that was suddenly in her throat. Putting on a small half-smile, she took a couple of steps closer to him.

"That's not the proper posture for a Fighter, is it?" she asked jokingly.

Etoileon stood up at once, and turned to see her smile. "Selene. You're here," he greeted her. His own smile started to form, but it faded once he saw that her eyes were not twinkling along with her smile. "What's wrong? Are you okay?"

"Me? Of course I'm okay." Selene's voice had a tiny infliction in it that told Etoileon she was fine, but she was not her usual cheerful self. Her eyes gleamed almost maliciously as she asked, "And what about you? Are you still sick?"

"Sick? I was –" he stopped and grimaced. Dorian must've told her to keep away from him because he was ill. Sometimes, Etoileon thought, Dorian could be a pain. But looking back at Selene, he struggled to maintain a level head. "I am fine, thanks."

She moved up to settle herself on the balcony's edge, on the opposite side from where Etoileon was standing. "Good."

That was when he was sure something wasn't right. As long as they'd been alone in the tower, she'd never in his recollection faltered in standing up close to him before, in reaching out to comfort him, or tentatively patting his back, or holding onto him while she leaned over the balcony wall.

"I think that something is bothering you," he started to say.

She cut him off quite nicely. "No, I said I'm very well, thank you. I'm fine, and everything is fine. Quit being so concerned."

He decided to try once more. Stepping a subtle step closer to her, he tried to look up in her face, which had been conveniently turned away from him at the moment. "Selene, are you sure –"

Her eyes snapped around at him, making him nearly step back. "Of course I'm good. I can survive a day without you hovering all around me."

So that was it. "Selene," he started, "Look, um … I'm sorry about what happened. These past couple of days –"

Again he was cut off as she broke into his sentences. "Don't worry about it," she practically snarled. Her anger was boiling at this point. "I said that I can live my life perfectly fine without you around."

Ouch, that hurt, Etoileon thought. "I don't care about that," he said. "I want you to know that I'm sorry I wasn't able to protect you."

"Protect me?" Selene's eyes flickered with tears. "Is that all? You're sorry you couldn't protect me?"

"Yes. I'm very sorry that Aemon hit you." Wrong answer. Etoileon could feel the stillness between them as it turned cold.

"Oh, I suppose your friends already told you all about what happened," Selene murmured. "Or maybe it was one of the maids, or the guards running around this palace." Her tears disappeared. As he began to confirm her assumption, she continued. "I don't care where you heard it from, but I can't believe you weren't there in the first place! You're supposed to be my protector, and then you disappear just as I … as I … " she broke off as her tears came back once again.

Etoileon didn't know what she was talking about. "Selene, if I'd so much as talked to you, your idiot brother would've had me thrown out of the palace, and then I'd never be able to see you or protect you again. I would've lost my job!" his hands were thrown up in exasperation.

"Oh, so instead you've just lost my respect! I never thought you would've let anyone try to marry me against my will."

"I told you, I couldn't! And besides, when I first came here, that was how it was laid down. I was supposed to protect you until you got married. And it looked like you and Aemon were going to get married!"

"I don't want to be married to him! You knew that!" There was no getting past it.

"Well, I hear he's going to be throwing a war instead, so you don't have to pitch the blame on me for that!" Etoileon couldn't believe how easily he'd fallen for it. She was angry with him, and now he was getting angry with her.

"Etoileon, can't you see? I don't like this at all. Dorian is my brother … and you, you're my … well, point is, you are both so important to me, and you both just stood back and figured that I'd go along with this marriage since it was Aemon threatening a war if I wouldn't! How could you?" She fell to her knees, crouched over.

"Oh, really, Selene, stop crying!" Etoileon insisted as he took another step closer to her. "I was scared out of my mind that I'd lose you!"

"And so instead of protecting me, you just stood back and deserted me?" Selene whispered softly as she looked up at him.

"No! I didn't stand back … " he thought about it. "Well, I might've, but I wouldn't have stayed that way, I promise! I was stuck in my room for the past two days, left to wonder what in the world was going to happen."

"Oh, I'm sure you would've thanked me for everything before I left to live on some island in the Sapphiran Seas. Thanked me for keeping you off the streets, having given you a good job and –"

He cut her off this time. "Hey, I earned that job! Do you know how many tests your stupid brother put me through before he consented to allow me to be your protector? It was more than necessary, that's for sure!"

Selene rose to her feet. With a look of indignation, she huffed. "Dare you interrupt me? Have you forgotten who I am?"

"Frankly, it's hard to tell just who you are at the moment. The Selene I know is never like this!"

" The Princess you serve can be however she likes!" Selene snapped angrily. "I'm a human too and I can be angry if I feel like it!"

"Serve? I serve you? Do you think I do all this stuff around here because I'm told to?" Etoileon asked, his voice still loud. "Well, guess what? I don't! I don't have to do anything you want or what anyone else wants!"

"Go ahead then," Selene shouted back. "I can see that since you do anything you want, standing aside while I was trying to be manipulated into a political marriage pretty much means that I'm not high on your list of priorities." She turned her back to him and scooted closer to her side of the balcony.

It was at this time the sky was starting to get dark. The mild sunshine was beginning to grow faded as the moons, one on each side of the circle of sunlight, started to shine their celestial rainbow colors.

Etoileon just stared at Selene's back as she glanced at the view. This argument was far from over, he thought. "Selene, I'm not finished. I was going to say that anything I do around here is because I want to, but -"

"I knew that!" Selene whirled around again. "I know that! You don't have to tell me!"

" What I meant by it is that there are sometimes when I can't always do what I want, all right?" Etoileon tried to lower the coldness of his voice. "I can't always break the rules or deny a request even if I want to, any more than you can roam around the city the way you want to."

"What's your point here?" she asked. "I'm getting sick of arguing." Literally, she thought. Her head was starting to hurt, and her vision was blurring over, more and more as the sky grew darker. She was starting to feel drained of her energy.

"My point is, there are sometimes when I can't control what I do. I wanted to tell you. I wanted to protect you. I want to be there for you. I sure didn't want this stupid argument!"

"So sorry to disappoint you," she frowned.

"Do you honestly think that I—or your brother for that matter—would've so easily let you go? That we wouldn't have tried to stop them from taking you? Do you have so little faith in both of us that you think we don't need you around here?"

She said nothing. Etoileon felt that, at last, he was getting somewhere. He reached out for her, but she took a step back from him again.

"Leave me alone," she whispered, turning away from him and trying to forget that he was there.

"No."

Her eyes snapped open and she looked back at him, about to demand that he leave at once when he'd caught her in a tight, uncomfortable hug. Her argument died on her lips as she felt his arms tighten around her. It was the first real time that he'd purposely attempted to hold her in his arms.

The moment passed. Remembering her anger, she elbowed him hard in the stomach and started to struggle against him, trying unsuccessfully to push him away from her. "Stop it! Let me go!" she squirmed as she balled up her fists and tried harder to get away.

But Etoileon was a trained Fighter. Nothing she did would be able to break his hold. Finally, after numerous attempts, she stopped hitting him and stopped trying to push him away, only to break down in tears.

She felt so betrayed, so confused. She'd felt so helpless to her anger. Selene knew that she should've been honest about it. But she couldn't help it. This was the first time that he'd ever let her down. This was the first time that she'd felt that maybe he wasn't as concerned for the future of their friendship as she was. Of course she'd probably just ruined any chance of remaining friends now, but it was only because … because … she didn't even know why she'd succumbed to this level. She thought he was giving up on her and her first instinctive action had been to hurt him for even allowing it to cross his mind. Her tears welled up in her eyes even more as she realized what a horrible person she was.

Her life was glossed over with joy that seemed incomplete, and habits that could not seem to allow her to acknowledge the fear she felt. She couldn't seem to be honest, even with herself. She didn't even realize that Etoileon was still holding her close to him.

As Etoileon continued to hold his arms around her, he fervently hoped that she would stop crying soon. He was totally confused by all this. Selene was usually all smiles, sympathetic and happy. This poor girl, her body quivering with sobs, was so unlike the person he knew she could be. His grip loosened on her slightly, his hands unclenching and rubbing her back. He was still trying to comfort her. "Don't cry, Selene," he said. "Please don't cry. It's okay. Everything's going to be okay."

Her eyes opened up at his words. Behind his shoulders, Selene could just make out the faintest tint of a dark rainbow beginning to show in the partly clouded sky. She sucked in her breath. Her head started to ache with pain. Pushing away from him once more, she at last escaped on his lightened hold. Her feet tried to carry her to the door, but even as her consciousness started to slip she could feel her knees hit the floor.

"Selene!" she could hear his voice as he called to her.

"Etoileon," she whispered back softly. Taking a deep breath, she let the world as she knew it fall away, as sleep descended on her like the rising tide.

"Selene!" he called out her name again as she slumped onto the floor in a dead faint. He knew that it was entirely his fault, too. He shouldn't have argued with her at all. Turning her over onto her stomach, he checked her pulse and was relieved to find that she was going to be okay. She'd just fainted. "Selene. I'm sorry that I let this happen to you."

His brain seemed incapable of logical thought as he let her slump against him. It took him more than a few minutes to realize that he could not leave her there. So Etoileon carefully placed his one arm under her neck and the other underneath her knees. Picking her up as carefully as possible, he looked down at her tear-stained face. Then he started to head for her room.

Reaching the end of the stairs, the thought that he would be blamed for this crossed his mind. He decided that when it came to defending himself, other than in physical combat, it was particularly not a good strategy.

***

He was not usually allowed in her room. This was her domain, the place where she and her handmaidens wandered almost as freely as the people did on the streets. This was the place where she got ready for the day and talked with her closest female companions. Etoileon had the feeling, from the way that her handmaidens were watching him so discretely vigilant, that he had been mentioned in more than a few of those conversations. He was not quite sure how to react to that.

Etoileon sat beside the Princess as she lay on her bed. His hand had reached out and taken a hold of hers some time before, but he was uncertain as to how long he'd been there.

Aura, whom he knew to be the Princess' governess, sat in a chair at the far end of the room, watching him every so often as he sat. One of her handmaidens, the one called Kadrianne, stood perfectly aloof from the situation in a nearby corner; if Selene hadn't told him before about Kadrianne's discretion, he would've said that she was paying him no mind at all. The glazed, faraway look in her eyes belied the surprising amount of detail she was taking in and analyzing. He figured there were more than just these women watching him. He knew that Selene had three handmaidens; Kadrianne was the only one in his present sight.

He sat there for a moment, grimacing as he recalled the harsh words he had said to Selene. It had been their first real fight, and he couldn't believe what had happened in the tower. He never would have said anything, if he had known that she would've collapsed from it. Her brother was no doubt going to chew him out for this later. She'd been so sad, and so angry. He'd never seen her like that before. Had he really hurt her that bad? His fingers took a firmer grip on her hand as he sat there.

"Selene," he whispered to her, just barely audible. "I'm so sorry. Please forgive me."

After a few more moments of silence, Aura got up and cleared her throat. Looking intently at Etoileon, he caught her gaze and sighed. She was clearly telling Etoileon that he was to leave now. He let go of Selene's hand, and got up.

Aura turned away, and Kadrianne also straightened up and moved to the other side of the room, helping Aura to close the Princess's curtains for the night. Through the window, Etoileon could see the starry night starting to take over the colored patterns of the Lunar Storms.

Etoileon knew he had to leave. Looking quickly back at the governess and the handmaiden, he hurriedly took one last look at Selene as she slept on, peacefully dreaming. He laid his hand softly on her cheek, affectionately brushing some of her hair out of her eyes.

"Sleep well, Selene," he whispered. Her lips were curled into a smile and she sighed happily, still fast asleep. He smiled a bit. It looked like she was going to be okay.

***

She was dreaming.

The water was all around her carrying her, supporting her. It was cool and relaxing; the only sounds she could hear as she floated in the sea were the waves, singing their quiet hymns. Her arms fluttered up and about slowly, trying to catch the rhythm of the water, moving with the infectious lull of it. She wanted nothing more than to be whisked away to another world—whisked away to be free of her bounds once more.

Her eyes for the moment were closed, as she tried to relax, to let the water take her along its path. She felt like she was floating on a cloud, making little or no effort to move along through the skies. She could feel her skirts swaying with the ripples, her feet dangling into the water's depth. There was a warm light on her face, calling her to the surface, almost as though it were keeping her there.

Selene has always remembered her dreams after she had awakened the next morning. But now there was something different. This was the first time she felt so awake, so very alive, during her dream. This was the first time she could feel the water beneath her, the air as it gently caressed her face. She could taste the sweetness of the ocean spray on her lips. She could breathe in the fresh crispness of the wind.

Selene opened her eyes, and marveled at the stunning beauty that surrounded her. "Wow," she whispered quietly.

THE MOONLGIHT PEGASUS

Her voice carried along the way, resonating into the sky. "This is amazing." It was almost as if she'd fallen down the waterfall, to find that the oasis had gone away along with the rest of the world.

Her gaze moved up to look at the sky above. It was a prefect shade of early night, a soft violet blue. There were even some tiny stars, despite the surprising amount of warm sunlight. There was a small glimpse of a moon's crescent in the far reaches of the sky, but it, too, had a strangely warm glow. Her hand reached up into the air, as though she was checking to make sure she was trying to determine if she was asleep or not.

Out of the sky, from high above her, a bright light flashed out. Selene's hands quickly flew to cover her eyes, and she suddenly found herself sitting on the sandy ocean floor, the bank of the coast just behind her. The sand clung to her skin and to her dress, making a mess everywhere. This is why I like the city life, she thought as she tried to brush off some of the scratchy sand. She paused in her task, as it was no doubt fruitless. She looked up into the sky once more, trying to see where the light had come from.

She glanced all around, and could not see anything. No hint of the incident was anywhere. Shrugging, she got to her feet and picked up her skirts, and headed for the coast. Looking around, she found herself a nice rock to sit on, to lie out on while she dried.

Selene had just sat down when her eyes caught sight of something glittering in the air.

"Huh?" she squinted, trying to make out what it was she was looking at. She stood up, planting her feet firmly on the rock.

That was when a great wind came, and it nearly knocked her to her knees. She flinched as she tried to block the wind from her face. It was over in a moment, however. Selene sighed. The wind had caused her sand-covered hair to whisk out in all directions.

She sighed and tried to brush her hair out of her face. Leaning down, she cupped her hands to reach for some water, in order to bring her windblown locks back into order. Another wind came, this one soft and light. Selene smiled once again, this wind feeling almost like a tickle against her wet skin. She was just about to touch the water when something fell into her hand. "What?" she examined the object and gasped.

It was a feather. It was a beautiful, soft, pristine white feather that caught the shining sunlight on the edge of the quills, creating an enchanting impression. Selene carefully brought her hands close to her, in order to get a better look. Seeing the sun's glimmer, she immediately recognized it to be what she'd seen moments earlier, glittering in the sky. Her fingers slowly stroked the feather, marveling at how beautiful and how soft and how perfect it was. Slowly she rose off her knees, her eyes still fixed on the feather. "It's so beautiful," she murmured, closing her eyes. And indeed it was. It was so magnificent and captivating, she could not look upon it for very long without hurting her eyes. Holding it close to her, it seemed as though the warmth of the sun had sunken into it as well as the light. Standing there, on the rock, she sensed a power seeming to radiate from the hidden folds of the feather.

She opened her eyes again, this time looking up to the sky. "But … where did it come from?" she wondered aloud, looking throughout the vast sky once more. Seeing nothing, her eyes looked down at her present once more. Her eyes closed once more as she found herself lost in the light of the feather. A moment later, her dream disappeared in a flood of shining, shimmering light.

A song seemed to drift out from the sky; she thought if she strained her ears, she could hear a sound in the distance, almost like a voice. But perhaps it was only the wind and the sea.

***

The Guardian looked down at his creation. The time had come at last; the Dark Plague's final days of ultimate power had arrived. There had been much loss, much death and a horrible aftermath, but there was also much hope now.

The Spirit had been brought forth; the gateway was clear for the Prince to depart soon. The Light of Hope was sure to shine through the darkness that surrounded the people of Sapphira.

***

"What?" Dorian's voice boomed as he shot up out of his seat and knocked over the tray he'd just been offered by a servant. His eyes were full of anger and shock as he looked down at his sister's governess bowed low on the floor before him.

"Your Majesty," Aura's voice was tight with distraught, "It is true. Your sister, Her Highness the Princess, has taken ill. Her protector informed me that she fainted while he was watching over her."

"That Orphan Boy," Dorian gritted through his teeth in anger. Turning back to Aura, he asked, "Not one day has passed and already the drama is resuming." He sighed. Where is she now?"

"The Princess's protector brought her back to her room and placed her in the care of myself," Aura assured him. "She will be fine, she just needs rest. Goodness knows that she's had a hard day today, with all the political agendas going on around here."

There was a subtle undertone to Aura's voice that made Dorian think for a second time about her words. He smiled ruefully. "You are not implying that I would be responsible for such a thing, are you, My Lady?"

Aura delicately fluttered her eyes at him with innocence. "I would not dare to ever even think such a thing," she said. She rose from her low bow and squared her shoulders. "However—"

"I knew it!" the King interrupted. "No doubt the Princess has said that she is blaming me for such a trying day. Am I right?"

"Not at all," Aura snapped, her tone surprisingly sharp. It was not like a lady such as herself to object strongly to the King. "She has said nothing to me on the matter at all. I suspect she hasn't said much to anyone"—she paused briefly as her face hardened in her expression—"except to maybe her protector about anything."

"Most likely she would tell him something," he agreed. Selene couldn't even let a day pass before she'd decided to go hopping off to see him again, Dorian thought. It looked like his worst fears were confirmed.

"Of course, Your Majesty."

"And he just brought her back after she fainted?"

"Yes, Your Majesty."

Dorian lifted a questioning eyebrow. "Do you like this protector of my sister's, Aura?"

Aura was surprised somewhat by the unusual question and even more curious at his tone. She looked up at the King and replied, "I do not think that he is traditionally suitable for her close company," she admitted with the pride of a member of the High Court. "But there are certain things that cannot be denied, and one such thing is their friendship."

"Do you think that he really is the one meant for her, despite all my hoping to the contrary?" His voice was soft and more wondering than condemning.

Aura sighed. "I'm sorry, Your Majesty, but it sure looks like it."

"I had a feeling that it was going to happen. I am left only with the question, then, of how this fits into the prophecy." His thoughts seemed to drift from the realms of reality for a moment. Still staring off into space, he asked, "My Lady, did you happen to sort out the handmaiden business for Selene?"

The governess nodded. "Yes, I spoke with the applicants earlier today, prior to lunch. The two I took into consideration for her are supposed to start tomorrow, Your Majesty."

"Good. It looks like you've done your job for today then," Dorian waved her off. "You're dismissed."

***

Selene shot up out of her sleep, her eyes practically jerking open. Her hand flew to her heart and found it was racing, but she felt like she had slept for a week. Seeing that it was dark outside, it took her a moment to realize it was early in the day, though dawn had not arrived just yet.

She leaned back and tried to relax. It was then the memories of the day before came crashing down on her. All her words, all the anger and frustration she'd thrown out … all of it directed at her protector, her dear friend. Selene felt more than sorrow at what had happened. She now felt guilty and angry with herself. All she wanted to do was have the pain go away. Better yet, she thought, it would've been better if the whole thing had never happened last night.

She sat still on her bed for a long moment, her thoughts pondering at the situation she now faced. A flicker of light in the corner of her eye suddenly caught her attention. She turned to face what had distracted her. A second later she was speechless in surprise.

It was a beautiful, familiar-looking white feather, brilliantly shining a faint light. Selene, deeply entranced by the feather's appearance, was suddenly able to recall what had happened that night while she had been asleep. With surprisingly steady hands, the princess reached out and touched it.

The feather was no less soft or delicate than it had been the first time she'd held it. The white quills all glittered with a soft light. Selene picked it up and held it to her heart, much as she'd done before in her dream. The warmth seemed to trickle into her very blood, sending a feeling of serenity through her. Such peace she felt. Hearing the footsteps coming up the hallway, Selene jerked out of her peaceful thoughts and hid the feather under her covers, just in time for the door to open.

"Yes?" Selene asked, seeing Kadrianne's anxious glance as her faithful handmaiden came in. "What is it, Kadrianne?"

"Good morning," Kadrianne bowed. "I'm so glad to see that you're awake at this hour, Your Highness. We all were quite worried about you when you fainted. We weren't sure when you were going to wake up."

A brief memory of the darkened hues of the sky flashed across her mind. Confused, Selene's gaze went up to meet with Kadrianne's. "Oh … I fainted? How long have I been out?" She started to move around anxiously as though she feared that she'd been asleep and hadn't moved for days.

"Oh, don't worry, Your Highness. You fainted only last night. You gave us all a fright." Kadrianne came closer and smiled softly. "Especially a particular young man."

"Etoileon." Selene thought once again about her quarrel with him. She felt the feather beside her as she held it carefully away from Kadrianne's gaze. She wondered suddenly if it had been a gift from him. Her thoughts of the matter disappeared as her handmaiden spoke up in answer to her question.

"Yes. He was here for nearly an hour after you fainted."

"Here?"

"Yes. Her ladyship, your governess, as well as Yana and I were all present. I was certain that the King would punish him. I haven't been able to find anything out in regards to that though, Your Highness."

"Why would he get in trouble?"

Kadrianne gave the Princess a meaningful look, one that said she knew more than she was letting on. "Because, no doubt her Ladyship would've told the King and that you'd fainted under his watch. You know how eager Aura is to get someone else in trouble other than herself."

She knew that Kadrianne was not exaggerating. Selene did not know what to say. She simply was determined to go find Etoileon and apologize at once. He did care for her. He had to. And she had to tell him how she felt about him. *I bet if I'd just been honest from the beginning, Etoileon wouldn't have gotten so angry with me in the first place,* Selene thought. She smiled a tiny smile as Kadrianne began to open the drapes and pick up some of the clutter in the room.

"Your Highness, the new handmaidens are to be here soon," Kadrianne reminded her as Chevée came into the room and Yana prepared the princess' wardrobe. "Let's hurry, shall we?"

Selene felt the sigh rise up in her chest. It looked like she wouldn't be able to seek out Etoileon until his practice session that morning; she was glad that it was still considered an important festival week, because the practices started a couple of hours later than usual. She had so much to deal with before she could even think about something as important as seeing her friend. Maybe if she hurried she could catch him.

Selene carefully hid the treasured feather in the large pocket of her cloak. She decided that she would find a safe place to hide it when she had some free time. Right at the moment, she had to deal with getting ready.

***

It was less than a half hour later when Selene, now fully dressed in her formal attire and feeling a bit more like her normal self, met with her two new handmaidens.

There was rarely a call for more than three handmaidens for a Princess, or even a Queen. They were not considered by the court to be necessary, even for a royal, because they were more like companions than anything else. However, all that opinion did was show the ignorance of the High Court and the public.

The handmaidens were much more than fancy servants or formally titled friends. They were highly trained in observation and local espionage, as well as the last line of defense for the Princess. Since in the past most had used their handmaidens for information in regards to just keeping up on gossip, the position of being a handmaiden was always much undermined by the rest of court. Had it not been for the oncoming threat of war, Selene thought, she doubted that Dorian would've been so quick to agree to let her add more help. As a charge under the King, Selene had not been allowed to choose her handmaidens herself. There was a delicate process to go about when one wished to become eligible for such a close position to the royal family members.

After meeting with Aura, the two handmaidens chosen were Cyerra, Ronal's not-so-secret girlfriend, and a young woman with kind brown eyes named Rosaria. Rosaria and Cyerra, who even without help or insistence from the Princess to be chosen, had been picked based on their wit, courage, and skill. They would be trained in more defensive weaponry with the new legions of foot soldiers at the palace. Selene gave them both a welcoming smile as she met with them.

"It is nice to meet you," Selene assured them as she greeted them. "Cyerra, I have heard much about you from your friend." Selene met Cyerra's eyes with a kind smile. They both knew she was talking about Ronal. "And Rosaria, I trust that Aura's judgment of you is accurate. I am looking forward to our time together."

Cyerra looked familiar, Selene thought. Huh. Wonder why. She knew from Ronal that Cyerra was Aemon's sister. Maybe that was why she looked so familiar. They were twins, after all. Still, there was a familiar gleam in her blue-gray eyes that Selene knew all too well. Her violet black hair was straight and long, and decorated with tiny island jewels. It was clear despite her time in Diamond City she was an Islander at heart.

Rosaria, on the other hand, was obviously born and raised in the city. She had her brown hair tied up in a fashionable bun, with expensive shoes and only the finest robes available. Selene wondered if like Cyerra, Rosaria had been introduced to her position by a way of a favor. Handmaidens were thought to be the eyes and ears of a Princess, held to be demure and respectable by society. They were to shape the Princess's views on everything with the truth, or as close to the real truth as they could get. Selene knew with the demand for information increasing, she had to watch herself when it came to saying anything in front of anyone, even her closest friends.

Kadrianne and Yana both started to instruct their coworkers with the rules of how things went as Chevée started to hand them the necessary supplies, robes, and insignia they were to carry with them at all times.

Selene felt herself grow bored as the hour dragged on.

Eventually, she stole a quick glance at the clock. It was nearly seven, and by the looks of it, dawn was approaching fast. Soon the Fighters' practice would begin. She could not wait any longer to see Etoileon and apologize. There was a rhythmic beat in her heart that had her absolutely driven to go to him. "Excuse me," she butted into Yana's speech, starting to walk away as she interrupted. "The extra help will be nice for Kadrianne, Yana, and Chevée, as well as the company. Cyerra, Rosaria … welcome to the Palace. I'll leave Yana to brief you in on what to do. Kadrianne is the senior Handmaiden and represents me in my absence." Selene knew that this was one time she had to choose herself over her duty. Even the disapproving look she was getting from Kadrianne and the shocked look she was getting from Yana could not halt her. They knew her well enough to know where she was going. "I'm sorry, but I have to go."

Before any of those around her could get in the way, stop her, or convince her otherwise, Selene dropped all she was doing and hurried off to find her friend.

"Princess!" Kadrianne looked over and met Yana's gaze with an incredulous look when Selene continued to hurry down the hallway. "What in the world do you suppose her problem is lately?"

Yana shook her head sadly. "I think she's in love."

The two of them sighed and turned to face their newest acquaintances. The Princess might be able to skip out of a job without qualms, but they were not. As Yana filled Cyerra and Rosaria in on their tasks, Kadrianne looked back at where the Princess had disappeared. She felt a shiver run down her spine as fear crept in. Something was not right.

***

The sun was still not entirely up when Selene made it to the hallway near the practice room.

There were no students there just yet, but she knew it wouldn't be long. Master Norio was just coming down the stairs.

She smiled warmly at the old man, and bowed respectfully in the way he'd trained her. "Master," she greeted him.

210

"Your Highness," he welcomed her. She was the only one who ever saw a smile on his face constantly. Even the King was usually on the receiving end of a cold stare. "For what do I owe this pleasure?" It was a pleasure for him indeed. In all his years of training students, never had one managed to capture his respect so much as the Princess. She felt more to him like a daughter than a student. Of course, the feeling was never mentioned, as it was considered untraditional, but it went without saying that he had a strong liking for this girl.

Selene laughed. "That's enough of that, Master," she giggled. "You know you can drop the wise formality act on me. I'm not fooled by it. I know you do not like it anyway."

He winked at her. "You insult me, Princess," he grinned, making his old face all wrinkled and creased. When Selene cocked an eyebrow, Master Norio just relaxed. "My, you are a perceptive one."

She nodded, and then got right to the point. "Master, the reason I came down here today was to –"

"To see if Etoileon was here," he filled in. When she raised her eyebrows, he bowed his head to apologize respectfully for interrupting her. "You are not the only perceptive one, My Lady."

"I can see."

"He is doing quite well, as you undoubtedly know. As long as he is with you, he can afford to miss today, if that is your wish … but remember, Selene, we are in a state of war now."

Selene's eyes twinkled in appreciation. She folded her hands together and bowed in thanks. "I am grateful for your kindness, Master. Thank you."

"Here he comes now, actually," Master Norio indicated, nodding his head to gesture to Etoileon's arrival. She turned and looked in the direction. Suddenly she had a hard time thinking.

Norio caught her expression and smiled thoughtfully. It was good to see such tender feelings could exist, with war no doubt on the way. He quietly slipped away as the two of them caught sight of each other.

She didn't move as Etoileon walked toward her. Her eyes caught and held his as he made his way to her. He stopped the respectable distance away from her, but his eyes never left hers. He was relieved to see that she was up and around again. Yesterday had been horrible for him.

There were more students coming in behind Etoileon. They all passed them in the hallway with a glance or two before seeming to dismiss the usual sight of them together. Despite the distractions, Etoileon's eyes never left hers. Rumors were sure to fly as soon as the other boys reached the locker room.

They were soon alone, standing in the hallway in silence a moment later.

Finally, Etoileon decided to try to say something. His gaze fell to the floor in embarrassment and uncertainty. It was then that Selene caught sight of the dark circles under his eyes. He must not have gotten a lot of sleep last night, Selene thought. Etoileon briefly looked back up at her and said, "Uh

THE MOONLGIHT PEGASUS

… It's good to see you're all right this morning, Your Highness. If you'll excuse me, I have to get to class."

The respectful thing to do was to wait until she stepped out of his way to let him pass by. When she didn't move, he said nothing. He didn't want to cause her any more pain. She'd been so angry that she'd fainted from it. This morning she still didn't look right. Selene was known for her royal glow; this morning she was so pale and light he thought she was feeling sick. Maybe I should quit, if all I'm going to do is fail in protecting her, he thought. When he looked up at her again, to see that she still hadn't moved, he breathed in deeply and stepped around her. He had barely moved two steps from his original position when her hand shot out and took his.

"Wait," she said.

"Why?" His question had been instinctive; he knew he was not one to question her but he could not seem to help it.

"Because I want you to come with me today … right now," she replied in a soft voice. When it was obvious that he was still hesitant, she gave his hand a gentle squeeze. "Please … will you stay with me?"

Her hand was warm and her offer was tempting. Still, he sighed and said nothing else as he turned around and began to walk with her through the palace hall.

They said nothing for a while. Etoileon watched as the last of the decorations were taken down, and the new, less formal ones were put up. Nearly every week there was another ball, another party, another celebration being held at the palace—the Lunar Storms were no doubt to be celebrated

THE MOONLGIHT PEGASUS

until the end of this week, but the big opening Festival night was over. The smaller rooms could be cleaned of their celebratory dressings. But the people couldn't seem to get enough of the moonshine, the food, or the esteemed company. Any cause to party was good enough for them, and an accompanying sky show was all the more reason to break out the decorations and costumes and party materials.

Eventually, the palace decorators disappeared from view and the two of them were left all alone.

Their footsteps made a soft echo on the palace floors as they wandered around. It was in the hallway of gardens that Selene turned to face him and slowed down in her stride. "Etoileon … I'm sorry about what I said," she apologized. "I mean it. I was so afraid that I was … I was scared that I was going to lose you. I was angry, I think, that you hadn't come to warn me, that I thought you were just going to let me go so easily." She looked down at the floor. "I know that I haven't been completely honest with you in the past. There are some secrets that I haven't shared that should be shared. You mean so much to me, Etoileon." Her cheeks were starting to turn a slight shade of pink. Looking back up at him, she smiled warmly and added, "I want you to know that out of all the people in this world, you are probably the only one I would cry on."

Etoileon said nothing for a moment. He could not hold a grudge against her, not if his life depended on it. Her words were true, and they were touching. He suddenly felt compelled to be completely honest with her for the first time since he'd met her. "I'm sorry, too. Selene, I haven't been any more honest than you. There are some things I should say that I don't. There are also some times when I … I should act on how I feel regardless of what the King says." He looked down and scratched the back of his head nervously.

"I love that I can be honest with you," Selene admitted. "Being a Princess is not easy. I told you that before. I mean it now, too. When I first met you, you saw me as a person before anything else. People around here, even Dorian sometimes, rarely recall that. I am supposed to be a standard for people to look up to. I'm on a pedestal and I understand that. But I don't want to be up there, and truthfully I shouldn't. I want to be normal … well, actually, I want to be seen as normal. I feel so trapped."

"It's not easy being your protector either," Etoileon offered. "The Fighters are easily discouraged from liking me too much. You're right about being honest. I like it that I can be honest with you, too. And I would be scared if you suddenly weren't there at all." He moved a bit closer to her and continued. "I like being here. I like being around you. I don't regret becoming your protector in the least. I do regret making you feel sad."

"Etoileon … " Selene sighed as she came to a stop. He followed her in manner and turned to look at her. "Obviously, there will be days, I think, where we will be angry again at each other. But please know that I would never hate you. I'll never forget the kindness and help that you've given me."

"I don't want that to happen again," Etoileon stated solemnly. "I like you too much to even think of causing you pain." His statements were followed by a silence. Both of them looked away for the moment.

She suddenly sneaked a peek at her friend. She suddenly wondered if maybe … he was certainly talking like he cared for her. What if he did? It was then that she decided it was time. She had to tell him, no matter what.

"Etoileon, I –"

"Selene –"

Both of them had tried to say something at the same time, and now both of them were red and laughing from it. Selene could feel the tension in her heart lift as she laughed. Etoileon felt a sense of relaxation as he looked up at her once again. He thought it was a nice feeling, considering the rapid beating of his heart. Etoileon was nervous, and for good reason. He wanted to tell her something important.

"Go ahead, Princess," he gestured a mock bow as he smiled up at her. "Your Royal Majesty."

Selene giggled again. "That's Dorian's title, not mine," she responded.

"Oh. Well, Your Highness then," he corrected himself. "What is it that you want to say, Selene?"

She always liked the sound of her name coming from him. The seriousness came back on her face, her smile replaced by an intent look. His kindness was not making this easy for her. She might've even run away, if her legs had not suddenly refused to work properly. "Etoileon … " her voice was low and sounded awkward even to her. Selene tried to look up at him and all she could do was blush. Resolve pushed past the embarrassment a moment later. She had to do this. She had to. Catching his eyes with hers, she tried to continue.

But there was a look on his face that mystified her; she could see every speck of silver in his eyes, faintly glittering in the first light of sunrise. His black hair was unruly and hardly tamed. It struck her all at once how unbelievably handsome he was. Her eyes traveled down from his eyes to settle on his mouth. She hardly noticed that she was leaning towards him.

He was having trouble breathing all of a sudden. She was so close to him. His mind was suddenly screaming at him to stop her, telling him to break off from this at once. But his heart wasn't listening. And his heart was finally admitting that he had wanted this a long time ago. He felt himself take her hands in his and pull her up closer to him. Leaning down, his eyes briefly met hers before they closed, and his lips pressed against hers in a soft and gentle kiss.

For a brief moment in time, the world seemed to stand still. The two of them clung to one another, their hands holding tightly to one another, as the sweet tenderness of their first kiss washed over them. It was a foreign act and somewhat awkward for the two of them, but for some reason, it was familiar to them, almost like a lost dream that they'd suddenly stumbled upon. Selene could feel the warmth of his breath against her mouth as her body stilled. She could feel quickened pace of her heart, and the rush of emotions running through her, yet she could not find it in herself to move apart from him.

Etoileon slowly backed away, his eyes opening just as hers fluttered open. He could see that the familiar blue eyes he'd come to love were glazed over, as though the kiss had left her thoughts in jumbled mess. The clarity pierced through seconds later, moving up to meet his. The corners of her mouth curved into a smile, and Etoileon could've sworn that the earth itself had moved by the tremendous force of his joy in that moment.

In fact, the ground beneath his feet almost seemed to rumble at the thought of it. Unusual, Etoileon thought, but the princess interrupted any further thinking when she took a step back from him.

She had not noticed the disruptions. Her face was slightly red as his hands dropped hers. Selene was certain that the time had come to tell him. She could feel her rapid heartbeat and the knots twisting in her stomach as she tried to summon her courage. Oh, why is it so hard to say? Her thoughts were muddled as she lost her composure. She shyly looked up at him, and finally spoke. Her voice was barely audible. " … Etoileon, I lo-"

A small explosion in the distance cut off her words.

Etoileon looked around. He'd heard the explosion, and felt the force of it. Dread trickled down his back. That rumbling seconds earlier was no illusion. Something was wrong, terribly wrong.

A much louder explosion rocked through the palace walls, this time accompanied by a blast that seemed to crash through the room. A foreboding silence followed before Etoileon could sense another one coming on. Looking at the shocked surprise on Selene's face as she wildly looked about, he grabbed her arm. "Your Highness, move!"

She was stunned more or less into a paralyzed state as shouting could suddenly be heard through the corridors.

Guards were ordered to take their positions. Maids were to hurry to the downstairs area. Fighters were to report to their trainers for instructions. Everything was in a panic, and Selene found herself floored. It was only due to Etoileon's swift action that she was able to start running.

"Etoileon, what's happening?" she yelled, as she stumbled over her dress and nearly fell.

He looked at her from over his shoulder and called back, "I think it's an air raid on the city!"

"But … why?" Her voiced thoughts went unanswered as the pair of them headed for the room exit.

They were almost out of the room when a small bomb launched itself into the courtyard next to them. Selene could feel the tremendous force as the bomb exploded, shattering all the windows. Etoileon and her were both knocked off their feet and thrown to the floor as the broken glass and the smell of smoke washed over them.

"Aemon," Etoileon sneered as he tried to wipe the blood off his scraped hands onto his pants. He winced at the number of lacerations he'd received on his exposed flesh. His arms and hands stung at the slashes. A growing irritation could be felt in his mind as he stood up. "He did this, no doubt."

"What?" Selene called out as she struggled to get back up on her feet. "What did you say, Etoileon?" She'd been pushed over to the middle of the room as she'd fallen. His words had been lost to her.

THE MOONLGIHT PEGASUS

"This is Aemon's work!" Etoileon yelled over the noise as yet another bomb was just being launched though the air. He'd heard the call for palace Fighters to go to their assigned areas, but with one glance at the princess and he knew he had to get her somewhere safe, and fast. "We've got to get you to safety, Your Highness!" He once again grabbed her wrist and pulled her after him as they headed for a safe place. "We've got to go, now!"

He could see through the windows as the enemy Fighter pilots streamed through the air, preparing, no doubt, to drop more explosives on the capitol.

She felt a panic arise as they wove a crocked path through the debris. The feel of Etoileon holding onto her hand briefly caused a blush to arise to her cheeks before another set of small explosions once again sent her spiraling into fear. Selene felt the ache of disappointment grow as she realized that she wouldn't be able to tell Etoileon how she felt about him. She'd been so close! She refrained from shrieking as they stumbled over a pile of rubble. Selene supposed that she'd just have to tell him later, when this battle was over.

***

Chapter 7
Unending Nightmare
***

Aemon stood on his ship with a feeling of triumph coursing through his blood. A smirk that had planted itself on his face said it all. The Rebellion had resurrected with his planned surprise attack on the capitol. His father would be proud.

Diamond City, long hailed as one of the most beautiful cities as well as one of the central political cities, was crumbling under the pressure of his force already. Buildings had holes in them, foundations were falling out, and the Diamond City's centerpiece, the Royal palace, was damaged - the crown of the Table was wrecked with the work of rebel firepower.

An official came up behind him, bowing his head. "Sire, the rest of the missiles has been assembled and the strike team would like your approval before firing the last rounds."

"Good, good," Aemon muttered more to himself than anyone. He took the charts that his worker had presented to him. After a quick look through, he nodded. "Very well. Tell them I approve. But a small request from me, if they don't mind."

The official glanced up at his leader. The grim look on his face seemed to highlight his determination. His jaw was set and he had a firm look in his eye. "Anything for you, Sire. I will see to it myself."

Aemon turned away, looking once again to the palace. His eyes centered their focus on the highest tower of the Royal palace, its walls untouched yet by any mark of violence. It seemed to almost mock him, as it stood as tall and as proud as the monarchs who held rule there. "I have it on good authority that the Princess loves to visit the highest tower of the castle often," he stated thoughtfully. "Take careful aim and bring it down."

"As you wish, Sire." The commanding official bowed once more and hurried off to give direction to the hands below.

Aemon smiled. The Princess would be sorry indeed that she had refused him.

He'd been left alone in the world with his sister when he'd been just a child. His aunt had seen to taking care of them, barely managing to bring them all to live in the city a few short years after they'd been orphaned. She'd tell them tales of their father, and his bravery, his resolve, his belief that the monarchy was completely wrong and the system had failed.

Aemon had been in the city for years, but the stories of his father's tragic ending had never reached him. It was only when he'd gone back to his original home, his Jewel Island, when he'd learned the truth.

His father had been a victim of more than a failing system; Ammos, his father, had been passionately in love with the lady from Diamond City, who had been chosen to become a queen. He'd been a victim of love, and all the dramatic calamity that came with it had followed.

It had been a crisis for Aemon. Having grown up being taught to admire his father, to grow up to be like his father, Aemon suddenly found his hero to be a suicidal lovesick soldier. And not only that, his father was one suicidal lovesick soldier who had abandoned his own family in pursuit of another. He hadn't really wanted to be with Aemon and Cyerra's mother, or their children. He had been a selfish romantic, caught up in his own dreams and regrets … a man who hated the thought of living without a city girl so much he'd fought for her, only to end up killing himself over his depression when he realized that she could never be with him in this world.

His father had hardly been a hero - much less one that Aemon wanted to be like. After discovering the truth, Aemon had vowed that he would one day make the world pay for what it had done to him. Not only had it caused his father an unbearable sadness, but it had in effect robbed Aemon of any chance of happiness in his life as well. And now, fueled by his vengeance, he was going to take his rightful place on the throne of this world.

Aemon drew his attention out of his reminiscences as he heard the field commander call out from the lookout post, signaling the alpha attack run.

"Fire!" His arms waved onward, a signal to all weapon stations below to commence the shooting. "All stations forward advance!"

The planes all swooped, turning to prepare for the upcoming attack, their deadly missiles gleaming in the glow of the dawn's early light.

***

Dorian was flung out of his bed as the royal bedchamber shook. He was flinging out his arms, flailing to grab onto something to anchor himself. Half asleep and still clinging to the night's infectious lull, Dorian was in no mood for an early morning wake-up call, let alone an early morning bomb raid.

"What in the world?" he mumbled as the floor steadied for a moment and he was able to stand up. "Russert!"

Russert, the King's royal valet, hurried in from the front room, nearly tripping over as an aftershock quaked through the area. "Your Majesty! It seems that we are under grave attack this morning!"

"Really? I had no idea," Dorian grumbled as he started rummaging around his room, looking for the necessary armory he'd need. He waved the anxious valet aside as he tried to bring the King the adornments for the day. "Never mind me! Call the troops, and the Fighter squad! Have the palace pilots get to the sky hangar! Go!"

Dorian rolled his eyes as he watched his servant head out the door. Just why had he hired him in the first place? Dorian wondered. More pressing matters at hand forced him to abandon the question and return to the task at hand.

He was dressed for battle in record time. Once he was finished, Dorian hurried to find his weaponry. Though the King did little fighting in battle, it was considered mandatory by tradition that he at least look the part of a warrior.

Dorian was just about to grab his sword when a huge piece of castle wall came sailing through his large windows, crashing and smashing everything. The glass broke into thousands of tiny pieces and scattered everywhere. Dorian dove over his bed just as the glass shattered. He managed to avoid all the glass shards, but as he pulled himself out of the tangled web of his silken sheets, he thought he heard the familiar voices of his crew yelling for help.

As more and more explosions rang out from the city's landscape, Dorian rushed through the palace to help. A deep rage was settling in him as he vowed to punish those who were responsible for this.

***

Etoileon only had a vague idea of where he was headed as Selene followed him, close at his heels. He'd decided that she'd be safest in the center of the palace, the throne room. It was the logical decision to make, considering that the palace had been built on a hilltop.

He could hear her breathing harder as she ran after him. His hand had remained firmly wrapped around her wrist, as they'd made their way from the Fighters corridors to the entrance halls. Jumping over a pile of rubble, Etoileon let her go and grabbed her hands to steady her. "Come on, it's just a bit further," he urged her forward.

"Etoileon, wait."

He noticed the concern in her voice and turned to face her. "What?"

"Your hands," she explained.

He blushed. "Oh. Sorry," he apologized quickly, letting go of her.

"No, no, that's not it," Selene blushed now, too. She took his hands in hers once again and turned them palm up, looking at the bloody cuts with concern. "You're bleeding, that's all."

"It's fine."

"Are you sure?"

"Yeah, it was just a bit of broken glass," he explained. "It's nothing. Come on, we'll worry about it later." As another rumble began to shake the floor, he pulled her along after him.

As they hurried onward, stumbling every now and then, Etoileon looked back and saw the worry on the Princess' face as she uneasily watched the floor she was walking on. "Don't worry, Selene!" he called back to her over the thunder of the explosions. "I'll protect you!"

Just as he finished saying the words, the doorway in front of him collapsed. Etoileon skidded to a halt at once, Selene bumping into him as he tried to back them up as the granite and the woodwork fell. The resulting pile blocked the doorway, releasing a cloud of dust into the air as pebbles of the wreckage could be heard falling. Etoileon managed a grim smile. If Selene hadn't stopped him a moment earlier, they would've been submerged in the castle's ruins.

The ceiling was gone, and in the distance Etoileon could see a plane. It looked like it was heading towards them, and most likely it was not for rescue. He knew that they had no choice. They'd have to go back the way they came and head in another direction to get to the throne room.

"Etoileon, we've got to go back!" Selene called, tugging on his sleeve.

"I was just thinking the same thing," he agreed. A sound above him caused him to look up. What he saw was the rest of the corridor ceiling beginning to crumble. A few of the larger cracks were beginning to grow even. "Move!" He pushed at Selene, forcing her back the way they'd come as the granite began to cave in. They barely managed to escape and turn the corner before the whole room was destroyed.

Selene could feel her body shaking. She wasn't used to taking the lead, for one thing, and for another, she'd never been in this kind of situation before. She'd never thought in a hundred million years that anyone would attack her palace, would attack the city, killing all sort of people and destroying their homes ...

Her eyes felt the sting of tears as she slowed down in her running. Etoileon took over the lead, until he noticed that she had slowed down to a stop.

"Selene?"

"I'm sorry," she whispered. "I just can't seem to deal with this, Etoileon ... I guess I'm a little shaken up." Her face fell into her hands as she tried to wipe the tears away and found that there were more. She could feel the sobs wrecking through her as she stood there, crying.

Etoileon froze, unsure of what he could say to make this easier for her. Selene had such a good heart, he thought. No wonder she was crying. She'd never imagined this kind of evil in her life before, let alone experienced it. The closest things

THE MOONLGIHT PEGASUS

she'd had to this were the heated arguments that broke out between himself and Dorian over breakfast.

He hesitantly walked up to her and reached out, touching her shoulder. "Selene," he started. "Uh … well … " he sighed. "Please don't cry. We can't stay here. It's not safe."

She nodded, her face still buried in her hands. Sniffing loudly, she lifted her now red face up to see him and swallowed harshly. "Okay. Sorry."

"It's okay, don't apologize," Etoileon smiled tenderly at her. His face turned serious a moment later. "We've got to get to the throne room now."

She nodded. Sniffing again, she wiped the wetness off her cheeks.

They continued running, this time at a slightly more relaxed pace. They didn't have a ceiling falling on them anymore; the sounds of the world outside the palace were muffled and faded against the people running past them, calling for this and that, carrying supplies, demanding supplies, crying, weeping, screaming, grimacing, or looking off into space, too emotional to be anything but stoic. No one bothered the two of them, as Etoileon reached out and took hold of the Princess by the hand and hurried her along down the damaged corridors towards the throne room.

They were just about three corridors away when a wall opened, causing Etoileon and Selene to halt momentarily. A secret passageway had opened up. A familiar face came into view.

"Your Highness," Kadrianne materialized onto the scene. "There you are, at last." Her voice was too practiced to reveal all of her relief. "We've been looking for you all over. We all were sure that you were dead."

"No, I'm fine," Selene tried to put on a convincing smile. Her smile turned more genuine as she looked over at Etoileon. "My protector was with me. We're both fine, thanks to him."

Etoileon felt his face turn warm from her praise. He would never feel worthy of the credit she gave him, he thought.

"I'm sorry, Your Highness," Kadrianne spoke up once again. "But I fear that you are not out of trouble just yet. Please, you must hurry after me."

****

Aemon saw the three Fighter jets he'd commissioned fly straight for the palace. He could feel the rapid pounding in his heart as his anticipation mounted. He only wished that his family could be with him in this moment of victory.

Come to think of family, where was Cyerra? He wondered when she was coming to meet with him. She'd been upset with him a few days ago, something about not being able to go to the Reception Ball with him … and then there was that issue with her being upset about staying away from the palace and the palace workers. Still, surely she was over it by now and her impudence towards him was done with. The guards had been unable to find her earlier, but surely they had located her in time for his moment of victory, Aemon thought as he glanced around. A sense of unease overtook him, as he still could not see her. He turned to his guards behind him. "Guard!"

His call brought forth a servant of his, one whose name he could not recall just then. The servant bumbled to Aemon's side, rigidly bowing. "Yes, Sire?"

"Guard, tell me … where is my sister, Cyerra? Is she onboard?"

The servant held his bowed position and answered hesitantly to Aemon's question. "No, Sire, Lady Cyerra has not been checked in on this ship," he responded.

"What?" Aemon's tone was tight between incredulous and irritated. "Why not?"

"It seems that she has acquired a new job," the servant remarked. "She was called in for duty early this morning and left the house before you had arrived in port. Her Highness Princess Selene has summoned Cyerra to her court."

"What!" Aemon was dumbfounded. It was one of the rare times he was caught off guard. "You mean she's in the palace as we speak?"

The servant nodded. "Yes, Sire."

Aemon felt a dread take over his body. He cared little for the fate of anyone in this world. But the one person he made an exception for was Cyerra. She was his twin sister, after all. He could not, and would not, abandon her as his father had done to them. He hastily picked up his two-way radio and fumbled with the buttons. A moment later, a voice on the other side responded to his call.

"Call off the attack!" Aemon yelled. There was a certain bite to his words and a growl in his throat as he issued the command. It was clear that he absolutely despised calling off his troops. "Retreat! I repeat, retreat!" He gritted his teeth in a cross of self-disgust and anger. "We've done enough damage."

"At once, Sir!" the commander on the other end complied.

But it was too late to call off all the attacks; it was only time enough to divert them. Aemon felt like cringing as a loud crashing noise met his ears. He turned around to see that the missile for the High Tower had been launched. The pilot had been ready to launch it just as the Aemon called for retreat—he'd pulled out of the attack run just in time to have the bomb released at the wrong angle degree. The missile was launched.

Time seemed to slow as the missile flew by the tower walls, missing them only by a few feet.

Rocketing into the palace keep with a loud blast, the explosion caused granite debris to be scattered everywhere in the nearby vicinity.

Aemon looked back to assess the damage. Large quantities of smoke from where the bombs had landed hung all over the once spotless, glittering landscape. The palace had a large hole in the center. A revived sense of satisfaction rose within him.

He hoped that Cyerra was safe. And if she was, he was going to give her the lecture of her life when he found her.

His hand clenched around his radio communicator in frustration. His sister was important to him. But her foolishness had cost him the ultimate victory against the monarchy.

The tiny machine he'd been holding broke in two. He turned and headed back to his ship quarters. The journey home was not going to be pleasant, he thought. There was an invasion to plan.

***

Selene and Etoileon followed after Kadrianne as she led them through a series of small, complicated hallways. Upon meeting up with the handmaiden, the princess and her protector had decided to follow Kadrianne down the servants' hallways, corridors that were used by the maids and chamber men to transport food, laundry, and messages, among other things. These hallways were forbidden to guests and high-ranking members of the court. It wasn't hard to see why the halls were prohibited to the court members, either. They were cramped and tiny, with barely enough room for two people to walk side-by-side down. The lighting was poor for the moment, with only a few lights still working due to the electrical lines that had been knocked down by the Rebel jets.

For a while the three of them walked briskly through the passageway without exchanging a word, before Selene broke the silence and spoke up.

"Kadrianne, wait," Selene piped up a moment later. Her voice bounced off the walls and echoed back, surprisingly loud for the soft tone she'd spoken in. "What happened? Who is attacking us, and why?"

"I fear, Your Highness," Kadrianne's jaw was set with a grim expression, "I fear that Aemon has taken the initiative to get the war started much earlier than anticipated. Our investigations and open communication lines have informed us that he had come prepared for rejection. Many think he would've attacked, whether you agreed to his wishes or not."

"I don't understand," Selene frowned. "He didn't seem like the kind of person to do anything like this. Why would he attack in the first place?"

"Your Highness, his father was the leader in the previous rebellion with your parents. History tells us that Aemon's father killed himself after your mother died in childbirth. This issue, therefore, carries a bit more weight than Your Highness'- augh!"

Kadrianne's words were lost, as another round of quaking seemed to streamline through the palace. The floor shook precariously beneath them, sending all three of them hurrying for a nearby wall or doorway. Kadrianne and Etoileon were thrown forward, while Selene flung to the side by the powerful quakes. The floor cracked and broke under the pressure of the shaking foundation.

"Lady Kadrianne," Etoileon asked as he held on tightly to a decorative tapestry pole, "Can the castle foundation take this abuse much longer?"

"I think so," Kadrianne shouted back. She'd managed to grab a hold of the doorframe and pull herself into a safer position as they all stumbled around. "But I'm not so sure about the rest of the palace ... we have to get Her Highness into the bomb shelter as soon as possible. The shelter's entrance is in the throne room!"

Etoileon grimaced and looked back at his charge as she struggled against the instability of the floor. He set his jaw and nodded firmly. "Okay!"

Selene lost her footing and nearly fell into the wall. She quickly regained her footing and, using the wall as a balance, she sidestepped her way toward her other companions. They were near the end of the hallway; Selene could see the once-majestic columns of the Throne room through the arched doorway.

"Princess!"

Selene looked up to see Etoileon reaching for her, his hand extended. She glanced past him for a moment to see Kadrianne not too far from him, clutching the doorframe in an effort to keep herself on her feet.

"Princess! Take my hand!" Etoileon's call jerked Selene's attention back to him.

She bravely shuffled her foot out, and reaching out unsteadily, she moved as close as she could to get to him. After struggling and straining her body to stretch out farther, her fingertips just brushed against his. "Etoileon!"

"Hurry!" Kadrianne called to them. "We have to get out of here!"

"We're coming!" Etoileon called back. "Please, Princess, just a bit further! You can do it!"

As the rumbling and shaking of the palace walls slowed, Selene could feel a bit more balanced and able to remain steadier on her feet. She bit her lip and scooted a bit more, managing to muster up enough strength to propel forward a few more inches. She felt a sigh of relief escape her as she felt Etoileon's hands clasp around hers and pull her over to where he was.

"Selene," he gave her a smile as the same sense of relief she felt poured over him. He'd been worried that he wouldn't be able to reach her. Lesson learned, he thought. Never let her out of reach again. This was certainly not the time to be worrying about formalities. Tightening his hold on her hand, he tried to navigate a path over to the doorway where Kadrianne had been waiting.

"Oh my." Selene could barely breathe as her gaze fell on the room before her. There were cracks in nearly all the windows. Some of the columns were still shaking warily, while a few had actually fallen over. The throne and its tree trunk remained untouched, but several of the tree's branches were snapped and hanging on by mere splinters. The floor was covered in fallen decorations, broken glass, and a surprising amount of what looked suspiciously like blood. Several of the High Court members were present, for once all disheveled and unkempt; some of them were still trying to rid themselves of rubble. Selene looked briefly down at her own hands and dress, only to see that she, too, was covered with dust and dirt, and she still had blood on her hands from Etoileon's wounds.

"Your Highness!" A voice called out to the princess as Selene made her way through the doors to the throne room. A moment later, the voice's owner came barreling out from around the base of the throne. It was Cyerra, and she was joyfully bouncing up and down as she hurried over to them. Once in front of the princess, she nearly fell over as she made a clumsy bow, and looked up to smile brightly at Selene. "We were all so worried, Your Highness. We all thought for sure you were injured."

"Thank you, Cyerra, I was worried for all of you as well," Selene warmly responded. Her eyes hardened again, and she commanded, "Kadrianne, please, see to anyone who needs help."

At once, Kadrianne bowed and hurried to help a nearby woman who was trapped under a layer of rubble. Selene nodded to Etoileon, who then followed after Kadrianne. Then her attention focused once more on Cyerra, who had not yet moved to help Kadrianne. Seeing the girl's anxiousness, her expression softened. "Please, tell me what is wrong."

Cyerra looked down. "I'm so sorry, Your Highness. This is all Aemon's fault. Word has reached us here at the palace that this indeed was planned—much more than we could have known." She wrung her hands.

"I see."

"There has been a significant amount of damage done to the palace, but not too much to the surrounding city. One or two buildings have suffered severe destruction, but that is all." Her gaze went even lower. "Sadly, there have been a number of deaths and many people are in serious medical conditions."

"We must help them at once," Selene stated. She almost started forward, but Cyerra stepped in front of her, effectively stopping the princess in her tracks. Selene was taken aback. "Don't try to stop me."

"I'm sorry," Cyerra nearly cried. "But I cannot allow you to work in here. It is drastically unsafe for you, Your Highness. Several of the columns are still unstable, and already three have fallen. The ceiling is also crumbling slightly in several areas … you would not be safe, working in here."

Selene smiled gently at her new handmaiden. "Cyerra, please stand aside."

As she took a step back, Cyerra was wide-eyed with shock and admiration. The princess hurried past her.

While Selene busied herself in the task ahead of her, Cyerra managed a small smile. Etoileon came up beside her, to tell her that Kadrianne required her help, but Cyerra spoke up. "Our Princess is such a lovely person. No wonder everyone loves her."

Yes, Etoileon thought, the princess was well loved here. "Lady Cyerra, Lady Kadrianne would like you to-"

"Hey, watch it!" A snapping voice suddenly rang through the dilapidated section.

"You're in my way, and be careful! I had to pay up a lot of currency for this robe!"

Now that the raid seemed to be over, the people in the room were trying to get out and get cleaned up as best as they could. But for the moment, all had stilled as two men were arguing near the base of the throne. Etoileon recognized one of the voices immediately.

"You're such an imbecile!" Trion was yelling at the top of his voice at a younger gentleman, who, until a moment ago, he'd been trying to help out of a high pile of debris.

The young man, managing to stand up, glared down at Trion. "I've never been so insulted in my life! I'm Lord Horatio of the High Court, I'll have you know, you arrogant ruffian!"

"Well, this ruffian might have arrogance, but I can sure beat you up," Trion stated darkly. His voice lowered and his eyes narrowed hatefully as his gaze burned into the man in front of him. "Who has the lack of respect here? I don't think it's me." He folded his arms in a taunting way. "What's the worst you can do to me? Ignore me?"

Etoileon recognized the stance that Trion took. It was one of the neutral stances from their Fighters' lessons. Remembering how he and Trion had fought earlier in the week, Etoileon started to head over. Horatio was no doubt in danger.

But he was too late. Trion jolted forward, pushing Lord Horatio onto the floor. Horatio grabbed at Trion, his lack of training showing even though he managed to pull Trion down along with him. The two of them fumbled for rocks and pebbles as they managed to hit and claw at the other.

The surrounding members of court were still watching; it was as though the scene had deprived them of the will to do anything but watch. A few people, noticing this, broke forth and headed over.

Selene was the first to reach them.

"Gentlemen!" she called in her most commanding tone. "Stop this at once, do you hear me?" *Why are they doing this? Haven't we had enough tragedy today?*

She took a step closer. Neither of the men stopped fighting, even at her insistence.

"Hey!" She tried again, this time several of her guards were coming up beside her. "Stop it! You're hurting each other. This is no way to behave!" Horatio looked over at the Princess with an indecisive look in his eye. Slowly, he pushed away from Trion and started to stand up.

Trion ignored the Princess' request and struck out his foot, kicking the feet out from under Horatio. His opponent let out a grunt as he landed hard on the floor. Trion eagerly moved in for another attack, the expression on his face clearly telling anyone he was not yet satisfied.

"Stop!" Selene jumped forward, grabbing onto Trion's arm. He skidded to a halt, almost losing his balance to the girl who'd just grabbed him.

"Get off, Your Highness!" he insisted, shaking his captured limb relentlessly. "I have been insulted by this man, and he must learn the price of such disrespect!"

"It seems that he is not the only one who needs to learn proper respect," Etoileon muttered as he came up and helped Horatio to his feet, seizing the opportunity to take the prize away from Trion's battle. Once Horatio was on his feet and scurrying away to find a safe place, Etoileon turned around to help Selene. She was having trouble holding on as Trion's struggling grew more violent and irritated.

THE MOONLGIHT PEGASUS

" Stop it!" Selene insisted. "Stop it right this —" Her sentence was interrupted as he managed to throw her off of him, sending her flying straight against one of the palace columns. There was a sickening crash! And the whole room hushed and fell silent.

For the moment, no one dared to make a move or speak a word.

Selene's face was tight with tension as she collided with the column. It was ridged and elegantly carved, and hard against her back, but other than the pain of impact Selene could feel nothing wrong with her. Her eyes had squeezed shut, but now they slowly opened to find everyone in the throne room looking her way with horror in their eyes. "Huh?" She wondered what they were all so worried about her—after all, she was okay - when she heard it. A creaking noise was emitting from the column behind her.

"Princess!" While everyone started yelling and screaming, Etoileon had rushed through the jumbled crowds.

He'd seen the marble crack near the base. He'd hoped that the impact wouldn't push it over. But it looked like it would fall anyway. Selene was trapped. If he didn't hurry, the column would fall right on her and crush her.

Selene glanced up and was met with a horrifying sight. She felt the scream rise in her throat as the column broke in two, causing a bunch of the ceiling to break and tumble down. She tried to scramble out of there, but it was too late.

The column fell, crashing down as the ceiling above it caved into pieces and rained down. A cloud of dust blew up from the refuse, tainting everything with a layer of gray.

Selene waited for the pain to hit her again. She waited for something to fall on her and leave her in a world of darkness. To her surprise, she felt none of these things. Her back was still numb from Trion's throw, but no new pain was bothering her. Without looking she could tell she was sprawled out on her stomach, with her hands protecting her head. But other than that, she was at a lost. She gradually opened her eyes. They instantly widened in shock.

She had opened her eyes to find Etoileon on his knees, crouching over her body. He had prevented the column from falling on her by letting it fall on him. His triceps contracted as he struggled to hold up under the weight of the heavy column.

"Etoileon!" her whispered exclamation caught his attention.

"Thank goodness," he grunted down at her. His smile was thin through gritted teeth, and there were beads of sweat appearing on his forehead as he held the column away from the princess.

"You—you saved me," Selene was awed. "But … but why?" her words ended in a cry.

"Selene, don't worry about it," he grimaced. "Of course I saved you. I told you I would always protect you, didn't I?" He paused and shifted his weight, and managed to give her a kind smile. "I'm sorry that I haven't always kept it, but I want to. I've always wanted to."

"Stop it! You'll be crushed!" she began to feel her eyes water. "Stop it, please!"

Etoileon groaned as he was starting to cave under the pressure. But he managed to shake his head. "No." He looked down at her intently. "Selene … get out of here, now. You can crawl out from under me, and you'll be okay."

"No! I'm not leaving without you," she declared, her voice a whisper. A sliver of fear crawled up her spine.

"Selene—do as I say, now. Or I'll be forced to let this go much sooner than intended,"
Etoileon smirked. "Without you there, I can let go of it and let it slide right off of my shoulder … I'll be fine. Just go."

Selene stilled. "Are you sure you'll be okay?" she asked, her voice a frightened whisper.

"I'll be fine … Selene." His gray eyes met hers, and remained that way until she sighed and began to crawl out from underneath him and the column. She would do what he wanted her to.

Once she was out, Selene realized that Etoileon had received some help from several of the guards that had been present. Under their quick direction, several ropes had been looped around the column as it had fallen. They were now anchoring the ropes down and tying them off safely.

Whew, she thought, it looks like everything is going to be okay.

Etoileon managed, with the aid of the binding support, to get out from underneath the marble column without any harm. He looked back at it as he was shrugging off the muscle cramps and sucked in his breath. He'd been lucky that there had been others here to assist him. There was no way anyone could've survived holding the entire weight of it.

He looked over and saw Selene relax and start to smile. Etoileon met her gaze and she blushed. But a moment later, her composure regained, she ran over to him and wrapped her arms tightly around him.

"I'm so glad you're okay!" she exclaimed into his shoulder.

Etoileon said nothing. There was a whole room full of people, some calming down from their recent scare, and some attending to the injured ones. The noise was so loud in the room that his words would have been lost anyway. So, for the moment, he allowed himself to enjoy the moment.

But it was not to last.

A rope that was bound down suddenly snapped. The column wavered, causing other ropes to break. People all around were once again fearful, and starting to shout for help or run for the exit as the column fell.

A cluster of screams could be heard as those in the crowd headed for cover. The large marble structure sank into the ground with such a force that it shook the building floor, sending a shockwave through the room. People stumbled and fell; others were thrown off their balance and wobbled precariously. The walls of the building even seemed to shake. The ceiling crumbled further. The branches of the royal throne creaked, several breaking with a loud snap!

What happened next occurred in only a matter of seconds. Selene felt Etoileon tighten his arms around her and hold onto her tightly as a shower of crumbled ceiling concrete rained down on them.

The noise was so loud that she thought she screamed, but she was not sure, because she could not hear it. She heard a sickening *crunch!* and then nothing more. Her world went black as she slipped away into unconsciousness.

***

The crowd gasped in horror as they watched their princess was buried in a waterfall of fallen ceiling. Several of the crowd started shouting, and as soon as the debris settled, only one person held back from helping to get those buried free.

Trion sniffed angrily. He was trying hard to keep the guilt at bay from him for the moment. He hugged his cloak around his shaking shoulders and headed for the exit.

Ronal briefly took into account Trion leaving the throne room. Ronal was too distracted, looking for his friends, to think to stop him.

Once Ronal stopped Cyerra among the people trying to move the crushed ceiling blocks, he hurried over. "Cyerra!" He called out. Ronal scurried over and was about to embrace his love until he was stopped by the expression on her face. Right away he could tell that something was not as it should be. "What's wrong?" he asked.

Cyerra's face had tears streaming down her face as she tried to explain to him just what had happened. "And now the princess and Etoileon are trapped underneath!" she finished, her last sentence coming out in despair. "It all happened so fast, no one could have done anything!"

"We have to get them out at once!" Ronal declared.

"That's what we're trying to do now," Cyerra explained gently. "We fear for the worst."

***

Dorian waded through the fallen bodies and crumpled rocks that had made up his home as he made his way to the Council Room for Wartime Activities. It was a rarely used room, so he and his attendants were trying more to focus on getting to the room as quickly as possible without getting lost to be concerned with the damage of the attack.

"Excuse me, Your Majesty," Russert spoke up between deep breaths. "The room is up there on the left."

"Thank you," Dorian answered brusquely as they all started to run down the corridor. They had to get to the room to discuss with the generals and military personnel what the plan was going to be.

As Dorian turned the corner to the left, he found himself in a room of the most hardened men of Sapphira looking weary and disbelieving. Some were clearly trying to hide their fear as they looked up at their king.

"Gentlemen," Dorian haltered in the doorway as they all turned to face him with the same looks on their face. Nearly twenty men wore a solemn, somber expression. The king sighed sadly. He knew that he had to do something. For the sake of his world, for the sake of his city, and most of all, for the sake of his men, he had to give them the encouragement that they needed in this time of anxiety and uncertainty.

He walked up to the front of the room and stood on the small platform next to the podium. He looked around and hurriedly tried to think of something to say. Dorian couldn't explain it, but he recalled what his old advisor, Haiasi had told him after the death and funeral of his father.

"Gentlemen, words cannot express the turmoil of the soul during times such as these. We have been faced with many trials in daily living, and it is not always so easy to see the light in the midst of darkness as consuming as this." As he paused, Dorian took note of the men looking up to meet his gaze. He nodded and continued. "However it is times like these that mold us, shape us, strengthen us, and most importantly, teach us. We cannot know what life holds in store for us, only that we must go on for the sake of those who have come before us, and for the sake of those who will come after us. We cannot know what will happen, or what may not happen, or how we shall ever deal with any of this in the end. But what we do know is, we must put forth our best efforts to eliminate the iniquity in front of us for the moment, in hopes of achieving to the next moment, until the light of day once again brightly shines from its eternal beacon."

The men all nodded at his words, some even smiling a bit. One of them started clapping, and eventually the others joined in. Soon, Dorian broke out in a grin and laughed. "Come on, you guys, it's time to get to work!"

Russert humbly approached him and nodded. "Great speech, Your Royal Majesty," he congratulated.

"It wasn't mine," Dorian admitted, "But it worked quite well, I will agree." *I hope that Haiasi doesn't mind,* he thought as he remembered the kindness of his late advisor.

It was times like these that reminded Dorian of the peace that he felt at Haiasi's assurances that there was a Guardian, and he watched over the monarchy like he promised he would. He recalled how Haiasi would tell him and Selene about the tales of the Guardian from the Sacred Book when they were younger. When Haiasi had died, Dorian put all that behind him. Losing his trusted advisor had been much worse than losing his real father. Dorian still didn't know how the King of Crystallon, in the World of Dreams, could ever let a man like Haiasi, who was so devoted to the Guardian's message, die.

Dorian shrugged the subject off of his mind. He had no time to worry about that now. He had a plan to discuss, and no doubt the council would be present soon enough to argue back and forth about the points of the counterattack. He was about to take a seat and call forth ideas from his compatriots, but the door burst open and a very rumpled handmaiden stepped inside the room.

Without even taking the time to bow, she pointed towards the keep of the castle. "Your Majesty! I am Chevée, a handmaiden to the princess. I have come to tell you that Her Highness is in trouble!"

"What?" Dorian and everyone else in the room froze. "Where is Selene?"

"She's been trapped by a fallen ceiling, Sire," Chevée wept. "We do not know if she lives or if ... if ... if ... " she could not bring herself to finish the sentence, hanging her head at the mere thought of such a tragedy.

Dorian bounded out of his seat and hurried to the door. "Take me to her, now!" Turning back to the military personnel and his wartime advisors, he pointed over to Russert. "Start planning, gentlemen! I shall return within a reasonable amount of time. Russert is in charge. I will be back." Then he looked back at Chevée and said, "Go, lead the way!"

***

It was hours later, unbeknownst to her. She felt surrounded by a dark and empty void. All at once there was an icy feeling all around, sending a prickling sensation through her body. She was aware that at that moment, she was not alone. There was no sound to be heard; there was only a chill in the wind.

"Selene … "

Hmm … what? Who's calling me? Selene struggled to open her eyes. A flicker of light caught her attention. *What's going on? Am I dead? Why does that voice sound familiar?*

"Wake up … my precious child … " the voice called patiently. "I am."

That voice, there it was again, calling to her amidst the darkness. A bubble of light began to sparkle.

Selene felt the dryness of her lips as she whispered, "Who are you?" It was a question born of wonder more than curiosity. The light bubbled again and she heard no reply. "Do I know you?"

But the voice did not respond. The light flickered again, this time flaring up bright. Selene felt the darkness disperse, almost sliding away from her as her eyes opened just enough to see that she was in a bright, white room. She was lying in a bed. She could feel nothing wrong with her, but she could not move. There was a tube in her arm, and bandages on her wrists, her hands, and also one on her left knee.

Selene could barely open her swollen eyelids, but she could just make out her handmaidens Kadrianne and Cyerra sitting by the doorway. Both were looking extremely worn out and tired, and it also looked like they had been crying.

She said nothing. She was rapidly awakening, and Selene could now hear the sounds of the heart monitors, the blood pressure readings, the humming of the air cooler, and the sound of doctors being paged over the paging system in the hall.

She sighed, causing Kadrianne to glance at her, amazed

"Your Highness!" she cried joyfully, nearly hopping over. She made her way to Selene's side, Cyerra close at her heels. "Oh, Princess, we were all so afraid for you!"

"Kadrianne?" Even to herself, Selene thought she sounded scratchy and hoarse.

"Yes, Your Highness, it is," Kadrianne assured her. "How do you feel?"

"Can you talk okay?" Cyerra asked. "Are you in pain at all?"

Selene nodded slightly. "What happened?" she just managed to get out. Looking around she realized that she was not in her palace room. "Where am I?"

"We are in the medical ward of the Silverton City limits, Your Highness. It is a town a relatively short transport from the palace. For the moment, there are several high-ranking court individuals here who are being treated for the wounds they had received earlier," Cyerra explained.

"Earlier, Cyerra?"

Kadrianne intervened here, stepping forward. "Yes. Don't concern yourself with that though, Lady Princess. You just worry about you for the moment. Cyerra, I'm going to tell Yana to tell His Majesty that the Princess has awoken. Stay here, please."

Cyerra nodded as Kadrianne hurried off. "There are no completely safe Medical Wards in Diamond City, so we came here, Your Highness, and that's why you're here in Silverton. Do try to go back to sleep though, Your Highness. You've had a rough day," Cyerra smiled. "Don't worry, I'm here. We'll all look after you."

Her words seemed to echo in Selene's head. The princess nearly jumped.

" Selene, don't worry … Of course I saved you. I told you I would always look after you, didn't I?" Her memory suddenly came rushing back to her. Aemon … The fight … the attack … the column … Etoileon. Selene could hear the roar of the falling debris, and could feel warm in the arms of her protector holding her tight. Then just as quickly, the warmth was gone. She shivered.

"Cyerra," Selene whispered softly. "Where's Etoileon? Is he okay?"

"Don't worry about him, Your Highness," Cyerra said in soothing tones. "Just worry about yourself for now." Cyerra hoped that the Princess would not push on the matter; she was avoiding a direct answer.

Selene looked up into her servant's eyes and saw the anxiety. Selene tried to sit up, but Cyerra shook her head. "Don't move, Princess, it is not good for you."

Silence descended on the room for what seemed like hours. Selene lay there, trying to listen to Cyerra and go back to sleep. But she could not. She felt like she was waiting for something, but she didn't know what it was or why.

Selene looked around, suddenly remembering the voice that had called to her. "Cyerra, who else was in here? Who was calling for me to wake up?"

Cyerra looked up at Selene with a confused look. "I'm sorry Your Highness," she said, "Yana and Chevée, as well as Rosaria, all of them remained at the castle to help with the minor injuries. There has been no one in here but Lady Kadrianne and myself for hours, and we have been silently waiting here for hours. You must have been dreaming."

"I see." Selene was certain that Cyerra would not lie to her, but who could have been the one who had called to her?

***

Yana looked on the king with sympathy as she waited to address him. Her brown eyes darted around as she looked around inconspicuously. As the princess's handmaiden, she was called to be on alert for all action. She stood still as she watched the scene before her take place.

Dorian was seated in front of military advisors and general lieutenants. For the moment they were listening to the report of the CCA, the Command Control Agency. The reporter was briefing the King on the series of retribution that the palace forces had managed to unleash upon the Rebels. Several of the judges had come to hear the battle plans as well, but it looked like there was not much of a battle anymore. It had been hours since the attack. The news was not encouraging.

"Sire, to conclude, we have been ineffective in preparation for and launching against this threat to international peace. It has been known for a matter of weeks that some of the Southern Sea islands were considering leaving the monarchy, but there was no solid proof to suggest that any arbitrary action would occur prior to –"

"This morning," Dorian interrupted smoothly. "We have no doubt figured this out on our own, Lord Melvin. We know that our city will need to be rebuilt, as your counterparts from the City Protection Agency have told us. We also know that the extent of the damage will cost several millions in currency. And I am half ashamed to call you members of this court." He stood up, surprising more than a few with his last statement. He waved them off. "These reports were not supposed to be redundant. What I want to know is where we go from here, gentlemen. I want to know their next move, and the one after that. I want spies sent out, people bribed, paid, information acquired. How many supporters are there for us? For them? How long until the countries of this world are all safe again?"

No one dared to answer the king. He was under control of his emotions, but his patience was starting to get the better of him. Dorian sat down again, aware that he had to remain calm. "Lord Melvin. I am sorry to interrupt you, but I want to hear more of our responding attacks."

"The responding attacks, Sire, well … they have not been well executed. Several of our planes were destroyed when a missile hit one of the landing hangars and a couple of the airplane runways. The pilot squadrons were not able to get into the hangar to get to their skyfighters because the power went out in that part of the city and the doors were unable to be opened. Soldiers on foot have been recruited to help move the dead and rescue those trapped alive in fallen buildings."

"So we have had no chance to counterattack?" Dorian asked.

"Not entirely, Sire. Some pilots were patrolling the coastline and were able to go into emergency attack mode. Some ships are sinking just outside the city harbor as we speak. Several members of the Imperial Navy have been called into action. But other than these legions, there has been no chance to counter."

"I see." Dorian was calm again. He stood up and gave a small smile to the audience. "Gentlemen, I do believe that I have heard enough for today. I will expect hourly reports on the developments. I leave the armies in control of Commodore Rosemont, who served in the time of my father, the late King Lukiahs. I trust his judgment and leave the controls to him for now. We will resume at first light tomorrow morning.”

He hesitated slightly before he continued. “I also ask that you forgive me for what I am about to say. Most of you who know me, know I am not a devout believer in the Guardian or his power. But I ask that those of you who are, or are willing to try for my sake, to pray for the safety of our dear Princess. Selene has suffered greatly from the attacks and is currently in the Critical Care Department in the Royal Hospital.”

The judges and a few of the men in the audience bowed their heads respectfully and murmured their assurances and promises at the King’s request.

Yana smiled at the King’s kindness. It was well known that the generations of rulers had not been particularly submissive to the teachings of the ancients as technology had increased. But it was heartwarming to see that he cared so much for his sister.

As the men filed out past her, Yana looked at the ground and humbly waited for the crowd to leave she straightened once they were gone, and moved to address the King.

As she approached, she could see the heavy black circles under his eyes, but he looked more than tired. He looked vulnerable. Yana quietly bowed and awaited his acknowledgement.

“Rise,” Dorian commanded, slumping into his chair. He gazed at her with heavy eyelids, but recognizing the insignia on her cloak, he knew that this was a handmaiden of Selene’s.

He had trouble remembering which one she was, but he knew that he'd seen her face before. Dorian mustered up all he could in order to pay full attention to the news; he'd been anticipating news of his sister for hours.

"Your Majesty," Yana bowed again. "I bring you good news. Your sister, Her Highness the Princess, has awoken from her unconsciousness. I have the report from Lady Kadrianne. Her Highness is slowly coming around. The doctors say that she will no doubt make a full, steady recovery."

Dorian visibly relaxed at the news. "Thank goodness," he muttered. "I was so worried."

"We all were, Your Majesty," Yana reminded him. Until then, her eyes had been on the floor in respect, but now she raised her eyes to meet his. "I know it is not my place to say so, but I would like to say that I was quite touched that you would ask your council to pray for her, Your Majesty."

Dorian was surprised and pleased with her remark, even if it wasn't her place to say such things. "Thank you ... I'm sorry, your name, please? I know you are not the one I met earlier."

"My name is Yana," she smiled. "You are most welcome ... Your Majesty." She blushed at her surprising show of courage.

"Please tell the doctors that Selene is to do what they tell her. If there is a problem, I shall handle it. But until she gets better, she is not to push herself. Please make sure that is understood, Lady Yana."

The handmaiden nodded, a silent understanding made; they both knew that Selene had a tendency to disobey orders from time to time, especially when she did not see how their reasoning could be right.

"Is that all you have for me?" Dorian asked.

"For now, Your Majesty."

"You may go then," Dorian nodded to her. He had to admit, as Yana turned and headed back to the hospital rooms, he was a little sorry to see the pretty girl leave; she had been by far his favorite audience.

***

Selene struggled despite Cyerra's earlier warning to elevate her head somewhat. Her mind was racing at this point, with the memories of what had happened before she'd blacked out. Her voice was ragged and her breathing quickened as she once again asked, "Where's Etoileon?"

Cyerra just looked at her this time, unsure. The princess truly cared for her friend, she knew. It would be wrong to keep it from her. But for her safety, should she? Cyerra heard a beeping noise and turned to find the stress level readings were peaking.

Kadrianne walked into the room, saving Cyerra from deciding. "Yana reports that His Majesty the King is at a meeting with the reconstruction assembly for the moment, but he has responded saying that he will come and see you soon, Your Highness." Kadrianne suddenly frowned. "Your Highness, you should really relax. Everything is under control now that you're awake."

"Stop it!" Selene ordered, on the brink of having a breakdown. "Tell me, now, Kadrianne, where is Etoileon?"

Kadrianne pursed her lips in mild annoyance. "He is in the room down the hall, Your Highness. Do not worry about him."

"Why?"

"Because you do not need to worry about him. However, if you keep up this stress level"—Kadrianne glanced at the heart monitor screen—"You will need to worry about yourself even more. And Aura will be down here to scold you."

"No, why is he there? What's wrong?" Selene's voice was coming back. As Cyerra stepped forward to pour the princess a glass of water, Kadrianne was unable to say anything. Selene started to push back her covers when Kadrianne finally responded.

"Your Highness, he is … Hey, wait a moment! Where are you going?" Kadrianne broke off as she watched as Selene had stumbled out of bed, and began pulling her medication tube along with her as a support as she headed for the door.

"Your Highness!"

Selene ignored Kadrianne and Cyerra's calls as she hurried out of the room. Her bare feet stumbled along on the cold floor. She felt her head spin and her heart beat furiously. Her hand clutched her stomach, which stung with every other step. Her eyes watered as her pain increased. It took an enormous amount of energy and will just to stand. But Selene

THE MOONLGIHT PEGASUS

was desperate. Her dearest friend was in pain, she knew. Surely if anyone should be able to help him, it would be her.

She looked in all the rooms as she went past, her focus blurring over more than once. She finally found Garth, the King's foremost guard, and rushed inside. Her brother would've sent his most trusted guard to watch over Etoileon until he was better.

Garth was staring off into space as the princess walked in. He nearly jumped in surprise. "Your Highness," he said, bowing his head respectfully as he stepped up beside her, "You should not be up. You are clearly still suffering from the attack."

"Etoileon," Selene murmured as she side-stepped around Garth and hurried over to his side. She nearly collapsed once she reached his bedside. She fell to her knees, clinging with weak hands to the sheets.

"Your Highness!" Garth softened his tone as he watched her struggle. He carefully took a step closer, in order to be nearby if she fainted.

Etoileon was lying peacefully on the bed, a bandage on his head and a few more on his limbs. There was a cut healing just underneath his left eye, and the areas of his arms not covered with medical bandages showed some sign of the cuts and scrapes he had endured in the palace raid. Selene reached for his hand but drew back. She was suddenly scared. "What's wrong with him, Garth? Is he going to be okay?"

At this point, Kadrianne and Cyerra had entered the room quietly. "Sir Garth," Cyerra spoke up softly, "You must tell her."

"Tell me what?" Selene asked. Her stomach turned and her heart began to sink.

Garth looked down at his feet. "Your Highness … Your protector has suffered several blows to the head. He is in critical condition at the moment."

Selene felt the air rush out of her. For a moment she was silent and unmoving, as though it took a while for her to absorb the news. "But … but he's going to be okay, right?" she asked. When Garth said nothing, Selene tried again. "Isn't he?"

"Maybe you should go back to your room, Your Highness. You have been under a lot of stress lately," Kadrianne suggested. "I can get a doctor to explain everything to you."

"No," the princess objected. Her eyes clouded over with unshed tears as she looked from Garth to Cyerra, finally resting her gaze on Kadrianne. "Tell me what happened! Why is he like this?! He is not going to … to … ?" She could not find it in her to finish the question.

Kadrianne found it hard not to squirm under her princess' gaze. She took a step back and looked away. Cyerra was wringing her hands nervously and Garth made no sound or movements at all.

Selene finally looked back at Etoileon. The last moments before she'd fallen unconscious flashed before her eyes as she was finally overcome. Suddenly all that was bright and good in the world seemed to grow faint. There was a great feeling of helplessness and fear as Selene felt her world come crashing down on her and felt herself hitting rock bottom.

"Why won't you tell me!?" Selene demanded, her eyes red and swollen. A teardrop slid down her cheek, falling onto Etoileon's hand. Selene sobbed as quietly as she could, her hand releasing the covers and reaching out to take his limp one in hers. "Etoileon! Please, wake up!"

"Your Highness!" Aura had come into the room, to find her charge weeping over her protector and everyone else silent and unmoving.

Selene didn't even hear Aura come in. She shook Etoileon's hand, once again pleading with him. "Etoileon … wake up … please wake up! Don't leave me here all alone," she sobbed quietly. Selene doubled over, crying. Her tears streaked her face incessantly, her hand tightly grasping onto his.

He didn't move or make a sound to indicate that he'd heard her call or felt her hand. He slept on peacefully, unable to wake up from his deep unconsciousness.

Selene felt her fingers being pried away from Etoileon's as she slumped over. Her head was splitting with pain and her stomach was feeling more twisted than ever. Her bruises were stinging and dizziness took over. Selene struggled to remain fully conscious as she straightened up. There was a feeling of warmth as someone behind her tucked her cloak around her shoulders.

"You must be cold, Your Highness," Cyerra's soft voice whispered as Selene felt herself being picked up.

Selene had taken a hold of her cloak, but nearly dropped it when someone tried to move her. "No!" she objected. "Leave me here! I want to stay with him!"

"Your Highness, don't be ridiculous," Aura's crisp voice cut through her like a knife. "He's ill. There's little chance that he will wake up anytime soon. The doctors need to be in here to watch over him and check up on him every so often. Besides," Aura continued as she started to pull Selene even harder, "You are not well yourself! You should be in bed!"

But Selene managed, with the small amount of strength she had left, to wriggle out of Aura's grasp. She surged forward, almost tumbling into the bedside cabinet. She hesitated a moment to catch her breath, before standing up as straight as she could. She looked up at Aura, and said weakly, "Aura, please … let me stay. I will feel much better if I know that I am doing all I can to help Etoileon get better."

"But you don't know that, Your Highness," Aura remarked. "You could be hurting him even more."

"I … I … I can't explain it, Aura, but I do think that I am needed here." It was almost like there was a whisper in her heart, telling her not to leave just yet. She looked up at Aura with imploring eyes. "At least let me stay for a few moments. I would not be alive, were it not for him." Selene looked intently at Aura with weary eyes. "I owe him my life, Aura."

Aura sighed. She was lost. "Alright," she agreed. "But only for fifteen minutes, do you hear me?"

Selene nodded. Normally she would've argued, but she did not have the strength to this time. She looked at the others in the room with an expectant expression. Her two handmaidens and Garth took their leave. Selene looked pointedly at Aura next, and the governess resigned herself to just outside the room. Once she was alone with Etoileon, Selene knelt by his bedside, fresh tears emerging from her eyes.

Why did he have to protect me? Oh, why did this have to happen?

Sapphira is a planet of peace, not war, she thought as she watched his chest rise and fall with his slow, deep breathing.

She suddenly shivered. Selene fumbled with her cloak, trying to get more warmth out of it, when something in her pocket stuck out against the soft folds of the fabric. Curious and almost annoyed, she reached to fix it when a surge of recognition hit her.

It was her feather. "Huh … I forgot about that." After a quick look to make sure no one was watching her, she took it out of her pocket and examined it.

The light it shined was no less radiant than it had been earlier, she thought with a small smile. It had helped her, in an odd way, to find peace for the moment. Looking back at her friend, Selene happened upon an idea. Remembering how she'd awoke that morning, with the light casting out all darkness to bring forth the morning light, she carefully laid the feather on top of Etoileon's heart.

She waited expectantly for him to awake. When nothing had happened after a few moments, Selene felt her face scrunch in disappointment. She put her face into the covers and began to cry again. "Please … Etoileon … " her voice was muffled and hoarse as she murmured into the covers. "Please! Why won't you wake up?"

The feather remained still as Etoileon continued his rhythmic breathing. Then suddenly there was a great sparkle of light, and the feather disappeared, fading away in thin air.

The light startled Selene, but she saw nothing for sure as she jumped up, her face red and splotchy from her tears. Seeing the feather was gone, she fell further into dismay.

"Huh? Where'd it go?" she wondered out loud. She stood up carefully, and looked around. But she saw nothing to show where her gift had gone. When she looked under the bed and all around on the floor, it was still nowhere to be found.

Aura tapped on the door a moment later. "Your Highness, time is up," she called. "Time for you to get back to bed."

"Wait, Aura! I lost something," Selene called back, still looking all over.

"Your Highness, now!" There was no patience left in her governess' voice.

Selene felt her heart sink further. It was not fair, she thought as she reluctantly got up from her position on the floor. Looking once more at her friend, she reached down and brushed a wayward strand of hair away from his face. Leaning down, she whispered, "I'll come see you again, I promise … my dear friend." Still seeing no sign of her feather, she sighed, past the point of being able to do anything. I'll have to get it later, she thought despairingly. I'm sure that it'll be fine anyway. Someone is bound to find it and give it to one of the nurses.

She headed out of the room more exhausted than she could ever remember being in her whole life. Aura was at the door, her foot tapping and her lips pursed in annoyance.

"I'm sorry, Aura," Selene apologized in a soft voice. "I can't seem to get my head on straight today. With all that has happened … " her voice trailed off and Selene could not find it in herself to confide her sadness and her torment to someone who would tell the entire court in a matter of days. Sometimes, Selene mused, silence is the best answer we can give.

Aura dropped her stance and helped the princess walk back to her room. When Selene was back in her bed, Aura looked down at her meaningfully. "Your Highness, I shall never know what to do with you. Every time I find that you've gone somewhere you should not have, I find that protector of yours is there too."

"It's a good thing, Aura," Selene gave her a tiny smile. "If he had not been there with me today, I would most likely be dead."

Aura drew back from Selene's comment. "Yes … I suppose so," Aura agreed after a moment. "Indeed, I doubt that I shall forget that moment when I saw the two of you unearthed from that pile of rubble. I almost had a heart attack."

Selene's eyes widened in surprise. "Aura, I didn't know you cared so much."

"Well, Your Highness, this place would not be the same if you weren't here to lighten it up," Aura admitted thoughtfully. "The attacks were enough to rattle us all, I suspect."

"When will the palace be rebuilt?" Selene asked.

"Reconstruction of the city has already begun. We've got several workers and machines on the job as we speak. It won't be too long, Your Highness … maybe in about three months, the city will be completely rebuilt and better than ever. The palace will be finished later, in order to get some much-desired renovations and additions up. One advantage about these attacks—we shall be getting some more room in the palace."

"That's good, I suppose."

"Well … it's not for you to worry about. Get some rest now; you have a long recovery to attend to, Your Highness."

"Will you call me Selene?"

Aura's eyes snapped up from their unfocused glance. "Beg pardon?"

"I asked if you would call me by my given name, Aura," the princess repeated patiently. "In light of this tragedy, I think it's only called for."

Aura shook her head. "It is not proper," she insisted. "You are royalty. One needs to look no further than your complexion to know it, and see your royal bearing to confirm it."

Selene looked disappointed but said nothing further.

Aura went on. "Your father would often insist that he be treated with no special titles. Only a few would listen to his request." She sighed and looked down back at Selene. "It must be a family trait." She paused here, as though she wasn't sure she should go on. In the end, she must have decided not to, because she simply sighed again and bid farewell.

Selene was surprised that Aura hadn't given in to her request to call her by her given name. It looks like no matter what happens to shake her up, it will not affect her convictions about social hierarchy, Selene mused.

Aura was soon forgotten as she thought once more about Etoileon. She was heartbroken at his trauma. How she longed to be with him, to be there when he woke up! She had to believe that he would. But as she lay in the hospital bed in her tattered clothes and many bandages, with pain screaming with every movement, Selene began to wonder what would happen if he didn't.

What if he died? What if he left her here? Would she be able to take care of herself? Would she be able to accept his death? He meant so much to her, and so much of what he was to her was unspoken and left unsaid. Of course that was her fault! It was all her fault that he was in the condition he was in, too. If she hadn't tried to stop that fight, both of them might've avoided all this trouble. He'd been so brave, to protect her. So devoted, too. And she'd called him on it just the night before! How blind she'd been. How ignorant. How undeserving. Her nose prickled with the oncoming of unshed tears. "How awful I've been," she whispered. What kind of person am I, to hurt someone like that?" Why couldn't it have been me who got injured? she wondered.

Selene rolled over and pulled the covers up high, shielding herself from view as she attempted to calm down. She curled up, pulling her legs up to her chest and wrapping her arms around herself. Shivering, she tried to gather up some true warmth, but she found little. Staring off at nothing, letting fresh grief surge through, her eyes were wide and unfocused. The only indication that she was somewhat aware of her surroundings was the teardrops steadily flowing down her face.

***

Dorian came to see her as soon as he could manage to slip away from his duties. It is not fair, he thought angrily as he walked down the medical ward hallway. Why is it that the king is the only one who can't have an hour to go down and see his loved ones?

Yana and Kadrianne were standing dutifully outside the door. Dorian had to have some sympathy for these ladies. They were only a few years older than Selene, and yet they looked as though they had not had a chance to sleep since the attack. They had most likely been watching over his sister for nearly a day.

Dorian gave a small smile to the women, smiling ever so slightly more when Yana, whose name he had vowed to remember after she had left before, smiled wearily back.

"Ladies," he addressed them. "Surely you are tired. Take a break. Get some rest."

The two women exchanged glances before Yana bowed her head and replied, "Your Majesty," she began to explain,

267

"We are currently on a break. Lady Cyerra is inside with Her Highness now. We have chosen to stay here on our own."

Dorian raised his eyebrows in surprise and then nodded. He understood. He'd probably be there himself, if everyone had not insisted that he take meetings with all of his advisers and officers. Selene was just as important and as loved by the kingdom as Dorian was. Taking a moment, he said, "I'll have my wards bring you some chairs to sit on, then. You cannot possibly be comfortable standing there all day."

Kadrianne bowed her head respectfully as she opened the door for Dorian while Yana peeked up at him and gave him a tiny smile.

Cyerra sat on the foot of the bed, her hands in her lap. She sat with the dignity of a handmaiden, and watched with the worried eyes of a friend. The sight of her heartfelt dedication to his sister filled Dorian with a sense of tenderness.

"Lady Cyerra," he spoke softly. "No, don't get up –" he ordered as she moved to kneel before him. "I have come to see how Selene is doing." Cyerra was still, unsure of what to do as Dorian moved forward and peeked over the mound of covers Selene was buried under.

"Brother," Selene murmured, "I am, as far as my body goes, fine." As for her heart, it was in turmoil. She could not even get to sleep she was so anguished.

"Selene … " Dorian reached out and put his hand on her shoulder. She shrugged away from him. "Selene, I'm sorry about this." He was her brother. He knew that she was more than sad about what had happened.

"Dorian, please. I am very tired," Selene implored. She did not want him to see her crying. "I have had a very long day."

"Is there anything I can do to make it better?" Dorian asked.

Selene shook her head. "Not unless you have the power to bring back the lost," she whispered.

There was a short silence following her words. It was then that Dorian turned back to the door. "I know you're concerned for Etoileon," he said stoically. "I was there when the excavation crew managed to pull you out."

Selene turned and faced him, her eyes red. She just looked at him and said nothing as her brother continued.

"There was blood everywhere. And then there you were," Dorian's voice cracked as his eyes looked away from her and found the floor. It appeared that even the king was emotional this day. "Lying there, so still. We were all so afraid in that moment. Several of the women looked away and began to weep for you. How much harder they cried in joy when we discovered that you were still alive."

"The ladies of the court always looked up to Her Highness," Cyerra spoke up gently. "They really admire your spirit, Your Highness."

Selene's gaze slowly shifted from Dorian's back to Cyerra's face. Instantly Selene felt her heart ache again. Cyerra herself was crying softly, no doubt at the memory. Even if the women of the court had hated Selene, Cyerra's concern for her well-being was enough to convince Selene that her surviving was worth something at least.

"Anyhow," Dorian continued, "I wanted to let you know that I'm glad that you're all right, Selene. And I want you to know that we are giving you and your protector the best medical care possible right now. I'm sure that everything will be just fine."

Selene nodded slowly. There was an undertone to Dorian's voice, telling her that he was doubtful for Etoileon's survival. Selene knew that nothing on Sapphira would convince her that everything would be just fine again, but it was nice to see Dorian was taking Etoileon's condition so seriously. "Thank you," she whispered, before resting her head down once more on her pillow.

Dorian looked back at her and sighed. He could not order her out of her obvious depression, but he hoped that he had at least comforted her somewhat. "I will see you later," Dorian told her, before he headed out the door.

Cyerra, having wiped her tears on a handkerchief, stepped forward. "Is there anything I can do for you, Lady Princess?"

Selene heard her title and flinched. "Cyerra," she said quietly. "Call me Selene."

"But why, Your Highness? It isn't proper that I should call you by your christened name," Cyerra tried to argue.

"I don't want to be a princess right now," Selene sighed. "Today has been long, and tomorrow will no doubt be longer. Why waste strength on such cold formalities?"

"Yes, Your High- I mean, Selene," Cyerra quickly corrected herself. She was a little surprised by the Princess' words, but she let it go, rationalizing that the Princess had not had an easy day, and that she had to be experiencing a lapse in judgment. "Get some rest. I'll be here if you need me to get you anything."

Selene nodded and waited until Cyerra had returned to her position by the door before rolling over on her side and letting her tears fall quietly. She did not, could not, go to sleep.

***

Aemon watched the dark water spilt as his ship coursed on his path to Jewel Island. He looked up to the sky and watched the moonlight of the two moons bounce off of the waves. A small smile flickered on his face as he thought of the reports brought to him moments earlier.

Diamond City was scarred with rubble and debris. The city would be in disarray for months, though it looked like the mobilization for war had started. He knew that the enemy's troops were already summoned, and that the armies would be trained in a matter of days. But for the moment he had great confidence in his victory.

He had heard the news about the Princess. Everyone in Diamond City it seemed had been hoping that she would be all right, and miraculously, she had awoken from her slumber just hours ago. He'd been surprised to hear that she'd woken up as soon as she did, considering that his intelligence forces had informed him of her injuries. She'd been proclaimed half-dead at the scene.

THE MOONLGIHT PEGASUS

He should've known that she wouldn't die. She was considered by many to be a mild thing, weak and naïve. But in the few days he'd been with her, Aemon had realized that no one who thought that about her could possibly know her well. Besides, he thought, she was the key to peace. If she died, so did the hope of peace for the whole world. Like anyone concerned with war and peace, he'd heard of the legendary tales of Selene bringing about peace in this world after she married and part of her died. What nonsense, Aemon thought. But it seemed that the people of Sapphira believed in that kind of nonsense. And what was conquering, after all, but capturing the minds and wills of the people? Aemon knew that if he could fit the prophecy, he would manage to do what no war had ever done: defeat the monarchy.

Aemon's smirk grew as he looked back over the horizon. "Sleep well, Selene … these next few months are going to be hard for you," he muttered.

***

Chapter 8
Pegasus
***

For many days, the princess remained in her bed under the doctor's orders. Her medical caretaker, Dr. Hamersley, was a constant presence at her side, running all sorts of tests. He was the first one to call attention to her unusual behavior.

It was almost always the same. She would be sitting up in bed, her eyes focused out of the window, when he came in. If she was not just staring off into space, she was writing on small scraps of paper she'd torn from her medical chart. It did not seem to matter when he was coming, whether it was in the dark hours of the morning or the middle of the day—she was always in the same position. He would wonder how much sleep she had gotten the night before, if any at all. Every time she would turn slowly and look at his face, her eyes wide and unfocused; there was no trace of a smile on her face.

"How is Etoileon doing?" she would ask in a soft tone, though she already knew the answer. Doctor Hamersley knew that the princess kept close watch on the condition of her protector. Her handmaidens had been instructed to keep her updated as often as possible on any developments. But for some reason, she continued to ask him. And if the Doctor didn't answer her, her eyes would turn a bright splotchy red. If he did, whether the news was good or bad or there remained no change (which was the answer in most cases) she would look away and sigh ever so softly.

It had been that way for two weeks. Today as he looked on her, Doctor Hamersley had a strong feeling that their

THE MOONLGIHT PEGASUS

routine would have little alteration. Looking in on her sad figure, he silently prayed to the Guardian that she would feel better this morning. It was such a lovely day outside.

He walked in, knocking a bit on the door as he entered. "Your Highness," he greeted her with a hopeful smile. He walked in and immediately retracted his steps. There were scraps of paper all over the floor. The Princess had been writing all night this time, it looked like.

She looked over at him. Her eyes were tired—more than usual. Again, he wondered if she had gotten any sleep that night. She nodded silently to acknowledge him. "How is Etoileon today, Dr.?" she asked.

"No change today, Your Highness, but don't lose hope." For a moment, Selene just looked at him. Then a small smile curved to her face for a split second, before it disappeared once more. Dr. Hamersley was almost certain that it hadn't happened at all, but he knew that there was no mistaking her flicker of a smile.

Before he could say anything else, she turned away and sighed. There was no response after that. The doctor took his tests as quickly as possible, so as not to disturb her, and then he bid her farewell. She just nodded to him again as he left, before her gaze turned back to the window.

***

Ronal felt his heart lift as he headed up the medical ward stairway to see Cyerra. It had been a somber time, and he could not even clearly remember the last time that he had to work so hard to be even remotely happy. Who could be happy when such tragedy was upon their land? War had broken out, and some of the isles were already fighting each other. Taking sides carried a hefty price, and it was all paid in pain and blood.

He held the flower that he'd bought down at the nursery in the city street market in his one hand as he pushed open the doors to the royal wards.

Cyerra was there, and he smiled brightly, his first genuine smile in a long time. But his smile quickly faded as he looked into Cyerra's tired face and saw her unhappiness and fatigue.

"Cyerra," he whispered, taking hold of her arm and pulling on her gently, urging her to follow him to the side for a moment. Cyerra looked at the other handmaiden attending to the watch duty, Rosaria, who waved her off with a wink. Ronal realized that it had to be a sign to tell Cyerra that it was okay for her to talk with him, because Cyerra nodded and then obligingly headed with Ronal in a direction away from the princess' room.

"Ronal, I'm so glad that you came," she whispered in a soft tone. "I am sorry that I cannot talk at the normal volume, but you must understand we have several patients here."

"That's fine, Cyerra, my dear," Ronal smirked, trying to get a laugh out of her. She looked so down that he thought she could use a lift. "How are you? You look tired."

"I am," Cyerra admitted. "But I am worried, too. Her Highness is not doing so well. I worry for her."

"I'm sure that the King will see to your pay, don't worry."

"It's not just that, Ronal," Cyerra frowned. "I happen to admire the princess very much. She has always been kind to me."

"I'm sorry, that was a bit mean," Ronal admitted. "I am, I assure you, deeply sorrowful as well."

Cyerra smiled knowingly. "Now you're just teasing me," she remarked. "But I know that you have had to deal with so much as well as I, so I will forgive you. I am sorry to hear that Etoileon is not any better yet. You are his best friend. I can't imagine how anxious you are for him to at least wake up."

Ronal nodded. Cyerra had struck a chord. "You're right," he nodded. "I miss having him around to joke and tease and fight with. He's more like my brother than a friend. Even in our training sessions, it's not the same without him beating me up during practice."

Cyerra and Ronal turned the corner and found themselves at the food court in the medical ward. It was a place for newly active patients, lackeys, and desk workers on break from their shifts. At one of the counters, Cyerra ordered a juice drink and Ronal got a small glass of water.

They headed over to the large windows and sat down with their backs to the glass. The grey sunlight had never seemed to be so unforgivingly bright. Cyerra stretched out and then drew her legs and skirts underneath her, tucking the smooth fabric in a discreet ladylike manner. She sipped from her juice glass and sighed heavily.

"What is it?" Ronal asked.

"Nothing," she said, "It's just that it's been so quiet and depressing around here. Her Highness insisted that I call her by her given name the other day."

"So?"

"So, this must be a terrible strain on her, for her to say that."

Ronal shrugged. "I don't think it's so unusual, Cyerra. You and I don't use formalities. And I know that Etoileon and the princess have been friends for years, calling each other by their real names. And anyway, you can hardly blame her. Etoileon once told me that she hated to be referred to as 'Her Highness'."

"Really? Why?" Cyerra asked.

Ronal looked up pensively. "I guess it's because when you focus so much on titles and prestige, you forget that you're dealing with an actual presence." He took a sip of his water and shrugged. "I suppose."

Cyerra gazed thoughtfully into the distance. "I never thought about it that way," she admitted. She gave him a small smile. "Who would've thought that names were so personal?"

They sat there quietly as her question hung in the air, never to be completely answered.

A moment later, Ronal cocked his head. "Have you heard from your brother?"

"Aemon disowned me, I'm sure," Cyerra frowned. She looked away as her frown deepened. "I am quite sure that I am no longer his favorite sister."

"But you are his only sibling."

"We actually used to have an older brother, but he was lost in the war as well," Cyerra sighed sadly, trying to give a small smile anyway. "And anyway, Aemon can and will hold his grudges against those who are opposed to him. I wish he wouldn't. Look at what this grudge has wrought; he has failed to see that the Sapphiran monarchy is not the responsible party for taking the life of our father."

"And now the planet's at war?" Ronal finished quietly, as a melancholy seemed to descend on Cyerra. She merely nodded and then dropped her head.

She looked up and shook her head. "How long do you think the war will last this time?" she asked him. "How long will it be until we talk of joyful things, of silly, happy times, and the beautiful things that war makes us forget?"

Ronal cocked an eyebrow at her, unsure of what to say, or even if he should say anything at all. He didn't really understand girls when they were like this. Cyerra was tired and emotionally overwrought. But as he thought about it some more, her words were strangely appropriate in a way that he could not explain. What was it about the passion for peace in the middle of all things, that brought down the soul to speechlessness, to a point of realization that there are millions of words, and yet all of them were meaninglessly empty went it came to expressing the feelings brought forth in silence?

***

When he walked outside the door and pulled it shut behind him, Dr. Hamersley found himself face to face with the Princess' governess. The doctor smiled in greeting. "Lady Aura," he welcomed her.

"Dr. Hamersley," Aura acknowledged crisply. "What is the news today? How is she? Any better today?"

The doctor nodded. "She is tired. If she would get more sleep, she would be completely healthy at this point. I'd say that you could remove the feeding tube now. Her complexion is pale, but not her usual brightness, so I suggest that you try to make sure that she eats at every meal. Her wounds are healing slowly, most likely due to her lack of rest." He let off on a sigh.

Aura nodded. "I see."

Dr. Hamersley looked at her sympathetically. "You appear to be worried for her, I see." The doctor took her arm and patted it comfortingly. "She is very dear to us all, my Lady. I assure you, we suffer as one."

Aura nodded. "Thank you," she whispered. "I feel so responsible for her. And she is not talking to me; but come to that, she barely speaks at all. I don't know what is wrong with her. All she does is sit there. She tells me that she's busy thinking when I ask what she would like to do. She tells her handmaidens that she doesn't want to talk when they come to watch over her. I don't understand her."

"Something tells me that the Princess is going through some kind of shock," Dr. Hamersley replied. "She is mourning, too. No doubt she is grieved to hear of war and those that are dying. Even if you do not tell her what is going on exactly, I suspect that she has a strong idea of what is."

Aura had wanted to interrupt him, but he continued. "She is a lot more perceptive than we think, my Lady. She really needs to get some sleep. It would do wonders for her heart, too. Being tired and emotionally distraught at the same time is never a good thing."

"Doctor, the other day when I came into her room, she was writing. I looked down at what she had written. It was a poem of some sort. Now that she is in the medical ward, she has not had her usual classes or any of her tutelage."

"I see. Did the poem make you feel uncomfortable in some manner?"

"Yes. I actually wrote it down on another piece of paper. It wasn't very long. In fact, why don't you tell me what you think of it?" Aura reached into her drawstring purse and pulled out a folded piece of paper. Unfolding it, she handed it to the doctor, who promptly read it.

"The dirt is damp and cold,
The air is stale and dry
Such little warmth to hold
As I lay inside my grave to cry."

The doctor folded up the paper once more and shook his head. "Quite interesting, Lady Aura. She is –"

"Going to need counseling?" Aura interrupted. There was a look on her face that was tight with tension and fear.

"No. But I think that she needs a friend right now. It appears that she is lonely and sad, which under the circumstances is only to be expected. But then, I am no expert in such matters."

"I will talk to her," Aura decided. "She is being rather childish about this war anyway. She must learn sooner or later that the people of this world will not always allow her to have her way."

"I think she already knew that, my Lady. And while she had such hope for the peace of this world, I suspect that is why she is full of remorse," the doctor said gently. Then he inclined his head respectfully and walked away, leaving the governess to stare at him with her mouth open in surprise.

When her surprise at being corrected was over a moment later, she shook her head and knocked on the door to Selene's room.

There was no response from the other side. Aura sighed and just walked in. "Your Highness?" She carefully walked over to where Selene sat unmoving on her bed.

Aura looked at the princess' eyes, their gazes meeting and allowing Aura to see that the doctor had made no exaggeration. Selene's eyes were indeed a bright red-pink in color and there were huge black circles under her eyes.

"Princess," Aura said, "You really must stop this. Staying up all hours of the day will not make Etoileon wake up."

Selene smiled ruefully at her. "I cannot seem to help it," she remarked. When Aura just scolded at her response,

Selene sighed. "I don't do it on purpose, Aura. I can't seem to relax in this room."

"Well, I suppose that you would feel a little uncomfortable," Aura reasoned. "When you move back into the Palace rooms tomorrow, I'm sure that you will be all right then."

"I'm moving?"

"Yes, Your Highness. In a while. The Palace has nearly been completely rebuilt in these pass two weeks," Aura informed her. "Several innovations have been made as well, to insure higher security, so Your Highness need not worry about the war while you are inside."

Selene made no comment. "And Etoileon?" she asked quietly.

"Don't be silly," Aura's voice had a hard bite to it. "He has to remain here, so the Doctors can keep watching his condition."

"I see."

Aura was surprised by the princess' ready acceptance. It was not like the princess to be so compliant, Aura thought. She was suddenly worried and suspicious, but looking at the sad, tired expression on her charge's face, Aura nodded and let it go. She almost wanted to comfort her, but she knew it was not her place to do so.

"Will I be allowed to visit him, Aura?"

Aura flinched. "Beg pardon, Your Highness?"

Selene looked at Aura intently, watching her governess carefully. "Will I be allowed to visit Etoileon while he remains here, Aura?"

Aura shrugged her shoulders and looked away from the princess' gaze. "I am not sure about that, Your Highness. I will ask His Majesty about it, and then we shall see," she answered finally. "But do not get your hopes up. It has been two weeks since he went into the coma. I cannot say how long it will be until he gets better. I'm sure," she said with confidence in her voice, "that you shall be concerned with other things that require your attention. You are a busy one, Your Highness. If His Majesty the king does allow you to come, it would only be every once in a while, I'm sure."

Selene nodded and turned her attention to the floor. After a moment of silence, she looked back up at her governess. "You can go, if you like, Aura," Selene murmured as she turned around to face the window once again.

Aura hesitated and then left. She hoped that the princess would feel better once she was back in her own rooms. It made sense that she would, Aura reasoned. There was something inexplicably gloomy about a medical ward.

***

It was night, but she was not dreaming. She was not sleeping either.

Selene remained curled up in her bed, the covers pulled high around her to muffle her soft crying.

283

"Etoileon … " she whispered quietly. "It's been two weeks now since you've been gone. I miss you." How she longed to return to the days when they were together! The times that they spent in the tower, the memories they shared … so much reminded her of him.

When she'd first heard the news, she'd been stricken with grief. There had been a foreboding shadow that had trickled down her spine, as if to tell her that she would not be seeing him a long while. Despite the news that he was doing okay, Selene worried that at any moment, she would be informed of his passing and thrown into a wave of loneliness and despair that would consume her. She feared that he would be lost to her forever. "I want you to wake up," she murmured, "But I know that only a miracle will save you now."

And then she cried even harder, sobbing into her tear-soaked pillow. Why was life so unfair? Why did this have to happen? What good could possibly come from all of this? As far as Selene could tell, her best protector was gone, the Fighter squad was missing its highest-ranking member, and the thought of the war outside taunted her, provoking her greatest fears to eat her up.

There was no way she could sleep. Selene finally stopped crying, her face sticky from her salty tears.

She rolled over on her back, and looked up at the ceiling. It was dark. She should have been afraid, she thought. But now that she no longer slept, Selene had grown accustomed to the darkness. When she'd been little, and the monsoon thunderstorms had awoken her, Selene had always been afraid to fall back asleep. Something about the dark had caused her skin to prickle with unexplainable fear. Now it was the opposite. How quickly her fear of night had turned into the fear of the day. The darkness seemed more like a friend to her now. Daylight only brought the sad truth of her life into focus—there was no one but herself that she could count on. Darkness seemed to sympathize with her, its cover allowing Selene to forget that there was anyone that she couldn't depend on.

She stared at the whitewashed surface until she could take it no further; she pushed aside her covers and swung her bare feet onto the cold surface of the floor. Grabbing a smaller blanket, she wrapped the warm cover around herself and headed to the door.

Silently, she opened the door and poked her head out. There were only a couple of people in sight; a nurse was at a nearby desk and an aid was filing something behind the nurse. Both of them were talking to each other quietly. Selene slipped out the door without making a noise, and quietly sneaked down the hall.

A few doors later, she reached her destination. Etoileon's room.

She crept inside and shut the door as quietly as she could. When the door creaked, she jumped and held her breath, hoping with all her might that she had not drawn any attention to herself or Etoileon's room. When no one came in after a few moments, Selene was reassured that she was safe.

Turning around, her eyes softened. The light of the two moons, Shira and Kuro, glowed pale against Etoileon's skin. There were no sounds except his quiet breathing; Selene could barely breath herself as she slowly walked over to stand next to him.

"Etoileon," she whispered, taking hold of his hand. She was shocked to find that his hand was warm. After looking at the monitor, Selene relaxed and gave a small smile. He didn't have a fever, but he was warm. It was a good sign to her.

She knelt down on the floor so she could talk directly to his face. "Etoileon, it's me," she said, her voice just above a whisper. "I know you can't hear me, but I want you to know that I'm here for you." Her gaze left his face and looked down. "I feel so alone, now that you're like this. I know that you're not … going to … to … " her voice faltered. Fresh tears came pouring out as she struggled to retain them. "But why won't you wake up?" she asked somberly. "Please, wake up!"

Etoileon remained as he was, lost in his coma. Selene smiled slightly and tightened her grip on his hand. "Please, my dear friend, get up!"

Still nothing. Selene lost her smile as she withdrew her hand. Looking down at him, she felt the sting of tears coming on once more. Just as she was about to cry, she heard the sound of footsteps coming down the hall. Startled, she held still, hoping that they weren't going to come into her now-vacant room.

The steps moved past her room and Selene felt her breath rush out in relief. She quickly jumped in surprise when she heard the click of a doorknob.

Oh no, Selene thought, the doctor couldn't possibly be checking on Etoileon now, can he? Her thoughts were quickly forgotten as she scrambled to hide. She moved behind a curtain and ducked down under a supply table, hurriedly moving to gather her pajamas close around her ankles. Her back against the wall, her arms were clutched around her knees in a crouching position.

She watched as the doctor's feet moved around the room as he began checking Etoileon's vitals and marking down his reports. She heard him emit a sigh as he removed his stethoscope.

"Doctor Hamersley?" There was a knock at the door. It was a nurse.

"Yes, yes, come in Fia. I'm almost finished on this patient."

The nurse came in and walked up beside the doctor, looking over the doctor's shoulders at the notes. "How is he doing?" she asked, more out of mild curiosity than anything else.

Selene felt her mouth go dry and her heart stop as she awaited the doctor's answer. There was a pause and then Doctor Hamersley let out a sigh. "It's not looking good."

The princess felt her heart plummet into her stomach.

"What's the problem?" the nurse asked.

"Well, it seems that there are a multiple amount of bruises, cuts, and scrapes. It took them hours to dig him and the princess out of that pile of rubble. He's lost a lot of blood. With the combination of fractures and the broken bones, it is probably for the best that he's knocked out. It's a miracle in itself that he's alive."

"Really? It's that bad?"

"I'm afraid it's worse than that." The doctor's voice fell as he looked down at the clipsheet that he held containing the reports.

"What could be worse than all of that?" the nurse whispered, with a touch of horror in her voice.

Doctor Hamersley shook his head. "It doesn't look like he will be waking up any time soon. His injuries, substantial as they are, would heal much more quickly if he were, even if he would be in pain. At least this way he's out of feeling any of the damage."

The nurse chuckled a bit, nervously. "Try telling that to the Princess. I don't think either of them would think this is the better way."

The doctor shook his head. "That is everything I need for now from this young man. Fia, go ahead and start preparing his medicine. Here's the prescription." A paper was torn off the doctor's pad and handed to her. "Let's head out, shall we?"

The nurse nodded and walked out promptly, heading for the drug counter. The doctor reached the door, but suddenly turned back. He looked at the peaceful expression on Etoileon's face and said, "We can only assume that you are much better off in sleep, young man. But I have a feeling that this is according to the will of the one who watches from above."

Selene waited until the doctor shut the door, so only a slit of light was shining from the hallway out from under the door. It was then that Selene relaxed, feeling certain that she had not been detected in the least by the nurse or Doctor Hamersley.

Safe for the moment, Selene thought as she poked her head out from underneath her hiding spot. Withdrawing, she slumped against the wall. Then she couldn't take it anymore.

Placing her head in her hands, she wept.

She cried for Etoileon, who was suffering and in the coma all because of her foolhardiness in the first place.

She cried for herself, because she was so lonely and didn't know what to do, or what to believe. She didn't know if she would ever be able to face the endless stream of days that held nothing but empty promises and hopelessness.

Who could she turn to, now that Etoileon was gone? She was left alone all over again. Her mother had abandoned her long before she'd given birth to her. Her father had left her all by herself until he had apparently drunk enough moonshine to poison himself. Her brother had neglected her to the lonely hours locked up inside her own palace, making the castle, with all its rich adornments and ornate decorations, to be her prison. Her handmaidens and her governess had left her to stand alone on a platform that was only given to her for her title, not her being. Even her subjects made her feel alone; they were all at war now. Etoileon had been her one true friend, who had called her by her name and treated her like an equal.

"Someone," she wept harder, "Someone save me from this misery! I cannot take it anymore! I'm so alone … "
Selene slumped over, falling prostrate on her hands and

THE MOONLGIHT PEGASUS

knees. "I can't do this by myself," she muttered. "Who can? Who can save me from this darkness?" Even if Etoileon woke up, she would not feel the same as she had before the war started. She closed her eyes, the last of her tears falling out. As she cried, the clouds began to cover over the two moons and hide their light from Sapphira. There was no light left in the room. It seemed that even the hall light from under the door had grown dim.

When there was nothing left inside of her, Selene listened to the quiet breathing of her friend. There was nothing but the rhythmic noise of Etoileon's inhale, exhale against the darkness of the night.

Suddenly there was great flash of light outside the window, its brightness filling the room with its brilliance. Selene looked up, and jumped to the window, but it was gone already. "What was that?" she wondered aloud. "Huh?" She suddenly felt warm. And sleepy. Her eyes flickered for a moment, but she felt the irresistible call to rest.

Selene felt her knees buckle and give way, hitting the cold floor. She was out; before the rest of her body hit the floor, she was sound asleep.

***

For the first night in a long while, Selene was dreaming.

She woke to find herself lying on a soft bed of sand. She looked up to find that she was once again in a vivid dream. Her hand went up to cover her mouth as she was filled with wonder. She was left speechless at how real and beautiful everything seemed.

There she was, on a sandy beach. The wind laced through her hair, and the sea mist blew gently across her face. Selene looked around; she'd been here before. It was the same place she'd been in after she had argued with Etoileon. She recognized the rock where she'd lain on before, and the pool of water that had given her the precious feather. The bright blue sky sparkled like the rarest of jewels, and the sea seemed to be bursting with knowing joy. The waves even seemed to dance. There was something about this place … something about it seemed so real, but it was so unnaturally real that it was completely ethereal.

She looked down at herself. Her feet were still bare, and she could feel the tinkling sensation of the warm sand beneath her. She was still wearing her plain white hospital pajamas. There was something wrong, though, Selene noticed as she examined her hands. There were no wound marks on her any longer, nor were there any bandages. Her skin was smooth and glowed with its natural brightness.

"What's going on?" she wondered. "Is this really a dream?"

A sound seemed to answer her from the realms of the forest behind her. Selene turned and looked at the forest, her voiced curiosity momentarily forgotten as she sucked in her breath at the sight of the forest. It was breathtakingly exquisite. The tree-like structures appeared to consist of a crystal formation, which the surrounding light cast out tiny colored streaks that flickered in the soft wind. There were some leaves on the trees, bouncing along in the wind. The ground progressed from sand to a striking dark green grass, and there was a cloudy fog that surrounded it. The fog added a foreboding feature to the setting, as if to ask each traveler if the truth was worth traveling through uncertain areas or not.

"Who's there?" she called out. "Hello?"

There was no response, but a stirring of sounds caused Selene to be curious once again. Carefully, she got up from her fallen position on the beach and took her first step toward the forest, a subtle determination seeping into each new step; she was overcome with the need to know what this light was.

The forest was confusing and full of distractions; regardless, Selene stopped for nothing, her hunger for the light to be realized. She began to quicken her pace as she felt herself drawing closer. "I have to see this!" she panted.

Suddenly, the forest cleared out, and there was a lake of crystal clear water before her. Selene nearly fell out of shock.

Walking on the water before her was a winged horse, a Pegasus. She could barely look at him, he was so strikingly beautiful.

His feathered wings were broad and long, the width of them seemed immeasurable; they were folded back against his body as he stood perfectly still on the water surface. It suddenly dawned on Selene where the gift of her feather had come from. His body was strong, his pure white hair gleaming in the cloudy surrounding. The mane and tail fluttered gracefully in the soft breeze. His steps were relaxed and seemed perfectly coordinated, as he slowed to a stop close to the edge of the sparkling lake. His eyes lifted to meet hers. Selene had never seen such a gentle kindness. Looking deeper, there seemed that a humble question was resting in the depths of his crystal fire eyes.

There was no mistaking the question his eyes held; she knew what he was asking her. He wanted to know if she wanted him to come to her or not. The choice had been left up to her. It suddenly struck Selene that he was waiting for her answer. Cautiously, Selene took a few more shaky steps to the border of the lake. She thought about wading in the water to go and meet the strange but magnificent creature, but she did not know how deep the water was or if she should just stay there.

His eyes met with Selene's, and she fell to her knees, her gaze never leaving his. Her thoughts stilled and dissolved in her mind, her body was left numb and trembling as she just gazed upon the beauty of this winged majesty.

Moments later, Selene somehow managed to find her voice. "Who are you?" she whispered softly, as he continued to meet her gaze with his.

He made no sound, no response. He merely came up to her and stood in front of her. With her hand shaking, Selene reached out to touch him. He did not move away from her; instead, he nudged his nose toward her. She suddenly wondered if he would be as real as the rest of her dream.

Her quivering fingers finally touched the soft texture of his nose in a gentle caress, and Selene felt a surge of power and certainty flood through her as she felt her dream fade away into a shimmering light.

He was the one who could help her. He was the Spirit of True Peace.

***

As Dr. Hamersley walked down the hall, a bright blast of light radiated at the other end of the hall.

Intrigued, he headed over to see where the light had come from. He found himself in front of the princess' room. Dr. Hamersley poked his head into the room to see if she had seen the flash of light. He half expected her to be still looking glumly out the window. He was amazed to find that not only was she sleeping soundly in her bed, but there also was a smile on her face.

He had to grin and stifle a chuckle of joy. The Guardian always worked wonders.

***

Selene woke up with a start in the morning. She sat up straight and was surprised to find that she was in her own bed in the hospital. Strange … she hadn't felt anyone move her or pick her up. She felt more rested and more relaxed than ever. She wondered why.

Then she remembered her dream. Selene's face broke out into the first genuinely happy smile that she'd had since coming to the medical ward. Her hands flew up to her mouth, to restrain the laughter that had bubbled up inside of her.

It was at that moment that she realized that she also no longer had any scars or scrapes from the disaster. Selene felt her happiness be replaced by awe as she looked down at her hands, fascinated, that she seemed better than new. Her royal glow was back, and there was no place on her body that she could find a remainder of an injury.

"This is amazing," she whispered. "What happened to me?" A memory of the kind Pegasus she'd seen in her dream flickered into her mind. Was it Him? Had He been the one who had done this for her? she wondered.

There was a knock at the door. Selene jolted away from her thoughts and looked up to see that Kadrianne was standing in the doorway.

"Good day, Your Highness," Kadrianne bowed. When she stood upright once again, Kadrianne's eyes flickered in surprise as she noticed the princess' recovery. "You are looking well today, I see," Kadrianne smiled. "How do you feel, Princess?"

Selene gave her a small smile, thinking of her peaceful dream. "I am feeling remarkably better today, Kadrianne."

Kadrianne came over and sat down at the foot of the princess' bed. "Good. We all worry about you so, Lady Princess."

Selene bit her lip, and then asked carefully, "Kadrianne, how is Etoileon today? Is he feeling better yet?" She reasoned out that maybe if she was better today, he would've been completely healed as well. Oh, how I hope so! Selene thought.

Kadrianne looked down and shook her head sadly. "No progress today, so far," she answered. "He is still doing the same as before, though. He has not gotten any worse, so that is good news."

Selene looked down and sighed softly. "I suppose you're right," she responded, though her voice sounded hollow. Still,

Selene thought, *I wish he would wake up. If I can make a miracle recovery, why can't Etoileon?*

She remembered the doctor's synopsis the night before and slumped down in her bed once again. It was a miracle that he was still alive, she thought. Maybe that was all the miracles that she was allowed for now.

"Your Governess, Lady Aura, told me to tell you that you will be moving out of the medical ward this afternoon," Kadrianne remarked, bringing Selene out of her trance-like state. "Your palace rooms are ready for you, Your Highness. His Majesty the King has taken great pains to ensure that you will be in the highest and safest amount of comfort possible."

"That's wonderful for His Majesty then," Selene replied. "I haven't seen him in here since I woke up."

Before Kadrianne could respond, a voice called from the door. "His Majesty has been very busy with the war, Your Highness." Kadrianne and Selene looked up to see Yana in the doorway, a small smile on her face. She'd already taken note of her princess' considerable improvement. She bowed and walked in, coming up behind where Kadrianne sat. "Your Highness, it is good to see you this morning," she said.

"Thank you, Yana," Selene murmured. *Had she worried her servants so much that they were moved to break traditional conversation lines?* It was a relief, but it was also a little frightening to realize how much her moods of the past weeks had shaken nearly everyone on the staff. *I'll have to bear this pain in my heart more quietly,* Selene thought with a sad smile. *Even if my dearest companion is not well, I can't worry everyone. It's too selfish.*

Yana continued, her brown eyes alive with excitement. "His Majesty has decided to open the palace with a ball in your honor tonight, Your Highness. Every member of the High Court is invited, and he has taken the liberty to order the seamstresses to make you a beautiful new gown, as well as gowns for all of your handmaidens! Isn't that kind of him?"

Something in Yana's voice caught Kadrianne's attention, but Selene apparently hadn't noticed. She was staring off into space again.

"Your Highness?" Kadrianne asked uncertainly.

"I'm all right, Kadrianne," Selene responded. She tried to give her faithful handmaidens a reassuring smile. "It's just … it's just that thinking of a party makes my head spin somewhat," Selene explained. "I'm still very tired and I don't know if I'll be up to it, that's all."

"Are you sure that's all, Your Highness?" Yana asked. Her words were chosen carefully as she asked further, "It doesn't have to do with a particular young man? You are not sad over something other than being too tired for a party?"

Selene looked up to meet Yana's gaze. "You needn't worry about me, Yana," she said truthfully. "Please, don't let me spoil your fun."

"Well … are you sure, princess?" Yana asked again. There was an eagerness to her features that clearly told anyone that she wanted to go to the party. It was a little surprising; usually Yana excused herself early from such celebrations.

Selene nodded. "By all means, we shall go. But I might turn in early, that's all."

"Thank you! Thank you so much, Your Highness," Yana bowed. "I shall inform His Majesty of your decision right away! He shall no doubt be most pleased." She bowed once again and then waltzed out of the room, a smile on her face. She nearly ran over Cyerra and Rosaria as they came into the room.

"Huh … Wonder what's gotten into Yana?" Cyerra asked as she looked back in the direction of Yana. Cyerra shrugged and turned her attention towards the princess. "Selene, you look like you've gotten some sleep at last. Are you well this morning?"

Selene smiled. At least she had convinced someone to call her by name. "Yes, Cyerra, I'm feeling better this morning."

"That's great," Cyerra smiled. "It's so good to see you smiling." Cyerra came and sat down opposite from Kadrianne.

"Thank you," the princess nodded politely. "Does anyone know what time I'm going to be moved to the Palace from here?"

"It's not that far of a transport, Your Highness," Kadrianne assured her. "You'll be shuttled over sometime after lunch, I'm sure. I will ask Lady Aura for the correct time, if you wish."

"No, that's all right," Selene replied. "I was just wondering, that's all." She looked intently at her handmaidens. "Is Etoileon going to be moved as well?" She dared to hope that Aura or one of her attendants would have pledged that he be moved along with her.

Cyerra and Kadrianne exchanged glances. Was it okay to tell the princess about her friend? Should they even tell her, now that she was finally showing progress?

Kadrianne shrugged and nodded. "We might as well tell you, Your Highness," she started.

"They decided that your protector would be better off here in the hospital, despite your questions earlier about moving him. The doctors are still watching his conditions," Cyerra explained. "They feel that he will eventually recover, but they don't know the exact length of time his internal repercussions or any of his injuries will take to heal."

Selene's eyes fell to the floor. "I … I understand," she managed. "But I wish that he would wake up at least."

"There is nothing we can do for him, but hope for the best," Kadrianne sighed. "I'm sure that he'll be fine in matter of time."

The question there is how long? Selene thought. How long would she be left without him? And how long could she go on without him?

A drizzle of warmth seemed to sink into her heart. Selene looked up and suddenly thought of her dream last night. It had been a wonderful, beautiful dream—her first one since the war started. Could it be a sign? A message? Was someone trying to tell her something? The more she thought about it, Selene realized that she could not possibly know for sure. She would have to go on, that was all there was to it for now. Answers would have to come later.

***

The palace of Diamond City had never looked more grand or more magnificent to the onlooker. The outer granite walls had been cleaned and scrubbed of all the debris. The windows had been replaced, as nearly all of the original ones had been shattered or cracked severely in the attack. The gardens were growing once again, and although some of the inner keep needed more reconstruction work, there was a certain liveliness to the place. The floors were mopped, the woodwork was dusted, the gold inlaid designs were polished, and there were all kinds of decorations hanging for the celebration. There was only one room that had not been completely restored.

It was more than a homecoming for the princess; it was a celebration of surviving the attack and bringing hope back to the people.

Selene was healthy enough to go home, but she sure did not understand why so many people believed that she could possibly bring the world peace. As far as Selene could tell, the war had decimated her in way that nothing else could have; her dearest friend and the one she cared for the most in the world was hanging on the edge between life and death. If she would ever talk to him again, see him awake again, she did not know. And she did not know what she would do if he did not survive.

Selene watched out the transport vehicle window as her subjects all lined the streets, some with flowers, some crying, some with gifts. A lot of flower petal confetti was being dropped from the sky by several airway ships. People were cheering for her as her vehicle sped by. Selene felt her body involuntarily shrink back into her seat. But she did try to smile and when Aura was watching her, she even managed to wave. There was nothing so important to Aura than appearances. She'd arranged for Selene to wear one of the more festive imperial outfits. It was quite pretty, Selene thought, as she looked down at her flounced gown. It was white and frilly, with gold inlaid sparkles and designs, complete with a matching gold-beaded headdress. Her hair had been brushed to a shine, let down for the arrival, and on her feet were the traditional golden shoes of Diamond City rulers. Selene managed a tiny smile.

"Now, Your Highness," Aura said as the vehicle slowed down in front of the palace entrance. "Please remember to behave. And smile, your people love you. Your Highness shouldn't want to worry them."

"Of course not, Aura," Selene assured her. A tiny smile came to her face as she added, "I would not have them think that they should worry about me. I suspect from their reactions, that many of them love me enough to worry on their own."

Aura, being one of them, looked over in surprise and then returned Selene a warm smile. "Yes, I think you are quite right about that, Your Highness." Aura watched the princess as she looked at the window on a crowd of people who had huddled as close as they could to the doorway. She really is such a treasure, Aura thought. Such a sweetheart, and very innocent. I just wish that she were a bit more serious regarding some matters.

But as she looked on Selene's calmness, she felt that if more serious were what this world had needed, then surely the reigning monarchs of the recent past years would've helped. Aura couldn't help but feel, as she continued to watch

Selene wave and smile at the people outside her window, that maybe the princess was the one who had it right. Maybe there was room in this world for a little harmless fun.

***

"Princess, Princess, over here!"

"Your Highness! We love you!"

"All hail Princess Selene!"

"Make way for Her Highness, the Princess of Sapphira!"

There were plenty of people shouting as the princess' transport arrived at the front entrance to the newly refurbished and rebuilt Palace.

Selene looked at her home and tried not to frown. It was still her home, but it had an unusual effect on her senses. She'd lived her whole life in that palace. Now she was going back to it after being away from it the longest amount of time in all her life. The realization hit her that she was going back to the place where she'd longed to escape from and caused her to falter in her movements as her door was opened.

She looked up the High Tower and felt a sigh rise up in her chest. She suddenly felt tired and weary.

An escort team of eight men huddled around her as two of them reached forward and extended their arms to her. She slid out of the vehicle and the surrounding crowds cheered all the louder. They knew nothing of the effort that Selene was putting forth in order not to look sad.

She walked in the center of her guards and remembering Aura's words, she waved and smiled graciously at her people. She was grateful that they cared for her, but she was also discouraged at the high amount of faith that they placed in her because of the prophecy for peace. She still didn't understand what she was supposed to do or when she was going to have to do something.

Still struggling against her inner chaos, Selene looked up ahead to see her brother waiting for her at the palace door.

***

There was no denying the feeling of pride as Dorian watched his sister come towards him. She was all dressed up in another one of her silly outfits, but Dorian had to admit, the white and gold color combination seemed to suit her. The sunlight seemed to make her sparkle like a little toy as she made her way to the castle's main doorway. Up the stairs, one by one, she walked with an air of matchless dignity. Her governess and her handmaidens, as well as a couple of maids and coaches followed her, all of them in their flounced matching garments. It made for a triumphant return, Dorian thought as he waited patiently.

Though he'd been busy the last couple of weeks with the rebuilding of not only the city, but also the reconstruction of hope in the city dwellers, he had not been able to visit Selene. Seeing her now, with her royal glow back to normal, and her wounds healed, she embodied the spirit of hope reborn. He imagined that the people would see no less.

When she reached the top of the stairs and stood before her King and brother, she bowed respectfully. Selene couldn't suppress a smile at the clinking of the beads on her attire. The crowd cheered and applauded as Dorian lifted her chin so that she no longer bowed. He winked at her, both of them sharing a brief, knowing look. The formalities were just for show. Dorian extended his arm to her and they walked inside to the melody of their applauding subjects. The princess' time away had brought questions to sound out loud throughout the community, one that could not be answered—had the time come at last, when man shall be freed of his captivity and sickness? Would the world be at peace? Was the prophecy to be fulfilled? Or was it hopeless to believe in such a miracle, hopeless to think, that their world, full of humans, was incapable to solve the crisis at hand?

***
Chapter 9
The Princess Makes a Friend
***

It was later that day during the evening that Selene headed towards her palace rooms. She had just finished with the celebratory dinner, and she was tired. She was also feeling empty, as if the hours surrounded by her people had done nothing to assure her that her trouble would be solved in time. If anything, it made her think that maybe she would be silently bearing this pain for a long time before someone noticed her actual condition, if they noticed at all.

"Well, I think that your return was a complete success, Your Highness," Aura grinned happily as she led the way through the inner-palace construction sites to the princess' rooms.

Flanked by all five of her handmaidens, Selene said nothing for the moment. She was too busy taking in all the wreckage and reconstruction of the place that she had once known as her home. Here and there, every so often, was a gaping hole in the granite walls, letting a small amount of moonlight to burst through. Though she felt remorse for the destruction of her palace, she couldn't help but think that the holes added an elegant touch to the fabric of the castle. The little moonlit holes illuminated the hallways, shining a sparkling light into the darkness of the corridors. It was a breathtaking moment, both sad and beautiful at the same time.

This is so sad, she thought as she watched some workers try to reassemble the pieces of a fallen vase. This place was not one of overwhelming happiness for me, she mused, but it was a familiar place at least.

It had been a place of beginnings for her, in many ways. Though she hated it and despised the place for keeping her from freedom, Selene knew that she was very loyal to her home. The walls that had once mocked her now cried out in pain, and she felt a sense of regret that nothing would go back to being the same as it had been before. An aching seemed to rise out from her heart as she turned her attention back to what Aura was saying.

"—and His Majesty was so handsome, too, all dressed up in the traditional garbs that he was in, don't you think so, Your Highness?"

Selene nodded. "Yes, Aura, I agree," she said. "Everything was really nice. Very nice."

Aura glanced back at her and asked, "How do you feel, now that you are home, Your Highness?"

"It is good to be back," Selene responded stoically. She looked towards the floor and added softly, "But I wish that everything could be as easily fixed as the palace was."

"What was that, Princess?"

Selene looked back up and said, "I just said that everything's gotten fixed up so quickly, Aura."

Aura smiled. "Yes, it really is a miracle that they were able to get as much done as they have, isn't it? The workers here must be working long hours. Just think, Your Highness, soon we shall hold grand balls and parties, just as we always have.

THE MOONLGIHT PEGASUS

Everything will be just like it was before, and everyone will be happy again!"

"I'm sure that it will be everything and more," Selene said dryly. She was getting tired. After the celebration for her return, and the luncheon that followed, and everything that had gone on that day, Selene wondered if she would ever get some time to herself. There was too much that was lying on her heart for her to enjoy herself. She watched as a support beam was being lifted back into its original place. Some debris fell off and scattered on the floor.

Aura moved quickly to avoid the small shower of dirt and dust, maneuvering through the piles of junk and broken things.

A few corridors later, Selene found herself back in her old rooms. She entered the room and felt a rush of familiarity, but something struck out as being different. She'd been assured by both her brother and Aura that nothing had been changed in the original design of her rooms, but now she was not certain that she could believe that.

"Aura," Selene questioned, "Has my room always been so … small like this?"

Her governess had wasted no time in giving directions out to the handmaidens, telling Kadrianne to open the curtains, Rosaria to fluff the pillows, Chevée to ready the princess' pajamas, and the like, but she halted at Selene's abrupt question. Turning to face her charge, Aura put on a confused smile. "Beg pardon, Your Highness?"

"I asked if my room had always been so small," Selene asked. "I feel cramped in here all of a sudden."

Aura shook her head. "The exact dimensions were used for the remodeling, Your Highness. This is your room. It is exactly the same as it was before." Then she grinned. "Maybe it is you that has changed, Your Highness." She started going on about how it was common for one who had been away to come back and not remember everything exactly as it had been, or to find something new, etc., etc.

Selene ignored Aura's chattiness as she prepared herself for bed. It was still early, but she'd been told by Dr. Hamersley to get plenty of rest over the next few weeks. He'd also told her that if she couldn't sleep, a good book would help. He'd laughed when she'd said that she agreed that her mathematics book would prove to be insufficient entertainment.

If it had been any good that had come from being away from the palace, Selene thought, it was that she'd been given some time off of her studies. Master Omni, her teacher, was very overzealous in his tutoring. Wondering about that, she turned to face Kadrianne, who had finished all of Aura's little tasks and asked, "When am I going back to Master Omni?"

"Your study sessions with the Master will resume the day after tomorrow, Your Highness. His Royal Majesty insisted that you go back soon after settling in once again, as you have missed so much in the past few weeks. He did not want you to fall behind," she remarked. Almost as an afterthought, she added, "It appears that he does not want you to get caught up in the world's war so much, Highness."

That figures, Selene thought as she pulled her nightgown over her head. It was nice to be back in her own clothes, she mused. The Medical ward gown felt too much like a burial dress to be completely comfortable. Remembering her manners, she nodded and said, "Thank you, Kadrianne."

"Your Welcome, Your Highness."

Soon all the handmaidens were dismissed. Selene was all tucked in bed as Aura headed out the door.

"Sleep well, Your Highness," Aura said as she waved goodnight.

"You too," Selene called in return, smiling to assure Aura that she was perfectly content. Aura smiled back, glad to see that her princess seemed to be much more relaxed and happy now that she was back in her own rooms. Once her governess was out of sight, Selene tossed off the covers and hurried over to her door. With her ear pressed against it, she listened carefully as Aura's footsteps disappeared down the hall. A few moments passed, and then there was nothing to be heard.

"Yes," Selene triumphed quietly as she turned around and put her back to rest on the door. "Finally, they're gone." As much as she was grateful for her companions, she was tired of trying to reassure them that she was okay. And she hated it even more that she had to pretend in front of them in the first place.

She headed over to the window and pulled the curtains aside. The familiar sight was warming somewhat. At Silverton, she had not been able to see as much of the night scene as she had hoped; the skyscrapers blocked the moonlight, and the stars were dulled against the bright city lights.

THE MOONLGIHT PEGASUS

But now a clear night was in view. Shira glowed at only half-light, while there was only a sliver of Kuro in the night sky. Selene felt drawn to their beauty as she watched the stars twinkle all around. "How long ago it seems," she murmured, "that the Moonbeam Festival had been here. And now, the festival is gone, and war has come. It seems that morning's light has only brought darkness of late. I wonder if tomorrow has any hope left at all?"

Selene frowned as she noticed a thundercloud forming in the distance. "I guess there is no hope, then." The monsoons were coming; a storm was brewing.

***

There were eyes watching the princess as she continued to mourn, watching out her window. The bloodshot eyes were sharp and carried the hint of slyness, the deceit of omniscience. The long black robes and scarred skin belied the age of the monster watching, waiting in anticipation, for his time to come.

At last, the time had come where the princess' light had weakened enough for him to attack and distort her mind; the time for his emancipation from his prison was upon him. In the late hour of the night, this one was in great anticipation.

This one below looked with twinkling eyes at his prey. She was a hard one to get to, but it had made the oncoming victory even worthwhile. After all those years of protection in the palace, she had been freed enough to be corrupted. His dark, wrinkled face looked even more twisted as he grinned.

Long, aging fingers swirled around the dark crystal ball as he watched the picture within. This one was the defiler, the bringer of Death. This one was Obsidian, the great enemy of the Guardian, who had brought the Dark Plague to the world of Sapphira and rejoiced with the iniquity he spread.

Obsidian frowned as he waited, remembering all too well the day that he had been cast away from the Throne of Crystallon. The Guardian had banished him, promising death to him for treason should Obsidian choose not to repent of his evil ways. The dark master smiled as he remembered fleeing into the world of Sapphira, and inflicting the word with the Dark Plague. Such a joyous day it had been, he thought. Now this day would rival it, as he convinced the Princess to forsake the Pure Light she carried; for she, as one of his enlightened children, was a bridge between Crystallon and Sapphira. There was an unmistakable presence living in her, working through her, one he had not felt so strongly in many centuries. As soon as he'd felt the radiance of her light, and the power it held through the hand of the Guardian, he knew that he had been waiting for her arrival; he knew that she was the one the prophecy called for. He sat back and thought of the royals spitefully. They had been the most difficult to corrupt throughout his rule over Sapphira started, though in recent years Obsidian had been able to gain some power over their family. To have this small girl threaten his hold over the entire world was too much for him to bear. He had to try to turn her to his side.

He'd tried so many ways to get inside her mind before, first calling out to her to go to the city, to go to a place of sickness and dreariness, the Gemstone Oasis. He'd even sent her the first son of the Rebel to meet her there. Obsidian's plan had worked, as the princess had taken to him at once. Even the king had played into Obsidian's hands, making the boy the princess' protector. But the Guardian had intervened once more, causing Obsidian's plan to backfire. The

Guardian had taken the memories of the son away in order, no doubt, to protect the princess. Obsidian thought about it sadly, but then deepened his furrowed brow—maybe there was a way to use the boy yet, despite the barrier Obsidian was faced with when trying to enter into the boy's mind.

His attention turned back to the princess as his crystal ball showed her climbing back under her covers. Obsidian gave a tiny smirk. "Sleep well, Princess … this is going to be a long night for you."

It was time to leave his confinement; there was no turning back after leaving. Once he did, Obsidian knew it would signify war between not only man on Sapphira, but war between the Celestial Prison and Crystallon. For a moment he stalled, holding back the demons behind him with a commanding look. A silence descended on the world almost, as the sounds of life faded as death stalked the sky.

Then he cried out, "Go forth, my loyal servants, and contaminate this world until the last of your power runs dry!" Charging forward, his black robes flapping in the wind, the Gateway of Blood that had allowed his voice to call out to the humans of the world, caved under his power, giving him a free reign at last.

His minions of evil flew out with him, scattering in all directions. Obsidian knew that while he and his servants were invisible to the blinded humans, the humans would fall easily under the power of darkness.

As he flew he began to hear already the sounds of havoc and confusion being unleashed down onto the Sapphiran people. A laugh bubbled up inside him chest as he headed for his own destination—the heart of the princess' dreams.

***

She was dreaming, but it was not peaceful. Selene had fallen asleep to find that her dreams were as troubled and as fitful this night as her heart was.

She found herself on her hands and knees, the sand hard and scratchy beneath her. The winds blew hard against her skin, and there was a chill in the air. She squeezed her eyes shut, to keep out the sand. She hugged her arms around her chest, and she felt the seas rolling as the water splayed up onto her from the shoreline.

"What is going on?" she asked loudly, her voice cracking. She looked up to the skies, to find that the sunlight had been covered by a sheet of clouds in the sky. There was no light to dance on the gray waters to comfort her. Some stray grains of sand blew into her eyes, causing them to water. Her dreams had never felt like this before.

A bright light appeared, and suddenly the wind blew easier. Selene wiped the tears from her eyes to find a figure approaching her. Squinting her eyes, she saw that it was in the shape of a Pegasus pony.

"Pegasus!" she called out to him, her worry fading as she saw his familiar shape. She took a step towards him, and then stopped as she saw how he was flying toward her. A smile jumped onto her face as she felt the laughter of happiness well up inside of her. Though she had only met him briefly before, she knew that he had come to bring her peace. Selene felt her heart start to race in anticipation, as the storm that she had fallen asleep to ceased to be remembered. The winged horse was almost within her reach.

He stopped and landed a few feet away from her, his wings beating up a little dust cloud from the sand below him. He straightened out and held his stature.

Selene wondered if he was going to come to her completely, or if she should risk approaching him. Not knowing what to do, she hesitantly took a small step toward him. When he didn't moved, she was encouraged enough to take another step, and then another. When she was just a step away, Selene looked at the Pegasus in the eyes and suddenly stopped, staring.

Were they the same eyes as before? The ones before had been filled with a crystal fire, a flame that flickered with life. These eyes were dull and grayish white, like the clouds of her dream's storm.

I wonder if he's feeling okay? Selene wondered as she tried to reason out why this Pegasus looked so different. She began to feel awkward, just standing in front of him like that. Not knowing what else to do, she began to reach for him like she had before.

Her smile slowly came back as her hand moved closer and closer to the Pegasus' soft nose. She watched as he made no move to avoid her touch, the confidence in her choice growing with each passing second. When she was an inch away, she broke out into a grin.

She was just about to feel the velvety texture of the Pegasus when, all of a sudden, he turned to stone. Selene jumped back and nearly screamed, causing her to trip over her dress and fall to the ground. She brushed away the hair in her face and looked up again to see that, indeed, the Pegasus

THE MOONLGIHT PEGASUS

was entirely made up of stone. "What?" she gasped. "What happened?"

She was about to get back up on her feet when a voice, different from all other voices she'd known, answered her question.

"He turned to stone, I'm afraid."

Selene jerked around to find a man, a very handsome man at that, looking intently at her as he sat on a nearby rock. He nodded his head in the direction of the Pegasus. "He is very weak, you know."

"Pegasus?" Selene asked. She was uncertain about this man. What was going on? She wondered if she could trust this man as she watched him get off the rock and head toward her.

The man looked surprised. "Yes, some do call him that, I suppose," he muttered to himself more than to anyone else. He stopped a few feet in front of Selene and put his hands in the pockets of his long robes. "It is a shame, really."

"What's a shame?" Selene asked, her curiosity growing as she wondered who this man was. He looked respectable, but she did not trust him completely.

The man looked back at her and met her gaze, and then sighed sadly. "It is a shame that he will not always be here. It really is a sad thing."

"What do you mean, he won't always be here? And … just who are you, anyway?" Selene asked. She wanted to know what he knew about Pegasus, but she had to assess this man's character as well.

The man shifted his weight and smiled warmly at her. "Let's just say I am a friend for now," he said.

"A friend?"

"Yes," he remarked. "I know of this Pegasus quite well, Your Highness."

"I see." Selene folded her arms across her chest. "What can you tell me about him?"

The man shrugged. "I can tell you that he's not to be trusted, Your Highness, that's for sure."

She gave him a small smile. "Can I assume that of you as well, friend?" her words had a bite to them. She did not trust him. No one in her dreams would call her by her royal address. How could he possibly know who she was? Wariness was growing in her heart.

He nodded. "I can see that you are smart, and very perceptive, Your Highness. But while I have not given you my name or stated how I can to be here, can you not say the same of your dear Pegasus?"

She did not respond. He had guessed right.

He pushed forward. "I have come to warn you of him, Your Highness. I have come to tell you that you cannot trust him, nor should you. He is dangerous, Highness. He will deceive you."

Selene looked back at the stone Pegasus, and then looked back at the man, only to find that he had disappeared. Once again, she turned to see the Pegasus and jumped. The man was leaning against the body of the majestic horse, his gaze still focused on her. Selene started to say something, but he held up a hand.

"If I may," he said. "I wish to tell you something about this winged creature, and how he comes and goes as he pleases, in and out of the dreams of this world. He likes beautiful dreams especially, which would explain why you have no doubt seen him before. He does not say any words of friendship, or of promise. But he has broken the hearts and shattered the dreams of those who wish to keep him with them."

"But … he is free to do so," Selene said in a hushed voice. Logic said that he had the freedom to go where he wanted, but the strange man had struck a chord with her; she did not want the Pegasus to go away from her so soon. She looked at the stone Pegasus and felt her heart ache at the thought of never seeing him, or understanding why he had come to her in the first place. She knew in her heart he was real, there was no question in her mind about that. She believed that he could help her, save her even. But why she felt this she did not know.

"Ah, yes, it is true … but Princess, would you keep him here if you could?" the man asked, causing Selene to look up at him with confusion in her gaze.

"I doubt I could if I wanted to," Selene responded.

"Then I will help you," the man said coaxingly. His hand reached up to do what looked like pet the horse's head, but a moment later, in the blink of an eye, a bright red bridle appeared on the horse. There was a small strap attached that he held in his hand. The man smiled.

Selene watched as he extended his hand with the strap in it toward her. She silently stood there, unsure of what to do.

"There you go," the man said, still holding the bridle strap out to her. "Take it, and you will have control over Pegasus. He will stay in your dreams for as long as you like. He will be yours, and nothing and no one will be able to take him away from you."

Selene just stared at the strap still. She wanted to get to know Pegasus, but … still, if she took control of him, to tame him, she would be altering who he was to make him be something else. And even if she just kept him in her dreams, then what would he think of her? Nothing good, I'm sure, she thought. I want to be his friend. I want to get to know him, but I don't want to take his freedom away in the process. It would be wrong.

She looked back up at the man's eager expression and was suddenly suspicious. Why would this man, who she had never seen before in her life, want to help her? It was true that he seemed to know her, but she could not trust him. She stepped back. "No, I don't want to do that," she said. "I would rather like to make friends with him. He would not even like me, much less respect me, if I started ordering him around. He has chosen to come into my dreams on his own terms, and that is how he should leave them … regardless of how much I might wish otherwise."

The man's face lost his smile, and suddenly grew twisted and ugly. His hair faded to white and then receded away to nothing, his eyes grew dark and blood-colored, and his robes, once bright and shinning, grew to a dirty black, beginning to billow with the fury of his anger. "You fool! You little fool!" he shouted at her. He advanced on her, towering over her, his true identity revealed. Obsidian smiled a cruel smile, and then laughed. "You simple little child! How foolish you are indeed, to have outwitted the master of evil. But you will regret that you did not follow my advice, little girl! You will see that your darling Pegasus will leave you yet!"

He pointed to the statue of Pegasus, and a stream of red lightning burst from his hand. The lightning struck the statue and blew it to dust. "No!" Selene cried out. "Pegasus!" The winds were blowing fiercely once more, catching the statue's dust and sending it towards Selene. She grabbed at it, trying to gather what she could. It was futile, however, for the dust disintegrated in her hands as she held it. "No!"

Obsidian threw his head back and laughed his cruel laugh once more. "You sad child," he whispered ominously. "There will come a day when you will see just what you gave up!" He straightened and charged toward her, ready to lash out an attack.

Selene tried to duck, but before she could move away from Obsidian's advancing form, there was a sudden flash of light in the sky. A brilliant white Pegasus materialized in the sky, chasing back the clouds and bringing forth the iridescent sunlight. Selene and Obsidian both shielded their eyes from the sight, Obsidian disappearing as he made his escape out of her dream.

The winds ceased, the seas calmed, and there was light in her dreams once more. Selene looked up at Pegasus, speechless in wonder. "Oh!" she awed in wonder at the beauty of the real Pegasus as he descended from the sky.

He set down gently in front of her, and she could see the familiar crystal fire blazing in his eyes. She smiled up at him, and it seemed to her that he smiled back.

She wondered if she should say something, but he said something before she could get any words out. His mouth never opened, but she could hear the words as surely as he'd whispered them in her ear.

Looking down at her, his eyes filled with delight. "I want to be your friend, too." The soft-spoken words echoed in her mind. His voice was deep and rich, as beautiful to her as a symphony of music. She nodded. It was all she could do for the moment, she was so astounded. Then Pegasus looked up into the sky and she could hear him tell her, "I had best get you back now. Your friends are worried." She looked up at him in confusion for a moment and then he nodded down to her. "Be still and know, my precious one, that you can trust me." He nudged his nose against her hand reassuringly.

Selene felt her mouth fall open in slight surprise as though she wanted to say something but was unable to; she merely nodded at his words.

She remained unable to speak as she watched Pegasus fade away into the bright light, as her dreams once again came to close.

It was seconds later that Selene found herself in her bed, surrounded by worried looks. Her handmaidens were there, as well as a few doctors. Aura was not present, which surprised Selene until she caught a glimpse of the clock. It was well past noon.

"What happened?" she asked, looking up at Kadrianne's concerned glance.

"We were unable to wake you up this morning, Your Highness. I was concerned after you did not get up at your usual time this morning, but I did not call the doctor until I was unable to get you to wake up," she answered.

Chevée looked up at the princess, her large eyes still wary. "Your Highness, we were all unable to wake you up. It was almost like you were in a deep sleep for a while there. Are you feeling all right?"

Selene recalled the touch of Pegasus' nose against her hand once more and nodded. "I am feeling so recharged," she said. There was a burning in her heart that had not been there last night. "I am sure that I am better than okay, Doctors." She looked up at Kadrianne and smiled wearily. "It is true that I did not get to sleep well until late last night."

Kadrianne studied the princess' face for a moment and then slowly nodded. "Okay … Your Highness."

Yana came up beside Selene and bowed her head. "The King has summoned you, Your Highness. He wishes for you to come and see him as soon as you are ready."

Selene sat up and brushed her wayward hair away from her face. "All right then, Yana. Let's get moving, everyone. The King awaits."

***

321

THE MOONLGIHT PEGASUS

"I am so sorry, Your Highness," the guard in front of the King's Library said, "But His Majesty is not here at the moment. He had a meeting that ran over. He contacted me to assure that he would be along within the hour, and to ask that you await him in here."

Selene had come shortly after she had awakened, but upon her arrival, she regretted her rushing about to come and meet with her brother. Dorian had not exactly been waiting for her when she headed out to his library. In fact, he was not there at all; the guard had been waiting for her arrival, to tell her that the King would be late. She nodded to the guard, and asked, "May I wait for him in his library?"

The guard concurred. "Certainly, Your Highness." He had moved out of her way and let her in.

As Selene looked in his office and around the room, she sighed. It had been several minutes ago that the guard had left her alone inside the library, and now Selene found herself wandering around the rows and rows of books with no particular goal in mind.

"Somehow I'm not surprised that Dorian is late," she murmured to herself, slightly disappointed. Dorian loved her, but he was quite busy these days. Though he would want to take time for her, he may have been caught up in a meeting with the councilors or the generals, or even the peace seekers.

Selene looked around at the newly furbished walls; there were murals restored, and several tapestries that hung from decorative rods. Selene smirked at the center of the library; there was a large, relaxing section, with comfortable chair and exquisite furniture there, placed for the comfort of the reader,

THE MOONLGIHT PEGASUS

and the enjoyment of the eye. This was a place for study perhaps, but it was also a place for grandeur and finery to be displayed. Dorian certainly likes his precious toys, Selene thought as she studied a picturesque vase on a wooden table near the end of a bookcase. Looking up, she saw a preserved depiction of Crystallon painted on the ceiling amongst the arched windows. Light streamed in, illuminating the library in patterns of the window shapes.

Selene decided to walk around. She had been in Dorian's library before, but she had never seen the whole room; after all, it was huge. It was not open to the public, but it had to be the biggest collection of books Selene knew of.

She turned down a row of no particular importance, and walked slowly, stopping every now and then, reading some of the titles on the book spines. Some were strange, some were clearly outdated, and a couple were faded and well worn. Selene was about to move onto another row when a book caught her eye.

It was a dark shade of silver, and it looked as though it had not been touched in years. It looked like just another book, except for one very distinguishing characteristic—the spine of the book was blank; there was no title.

Curious, Selene reached up and pulled it down. She sensed that she had seen this book before, but she could not remember where. There was no title on the cover of the book, only a picture of wings. Gingerly, Selene opened the book to the first page inside and began to read out loud.

"There was a time, once long ago, when all dreams had been beautiful." Wait a minute, Selene thought. I have heard this before. It's the storybook that Dorian and I used to have read to us before we would go to bed when we were younger.

"There was a time, long ago, before the Guardian had dreamed of Sapphira, that the world of Dreams existed, powered by the Everlasting Life." Reading on, Selene smiled as she could almost recall the story word for word. She stopped after the next couple of lines and shut the book, carefully holding it in her hands. There had been a man, an older gentleman, who had treated her with a kindness back then, who had called her special, who had treated her like a father would treat his daughter. He was the one, Selene recalled, who had first told her the stories of the Guardian.

She was searching her mind for the memory of his name when the door to the library opened up, and she jumped at the unexpected intrusion. Still clutching the book in her arms, she made her way to see if it had been Dorian who had come into the Library or not. She peeked around the corner and saw that it was Dorian.

"Selene!" he called out in joy as he noticed her. He headed over to her with much enthusiasm in his step. As she came closer to him, his arms opened up and embraced her tightly.

"Dorian," Selene muttered as he squeezed the air out of her playfully. She did smile though, once he released her. He had not hugged her in a long while, she thought wistfully. She had missed it more than she'd realized.

"How are you, sister?" he asked as he stepped back from her. "Are you feeling better now that you are back in your home?"

"Yes, but I think for other reasons than just that," Selene admitted. She looked thoughtfully at him. "And you, my brother? Are you well?" He looked tired, Selene thought as she studied him. If it weren't for the impish grin on his face, he would look much older than thirty, she decided.

He nodded. "I know that it does not look it, but I am happy to be home here," Dorian said. "I have been making checks on my soldiers every so often these past few weeks and there are some that are so angry, some that are so weary, and some that have no hope for us. It's very hard to encourage those who do not seek encouragement."

"I'm sure that your presence alone does lift their spirits, in a way," Selene replied. "You are a true king, to be at battle with your followers, Dorian. The people admire that."

"Would you be a warrior princess then?" Dorian questioned. They started to walk in the library, heading for Dorian's study on the other side of the room.

Selene shrugged. "Maybe someday I will –" she broke off as she looked at him intently—"If I ever get the chance to get away from here."

Dorian rolled his eyes. "Wasn't three weeks enough?"

"It was only two."

"Oh, all right then. Wasn't two weeks enough for you?"

Selene looked up, her cheerfulness gone as her pain came rushing back to her. "The time I spent away, though it was away from here, was not free of the same burden I feel here."

"You will find that feeling everywhere, Selene," Dorian said gravely. "I know what you feel, believe it or not. I was once your age, with your dreams. I wanted to be free of all my burdens, my duty most of all. I grew used to the feeling of imprisonment, and it no longer plagues me. But the dreams of freedom elude me now, so that they are gone, except for a fragment of a memory from long ago."

His words were not condemning, nor were they trivial. Selene could see that Dorian was being honest with her, in a way that would be frowned on in the Council or the High Court. Her heart heard his words and felt sad for him, because that was where they differed; Selene believed that one day her dreams would come true, while Dorian had finished dreaming new dreams all together, finding only reality to fulfill his destiny.

"I feel sad for you," she admitted after a long pause.

"Why? Because I take life as it comes, not what I think it should be?" he asked, as they continued to walk together much as Selene had done earlier, through the halls of bookcases.

"No. Yes. Sort of." Selene sighed. "What I mean is, you can't stop believing that there's something bigger, something better out there, because of the trouble in life. Dreams fuel the passion for wanting to do good for the sake of everyone."

"Not always," Dorian interrupted.

Selene nodded. "When I say dreams, what I mean are dreams that are not ... corrupted by evil, I suppose."

"It is too hard to live to such pure standards," Dorian replied gently. "Especially when the whole world is counting on you to make the big decisions."

"Maybe the decisions you mean aren't so big, then," Selene remarked. "Maybe the biggest decisions a person can make are not about taxes or battle strategies, but what kind of person he wants to be, the person he can be."

Dorian sighed. "You are so idealistic, my sister, and this surprises me," he said. "But it is one thing to say something, and another to do something about it. And it's also another thing to expect everybody to go along with you. There will always be some who are unhappy."

"That may be true, but sinking down to their level will bring nothing good out at the end of the long run," Selene argued. "Dreams are one thing everyone has in common. Everyone dreams of something wonderful, something beautiful, I'm sure." She glanced over at him. "Do you remember, brother, when we were young, and that kind man used to read stories to us, about the Guardian of Dreams?"

Dorian stopped walking for a moment. His fingers clenched in a ball as he thought of that painful day so many years ago. "Yes," he admitted stonily.

"What was his name again?"

Dorian felt dryness in his throat as he answered her, saying, "Haiasi."

"Oh, yes, now I recall," Selene smiled. "He told us all about the Guardian and how Sapphira was created and all of that, remember?"

"Yes." It was the same curt yes as before.

"Well, Dorian, I remember that he told us once that there is nothing in life that was constant, and that only the Guardian's love and power remained the same, from day to day. Do you believe that?"

"Selene … I do not think that there is really a Guardian, okay?" His words silenced her and caused the smile to leave her face. "If there was a Guardian, who was in control of everything here on Sapphira, don't you think that this world would not be so full of fear, or of hopelessness? Wouldn't there by much more peace and prosperity, and life and laughter, not war and destruction, not evil and those who seek relentlessly after power?"

Selene could say nothing. She was still horrified that her brother was so pessimistic. Finally, she managed to get out, "Dorian … I know this world is not perfect, and as a king, you are exposed to all of the evils of it every day. There is no end, I would imagine, to all the problems that must be solved and to the people to deal with." She paused here, and thought of her dream last night. "But I do not think that it would be the Guardian's fault that people are so corrupt. If the people are lost, and in the darkness, it is because they have no love for the light, nor do they have the will to seek it. They have fallen, and are content to lie down and die."

Dorian looked over at her, thinking about what she was saying. "Then why does the world continue on with such a pitiful future? Why do we go on living in such a way if all we see is bleakness and woe?"

Selene met his eyes, her gaze sure. "Because those of us who find the strength to stand up again believe that there is hope, and it is worth getting back up for."

Dorian shook his head. "It is people like you, Selene, that the world needs more of."

"No," she shook her head. "It just needs people that will listen and have faith."

They were silent in the next few moments, before they arrived at Dorian's study. Walking inside, Selene sat down as Dorian headed behind his desk.

"Well, Selene, since you are feeling as good as you were expected to feel by now, you will be resuming your lessons with Master Omni tomorrow morning," Dorian said as he rummaged through his collection of papers and notes on his desk. "Ah, yes, here it is." He held up a piece of paper and read from it. The note said:

To Her Royal Highness, the Princess of Sapphira and Heir Apparent to the Throne of the World,

On the occasion of this strenuous time in history, I humbly write this message in hopes that the king will hasten you to study several of the courses listed below. I ask especially that you be on time for class, in the East tower classroom, at nine o'clock beginning tomorrow morning. Your handmaidens will escort you and I am instructed to allow them to study along with you, but not to help you, as I am currently living in the inner city area, and cannot be in the palace to teach you all the time. I humbly thank you and wish you the best of luck in your educational endeavors.

Your Servant and Teacher,
Master V. Omni

Below the signature were several subjects, including writing, history, mathematics, logic, and literature readings. Selene had to stifle a groan as Dorian read off the list. She had always dreaded doing her schoolwork.

"Is everything clear on that?" Dorian asked her, as he studied her profile carefully. He knew all too well about how Selene was reluctant to stay on schedule with her studies.

"It is fine, Dorian," Selene assured him. "But I am not looking forward to it, that's for sure. I wish I was old enough to pursue other interests I have."

"You can do that in your free time," he pointed out.

Selene looked down at her lap and saw that she still held the silver book. "Does that mean that I would be able to borrow a book from you if I asked, Dorian?"

He shrugged. "I don't see why not, sister, so long as I get it back."

"I'll take care of it," she promised. "I want to borrow this one." She held up the silver book and showed him. She wanted to see if he recognized it as she had, but he did not, so far as she could tell, because he waved her off a second later.

"That's fine," he said. "Take it if you want." He stood up from his chair and nodded to her. "You may go now, Selene. I have another meeting I have to prepare for, if you don't mind. I would like to get ready in the last few moments I have."

Selene nodded and started to leave when she suddenly thought of something. She turned around and pursed her lips, unsure if she dare ask him. When he looked up at her, she decided to voice her question.

"Dorian … do you think I would be allowed to go visit Etoileon in the Medical Ward every once in a while until he gets better?"

Dorian felt the old irritation with the boy come rushing back, but he knew that the twerp had saved Selene's life. So for a moment he just looked at his sister, with her hopeful expression. He moved to find a reason to reject her request, but she interrupted him before he could speak.

She looked up at him with a somber expression on her face and reminded him, "After all, it is my fault that he is there. He saved my life, Dorian, by laying down his own."

Dorian sighed, feeling defeat. "I suppose you are of age to start making decisions on your own," he reasoned. "But only once in a while, do you hear? I won't have you going to see him every blasted day. And you will not go if I hear that you are skipping your studies. In fact, why don't you wait until you have your studies started up regularly before you go? I think that would be best."

Selene felt her face break out into a large grin and she wanted to bounce with the happiness she felt. "Thank you so much, Dorian! I will go once in a while, as promised! Oh, thank you, thank you, thank you! Now I cannot wait to start my learning sessions up again!" she exclaimed joyously. Clutching her borrowed book to her chest, she nearly hopped out of his library.

Dorian couldn't help but smile at her childishness. She was a wonder all right, he thought. There was no getting past it. There was a sparkle in her that made him wonder if she was right about all that idealistic rubbish she'd told him earlier.

***

"Augh! Augh!" the screams of fury from the master of darkness could be heard into the distance as he tried to gain control of his anger.

He tried to calm down, but his frustration ate at him. Once again he had been thwarted by the power of that annoying Guardian. Grabbing a hold of a nearby rock, he flung in away in anger, causing the rock to hit the ground a long way off with a loud crunch! Obsidian felt no release of his irritation.

" What a little monster, that princess is!" he muttered spitefully, grabbing onto more rocks and slamming them together with enough force to shatter them both. "How dare she refuse me! How dare she! I will make her rue the day that she turned me down!" He looked around at the barren lands, covered in sand. "And it's all that Pegasus' fault that I'm stuck here in this wilderness!"

Obsidian had fled to the farthest reaches of the desert earth to hide. He had taken shelter in a rocky formation in the Great Desert of Sapphira, as he could no longer return to the starry prison he'd been kept in for these past millennia. The time had come when at last he had been let free from the Four-point prison, and he had hurriedly escaped. He knew that it was better that he be stuck here on the planet then in that endless hole once again. He began to pace around his rocky dwelling, trying to think of what to do.

He had tried to get the princess to choose a life of darkness, but he had failed to manipulate her in the right way. He needed to find a way to get her to see things his way. He walked around and around, his mind preying on the different things he could use against her.

She was the key, he knew. Obsidian also knew that if he could lay claim to her soul, the bridge between humankind and the Gates of Crystallon would be broken. The Guardian would be cut off, and that would be the end of it. He could rule freely over this desert world in darkness, eventually bringing the Dark Plague to all things, allowing a bleak silence to consume all that was bright and happy in this world. Obsidian could feel his mouth watering at such a notion. He hated man, and despised the Guardian who loved them with a great passion. He wanted nothing more than to see the world suffer for all eternity.

"Let me see, then," he murmured to himself, using his demonic magic to conjure up his crystal ball. "There is a war, and not just any war, but a civil war pitting the nations against the monarchy. That I can use."

He knew that the princess often suffered from loneliness. That he could use as well. He sat down on a chair he had called out from the depths of the planet's core. Looking into his crystal once again, he tuned into what the princess was doing for the moment. He looked to see that she had looked up from her studies to gaze out her window. Her focus seemed to be on one of the castle towers, the one that raised above all the rest. All of a sudden, it came to memory that she had great feelings for one besides the Pegasus ... that boy, the first son of the rebel Ammos, who was trapped in a coma in Silverton City. Obsidian sneered at his discovery; what a plan it would be, to pit the princess between her two great loves—the human or the spirit, the boy or the horse.

He leaned back and relaxed, taking the time to laugh cruelly. "That is it!" he exclaimed with renewed enthusiasm. "The princess will be torn in two … it is perfect. Her love for that young man will be her greatest undoing yet. Love is such a weakness. Humans are so stupid … they do not realize that the more they love, the more they can be hurt in the end!" He laughed again, nearly doubling over with the force of such laughter.

***

Selene looked up from the book she read and sighed, just letting the words mull over in her mind. They were not hard to understand, but the style was very symbolistic and slightly confusing. Though the book was very interesting and made her want to continue reading it, she wasn't sure if any of it would be made clear to her or not.

Her room was silent; she had allowed her handmaidens a free day, and Aura was still being called on by her social cliques for the latest news about Selene's condition. Selene decided that she liked being alone in her room; somehow she felt that she was lonely, but she was not alone.

Turning her head, she looked out her room's windows and noticed the High Tower in the distance. Suddenly she missed Etoileon so much, there was a great pain in her heart and she ached with a longing to see him. She slumped over, putting her head down on her desk. Ever since that night in the Medical Ward that she'd heard the doctor tell the nurse that it would be unlikely if Etoileon would wake up again, Selene had been fearful that the doctor was right. She was heartbroken over his concussions, and she could do nothing to make herself feel better about the matter. She glanced once again at the High Tower, and realized that she did not want to go back there without her friend.

She sighed, and found her eyes were wet with tears. "Etoileon … " she murmured as she laid her head to rest in her arms once again as she let her tears go out silently. She felt her heart cry out in pain for his companionship, his company. She missed his smile, his laugh, his kindness.

She felt herself drifting off to sleep as her tears slowed. There was a numbing feeling in her body as she was whisked away to another world.

***

Selene opened her eyes to find herself on her little island of dreams once more. She was lying on the beach with the warmth of the sun tickling her cheeks, as though to wipe away the tearstains. She sat up slowly, looking around. Despite that evil man leaving her dream world, she couldn't completely shake off his words of Pegasus leaving her. Selene stood up and began to look around carefully. "Pegasus?" she called out.

A moment later, there were footsteps coming out from the forest, and her face broke out into a smile. "Pegasus!"

The horse almost seemed to smile back at her. The crystal flames of his eyes sparked with a playful cheeriness. "Selene."

Selene suddenly stopped in her tracks. "Wow! How did you know my name?" she asked. "I don't think I ever told you before." She was a little scared all of a sudden.

Again, the creature seemed to smile. "My friend, I have known you for years," he said. His mouth never moved, but his voice was clearly heard. It called to her above the wind and the water, rang in her heart and in her thoughts. "I have been with you since you were conceived, and I had known you long before. It is the same with all my precious ones."

Selene walked cautiously up to him. "Who are you?"

"Who do you say I am?" he asked her softly. When she could not answer him, he nudged her hand with his nose. He then turned and took a step toward the beach. "Come, follow me," he invited.

"But I have so much to ask you," Selene stammered. "There is so much I am confused about. Why are you here? What is it that you do? Where did you come from? How is it that you know me, and knew of me so long ago? Is this really real?"

He shook his head slightly. "I cannot tell you all the things you wish to know, dear one. I must ask that you trust me on certain things."

"Will you give me the answers to some of my questions?" Selene pressed.

He smiled patiently. "With time, you will see all that you need to know. With faith, you will understand all that you need to know."

She did not hesitate to follow him after that. His words held no note of falseness, only of the truth. Selene picked up her skirts and caught up to him as he walked. She could not take her eyes off of him, she was so entranced by his beauty.

He turned towards her as he walked. "This is a lovely dream," he said.

Selene was a bit surprised. "Thank you … but I thought that it was you who made it beautiful, not me."

"All of the humans on this world have a choice in such matters," he told her. When she just looked puzzled, he went on and said, "There are some who try to read the mind of the Creator, and say, 'Surely a man is destined to be either good or bad,' and think that no matter how good or bad he is, he will hold true to his fate. But I tell you, all have been given the free will to choose. Though the outcome may be known, the path of fate is not one of a simple journey to an end place. It is one of discovery."

"What do they discover?" Selene asked.

"Each one will discover his own darkness," Pegasus replied. "But it is then that the decision of their fate is before their feet. Will they turn away from their inner darkness? Will they embrace it? Or will they choose to get rid of it?" He looked up. "Only the Guardian knows the fate of each one; but it is not his will that any should choose the darkness over the light."

"Why?"

Pegasus looked down at her. "The Guardian's most precious dream is Sapphira, Selene. As his most precious dream, he wants the people he created to love him as much as he loves them. He is their Father. For their own safety, not to mention their own good, he also wants them to listen for his direction. He can see the trouble ahead and does not want us to fall under its shadow. He wants to protect them. But if they do not want him to protect them, if they want to go out on their own strength, then the Father has chosen not to intervene."

"Why not?" Selene asked. "The advisors at the castle intervene all the time to prevent bed decisions being made."

"A father must let his children choose their paths freely. If he controlled them, and made them love him back, how empty would their love seem?"

Selene thought about it, and suddenly she understood. "Pretty empty, I would say," she said softly.

"Love is willing to wait, Selene," Pegasus explained. "It takes time for a relationship to grow. In the same way, the seeds of a flower are planted, but only with the proper nutrients can it flourish."

"But in the end, the gardener would rejoice?" Selene asked.

"Yes," Pegasus nodded, smiling kindly down at her. "Nothing worth having is ever easy. That is why Sapphira's people have been given the free choice. It is not a decision that is always easy to make."

Selene nodded, thinking of Dorian. "Do you believe in the Guardian then?" she asked.

Pegasus smiled, his eyes twinkling strangely. "Yes, I do. It is on him that I cast my faith, my trust, and even my life. I tell you the truth, whoever does not believe in him and his great love, or have faith in the Prince, shall never see the Great Light of Crystallon."

Selene bit her lip. "I want to believe in such a love," she said quietly. "But how do I know if I am even lovable? Do I even deserve his love?"

"Dear child, I told you it was not his will that any should die in darkness," her friend responded. "He loves you, and wants to be there to help you through all things. He has given you many gifts, has he not? He has formed you to be original and unique among all that he has created. If his love has made you, then you are capable of loving him back."

"But I am not perfect," Selene insisted. "I'm not very nice all the time, and I do not always tell the truth, and I have doubts about some things, and all these other things." She looked up at him and sighed. "I am sorry, Pegasus. No one has really told me of the Guardian since I was a little girl."

"Ah, yes," Pegasus nodded. "Haiasi was a good man, a very devout follower. He was filled with the truth."

"You know him?"

"Of course."

"Will you tell me how?"

"Not yet. Tell me what he taught you," Pegasus urged her. "I will listen."

Selene thought about it for a moment or two before she began. "Well, he told me that all the people on the world had been corrupted. He said that they all knew what the difference between good and evil was, but they choose evil over good many times and that the Guardian, though he loved them, could not dwell with both goodness and badness in their hearts." When Pegasus just nodded, she continued. "I read in that book I got from Dorian today that all who carried something called the Dark Plague and were evil must die apart from the Guardian."

"That is true," Pegasus nodded. "Every human since the birth of man has had the Dark Plague in his heart, passed on from the first infection."

"Then how can anyone ever hope to see Crystallon?" Selene asked. "Is there no way for the Guardian to overlook sin?"

"No. But there is a way to get rid of the Dark Plague. You have managed, all these years, Selene, to hold off the symptoms of it, because you believed in the power of good dreams, and though you may not realize it, you also believed that they were given to you by the Guardian. There was a conviction in your heart that most do not have, because you chose a long time ago to believe in those stories that your mentor shared with you."

"I did believe in them," Selene agreed. "They were beautiful dreams, and I was surrounded by loneliness. I think they saved me from being consumed by the darkness. But I know still have some in me." She thought of Etoileon, and the guilt in her heart over his injuries, the war, and Dorian's disregard of a higher authority. In a way, she felt that her actions, or in some cases her inactions, had allowed the darkness of the world to get at those she cared for.

Pegasus stopped. "There is only way to get rid of darkness completely. The Pure Light will absorb it, kill it, gather it, and lock it away from the world … but for such a gift, the world has its own price to pay."

"Price?"

"Yes. There is something that humans must give to the Guardian for his gift of redemption."

"What is it? Is it very expensive?"

"It cannot be purchased, but it is more priceless than all human wealth," Pegasus told her. "It must be freely given."

"Not our free will though, right?"

"No. The Guardian has promised never to interfere with that, and he has never gone back on his word, nor shall he ever. At first it is a simple gift, but it will be hard for some."

"What is it?"

Pegasus looked over at her, and Selene began to feel the familiar sensation of waking up begin to stir around her. As her dream faded away in the shimmering display of light, Selene could hear his whispered response.

"The faith that grows from love."

And with that, Selene felt her dream fall away from her and the human world settle around her once more.

***

She woke up to Cyerra standing over her, shaking her shoulder slightly. "Princess?" Cyerra asked quietly. "Are you well?"

Selene straightened up at her desk. "Yes," she said, shaking the remnant of her nap away from her face. "I'm … quite fine, actually. I guess I was just tired, that's all."

"You do need your rest for tomorrow," Cyerra agreed. "I walked by Master Omni's schoolroom and heard him getting things all prepared for you. He seems to be a likable instructor."

"He is, most of the time," Selene agreed. But then she yawned. "But his lessons are rather dull some days. Still, he has been a wonderful teacher, and I have learned much from him."

Cyerra nodded, and then replied, "I came to let you know that all of your handmaidens are back on duty, Highness."

"Selene, please, Cyerra."

"Oh, right … sorry."

"That's quite alright," Selene brushed it aside. "But I like to be called Selene by my friends, that's all."

Cyerra smiled brightly. "Thank you, Selene." She broke into a grin at the thought of being a friend of the princess. "Did you have a nice nap? It couldn't have been too comfortable sitting at your desk there."

"Huh? Oh … Well, it was a good nap," Selene said cheerfully. "I definitely feel refreshed. I think … I think I would like to go and take a walk in the gardens before dinner tonight."

"Okay. If Aura comes by, I will tell her that you'll be back to dress for dinner in a couple of hours, right?"

Selene cocked her head thoughtfully. "Why don't you come with me, instead, Cyerra? I can't imagine that you'd like to defend me to Aura anyway."

"If you want, sure," Cyerra agreed. She smiled again. "That sounds much more preferable to getting the heat from Aura, yes." They both giggled over that while Selene grabbed her cloak.

A few moments later, they were walking in the Courtyard Garden Hall on the main stone path. Selene and Cyerra chatted for a few moments of the beauty of the place and how glad they were that the reconstruction workers had been able to fix it up without harming any of the flowers. After a brief period of silence, Selene looked over at Cyerra and asked, "Cyerra, what was it like to grow up in the city? Was it nice?"

"You mean what was it like to grow up outside of the palace?" Cyerra asked, a little startled at the unusual question.

"Kind of, yes. I have not been outside the palace much. Certainly not enough to know what it is like to live there. Would you tell me?"

So Cyerra complied and told Selene about her aunt, and the shop that they ran. "It's just a little shop," Cyerra said, "But it's quite charming. I help decorate it. It's funny, but I actually miss it sometimes. The palace is nice, don't get me wrong, but I think one has to be born here to feel at home here."

Selene nodded. "Maybe. I don't really feel at home here right now."

"I'm sure it's just because of all the walls and windows that are still being worked on," Cyerra assured her.

Selene nodded. "I hope you're right. But I think something else is missing, too. It's more than that, but it's too hard to explain." I don't feel as trapped here as I did before, she realized. There was always something confining about being here, but now it doesn't feel so ... hopeless, I guess, to be free, she thought.

Cyerra studied her for a moment, trying to decide whether or not to bring up Etoileon. She had heard the news that he was still showing no signs of improvement, as usual. But before she could mention him or anything else, Selene spoke up.

"Cyerra, tell me," Selene implored, "Do you think your brother will call off the war anytime soon?"

Cyerra shrugged. "I guess I don't really know him as well as I thought I did," she remarked. "I wouldn't have guessed in a million years that he would grow up so cold and so prone to take revenge. I suppose that deep down, I may only ever remember him as Auntie's little helper. It certainly is a better choice over leader of the rebels."

Selene sensed Cyerra's heart was full of pain, just as Selene felt for Etoileon. Somehow both of them had lost someone that they deeply cared for. "I'm sorry," she said. "I shouldn't have brought it up."

Cyerra nodded. "It's fine. It's actually rather nice talking with you, you know. I wish more of the monarchs were like you, Selene."

Selene shook her head. "I don't think I would make a great Queen. I would happily resign my title, if only Dorian had a family. But he tells me that he likes it, being just the two of us. He says that he doesn't want a wife under the conditions like our father's. I don't blame him, in many ways," Selene admitted. "People around here still won't talk about my mother to me."

"It is good that they don't," Cyerra told her. "Let your mother remain in your heart as you recall her, and if you can't, then her memory needn't be tarnished by the hurtful gossip that plagues this society. I'll have you know, princess, that not one Lord or Lady in court would stand the idea of her not giving us you."

"That may be," Selene responded. "But –"

"No buts about it," Cyerra interrupted her. "People here love you."

"Only for the prophecy."

"No, no … surely not. There are so many good things about you. There is so much good in you," Cyerra insisted.

Selene hung her head slightly as she recalled Pegasus' words about the Dark Plague. Every human had it, he had told her. "Please. Do not say such things. For while I may have good intentions, I am not so good. I know where I stand, and I know where I want to be. That is all."

***

"Pegasus," Selene asked as she turned to face him, "What do you do while I am awake?"

Selene was back in the world of her dreams, and talking once more with her new friend. She loved that he was there for her, waiting for her to come back to him, but she couldn't help but wonder what he did all the time she wasn't there.

"This is a good place to be," Pegasus answered. "It is not so boring as it would appear to a human."

"Really? You're just here all the time?"

"Selene … I am not a human. I am from the dream world, the Spirit. I can be many places at once. And besides," he smiled at her, "When you are awake in the human realm, you cannot, with those darkened eyes, see any of the dream world."

"So you can actually see me all the time?" Selene asked.

"What do you think?" he asked her. The glimmer in his eye suddenly made her feel very afraid. I wonder if that means he knows all my thoughts, too, she wondered silently.

THE MOONLGIHT PEGASUS

"Since the day that you invited me in, Selene, there has been power set into motion, working to create new beginnings in you," he told her.

"I don't remember inviting you in," she said.

"But I do," he replied. "It was the day that you were in your room, and you prayed aloud for someone to help you. I was the one who was sent from the one above to comfort you, and give you peace."

"I only had to ask for it?"

"Yes. And you did. And then you believed."

Selene nodded. "I remember now. Later on that day I had my first fight with … a friend of mine."

Pegasus pulled off the path and beckoned her to follow him. She did so, but she was not sure where they were going or why. She continued with her story though, as he remained in expected silence.

"I was not very nice to him. It was then that I learned that trying to control people that I cared for by being assertive and commanding was not the way to keep their friendship."

Pegasus' eyes glittered. "An important lesson to remember," he agreed. For a moment Selene just looked at him, and then they both laughed.

It is so strange, Selene thought as she still laughed, that this was a spirit sent from the world of dreams, and here he

THE MOONLGIHT PEGASUS

is, listening to my problems, laughing with me, acting so … so human.

"The next morning I went to find him and apologize," she finished. "Even though I did apologize, I felt awful that later on, during the attack on the palace, he got hurt. Really bad, too." Her eyes lowered. She put her hand on her heart, aching for him. "I'm not even sure that he'll wake up again. I would give so much if he would just be okay." Two small teardrops fell to the ground.

She did not move, but she did not hear any movement as Pegasus encased her in his wings. His wings spread out to full wingspan, and then folded her up in their broad warmth. She felt him draw her close to his heart in a tranquil, though untraditional, hug.

"There is no human on this world that can know the future," Pegasus whispered down at her. "My precious one, it is important to keep your faith in such trying times. I can only assure you that all things work together for the glory of the Highest. If you long for his will to be, then you shall not be disappointed at the end."

Selene nodded into his warm chest, her arms relaxing against him. It had been a long time since anyone had held her with such reassurance of love. Even her brother's hugs grew short and full of habit, to the point where he rarely gave her any at all.

"Let not your heart trouble you," he said. "For I have come, and I will help you bear this pain."

"Pegasus … " Selene looked up at his face and gave him a tiny smile. "Thank you."

***

The next day, it was raining again. The monsoons were close to being over for Diamond City. They started nearly every year with the coming of the Moonbeam Festival celebration, and lasted for about a month and a half. It was the first time most could remember that the city was almost clear of people, both travelers and even people who had lived there were moving out, more and more by the day.

Selene was partially disappointed that the season's rain was nearly over, because she always loved seeing the sky's water feeding a renewed sense of life into the city's renowned gardens and plants. She had been away for the beginning of the season, when it always rained hard for several days in a row. She'd been in Silverton then, where there was little to see in the sky but skyscrapers. However, she was glad that the rains were slowly coming to a stop. Dorian had promised her, after she got back on her studies, she could go to see Etoileon on a clear day. So she was hoping for not too much rain.

She was also hoping that Master Omni would go easy on her, trying to understand the situation Selene found herself dealing with. But as soon as Selene waltzed back into the Palace schoolroom, she knew that Master Omni was not going to feel too sympathetic towards her.

"Your Highness is late," Master Omni scolded. He looked down his long nose at her and frowned.

"I'm sorry," Selene responded at once. She had been busy this morning, rummaging around to find all the books she was supposed to bring. In addition, she had brought along the silver bedtime book, because she had been meaning to read more of it of late. "I had to sidestep a few passageways because of the repairs on the palace," she explained further as he continued to look at her in his unpleasant way. She feared that he would go on about her lack of discipline in punctuality, but he looked back down at his papers and waved at her to sit down.

Selene sat at her usual desk, front and center to the room. When Etoileon had come with her before, he had been allowed to sit down as well. Since it was only going to be Selene and her handmaidens, the extra desks for her ladies in waiting had been moved the respectful distance away. She pulled out her notes and her extra data sheet, hoping that he was going to go easy for the first day.

It turned out the Selene was tuned out by his second lecture.

She had tried to pay attention during the mathematics speech, but her mind just would not remain still. She thought about several things (mostly food) until her thoughts centered on Pegasus.

She missed him already, she realized. How she longed to take a nap and see him. He was becoming so important to her so quickly. She suddenly remembered Obsidian's warning about Pegasus leaving her without telling her. Was it true? She wondered. How could it possibly be true? There remained some doubt about that, but she didn't think it was anything to worry about. She was sure that if Pegasus did leave, he would tell her why. That was, if he left her at all. Selene, for her part, did not see any reason that would get in the way of her seeing him again.

THE MOONLGIHT PEGASUS

She loved him. There was no mistaking it, the feelings in her that were produced when she thought of him. He was so gorgeous, she thought, such a striking white coat, and his enchanting wings! And his wisdom! Such profoundness she had never heard before with such simplicity. His voice, his eyes, his gentle expressions and his sincerity … she loved all these things about him, but most of all she loved his voice. It caused a sense of peace in her, one of comfort, even when she did not want to be comforted.

Selene had to admit that she'd never felt such a connection before in all of her life. Not with her brother, nor any of her handmaidens. Certainly not her parents, or Aura. Not even Etoileon's friendship or her secret feelings toward him caused this same rapture of the soul. She felt so much more of herself, yet less of herself; she felt like she could love herself more, yet she hated more of herself as well. Though the feelings in her were complimentary in a positive and negative way, both sides could be true. Such a change he had brought upon her, in such a short time. Such things can only be described as miraculous.

As she thought about his messages to her, she began to scribble down on her datasheet her thoughts and tried to start a poem about it, she was so inspired. As she sat there thinking, she barely noticed that her handmaidens had arrived silently and Master Omni had begun asking questions.

Suddenly Master Omni's voice sliced through her reverie. "Your Highness, can you tell me what the basic theorem helps one to accomplish?" Selene felt her face flush red and her head jerk up to look at the teacher once more.

"Uh … well," she started to say something and then gave up. "Um … what was the question again?" she asked.

Master Omni was clearly irked by her question. "Your Highness, if you cannot pay full attention to me while I am attempting to teach you in the necessary ways that you will need to know someday in order to be an enlightened monarch, you will fail to prove capable in the eyes of the court and the general public."

She looked back down at her datasheet and mumbled, "Sorry."

"Sorry is not going to allow your shortcomings to be overlooked by your subjects, Highness," Master Omni scolded, his words stinging. "Now, I will explain this once again. Basic theorem allows one to grasp the logical fact that in mathematics there is always a particular and individual answer as an outcome for a unique mathematical function."

Selene nodded, her brain already going blank as she tried to comprehend what her teacher was saying to the full extent. She sighed inwardly. *I wish things were as easy to understand as Pegasus explains them,* she thought. Although, she admitted silently, her friend had not told her everything about himself. She had enough sense to realize that he was not from this world, and he had told her that he had been sent to her from 'the one above'. *Did that mean the Guardian?* She couldn't be sure about that. And there were always the words of Obsidian to plague her mind. *I wonder,* she mused, *if knowing Pegasus is part of my destiny? Could he be the one who would bring peace to the world, through her?* she wondered. "I'll have to ask him," she muttered subconsciously.

"Ask who, Your Highness, about what?"

THE MOONLGIHT PEGASUS

Once again Selene found herself at the end of a cold stare from her teacher. She looked away, ashamed that she had once again allowed her mind to stray so easily. "I'm sorry, Master," she apologized once again. "I guess I'm still not quite ready to study about all this in light of the war and my recent injuries," she tried to excuse herself in a logical way.

Master Omni looked skeptically at her, and then frowned more. He was not satisfied with her answer. "Your Highness, I beg that you forgive me for this, but I can see no reason why you would not be able to perform what is expected of you. You are so far behind already in your teaching, and I can see for myself quite clearly that you have not so much as looked at the books I asked His Majesty the King to have you study beforehand. I am your teacher, and I am responsible for your education. I realize that the war going on would affect you somewhat, but that is all the more reason to study. It is through study that you will learn how to effectively deal with the problems of the world war at hand. It is also very important for you to have a sense of normalcy and of routine while the war is going on. That is the main desire of the King."

Dorian wants me to keep busy so I won't be a bother is what he means, more likely, she thought. "I pray that you will forgive me then, Master, as I fail to see what mathematics have to do with ending the war," Selene retorted. She was getting irked herself. "And furthermore, maybe if I felt I was learning something that would help the war end, I would not be so apt to not pay attention." She was angry with him for not caring, but she was also angry with herself for not trying as hard as she could have to stay on task.

Master Omni had never been shocked to the point of speechlessness before, and now was no exception as he sputtered out nonsensical sounds as his mind reeled in trying to get out a reply that would not be considered treasonous to the crown. "Your Highness," he finally managed, "Why don't we learn what is in front of us now, and see if it is so useless later? You might be surprised at how helpful some of this could be to you. And besides –" he nearly glared down at her as he finally recalled the most forceful mediator he could use in regards to the princess' behavior—"You know that Dorian will not allow you to go and see your little friend in Silverton if your behavior and your prudence in my classroom does not improve quickly."

Selene eyes shot up to meet his, and he knew that he had hit his mark. She lowered her eyes and reluctantly said, "Let us get on with the lesson, then."

"That's the spirit," Master Omni praised her. "Now, as I was saying, the basic theorem … "

Selene did not allow her mind to wander off as she took notes. Master Omni had proven to be a formidable opponent when it came to arguing. He had given her the correct motivation that she needed in order to place her daydreams aside.

***

Dorian sighed as he glanced out the window as it began to rain again. Though he longed to see the sunlight, he couldn't help but feel that the weather matched his mood. He stood up from his desk and began to pace, letting the progress of the war mull over in his mind.

His troops were gaining ground, and fighting off the enemy forces quite well on the land. But on the seas it was a different matter. Dorian had issued firmer training on the naval forces, but they were no match for those who were more familiar with the surrounding waters. Still, he had no doubt in his mind that taking down this Aemon character would be nothing too difficult. It was only luck that Aemon had managed to elude being captured by the royal armies.

He heard a knock at the door and looked up, surprised to see a familiar face poking through his doorway. It was one of Selene's handmaidens, the one he had met with before. Instantly, he put his worries behind him and replaced the look of quiet contemplation on his face with one of happy surprise. "Lady Yana," he greeted her. "Do come in, if you wish."

"Your Majesty," she acknowledged, bowing low before him. When she looked up at him, she said, "I have come to tell you of the princess' progress."

"Oh, I see," Dorian said. "Well, tell me then, how is my dear sister?"

Yana perceived a bit of a smirk on his face as he bid her to inform him. Yana gave him a small smile before saying, "She is sleeping almost all her free time."

"Good, good," the king said, sitting down at his desk. "Her doctor told me that she should rest up as much as possible."

Yana hesitated before asking, "Is Your Majesty quite sure that she is supposed to be sleeping as much as she is? Lady Aura is quite concerned about her."

"Well, that would be something new for Aura, I'm sure," Dorian said playfully, "But Selene is considered an adult, now that she is of age to be married. I'm sure that she is capable of taking command of all her senses."

Yana slowly nodded. "Yes, Your Majesty." She paused here, and Dorian motioned to her to continue her reports. "Her Highness is actively pursuing her studies with an unusual enthusiasm, but her color and her vital signs have all been checked out with the on call medical staff here, and they informed us that she is normal in all areas."

"That is wonderful then," Dorian nodded. "I was worried that she would not be doing as well as she really was. Selene is quite strong, but I know that she can be frail at times. She is so careful not to draw worry to her, showing an illusion of strength to her public."

"She certainly has enough excuses," Yana agreed.

"Well, that is good enough to hear for now." Dorian stood up and nodded to her. "Thank you, Lady Yana. Might I say that you are a gift to have around here? I would not be half as glad to hear of my sister's recovery if it was from anyone other than you."

Yana blushed. "Thank you, Your Majesty." She bowed and turned to leave, but before she walked out the door, Dorian called out to her.

"Lady Yana!" He came around from his desk and took a couple hurried steps up closer to her.

"Yes?" She turned around to face him. "What is it, Your Majesty?"

"Uh … well, that is … I will need to watch over Selene's progress over the course of this period of war," he said thoughtfully. "I do not want to have her affected by the fighting."

"I understand that, Sire," Yana agreed. "As one who is also participating in Master Omni's classes, I can relate to how hard it is to stay on track with new information coming into the castle every day."

"Yes, well, I was thinking that it would be a good idea then, for me to assign a … a reporter of some kind. What I mean to say then, Lady Yana, is that I would like it if you would inform me of how she is doing in her subjects and tell me of any other problems and such that she may be having."

"You mean, like a spy?" Yana frowned. "Your Majesty, I could not."

"No, it's not like that," Dorian tried to reassure her. "I just want to know —"

"What she is doing, how she is doing it, and so forth?"

"No. Yes. Sort of. Not in the interest of spying on her for my own benefit, if that's what you are wondering. But I mean in the interest of her education, her surroundings, and for the future of our people. You would not want her to rule the people with an unsatisfactory education, would you?"

"No, but I still think that if maybe you would just talk to the princess herself, there would be no need for that kind of surveillance," Yana argued. "Have dinner with her, keep her close at your side. Act like her brother, for goodness sake.

You cannot talk of war when you are with her anyway. Why not ask about how she is doing?"

"She will not always tell me!" Dorian exclaimed in frustration. "I cannot keep constant tabs on her the way you can."

"Do not ask me to do such a thing without her knowing, then," Yana asked. "I will do what my Lady asks of me, but I will not allow her to be subjected to unfair demands, Your Majesty … even if they are from you." Her eyes cast low, her head bowed in reverence. "Excuse me." And then she exited the room.

Dorian waited until her footsteps disappeared down the hall to walk behind his desk and sit down. His mind stirred over how he had let her get the better of him in that argument. He couldn't help but smirk. Though Lady Yana was quite pretty, she sure could be maddening. Dorian would not have thought that she would ever fight with him until today's conversation.

"Well, Selene sure has a loyal crew," he muttered bitterly as Yana's parting words mulled over in his mind again and again. "I will have to speak with her about such a subject then." He looked at the water clock and saw that it was almost time for him to go inspect the Fighters training sessions. "Perhaps later," he decided. Reaching down in his bottom desk drawer, he pulled out a decanter of moonshine and took a long drink. The luminescent liquid burned on its way down, refreshing him. "I must go now."

He did not notice that the rain outside had begun to fall harder down on the sandy earth.

***

Ronal had not heard that the king was coming to watch them that day. It was as he came into the training room that several of his friends and colleagues all came rushing up to him, eager to share the rumors and information.

"Hey, Ronal," a younger boy, whose name was Austen, called out to him. "Did you hear the news?"

"What news?" Ronal asked, picking up his training uniform and grabbing a hold on some of his fighting equipment.

Austen's young face was lit up with nervous excitement as he came over with a few of his friends in tow. "The king is coming today, to oversee our work." A nervous laugh escaped him as he tried to appear levelheaded. "Word has it that he's thinking of sending us overseas or into battle soon."

"I doubt it," Ronal retorted, nearing laughing himself. "Fighters like us don't usually leave the city, even during war. My uncle was a Fighter during the Rebellion years ago. He and all the others were stationed in the city as a last line of defense."

"That may be true," another kid piped up, "But that was when there wasn't so much technology available to the public. If Diamond City becomes a target, we could all be killed and that would leave the monarchy open to threats."

"Oh, come on," one more voice interjected. "We had Fighter pilots and skyfighters back then, too. Surely no one would be that thick to attack here again."

Austen turned to face his friends behind him and said, "I'll bet they're thinking that if we go off into battle, the war would be over much sooner, since with all our advanced training and stuff we could easily kill any of our enemies."

Ronal rolled his eyes and turned his attention away from the argument as he got ready for class. He secretly hoped that they would not leave the city, if only just because he did not want Cyerra to be worried about him. She was worried enough about the princess and her brother. Tightening his knuckle guards, he set his jaw determinedly. He did not want to go, but if he had to, he would stop at nothing to destroy the adversaries that got in his way. Being a Fighter meant that it was his duty to protect the crown and all the good it stood for. And so he would.

It was not too much longer before Master Norio called all the students to line up before practice. The king sauntered into the room in regal armor, his faction of guards positioned around him, all in matching suit.

Ronal could feel nearly every Fighter straighten and assume the proper posture. A small grin flickered on his face. There was no slacking off for today, that was for sure.

Master Norio made the announcements, calling the students entrusted to his training to acknowledge the sovereignty of the King. At once, all of the nearly two hundred students bowed respectfully.

"Arise," Dorian instructed. When all eyes had turned to face him, he put on his most solemn face and continued. "Your Master Norio has kindly allowed me to take over your class for today. I am not going to be teaching you anything, but I will want to see what you have learned. I have decided, along with the approval of the Council of Judges, that there will be several legions of Fighters deployed throughout the world."

There was a wave of murmurs in the crowd at his words, but Dorian did not allow it to affect him. He raised his voice slightly and said further, "The younger ones who are still in training will not be leaving the palace, not for quite some time yet. The war has only just started, merely a month ago. The rainy season has come, and we are all suffering in some way. Already there is much causality on both sides. But there is a price to pay for peace and we all know it. There is a price for freedom, and we all know that as well. Men, understand that I ask of you something that I have no right to ask. The decision to go or to stay rests entirely on your hearts. The cost is great, but the reward is greater."

Dorian looked around the room and said, "Who would like to be tested first?"

One by one the rows of boys all looked at each other. No one seemed to know what to do; the shock of their eventual departure seemed to have rattled them all. Fighters had not been sent out of the city since the Great Wars of the Ancient Days.

Dorian asked again, "Who would be the first to be tested?"

Ronal stepped forward. "I will, Your Majesty," he said. Ronal did not feel as brave as he sounded. But he knew that his fellow students needed someone else to take the first step in this case. Ronal also knew that if Etoileon had been present, he would have stepped forward without a second thought.

Dorian walked over to him and looked at him. The room was silent. No one dared breath loudly or speak a word as the king looked down at his willing servant. "I've seen you before," the king said softly. "You were a friend of that brat who guarded Selene."

Ronal nodded. "I am a friend of his, yes."

"You were also the one who informed Selene of the Jewel Island Representative's plot to marry her to gain the throne, despite any orders to be silent."

"Yes, I was." Ronal could feel a bit of anxiety rise up in his stomach. He had made a bad reputation for himself in King Dorian's eyes, no doubt. When the king made no immediate reply, Ronal began to wonder if he had made the right choice in speaking up. Suddenly he heard the unsheathing of a sword, and dared to peek up at the king's face. He was surprised to see an expression of thoughtful delight looking down at him.

Dorian had pulled out his sword, and gently touched it to Ronal's right shoulder, and then to his left shoulder. "I dub you, then, Courageous Knight of Sapphira. May you fight with strength and honor in your battles, and triumph in your deeds of mercy. Arise."

Ronal felt the shock hit him full force. He couldn't stop himself from blurting out, "You're making me a Knight?" It was considered one of the highest honors a Fighter could earn. Only rarely was it done before a Fighter was thirty years of age.

Dorian nodded. "It takes a special kind of bravery to stand up for what you believe is right," he said, "Especially when your peers are content to say nothing." Dorian gestured toward the crowd behind Ronal and explained, "Out of all these men, you were the first to step forth. And yet you are an unlikely candidate for such a task, considering we have not always been of the same opinion. Your loyalty lies with justice, not with me … and that I can respect, since my loyalty is to justice as well; although I have strayed more than once, I will admit."

"Thank you," Ronal said, bowing. "I am very grateful." He looked back up at King Dorian and said, "However, Your Majesty, I feel compelled to tell you that I was not the first to stand up."

"Oh really?" Dorian chuckled softly. "Then who was?"

"The first was your servant, the Fighter Etoileon, Sire. His gift of protection to Her Highness is far more deserving of Knighthood than mine," Ronal told him, humbly looking away.

Dorian stood still for a moment before he said, "You have much to do, Knight. Go do it."

"Yes, Your Majesty."

Dorian watched as his new Knight walked out of the room with one of his royal guards before turning and facing the rest of the room. Suddenly, another boy stepped forward. "Your Majesty?" his small hand went up in the air, and his cracking voice caught the attention of the occupants of the room. When the king turned and faced him, the boy nervously bowed and said, "I will go! Send me!"

One by one, more voices began calling out to be sent. The king smiled at their eagerness before he took a step back from them, saying, "There will be much tribulation in your path, should you choose this destiny. It is not one for the faint of heart, but for the heart of faith. You believe there is a chance for a better world than this one. This you must do, because looking at the here and now, you will only see trouble. But look to the future, my people, my Fighters. You will see much more than what I can promise awaiting you and your loved ones there, should you all choose to stand against your enemies for the time being."

The room filled with cheers. Dorian looked at it, and thought that it looked like these young men had hope at last.

***

It was a week later that all the official military reports came out. The Fighters who volunteered to go abroad had been selected, assigned, and prepared for departure within the next few days.

Selene had remained unaware of all that was going on. She had spent all her free moments in the last week studying, reading, or taking naps. She had even skipped a few meals here and there, in order to be able to convince Dorian that she was caught up enough in her studies to be able to go and see Etoileon over the weekend.

She had been told that several of his internal bruises were apparently healed, but there were still problems. He never made a sound at all in his unconsciousness, but his vital signs remained steady. The doctors were stumped as to what was keeping him from waking up, but they thought it had something to do with a psychological problem. When Selene asked what that could possibly mean, the informant had shook his head and replied, "Any number of things, I'm sure."

Sitting on the floor by her bed now, she sighed. There was a dullness in her spirit as she thought once again that it was all her fault for his present condition. She could not think of much else. It was only her time with Pegasus that she truly felt any joy at all these days. Her studies distracted her, and all of her companions were concerned with the developments of the wartime activity. Selene became so depressed over hearing of the losses and all the troubles the army was having in the seas that she tuned it out, trying to think of more pleasant things.

She found herself remembering the good times with Etoileon and Pegasus, and the times with Dorian when he had not been so grown up. She recalled some memories with Aura even, when the woman had not been so concerned with trying to be regarded as a true Lady of the Court. Selene also thought of the countless sunsets and sunrises she had been in awe of, the different palettes of color that were painted on the sky each day and night. She recalled the Lunar Storms of the years gone by, and the special night of the lunar rainbow when she and Etoileon had first become friends. All her good dreams came forth too, as though to guard her heart against feeling the dark pain of her world.

She was thinking of going to see if the kitchens were still open for a bit of hot chocolate, but it was then that the door to her room opened and Cyerra came rushing into the room. Selene peeked over the top of her covers to see that Cyerra had teardrops falling down her cheeks.

Cyerra tried to brush away the tears, but she just stopped and cried into her hands. Selene hesitated before speaking up.

"Cyerra?"

The handmaiden sniffled and tried harder to compose herself. "My Lady?" she asked. She had not noticed when she'd come into the room that there was someone else in there.

"Over here," Selene spoke up as she got up from her bedroom floor. "Are you all right?"

"Yes," Cyerra said, her voice heavy with sorrow. "I'm so sorry, princess," she blubbered. "I'm afraid that I've just received bad news."

"What's wrong? What is it?" Selene walked over to her and offered her a handkerchief. "Surely we can do something to help you out."

"No, it's not about me. Or at least, not directly. I just got word from Ronal that he is going to be sent to the north of the Continent for battle. It's official this time, too, so it will be done." Cyerra looked up sadly. "Before it was just a rumor, a possibility. Now … " she laid her hands palm up on her lap as she crouched down where she stood, unable to stand.

"A battle? In the north?" Selene asked. "I had no idea that there was a battle going on there. Oh, Cyerra, I'm so sorry."

"It's not your fault, princess," Cyerra sobbed. "It's just that … I worry for him so."

Selene nodded. "You must care for him greatly," she said slowly.

Cyerra looked up and nodded. "I'm sorry, Your Highness," she said. "I can't seem to help but cry. I love him."

Selene could tell that her words were sincere, and she nodded. Crouching down next to her handmaiden, she reached over and put her hand reassuringly on Cyerra's. When Cyerra nearly jumped in surprise, Selene caught her eyes and said, "Then you should not worry what I think. Go ahead and cry. I cannot hold it against you for such a reason as love."

Cyerra just stared at her for a moment and then nodded. "Thank you."

Selene gave her a tiny smile. "Do you want me to see if I can get Dorian to keep him here?"

"No," Cyerra shook her head. "Ronal was promoted to a Knight in the Fighter squadron. He can't stay here now. He is a leader of a legion of men. Telling him to stay would only dishonor and offend him."

"I see." Selene could think of nothing else that was possible. "We can only believe that he will know what to do when the time comes for him to fight," Selene said slowly. "And we must hope that he will be careful." When she finished talking, Cyerra lowered her head into her arms and cried. Selene placed a hand on her shoulder and said nothing more, just silently assuring Cyerra that she was there for her.

It did not take Cyerra long to compose herself entirely, but her eyes, Selene noticed, still held a sadness in them. They stood up, and Selene felt like she should try to make Cyerra feel better somehow. "Cyerra, why don't you go and stay with your aunt in the city for a few days? I'm sure that Dorian would allow you to if I ask him," she offered.

Sadly, Cyerra sighed. "Not at this time, if you don't mind, My Lady," she replied. "Ronal will leave at the end of next week. I would like as much time with him as I can get before he departs the city."

"Oh, I see … I'm sorry," Selene apologized. "There is nothing I can think of that would help you too much."

"Thank you anyway," Cyerra smiled at her kindly. "That is enough for me, that you would go to such trouble. But there is nothing to be done about it, and that's that I'm afraid." She frowned at her bitter words and then slumped over a bit.

Selene bit her lip in uncertainty. "I know how you feel," she said softly. "We do not have the exact same situation, but I know what it is like to have someone that you love away from you, outside of your reach."

Cyerra looked up and nodded. "Etoileon will get better one day, princess. I am sure of it."

Selene gave her a tiny smile. "Thank you, Cyerra, but please, call me Selene."

"It sounds as if we both could use some comfort," Cyerra remarked after a moment of silence. "If you don't mind,

Selene, I'd like to go to sleep now. I'm very drained and I can use the extra rest."

"Go ahead," Selene nodded. "Get some sleep. Take tomorrow off if you wish, even. Yana, Kadrianne, and the others can handle me for a day without you. In fact, I insist that you take the day off tomorrow. Spend some time with Ronal, between his training sessions."

Cyerra's eyes lit up briefly. "Really? That sounds wonderful." She bowed low and replied, "Thank you, Selene. I appreciate all that you do for me, so much."

Selene waved her off. "Go to bed, Cyerra. Things will look better after you've had some good rest. And I think the same goes for me. I think I will turn in early too."

"Good night, Selene," Cyerra said as she bid the princess farewell for the night.

"Sweet Dreams, Cyerra," Selene turned around to say goodnight, but Cyerra was already gone.

***

A short while later, Selene found herself once again surrounded by the comfort and peace of her Pegasus friend.

"You seem so sad lately," Pegasus said as he approached her.

"Yes, I have been sad," Selene admitted, a little uncomfortable at the thought of telling Pegasus why she was so glum. She looked down at that ground. "Today Cyerra, one of my handmaidens, found out that she was going to

THE MOONLGIHT PEGASUS

have to say goodbye to one that she loves. I tried to help her out, but I couldn't do anything for her. At least, not much."

"Selene, you are a good friend to her. I'm sure that knowing that much gives her much more comfort than can be expected."

The princess peeked up at him. "Couldn't you go and comfort her?" she asked. "You are a spirit who lives in the heart of dreams, right?"

Pegasus shook his head. "Though I have the power to do so, I can only knock on the door of her heart. She must decide to let me in or not, and must ask it of me. I would never refuse such a request, but they have to be the ones to ask for it."

Selene nodded and sighed. "I understand. Sometimes I wish that you could bypass that rule."

Pegasus gave a small chuckle. "Nothing worth having is easy, and it usually takes a lot of time to get it just the way it should be. Humans do not usually take to asking for help too easily; there are exceptions, of course, but the human race is a proud one. It is too humbling to ask for help in their eyes most of the time."

Selene nodded. "There are some things I don't like to ask for help with," she agreed. "I want to be able to know that I can do certain things on my own."

"There are things that we all must learn to be able to do on our own. But no one should feel so independent as to try to do everything or even most things on his own," Pegasus shook his head. "Doing things on our own, even for others, is a way that pride can corrupt our thinking. It is only when good is done when credit is taken. When something goes wrong, it is then that the credit becomes blame."

"Why is pride so dangerous?" Selene wondered out loud.

"Pride often leads to mistakes, and mistakes lead to shame and regret. Pride will take you away, and shame will keep you away. And regrets will haunt you."

Selene thought of how she had caused Etoileon to get hurt and shook her head, trying to disperse the image. "I can see you have a good point there."

"That is why it is best to learn from the mistakes of others," Pegasus said. "Humans do not always have such a luxury, however."

"That's sure the truth."

"Selene … if you have a problem, you know that I will help you, if you only ask for it."

Selene looked up to face Pegasus at his words. Was it possible that he wanted her to tell him about Etoileon? Was that safe to do? She swallowed hard and replied, "I know."

He just looked at her for a moment longer in silence, saying nothing, not even moving. Then his head nodded slowly and he said, "That is good to hear."

Selene stopped to sit down on her rock on the beach. Pegasus lay down on the sand beside her dangling feet, his wings folded back gracefully, as though he was there to guard her. The princess looked down at him and leaned back, sighing happily. "Pegasus … I'm so grateful that you came to help me. We're going to be friends forever, right?"

"Yes," he assured her. "We are."

"And you'll never leave me, right?"

Pegasus shook his head. "No, I will not leave you." Selene smiled, just starting to relax as Pegasus continued on, saying, "But the one who is coming through the Light, as I am here through you, will be the one that will make that promise to all people."

"What?" Selene sat back up and looked down at him. "Someone else is coming?"

"Yes."

"Who is it?" she asked. "One of your friends? Is it another Pegasus?"

Pegasus laughed and then turned his head to face her. "You will see Him, and you will know who He is. There will be no doubt in your heart as to who He is."

Selene blinked, unsure of what to make of that statement. Ultimately, she decided that she would just have to trust Pegasus' word on the matter. She did not fully comprehend what Pegasus was telling her, but she had to have faith that all would be revealed in due time.

***

Obsidian had begun to formulate his plan. His hands seemed to grow restless as they encircled his all-seeing orb, calling forth his demonic power to feed him the information he sought. Below his rocky throne, his servants were hard at work, digging out a larger chamber in the cave.

His makeshift home had grown dark and cave-like over the last days of his presence. There glowed an evil shadow around him, and his servants had come to his call. The Demon Chasers, as those who followed the Light called them, had come crawling to feed on the dark energy provided for them from Obsidian. He was their ruler, and they depended on him for satisfying their dark pleasures.

They worked day and night, tiring quickly but never ceasing, in their work to accommodate their master. Black fire roared up from the deep crevices of the tainted earth, and smoke filled much of the cave. The Demon chasers, spirits and humans alike, worked to carve out of the heavy earth a suitable place to reign.

Obsidian turned with great delight to his minion, Sulfas, who had led the Demon Chaser spirits. "I have broken free," he remarked scathingly, "from my celestial prison to find, that you, Lord Sulfas, have done well in gathering unto me all those who wish to be lost."

"It was only through your instruction I was able to do so," Sulfas bowed deeply as his shadowy outline hung in midair.

"Repeating my instructions to those humans seeking to contact the lost spirits was inspired," Obsidian praised. "Who is their leader?"

"A man, a piteous and foolhardy man named Emanon," Sulfas replied. "He is from Jewel Island."

"Ah … I see. A relative to that Ammos fellow, am I right?" It was not a question that Obsidian asked, but a statement of fact. When Sulfas nodded, his fangs still exposed, Obsidian sneered. "I hope that he listens better than his brother, then."

"I rather liked Ammos," Sulfas said, "But it is true that he was a lovesick fool. It was genius of you, Master, to have him kill himself."

"But he did not listen to my instructions as I told him," Obsidian scowled. "He was too much influenced by that woman of his. When she died, he killed himself. I told him to kill himself only after he had established a suitable successor. His son was only a small child then. He was of no use to me when Ammos died."

"It makes no matter about the boy, anyhow," Sulfas shrugged. "His twin brother and sister were born only a few months later. And the Guardian interfered with the boy and separated him from the rest of the troops. There was no way that you could take control of his mind."

Obsidian retaliated in a matter of seconds at Sulfas' unintentional insult. "Never reference that one again!" Obsidian shouted as his blow struck Sulfas squarely in his wispy smoke. Having power over the lost spirits, Obsidian's attack sent Sulfas splaying backwards, trying to steady himself. Now, at the receiving end of the dark master's anger, he cowered fearfully on the floor before his leader. Obsidian advanced, his voice crackling with an outburst of rage. "You dare to think that I am not as strong as Him!"

"Forgive me, Master," Sulfas begged, falling prostrate as his ghostly hands took hold of Obsidian's flowing black robes. "I did not know what I was saying."

Obsidian resumed his cordial position on his throne and waved the spirit away. "It makes no matter, Sulfas. I will not forget what you have done, but I will overlook it this time. Besides … you should know that I have other plans. And the time to enact them is approaching us."

"Yes, my master," Sulfas bowed low. "I thank you. I will put all my effort into putting your perfect will into place."

"Good. I need you then, to contact an old friend of mine."

"Who is it that you wish to reach, My Lord?"

Obsidian's grin was sinister as he glared maliciously into his crystal ball. "A woman I know, one who lives in Diamond City."

***

Chapter 10
Knowing Love and Guilt
***

Selene could hardly stand still. This day was the day that she was allowed to go and see Etoileon. She'd waited so long, it felt like ages had passed since she'd last seen him. Now, as she grabbed her cloak and headed out of her room, she was filled with a rush of emotions that she could not completely identify.

Dorian had consented that she be allowed to go, mostly because of her good behavior. He had arranged that she could go with only two of her handmaidens, Aura, and a set of guards. For Selene, it was too much. For a princess, however, it was considered barely enough.

As she watched Kadrianne and Rosaria climb into the transport vehicle, Selene looked back up to the palace. It was a rare sight for her to see, the picture of her home. While she lived there, she could never recall just how it looked to the outsider. From her vantage point, she could see the granite walls off the outer keep, and most of the higher walls of the inner palace. Rising high above it all was the High Tower, superficially unscathed and recently polished. While the palace exclaimed a picture of warmth and comfort to those on the outside of its walls, but Selene knew how much of a prison it could be.

"Princess?"

Selene turned around and saw Kadrianne was looking out at her. The princess gave her a smile. "I'm coming," she said. Glancing once more at the palace, she let her gaze linger a bit longer on the High Tower and then sighed, her heart full of heaviness. "Let's go." She climbed inside just as the engines started.

She was silent for the trip, saying nothing as Aura and her handmaidens went over procedure together in the rear seats. Selene just looked out the window, letting her thoughts circle on how she could try to wake Etoileon up when she could see him. She decided that it would be best to ask for a few moments alone with him first, just to keep suspicions low enough.

When they arrived in Silverton City, Selene felt her thoughts and plans being pushed out of her head as she viewed the city skyline. The last time she'd been here, she had been feeling hopeless and troubled. While she was still suffering, she was better to the point that she allowed herself to be distracted by the unusualness of the city landscape.

In Diamond City, there were larger streets, not too much traffic, and a bustle of colors and shops all lining the city streets. As Selene watched the passing scenes out of her window, she saw that Silverton had small, crowded streets filled up with hover vehicles and turbojets. There were people and shops everywhere, but while Diamond City seemed to have an array of colors and tones, Silverton had nondescript and dull shades of silver gray. It seemed to make sense, Selene supposed, as the City was named for the silver found in the mines below it.

The vehicle pulled up to the entrance to the Medical Ward and Selene, along with her companions and her guards, headed for their destination. Selene felt a foreboding sensation trickle down her spine as she looked up at the structure. She could not recall what the building had looked like the last time she'd been here, but she didn't remember it being this unusual. She shook her head. It had to be her imagination, she thought.

As she made her way up to Etoileon's room, Selene passed by Dr. Hamersley in the hallway. He was going over a chart with one of the nurses when he saw her go by, and he paused for a moment in his work, as though he wanted to be sure that it was really the princess. He was certain it was Her Highness, though, a moment later, because of all the guards and court ladies following her. He chuckled when he saw the direction that she and her group were headed in. He looked back at the nurse and handed her the chart. "Excuse me," he said, hurrying to follow after them.

When they got to the correct floor, Selene turned to her troop. "Everyone, I would like a few moments alone with my friend, if you don't mind." Looking at Aura, who wasted no time in scowling her scowl of disapproval, Selene continued, "Just for a few moments. I just want to see how he's doing for myself. Until then, why don't you all have a seat in the waiting room, or better yet, why don't you go out and get some lunch? You all must be hungry after being transported here." When even Aura could not argue with the princess' logic, they all agreed to be ready to leave the city in two hours.

Selene cautiously opened the door to Etoileon's room and peeked inside. She was surprised to find he was not in there. Walking in, she shut the door behind her and started to look around. "Etoileon?" she called out. Maybe he'd woken up, she thought hopefully. "Etoileon?" She called out his name again, but there was still no answer. She was about to try once more when the door opened up behind her.

She turned to find the kind face of her elderly doctor smiling at her. "Your Highness," he bowed. "How unexpected, and yet expected, to see you."

"You knew I was coming?" Selene asked, confused but pleased to see him once more. "I didn't think that Dorian would tell anyone I was coming."

Dr. Hamersley shrugged, still smiling. "I knew that you were concerned for him, Your Highness. You share a deep bond. It was only natural to assume that you would not be long in returning to him."

Selene felt her face flush over slightly. "Yes … but where is he?" Her face broke into a tentative smile as she asked, "Is he better?"

Dr. Hamersley hated to be the one to tell her. "No, Your Highness." He sighed. "The doctors here, myself included, have done all we can for him … medicine, bandages, and everything else. But he has not awakened yet."

"Then where is he?"

"He has been moved out of the Intensive Care Unit to the bottom floor, for resident patients. He has been given his own room, where the nurses can check up on him regularly and give him his medication every time he needs it."

So he hasn't gotten better, Selene thought glumly. "Can I see him?" she asked.

"For the Princess of the World? Certainly," the kind doctor replied. Looking at her saddened face, he hesitated before going on. "I should tell you, Princess, that it is really unpredictable what is going to happen to him. He could wake up tomorrow. Or he could sleep for months. There is no certainty in his condition. We are all stumped as to what it could be that is holding him back from full recovery. Therefore, we can only guess that it is something that we haven't been able to detect, or it is psychological."

"But he is safe from dying?"

Once more, Dr. Hamersley hated that he had to be the one to inform her. "Not quite yet, Your Highness. His wounds have all healed on his body, but there is a mess of stitches inside of him yet. And there is always the possibility of something going wrong."

Selene stood still for a moment, letting all the information soak into her. "I see," she remarked at last. "Take me down to him, if you please," she said.

He nodded and gestured toward the door. As they left the empty room, Selene suddenly looked back up at him and tried to put on a brave smile, though she was not very successful. "Thank you so much, Dr. Hamersley. I appreciate all the work you've done to help me and Etoileon."

He bowed his head and said, "It is always a privilege to work for a princess as kind as you are, Your Highness. You give such hope to this world, and I'll have you know it is not merely because of that prophecy. You really are most welcome."

Selene felt his words warm her in a comforting way. She respected him, and was honored that he would praise her. But inside she did not know if she could agree with him.

***

Etoileon's new room was located on the west side of the building. It was small and in order, and it was, for a wardroom, cozy. Selene looked inside and felt her nose start to prickle as oncoming tears threatened to overwhelm her.

She looked at Dr. Hamersley, who nodded, and gestured toward the far end of the hallway, silently letting her know that he would be waiting for her down there. She bowed her head low in respect and thanks, and he seemed to understand. He turned and left her there, all alone, with the boy that she had missed so much in recent weeks.

"Etoileon," she murmured, after closing the door and walking over to him. He remained still on his bed, his black hair slightly moist with sweat and his eyes closed. Selene stood over him and was glad to see that he did not have as many bandages on him as he had before she'd gone back to the palace. There was a small bandage on his forehead near his temple, but other than that his face was all healed and looking as though nothing had happened to him. She looked down his body to see that he still had bandages on one of his arms, and a few more under his shirt. She could not tell if there was any more damage below his waist due to the thick covers he was under.

"Hi," Selene whispered, bending down to talk into his ear. Her hand reached down and tucked itself into his free hand, her cold fingers finding warmth as they curled around his. "I came back to see you, Etoileon. I missed you." She tried to smile, but her eyes filled up with tears. "I wish you would wake up so much, so I could see you smile again," she whispered shakily, her voice affected by her uneven breathing.

She took a deep breath and tried to relax. "I had to go back to the palace last week. But Dorian was kind enough to allow me to visit you, even though you are out of the palace grounds."

Selene was close enough that she could feel his deep, even breathing on her cheek. She smiled a bit and said, "I hope that they're taking good care of you, Etoileon. I want you to know, also, that Dorian has not assigned me another personal protector. I do not think he will, either. It seems that while he disliked you, you are the only person for such a job in his eyes."

There was no response, but Selene squeezed his hand and kept going. She told him of her studies, and of her companions, and only a little about the war. She eventually sat down and rested her arm on his shoulder, still talking to him. She wanted to tell him about her beautiful dreams of late.

"I have a wonderful new friend, too. He comes to me while I am dreaming," she spoke in her hushed voice. Her tears dried up as she told him of the wisdom of Pegasus, his beauty, his goodness to her. There was even a smile on her face as she told him of walking with him. "I am a little scared to talk to him about you," she admitted, dropping her smile for a moment. "I want you to get better so much, and I am scared that he won't be able to do anything for you." She frowned sadly as she said, "Out of all the people in this world, Etoileon, you have been the closest to me. Out of everyone, the one I fear losing the most is you … I should've told you earlier how much you mean to me … but … " her voice broke off as at last her tears began to break free. "But I did not think I was going to lose you!" she finished, as she

THE MOONLGIHT PEGASUS

laid her head down on his, resting against him, holding him close to her.

Leaning down, she whispered, "I would give anything if you would just come back to me."

His hair was sticky against her face, but she paid it no mind. Careful of his wounds, she stayed there, close to him, as he continued to sleep.

***

Back in Diamond City, Sulfas was calling upon one of Obsidian's well-known contacts of the human world. Though he was one of the spirit world, this woman was said to contact the dead constantly.

He was there, in her house, pictured in one of her dark magic objects, known as the Gateway to the Grave. It was a mirror-like object that allowed passing sprits to look in on the mortal world, and, for those humans who had been deeply absorbed by dark power, to look back and talk to them.

The old woman never moved an eyelash as she listened. She was old and wrinkled, and if she were not a human, Sulfas would say that she would have been the bride of Obsidian. Her hair was thin and white, flimsy in nature. Most of it was piled up in a large turban decorated with beads and various jewels. Her eyes were sunken and a dark black color, as though it was bringing her mystical power into her very body. She, like a true Demon Chaser, wore dark colors, and she also had painted her long, scaly fingertips a gloomy shade of black.

THE MOONLGIHT PEGASUS

"Our Lord Obsidian has called upon me to ask of you a favor, Seer Melantha," Sulfas said. "I have come at his biding, that you might do this favor for our side."

She still did not move, but merely stared at him. He continued on, saying, "He wants you to go to the palace, and get an audience with the Princess herself."

It was this order that caused Melantha to cackle with laughter, her old, scratchy voice causing a sinister laugh to rumble within her throat. "I see then. Lord Sulfas, I take it that I therefore can assume that the time has come?"

Sulfas grinned evilly, knowing that it was a celebratory time. "Yes, you are correct, Seer. Obsidian has broken free of the Celestial Prison, and taken refuge in the Deserts of the Continent. The Great War is upon us."

Melantha smiled, making her ancient face more twisted and more distorted than before. "I was hoping it would come, that Our Master would finally over throw the Guardian and take his seat on his throne in Crystallon." She stood up from her chair, a new sense of anticipation and eagerness taking hold of her. "Where is the Pure Light? Where is he?"

"He has come to reside in the light of beautiful dreams," Sulfas explained. "The Princess Selene is where he is residing now."

"But she is only a child," Melantha sneered. "Why would he choose to bridge the worlds through her? She has no strength. She will fall easily into our hands."

"Lord Obsidian has witnessed her loyalty to the Light himself. He feels that she will need a more focused persuasion in order to stumble and fall away from the Light, although he says that it will take only a little to render her useless for the Light. He has waited patiently, watching for any sign of such a weakness in the princess."

"So, since you are here, he has found it?"

"Yes. Indeed he has," Sulfas nodded. "This is what the Master has commanded that I tell you to do."

Melantha eagerly listened to the plan. When he was finished explaining it to her, she laughed her wicked laugh. "What genius!" she exclaimed. "I shall prepare to go at once."

"I will inform Lord Obsidian of your intents, then," Sulfas agreed, and with that, he hurried off, his image disappearing from the Gateway in a twinkling of an eye.

***

There was a soft knock on the door a while later. Selene looked up from her position, as Kadrianne opened the door.

"Your Highness? May I come in?" Kadrianne asked.

"Yes," Selene responded, a feeling of regret coming over her. "It is time to leave then?"

"I'm afraid so," Kadrianne nodded solemnly. "Your doctor was kind enough to inform me of your whereabouts. He told me that you had been here for a while. Are you all right?"

385

Selene nodded. "Just a little tired, I think," she said. "But also sad." Her lip quivered as she said, "I wish he was all better, Kadrianne. I wish he would wake up for me."

Kadrianne nodded sympathetically. "I wish it were so as well, Your Highness. He brings you so much joy that it really is a shame that he is not awake. I'm sure that he will eventually wake up. Don't worry about him, Your Highness. I have no doubt that he would be the last person on Sapphira to give into death when he has you to see when he wakes up."

Selene gave Kadrianne a small smile. "Thank you for saying that, Kadrianne," she said, her voice hushed. "I'm very grateful … but you can call me Selene, you know that right?"

"If it is your wish," Kadrianne said, "But tradition usually calls for formality between royalty and commoners."

"There are two things wrong with that statement," Selene said as she turned to face Etoileon once more. "One, I am your friend. Friends do not use titles, even in Court, except in public. And two … " She turned and looked over her shoulder at Kadrianne, "There is nothing so very common about you, Kadrianne."

Kadrianne bowed low. "Thank you. It is very kind of you to say so."

"You will become a great Lady of the Court one day," Selene told her. "I have no doubt of that."

"Thank you, again."

"Now why don't you go and get Aura and all of them ready, while I say farewell to Etoileon?" Selene asked, smiling as brightly as she had all day. Kadrianne nodded and left, leaving Selene alone with Etoileon once more.

Leaning down, she placed her head on his heart and gave him a hug, although it was awkward and a small embrace. "Please wake up soon," she whispered. "I … I care so much for you, Etoileon … but honestly … I wanted to tell you that I'm -"

"Princess, are you coming?" Aura's voice called out as the door opened partially. "We have to leave right away if we're going to be able to get back to the palace on time. We wouldn't want His Royal Majesty to worry, would we?"

Selene scrunched up her face in a sad, annoyed expression. "No, Aura," she responded. "I'm coming." She remained there for a moment longer before she got up and left the room, glancing back for only a second. He had not moved, nor was there any indication that he had heard her.

***

Cyerra and Ronal were enjoying one of the rare times when they both had time enough to spare for each other. Since being knighted, Ronal had been attending not only strategy classes, but also strategy meetings. Cyerra was only free because she had been given time off as the Princess made her way to Silverton City and back again.

They talked as they strolled down the streets of the city. It was near noontime, but there was little sunshine out. The days of late had been gloomy and dreary, due to the weather of the monsoon season. There was some rain, much more than at any other time throughout the year. It was humid until sundown, and then it grew chilly.

Cyerra had invited Ronal to come and meet with her Aunt Rou for lunch, which he had accepted hesitantly. He wasn't sure that he wanted to meet her family yet, considering he had just been assigned to fight against Cyerra's brother in the war. But Cyerra had convinced him that her aunt would love to meet him. She had also agreed not to bring up the subjects of Aemon or the war. He had settled for that. Ronal also agreed because he had been at the palace much too long and he wanted to get away for a while before he left it for the North.

"Are you sure I should wear this?" he asked, pulling at the formal cloak Cyerra had insisted that he wear. "Isn't it a bit too … dressy? What if your aunt's just wearing a housedress or something? Won't that be showing her up or something."

"Auntie Rou is excited to meet you," Cyerra insisted. "I want her to be impressed with you. I want her to like you."

"Oh." That really didn't answer all his questions or address all his concerns, but he let it slide. If nothing else, he decided, he could just attribute the formality to Cyerra's insistence. "Okay."

"Relax, would you? She'll love you."

"Okay," he said again, his voice clearly telling anyone who was listening that he was still not sure about that.

They arrived at the shop to find it closed. "That's odd," Cyerra said. "I guess maybe after she heard we were coming, she wanted to close the shop for today." After a moment of thought, she gestured toward the alleyway. "Let's try around back."

"Sure," Ronal agreed. He wondered if anything was wrong or not. It didn't feel too suspicious, but his feelings had been wrong about certain things before. He was suddenly glad that he was with Cyerra. He wouldn't want her to get hurt. He looked up and all around at the enclosing walls of the alley, glad to find that nothing seemed amiss. "Cyerra, I don't see anything -" He broke off as Cyerra gasped in horror.

"Oh no!" she cried.

"What? What is it?" he asked, his hand reaching for his hidden dagger in his belt.

"The door!" Cyerra pointed as she shrunk back next to him. "Someone's broken in!" Ronal looked to see that the back door had indeed been thrown off of its hinges and the doorframe mutilated. Looking past that into the house, he could see that the house had been ransacked. When or how, he could not say. All he could tell from where he was standing was that it looked like the intruder, or intruders, had done a thorough job.

Her eyes suddenly grew wide as she was struck with a sudden thought. "Oh my! Auntie Rou!" she exclaimed. She hurried off to find her aunt.

"Cyerra, no!" Ronal shouted after her, quickly running after her. "It could be dangerous still! There could be burglars still inside!"

She did not hear his warning as she jumped over the mess on the floor and wove her way through the building that had once been her home. Well, we were going to move soon anyway, she thought, but this was terrible. "Auntie Rou? Are you here? It's me, Cyerra!"

Ronal came up behind her. "Cyerra, hang on," he said. "Be quiet a moment." He strained his ears to listen. There was nothing. "She's either not here or she's unconscious," he said. "I don't think anyone else is here, either."

"How can you tell?"

"There are no subtle movements, or even any motion at all in this house," he explained. "Let's check upstairs."

"Okay," Cyerra agreed. "The steps are over there," she said as she pointed.

Ronal bounced up the stairs as stealthily as he could. Right away he knew that there was trouble. All of the doors he saw were opened, and all of them except one were turned completely upside down. He wanted to take a look, but Cyerra interrupted his thoughts.

"Auntie!" she screamed, as her eyes fell to the floor in one of the looted rooms. Ronal had not realized that the pile of flower-printed robes on the floor was a real person. Cyerra pushed past Ronal and hurried over to her fallen aunt's side, to see if she was still alive or not.

She was, but she was very pale and her breathing was shallow. Ronal saw that her careworn features were stressed and there was a large bump on her head. "Careful," he warned Cyerra as she started to try and move her aunt. "She's

THE MOONLGIHT PEGASUS

been attacked, and I think it's been more than a couple of hours since it happened. It might've happened this morning."

"But why?" Cyerra asked. "Who would do this?"

"I have an idea," Ronal muttered as he looked back to the spotless room once more. "Is that your brother's room right there?"

"Yes," Cyerra looked up. "But I don't think it was Aemon who did this, Ronal. He was raised by our aunt, the same as I was. How could he turn on her, and to this degree?"

"Didn't you once tell me that he found out that he had been lied to about his father?" Ronal asked. "And that he was angry about it?"

Cyerra's eyes dawned with understanding. "I don't know about this, Ronal. Why would he try to attack her now, of all times? He isn't even here, is he?"

"There's only one person who can answer that question now," Ronal said, looking from Cyerra down to Auntie Rou's face. "Let's get her to the Palace Medical Ward. It was just finished about two weeks ago. It should be running now."

"Yes, let's hurry," Cyerra agreed. She watched as Ronal leaned down and scooped up her aunt, cradling her in his arms. Cyerra stood up and led the way out of the house towards the royal hospital.

***

It was hours later that Selene was sitting once more at her desk, trying to read. She suddenly realized that she'd been attempting to read the same page for the last twenty minutes and sighed. She stretched, breathing in deeply as she tried to concentrate.

A few moments later, she gave up on it. The little silver book had proved to be a wonderful book, but there was too much on her mind to let her pay any attention to the words. And anyway, she'd discovered that the book was full of blank pages in the back of it. Hundreds and hundreds of blank pages. What was she supposed to do with that? She shrugged and looked away.

Selene's eyes caught sight of the note that she'd been given as she'd left the dinner table. Looking for a temporary distraction, she picked it up and read it again.

It was from Cyerra. She'd written to tell Selene that she would be spending the night in the Medical Ward with her aunt. Selene hadn't been told anything in regards to what had happened, but she understood. It was only natural that Cyerra was worried about her aunt; from what Selene had gathered from her small talks with her handmaiden, Cyerra regarded her Aunt Rou as a child would her mother. She put the letter aside and frowning down at her workspace, she did the same thing with her book. She would not be able to give it her full attention; at least, not while she was distracted. Selene silently promised herself that she would return to later.

She got up and stood at the window, very much like the night she had become friends with the Pegasus in her dreams. It was not raining, but it was cloudy out as she looked up at the night sky.

THE MOONLGIHT PEGASUS

It was then that something caught her attention, and she felt her mouth drop open in surprise.

There was a star missing. "Where is it?" she asked, squinting into the dark blue sky. She could find no trace of the familiar sparkle. "How unusual … " her voice trailed off as she turned her thoughts back to the night when she'd noticed that the star was flickering. She'd been with Etoileon then.

Her eyes left the star's empty spot to look over at the High Tower. Should she go look from there? she wondered. A moment later she shook her head. I can't, she thought. I can't face the place where too many memories of Etoileon are. Not yet.

She forgot all about her concern for the blackened star as her hand went up to her heart and thoughts of her cherished friend came to her mind. "Oh, Etoileon … " her voice was soft and full of unspoken pain. "How I wish … I wish you were here."

Selene turned away from the window and subdued her oncoming tears. She was growing impatient for him to wake up, she realized. The belief in his eventual recovery was weakening. She'd resolved that she would never doubt his getting better, but now, with her heart nearly empty of conviction, she considered the possibility if he did perish. She did not have to dwell in her dark thoughts long to know that she would no longer want to live without him in this world.

She buried her face in her pillow and tried to quiet her mind. She wanted to see Pegasus. He always brightened up her days. In many ways, she thought, it was almost like he had come into her world to replace Etoileon. She suddenly regretted that thought. No one would replace Etoileon, and she should not have even thought that. "What kind of love gives up so easily?" Selene asked softly into her folded arms. "How dare I think such a thing." She sighed. "I am not worthy of anyone's love."

"No one is ever worthy of a perfect love," she heard Pegasus whispered, tickling her ear with his mane as he bent his head to look down at her.

She found that she was lying on the sand of her dreamland, her arm shielding her eyes from the bright, yellow sunlight as she lay there. Selene removed her arm from her face and looked up, realizing that she must've fallen asleep. "What?" she asked.

"Not one human on all of Sapphira, since the beginning of time, has there been a human being worthy of perfect love," Pegasus repeated. "All humans have been infected with the Dark Plague. And while they are sick, no one would love them. No one would love their sickness."

Selene sat up and brushed the sand out of her hair. "But what about you?"

Pegasus flicked his tail. "The only one who can love them even though they are sick is the one who created them, who has known them since the beginning."

Selene wasn't sure if he had answered her question or not. "What about when we are healed?"

"There will come a time, a time that is fast approaching, where all the humans will be able to be cured," Pegasus told her. He smiled. "You should know that better than anyone, Selene."

"Huh?" She looked at him, not sure what he was talking about before it clicked. "Oh, you mean the prophecy."

He nodded. "You are the one who will bring peace into this world," he said. "But you are not the peace itself."

"I wish that was so easy to explain to Dorian," Selene muttered, her cynical remark almost a reflex reaction.

"Tired of hearing about it?" Pegasus asked.

"Very," Selene agreed. "I don't even know what I'm supposed to do! Or how, or when, or any of that … how can I be expected to do something I don't even know what it is? I mean, I could've already missed the chance to bring peace to the world by rejecting Aemon's marriage proposal."

"It is hard to be faced with fear," Pegasus said. "But I tell you, it is not fear that shows our true characters. It is by fear we test our faith."

Selene said nothing, merely nodding. "I wish that people would not look up at me for a solution, Pegasus. I can only do so much. I will not refuse my heart and be married to someone all for the sake of peace. I want … " She trailed off, turning a slight shade of red.

"Go on," Pegasus smiled kindly down at her. "I will not laugh."

"Well … " She hesitated for only a moment, before continuing on. "Well, I want to fall in love, like anyone else. I

THE MOONLGIHT PEGASUS

might have a title and live in a big house, but I am the same as everyone else. I want to be happy, but I do not consider that top priority and I know that it may not be the case. I want to have a family of love someday, but I know that I can be happy without it if I don't get that. I want to have adventures, and dream … just like everyone else, I have dreams." When she looked up, she saw that Pegasus was nodding, silently agreeing with her. "The only thing that's different about me, besides the prophecy, is my title. How can that be something to cause me to be a hero to someone, especially for something that I might not choose to do in the first place?"

Pegasus was silent still as she slumped over, her eyes cast to the ground in despair. Finally he spoke up. "Listen to me, Selene. Humans want to have a hero to look up to, you're right. They long to have a leader, someone worthy of their admiration and love. And yet, they ignore the one who has dreamed of them. They are not able to see the divine, because they don't want to. They gloss over miracles; they find doubt in every corner that is not explicitly explained. Gone are the days of faith. With all the technology in the world, while it has made human life more comfortable and safer, it has robbed them of the feeling of living in the wild. There was a time on Sapphira that people had to believe in a greater power, because it was a part of survival. Now, with all their devices and gadgets, they feel like they have tamed this world, figured out all its secrets."

"What are you saying, Pegasus? I don't understand," Selene confessed.

"You will," he said. "I am merely telling you that humans want to have someone to lead them who is like them, or someone that they can control. They long to have a leader who will model the perfect life and will give them the secrets to a higher living, a more meaningful existence. But no human is able to fit such a form."

"Because we all have darkness?"

"Yes. Only one who is perfect can be what the people want, but that is a contradiction. There is no such thing as a perfect human. The only one who is pure is the Guardian himself, but the people will not accept that."

"Why not?"

"Most of it is because humans, for the most part, do not want a leader who has such power over them. Like the young man who wishes to leave his Father's household, he does not want to remain in a place where he has to answer to someone, with the rules of someone else to consider. But also, the people of Sapphira fail to realize that the Guardian is still speaking to them. You have read some of His book, and have heard His whispers of righteousness, his promises for love and judgment?"

"Yes, I have read the book. And I understand what you're saying about him speaking while I'm reading the text. I can almost hear his expression, and sometimes I can imagine him actually saying the words, like I was watching him make a speech or something. Does that make sense, Pegasus?"

"Yes, I know what you are telling me. But, dear one, realize this: the voice of the Guardian does not stop once you shut the book. His promises are not stalled because you have finished reading. His kindness does not stop because you have fallen. His love does not end because you have failed. Life goes on, regardless of what happens. There is nothing that will make this world's time stop, even if there are ways to step out of the world's timeframe."

"Such as when I am here with you?" she asked.

He nodded. "This world is as real as the world you live in when you consider yourself awake. Soon these worlds, at the Guardian's command, will be able to meet, and you will see the wonders of His love in the flesh. That is a promise, my dear Selene."

She felt a warm smile on her face. She loved it when he gave his promises to her. There was always a resolute feeling with each one, that for that small instant of time, she could believe him perfectly. With each step into reality, however, meant there would be more doubts and uncertainties would arise. She stopped thinking about this as Pegasus continued.

"I also promise you this, Selene. If you listen and truly wish to hear, you will know what the Guardian is speaking to you. His is not a voice that will not always be heard in the air, but one that is always heard in the heart. Call out to him, and He will hear … you remember that He had heard you before?"

"And that is why you are here," Selene nodded. "He will always send an answer like you?"

Pegasus shook his head. "No. He will not always give the answer that one would want to hear. Sometimes humans desire things that are not good for them. That is their downfall."

"I see," Selene murmured thoughtfully. Maybe she could ask the Guardian to do something about Etoileon. It couldn't hurt, she thought. "Thank you for comforting me, Pegasus," she whispered softly. "I am feeling so much better than before. I'm so glad that you will always be here to help me through trouble."

Pegasus nodded his head. "You and I will always share a bond," he told her, "but you must know you will not be able to see me all the time. As time goes on, and the Light draws closer, the time that I share with you alone is coming to a slow end."

"What?" Selene's eyes jerked up to meet his face. "What are you saying? You can't leave me! I thought we were friends!"

"I will not leave you," he tried to tell her, but she paid him no attention as she cried into her hands. "You will not be able to see me, because the darkness allowed to grow in your soul will not let you. But I will not ever abandon you."

"But then how will I know you are really there?" Selene asked, her voice condemning as her heart broke. Suddenly all that she had believed to be certain was coming apart, falling down. Once again she was struck with a feeling of nothingness in her heart. Pegasus merely nudged his head against hers, one of his wings gently wiping her face of her tears as she looked back up at him.

"By faith."

She suddenly wondered what would happen if she would leave him. She stood up and turned away from him. She did not look at him, did not see him with her eyes. And suddenly she knew what he had meant when he had told her that he would not leave her, but he would always be there for her.

He had meant that she would be the one to shut him out, that the sickness that plagued her mind would turn away from him, losing sight of him. If there would be one who would break away, Selene realized, it was she that would leave. Not him. She would choose to leave. But He had chosen to stay with her, and had promised not to leave.

Feeling ashamed, she broke off her dream to fall into an empty black nothingness, some part of her aware that she was doing exactly what she had least wanted to do—run away from Pegasus, whom she loved because he knew her, yet loved her, and wanted her to follow him in the way everlasting.

***

He was dreaming, but he was not in a dream. He was in a nightmare.

Etoileon was caught in a world of endless gloom. Once the darkness had managed to worm its way into his dreams, it had engulfed him. For countless days and fathomless hours, too long for him to know, he had been at the mercy of Obsidian. His hands were bound, his body was chained to a rocky wall, and his mind was corrupted by the hand of the dark master himself. Etoileon's will to keep out the dark master would prove futile; it was only by grace that he had managed to hang on this far.

Etoileon grimaced as he looked up from his position. His wrists were bleeding as he hung there. Obsidian's minions keep watch over him as he struggled against his bonds.

"Why are you doing this?" he yelled at them once more. He gritted his teeth in anger. They never responded to him; they merely laughed cruelly and tried to attack him once more.

A Phantom Guard stepped forth; his sever was held at the ready. "Silence, boy!" he shouted in his scratchy voice, raising the curved blade at the ready, and then swung into a striking blow.

Etoileon didn't even blink as the blade collided with a force field of light. The small force shielded Etoileon from the darkness, but it could not help him escape. He watched as the Phantom continued to lash out his useless attacks, each one thwarted by the light.

As the blade came down again, Etoileon nearly rolled his eyes, but it was then that something caught his eye.

"Huh?" He noticed that when the blade struck the force field, a bright light emitted, but it wasn't until this time that he noticed that the light shot out in the form of a shape. He tried to get a more focused look, squinting at it. He noticed that it was in the shape of a small, bright feather. He felt a jolt of shock. "What?"

As another attack came charging at him, Etoileon watched again for the light. When he saw the feather, a small smile crossed his weary face. He'd heard tell of the Spirit of the Guardian, the one who could be seen sometimes in pure dreams. Maybe it was a sign, he thought, that his call for help had been heard despite the demons within him.

Etoileon didn't even understand why they were here. He was at a loss for how keeping him trapped in his mind was helpful, but then again, he sneered, the tainted powers of the forsaken world didn't always need an excuse. It was enough to have him away from the Light.

Etoileon was just about to shout at the Phantoms for being imbeciles when he felt a surge of power break into his dream world. He let out a painful yell, as he felt his mind being filled with a more gloomy and dreary power than he had ever felt. His eyes widened as the pain increased, and he tried to put his hand over his aching heart. When the surge was over, Etoileon scrunched up his face in pain, squeezing his eyes shut in order to bear the pain more easily. When he weakly opened his eyes, he was shocked to find bloody eyes staring at him closely.

"Etoileon, Son of Ammos," the raspy voice called out scathingly. "So we meet at last. Your father was quite a fool, but that is no reason that you should be."

"Ammos? My father?" Etoileon narrowed his eyes. "Who are you, and what do you want with me?"

"Who am I? I think you know who I am," the red eyes glimmered. "To some, I am a beacon of Light. To most, I am known as the dark master of the anti-world, Obsidian."

"Obsidian," Etoileon scathed. "So you have escaped from your prison then."

The dark master's eyes widened slightly in surprise. "You know your history, then, I see. How impressive. How did you come to learn of my past?"

Etoileon continued to glare at him. "My first Fighting Master, Master Liu, the one who took me in, was a believer in the Light. He told me all about you as he taught and took care of all of his students.”

“Ah. I see,” Obsidian murmured. “By why did you not talk more of me to your Princess?”

Etoileon’s suspicions heightened. “What does this have to do with her?” he asked, before his temper grew. “You leave her out of this, do you hear!?”

“I cannot, unfortunately,” Obsidian told him, beginning to pace around in a circle. Etoileon’s eyes followed him, watching for any kind of warning. “She is already involved. She is the one who carries the Pure Light.”

Etoileon felt his heart stop. “No!” he cried out. “No!” Tears came to his face, as his weariness and suffering reached a maximum. “She can’t be! You’re lying!” Selene, he thought despairingly. No. Not her.

“I wish I was,” the dark master smirked. “She is most hard to get to, surrounded by those anointed walls of the palace. Of late, though, I am pleased to say that I have managed to get in much more easily.”

“Stay away from her!” Etoileon yelled again.

Obsidian just laughed. “I told you, I can’t. If I am to rule Crystallon one day, I need her on my side. If the Pure Light cannot shine, he will be unable to bring forth my greatest foe.”

“You will lose in the end,” Etoileon said. “You will never get what you want.”

"On the contrary, my boy," Obsidian remarked. "I have already gotten much of what I want. And I just need your assistance in getting to the next stage of my genius plan."

"I'll never help you!" Etoileon cried. "I would never let you hurt Selene or destroy this world!"

Obsidian laughed harder at this. "Haven't you heard what I've been saying? I am of the anti-world. You have no free choice in the anti-world. Only suffering is awaiting you there!" With this, Obsidian lashed out an attack, thrusting out bright red lightning flashes towards Etoileon. This time, the Light was only able to protect Etoileon a little as Obsidian's power laced around him.

"No!" Etoileon cried out in anguish, as his body twisted with unspeakable pain. He slumped over, his weariness and blinding agony taking their toll on him.

All the while, Obsidian cried out happily, "Yes! Yes!" and rubbed his hands together excitedly. His moment was approaching.

"Selene," Etoileon muttered into his chest. "Don't fall for his tricks. I need to wake up. I need to! I have to stop this evil!" he shouted. "I can't stop you now, but someone will stop you, Obsidian!"

The dark master shook his head. "Foolish one," he scolded his captive. "Surely you are a witness to my awesome powers. No one will be able to defeat me!" And he laughed again, watching as the human boy tried to wriggle his way out of his bonds.

Obsidian watched him and grinned. The son of Ammos had reacted just as Obsidian had expected. His plan was working. Soon the boy's body temperature would be up dangerously, and his condition would grow worse. Once the princess was out of the palace and in the hospital, her grief strong and, thanks to his quick thinking and subtle actions, with her connection to the Light weakened by her sorrow and fear, he was sure that his servant Melantha would be able to seal the final fate of the princess.

***

Selene woke up groggily, feeling guilty. She was upset with herself for running away from Pegasus. She had not wanted him to leave her, so she went and left him. Selene sadly shook her head. What kind of person did that? She had to wonder. Only a fool, she decided. She also decided that she would apologize as soon as she fell asleep later that night.

She had work to do for now. Kadrianne had already opened the curtains, and the sunlight was just shining enough through the clouds to allow Selene to see the outline of her room's contents clearly.

Chevée came in, and began to do the princess' hair just as breakfast time came around. Selene recalled that it was the first day of the new week, so Dorian would be present at breakfast, so long as another battle had not broken out yesterday. Putting on a gray dress, she hurried down to the breakfast chamber.

As she walked down the halls, she thought of how quiet and alone she felt. Etoileon was not there. She had turned her back on Pegasus and ran away from him. Though he had told her that he was with her, she did not think that she could feel

405

him. She wondered if this was where faith was supposed to come in, but she did not know for sure.

Looking out of the Main Hall windows, she saw that it was going to rain later. There were huge, puffy clouds hanging in the sky, nearly blocking out all of the sunshine. The rains of the monsoon season sometimes lasted for days, she recalled, but they would eventually clear up. Selene didn't mind that it would rain; she felt that the rain seemed to coordinate with her current temperament all the more fittingly.

As she walked into the Great Hall, she noticed that several people were there already. Yana and Kadrianne were present, Kadrianne standing contentedly, and Yana looking over at Dorian every so often as though she wanted to say something. Aura was also there, already sitting down and sipping out of her teacup. Selene was filled with a sense of relief, as she was suddenly aware that there were no guards or military advisors around. But she was unnerved at the silence that seemed to fill the room.

She sat down at Dorian's right side, and began to pick at the food that was placed in front of her. As the silence of the room continued, she began to lose her appetite more. She finally looked up at Dorian and said, "It is good to see you, Brother."

"And you," Dorian nodded. He turned his attention to her but did not say anything else.

Selene was suddenly very frightened. Something was wrong. Something was very, very wrong. She threw down her fork. "You may as well tell me," she said in huffy voice. "I know that you are hiding something from me."

Dorian flinched at her perceptiveness. "Curses, Selene," he muttered. "This is not going to be easy for you to hear."

"Well, what is it? Did someone die?" Selene spat out. Her patience was gone for the day. She was upset with herself for losing control of her emotions, and she had not meant to sound so irritated. But as Dorian shook his head, she was suddenly impacted with her own words. "Oh my goodness," she began to gasp, "No. Tell me no. Not … not … not Etoileon!"

Dorian sighed. "No, he is not dead, but he has taken a turn for the worst," the king told her. "This morning I was informed that his vital signs are weakening significantly and he is running a fever."

Selene sat back in her chair and for the first time she could remember in a long time, she allowed herself to cry in public. "No!" she wailed as her grief swallowed her up. "No, no, no! This is all my fault!"

"How is it your fault, Selene? Really, you are being quite irrational. And please, if you are going to cry, have some care. You are a princess, and you should act accordingly," Dorian whispered sharply.

Selene wanted to hit him and tell him that she was a person first, but she was sobbing too hard to see through her tears. Eventually, she felt someone take a hold of her arms and lead her away from the table.

"Now, now, Your Highness," Aura's voice washed over her, "You must not be worried about this. The doctors are taking good care of him, and he is being treated with the best help in all of Sapphira. There is little more that you can do for him. Besides, your people will always stand behind you for support.”

Selene nodded, and was about to say “Thank you,” when Aura continued, going on to say, “I’m sure that this is for the best, anyway. You need to concentrate on your studies and on staying well yourself. You do not need to waste your time worrying about that silly boy.”

Selene jerked out of her governess’ grasp, blinking away her tears as anger took the place of sadness. “Aura!” she exclaimed. “You should be ashamed of yourself, talking about Etoileon that way, talking to my face that way! He saved my life more than once, I’ll have you know!”

“Really, Your Highness, I’m sorry to have to be the one to tell you this, but he is a commoner, and you are royalty. His life is nothing compared to yours. It is only expected that he should give his life for yours,” Aura sniffed indignantly.

“That is enough!” Selene stomped her foot on the floor. “After all these years, Aura, I have come to see you for what you really are! For all your grace and beauty, for all your intelligence and gifts, you are nothing but a bitter, old, cynical woman, incapable to believe in any love at all!”

Aura took a step back, as though the princess’ words had struck her. “How dare you!” Aura snapped. “How dare you insult me? I practically had to raise you.”

“There are some days,” Selene said, her voice hushed and serious. “When I think that I will never be like you, and I despair because I will never have anything that has made you so influential in court. But then there are days when I realize that this is a good thing, for more people will revere me because of love, than those who heed to you for fear. You might have raised me, but you never truly loved me!"

"Oh, and I suppose that Orphan Boy did?" Aura huffed as her face burned with anger and shame.

"Yes, and I love him!" Selene shouted. Her hands flew up to cover her mouth. Once again, her words escaped her before she knew what they were. She stalled and sucked in her breath at the unspoken revelation that she had kept hidden in her heart for so long. She blushed, having never truly said it aloud before. She started to tremble and felt weak in her knees. Aura stood in silence for a moment before she turned around and walked away, unable to say anything.

Selene just stood there, not even watching Aura leave the hallway. She was still in shock at having revealed her true feelings at last. "I love him," she repeated. It felt so strange to hear such words. Tenderness, love, and things that were considered to be 'the softer emotions' were not talked about too much in court. They were feelings that were chided and viewed as rare and weak in the eyes of the High Court. So many of the members reserved their deepest cynic opinions for the discussion of love.

But Selene did not think it was so. Love was a beautiful thing. She had seen love incarnate in the Spirit who resided of her dreams, and she did not think he was weak at all, and he had told her that since he was a spirit, he could be anywhere and in all places at once, so how could it be rare? Maybe a human choosing to accept others, to love others, was rare, she thought, but not love itself.

She loved Etoileon. She had to go to him, she realized. She had to go and see him again, to be with him. This was probably a result of her turning away from Pegasus anyway, she thought carelessly. Selene turned and ran to for her room. She had once promised Dorian that she would not leave the castle again, unless it was necessary. She didn't know about Dorian, but Selene considered this venture more than necessary. She just could not stay away.

****

The hour was late but the palace was still lively. There were always guests, it seemed, to fill up the palace and keep the hosts entertained well past the midnight hour. The princess had excused herself to her room hours before, but not to sleep; little did any in the palace know, she was planning her second escape. Lady Aura was not present at dinner, not having been seen since early morning before she'd locked herself in her room. She'd told more than one maid that she was suffering as a result of 'traumatic conditions', so no one had called upon her in some time. The dining hall and the Great Hall were packed with people, a couple of them still present since the Islander Reception, not only due to the outbreak of war, but because of the hostile sea conditions due to the monsoon season. The castle was full of laughter and talking, and even some midnight dancing.

There was one place in the room that was not so lively, however. Cyerra looked in on her aunt for the third time in the last hour, her eyes tired and dry with lack of sleep. Ronal had left her, to his regret, in order to get to his classes and meetings for the day. She had stayed there, watching over the care given to her dear relative, since they'd come back from the city.

Cyerra watched as the water clock dripped, the time passing slowly to her. She sighed and hoped that if Ronal would come, he would bring her some dinner. She had forgotten to eat earlier, but she had received the news that her aunt was bound to wake up any moment. Cyerra knew she could not afford to leave at a time like this.

As she sat in the waiting room, she saw a flicker of movement in the corner of her eye. She waited a moment, carefully trying to see if someone was actually there or it had been her imagination. She shrugged, seeing nothing.

A few minutes later, there it was again. Cyerra turned her head quickly, but it had stopped moving once again. She waited, this time not to be distracted by her concerns. When she saw it this time, Cyerra could see that it was indeed a person, in a long palace robe, heading slowly for the door. Cyerra normally would not have said anything, but the next time she saw the movement, she noticed the gait of the walker and recognized at last that it was the princess.

"Your Highness?" she asked, moving over to stand next to her. She found Selene crouched behind a doorway, looking guilty.

"Cyerra," Selene greeted. "How are you doing?" She tried to smile, but Cyerra shook her head, and the princess could tell that she was caught.

"Princess," Cyerra started, "Selene, where are you going, at this time of night? Shouldn't you be in bed?"

Selene sighed. "I want to go see Etoileon, Cyerra. I cannot possibly wait until next weekend. His condition has worsened, and I feel like I have to go see him as soon as I can. I don't care what Dorian says, I feel in my heart that I am supposed to go."

"Selene, it is dangerous," Cyerra said. "You shouldn't go alone."

"I know," the princess shrugged, looking down. "But Cyerra … I can't help this feeling in me. I know I must go, no matter what, because … because … " her voice trailed off, her face growing red.

"Because you love him so?" Cyerra finished carefully. When Selene nodded and looked up at Cyerra with a questioning look, Cyerra found it in herself to smile. "I have sensed ever since I've been here, as long as I've known you, that you've held a special place in his heart," she explained.

"I must go, Cyerra," Selene insisted. "I know that you may not agree, but I am asking you to not tell them that you saw me here."

Cyerra looked down. "I will not tell them, Selene. You are my friend, and we all have to do certain things for love. But I would rather not be confronted with such an issue if possible."

"I understand," Selene nodded. "You are a good and true friend, Cyerra. I hope that your aunt does get better soon."

"I hope that you are able to help Etoileon get better as well," Cyerra said. "Now go. I trust that you have transportation?"

Selene's eyes twinkled in excitement. "Yes, I do. There is a transport waiting to escort a maid to her hometown, where one of her relatives is near death."

"Go then," Cyerra said, bowing her head. "And be safe."

"I will," Selene promised.

Watching her go, Cyerra felt a small smile come to her face once more. The princess would go through such trouble for someone that she loved very deeply. It was a heartwarming notion.

Turning back to her waiting room seat, Cyerra turned to find Ronal coming up the hallway with a small package in his hand. "Cyerra!" he called out, waving. He picked up his pace to a canter, quickly stopping once he was in front of her. "I'm so glad to see you!" he said. "I'm sorry that I was gone so long, but I was needed at the gala tonight for a while. And I wanted to get you something to eat. I figured that you probably haven't eaten all day, have you?"

"No," Cyerra grinned. "Thank you, Ronal darling. Let's go sit and talk for a while over here."

"How's your aunt doing?"

Cyerra bit into one of the small meat cuts that he'd brought her and felt her stomach almost rejoice. She swallowed before she said, "She's bound to wake up at any moment, according to the doctors."

"That's great then," Ronal replied. "No internal damage? No concussion?"

"Nope. She's just asleep for now," Cyerra said. "But they did ask a lot of questions that I couldn't answer. They wanted to know what happened to her and I had to tell them that I didn't have any idea. Poor Auntie Rou. She must've been beat up somewhat, before she was knocked out. I didn't know what else to tell the nurse."

Ronal thought about it for a moment, before saying, "Well, you've done all you can, Cyerra, so that's good enough for now. Who knows? You might've even saved her life today."

"You helped," Cyerra blushed.

"Just a little," he shook his head. "That's nothing."

"Sure it is," Cyerra insisted. "But the question I wanted to answer the most was who did could have possibly done this to her." At this Ronal just looked at her, unable to give her answer. She knew that she had no more luck in figuring that out than he did.

"Maybe when she wakes up, she'll be able to tell us something," Ronal said slowly.

Cyerra nodded. "Maybe."

***

Selene watched as the city lights of Silverton City came into view. She was left alone, the only one who was really in the transport. There was a royal guard watching from the hallway connecting to the pilots' quarters, but that was it.

She put her hand on the window, feeling as though her spirit would rise out of her body in an attempt to get there faster unless she managed to keep it in check. She felt a sense in her heart that she had done wrong, but she could not abandon her plans now. She was more worried for Etoileon than she was what Dorian would say, anyhow. She would gladly trade places with him, if only he would be saved. Besides, her absence might not even be noticed, all things considered. It wasn't like Dorian didn't have more pressing issues to attend to.

She arrived at the hospital only a couple of hours after she'd left the palace. She headed around the corner and turned, and at last she caught sight of her destination.

There were only a couple of nurses that were on duty on the bottom floor this late at night, she noticed. That would prolong the discovery of her being there for a while. She waited until the hallway was clear, and then she went inside. She opened the door to find Etoileon was still in his bed, in about the same position he'd been as she'd last left him, but he didn't look as peaceful this time. His sheets were soaked with sweat, and his face was red from the heat. Selene rushed over to his side, taking his clammy hand in hers and squeezing it in both of hers.

"Etoileon," she exclaimed. "I am so happy to be here for you! Once again, I have broken free of the palace. And once again, I find you waiting for me," she whispered gently. His hand was limp and cold in hers. She drew his hand and lovingly laid it against her cheek as she smiled contentedly.

"You must love the boy a lot to risk breaking out of the palace."

Selene felt her breath catch in her throat as she slowly turned around. There was a woman in the room, watching her. The woman had gnarled hands and a wrinkled face to match. She'd painted on more than half of her eyebrows, and her eyes were shadowed with too much smoky eye paint. Her cheeks were dusted a very bright pink, and with all her other features, she looked like a poorly designed clay figurine. Her outfit seemed to match the rest of her person; the black fabric was made to last, but it was faded and stained in certain spots. Selene could find no words to say as she just stared at the woman, a look of half-guilt and half-fear written on her face.

The old woman smiled. "Relax, child. I knew that you would be here. I have not told a soul," she crackled, as though she were sharing a private joke with someone that Selene could not see.

"How could you know I would be here?" Selene asked carefully. "Who are you?"

"My name is not important," she said. "But just for kicks I'll humor you. I am known as Melantha the Seer. One who is not of this world has summoned me here to help you. He knows of your trouble with this boy's condition, and he has convinced me to come here and assist you."

"Really?" Selene's voice was breathless. Could it be that Pegasus had sent this woman? "You can help Etoileon?" It was too good to be true.

"Yes. I know that the darkness has plagued him, child," Melantha spoke, her hypnotic voice almost entrancing Selene away from Etoileon. "I can bring him back to this mortal plain, for he is hanging between this world and the next."

"You can really do that?" Selene felt her heart start to beat faster as she began to feel that surely this was an answer to her call.

"Yes, I can. And I will … for a price, of course," she said.

At her last words, Selene snapped out of the trance she'd found herself in. "Excuse me? I beg your pardon? There's a price?"

"Yes. All things have a price, remember?" Melantha frowned. "I am sorry, child, this does not happen to me very often, that I am wrong. I was certain that you loved this boy, but I guess that I was mistaken about that –"

"No! No you weren't!" Selene said, waving her hands to motion to the woman to stop her from leaving. "No. I'm sorry." She sighed. "What is the price?"

"Only one thing shall do. If you want the boy to wake up, which is quite a lot of work for an old, weak woman like me," Melantha started. "But you seem like such a sweet little girl, that I will give it to you at a discount." Melantha looked around and said, "Hmmm. I will take the boy's memories as the price."

"What?" Selene asked. "His memories?"

"No, no, you're right. That's too much to ask. I'll settle for his memory of you," the woman smiled. "That's a big discount there girl. I'd take it if I were you."

"But how … but how would I … ?" Selene searched around for the right words, but couldn't find them. She shook her head. "I can't do that," she said. "That's too much of a price."

Melantha shrugged. "Well, he had a good life. I'm sure that he will find peace in death. Maybe he'll even remember you when you join him, and then you can finally be happy, too. I suppose that it'll be hard to deal with his loss, but when you push yourself, it's amazing what you can —"

"Wait." Selene stopped her. "Okay. Do it. I'll pay the price." She took Etoileon's hand in hers and held on tightly. "I can't live in a world without knowing I could have saved him and didn't at least try it.

Melantha grinned. "You've made a wise choice, girl." She stood up and waved her hands, calling forth her powers granted from her master. Her hands swirled around, her fingers shaking. "I was this boy's guardian at one point in time, you know. I was the one who told him of the place of real power. I know for a fact that he would thank you for doing this service to him."

There was something in her voice that made Selene cringe. Recalling how Etoileon had told her long ago that he'd never really had a guardian that he had liked before, aside from his first Master, a man named Liu, she immediately regretted making her choice. Selene was about to tell Melantha that she'd changed her mind when Melantha starting chanting.

She whispered softly, murmuring indecipherable incantations as she stood in front of Etoileon's body. Selene suddenly had a feeling in her heart telling her this was wrong; this was too wrong. She could not choose such a life for her friend. And maybe there was a chance that he would wake up on his own yet.

Suddenly, his words seemed to echo straight out of her heart. "It's kind of nice to think about how you'd be different if you had no memories, and grateful that you're who you are because of certain people."

"Wait!" Selene called out, just as Melantha's eyes rolled to the back of her head and her head turned to face Selene. "I changed my mind!"

There was foam bubbling out of the old woman's over-painted mouth, and her face turned dead white. She laughed a crazy laugh. "Too late! It's too late! You have chosen this path, and you cannot turn back!"

"No! Stop!" Selene said, grabbing a hold of Etoileon's hand and trying to pull him away from the demon-possessed woman. Melantha shrieked with a bloodcurdling howl, and Selene had to press her ear in with her free hand as she tried to break free of Melantha's curse.

She fell to the floor, but kept her hand tight around Etoileon's hand. She curled up in front of Melantha, stopping the woman from getting too close. "Etoileon, I won't let her harm you!" she called out, as a great wind blew through the windows and smoke began to billow everywhere. Selene had trouble breathing and coughed. Her eyes watered, and she felt Etoileon's breathing start to heave. "No!"

She grasped tightly to Etoileon, pulling herself up to him. She leaned down and protected him from the smoke as best as she could. But there was nothing she could do. "Old

Woman, go away!" she yelled as she turned to see her foe once again.

At this point Melantha had begun to hang in the air, and when she spoke a new voice called to her. "You have fallen, Princess! I have you at last! Your light is smoldering; you can no longer house the Pure Light! I have won!"

Obsidian's laugh was cruel and scathing, and Selene could feel the sting of it. "No!" she cried. "Pegasus! Help me!" she called.

"Oh, Pegasus, help me, help me!" Obsidian mocked her in his best girl's voice. Then he laughed again. "Oh, Princess Selene, you are so funny. You have chosen this pathway, turning against your darling Pegasus. And best of all, I still have your dear friend there trapped in the realms of his own dream world."

"Give them back to me!" Selene yelled at Melantha's form.

"They were never yours to have," Obsidian laughed again. "They were always mine to be taken. The son of the rebel, Ammos, has eluded me for years, safe in the protection of the palace."

"What?" Selene narrowed her eyes. "What do you mean, the son of Ammos? You can't mean that Etoileon … " her voice trailed off as a memory of him surfaced in her mind, of him telling her of his earliest memory.

She remembered what he'd told her. A black moon, she thought. Could that be … an eclipse? She gasped, as it all fell into place now.

"Yes," Obsidian answered her question. "I had led his father to bring him to the City, to establish him as prince once the rebellion took over the monarchy, but the fool was too busy planning how to talk to his true love, the Queen, your mother. He let his oldest brat out of his sight just as the eclipse took over. His son, Etoileon, was playing around the water at the Gemstone Oasis when the darkness took over the sunlight. Ammos hadn't listened to me, because I knew the Guardian would interfere. And so he did. The Guardian must've taken away all the kids memories somehow, because none of my followers could find him for a long time; even I looked from behind the celestial prison and could find no trace of him for a while. But he proved useful in the end, huh? I used him to convince you to give up the Pure Light."

"Pegasus!" Selene gasped. "No! No, he will come back to me!"

"But he cannot live in you any longer," Obsidian smirked. "So he won't come. You will rot all the days of your life in darkness, your inner light fading away to nothing as you wallow in your grief."

Selene broke off into tears, realizing too late her mistake. "And Etoileon?" she asked.

"His memory of you belongs to me," Obsidian said. "I will keep true to my word, and I will release him from his prison, but it matters not. He is still trapped in his own mind, thanks to the darkness I have kept there. He will soon be killed in battle, as my forces rally to attack."

With this, Melantha slumped over, and Etoileon's eyes flickered open. Selene was still crying. The winds were gone, the smoke had vanished, and there was no evidence that anyone in the hall way had heard the commotion that had gone on. Seeing that her friend had awakened, she wiped her tears away with a hopeful, desperate wish that he hadn't been affected by her deal with Melantha.

"Etoileon," she muttered, struggling to push Melantha's limp body to get to him. She sat down next to him and looked down at him. "Are you all right?" she asked. "Etoileon … is it really you?"

He rubbed his aching head with his free hand, and then looked up to her, allowing his eyes to focus on her for a moment. He just stared at her, as though he was trying to remember where he had seen her before. Then he slowly, shakingly, raised his hand to reach up and touch her face, his fingertips brushing over her cheek.

She cried, and whispered, "I love you, you know. And I guess that you don't remember me at all now, because I was so scared I was going to lose you before, I tried to take the fast and quick way out of it … I'm so sorry, I'm so sorry, Etoileon! It was only because … because I love you so much!" She looked down at him once more, to see that he was smiling up at her weakly.

"Selene … " it was a soft whisper, one that could barely be heard even in the silence of the room. But it was real, and he had said it. Selene felt her eyes fill with happy tears as she slowly smiled, amazed that he had been protected from Melantha's curse.

She was about to ask him if he was feeling better when all of a sudden his beautiful gray eyes lost their focus on her, lowering to the bed. His eyes closed slowly, and his body went limp as he slouched back in his bed. "No!" she cried out.

The door suddenly opened and a nurse came in. "What is going on here?" she asked. "Who let you in, hun? Shouldn't you be in bed now? It's after visiting hours."

Selene just shook her head and said, "Please, Nurse, please, go get Dr. Hamersley! Etoileon needs him, now! Go, I beg you!"

The Nurse looked down at Etoileon and sighed. "Beg Pardon, sweetheart, but he's just asleep still, that's all. He's fine. In fact –" she looked over at the medical readings coming off of the screen and quickly summarized the facts— "He's doing much better than he was yesterday. This is good news. I will go inform the doctor of this. You'd better stay here."

The nurse hurried off and Selene let a long breath exhale from deep within her. "Etoileon's okay," she whispered. "He's okay." Then she let go of him and fell forward onto his bed, laying her forehead down by his side. "Thank you, Guardian! Thank you, Pegasus! I know that you were the ones who saved him. I couldn't even save myself back there!"

She knew that there had been a higher power that had intervened and saved her and Etoileon from a cruel fate. But she would be punished, she knew. She could feel the conviction in her heart as she started to cry. She'd disappointed so many people, she thought. She'd run away from her home without permission, she'd lied to the transport crew, she'd wrongfully asked Cyerra to keep it all a secret, and she'd made a deal with the dark master's servant to bring back the only other human that had ever seemed to care for her! She'd disobeyed Pegasus' command to follow him, and she'd traded away her inner light in order that Etoileon be saved from death, at the cost of his memory of her. How could she go back to Pegasus? Would she even be able to find him now?

She fell asleep, but she did not dream, her heart still believing that she was unforgivable.

***
Chapter 11
"My Precious Child"
***

Dorian felt his stomach turn over in his body as he heard the words of the trembling woman before him. Sitting on a makeshift seat in front of the still-damaged Tree Throne, he just stared down at the handmaiden in front of him. "What?" he spurted out. "What do you mean, you can't locate the princess?"

Yana looked up, shaken by the king's reaction as well as Selene's sudden disappearance. She tried to sound calm as she once more told the king what she had found out. "The maids and the chamber men have all confirmed the reports, Sire, that the princess is not here."

"Where is she then?" Dorian roared, his frustration taking over.

"I … I don't know, Your Royal Majesty," Yana spoke softly. "I cannot tell you anymore, just that I know that she went to her room last night early. She has been unaccounted for, as of now, for nearly ten hours. The staff is still looking; some have even gone into the city, trying to find out if any had heard the whereabouts of rebel spies of late."

"You think it is possible that the rebels kidnapped her?" Dorian asked incredulously. "What are the chances of that?"

"Any number," Yana told him. "It could be possible that a member of the Court or the staff was blackmailed or bribed into getting to her. However … " her voice trailed off, as she let her gaze slip to the floor.

Dorian could see what she was trying to say. "However, you don't believe that such is the case, right, Lady Yana?"

Yana's eyes shot back up to meet his. "No, I do not," she agreed. Sighing, she said, "I have a feeling that this has something to do with Sir Etoileon's relapse in the Silverton City Medical Ward."

"Really? What makes you think that is so?"

Yana shook her head. "There is no mistaking her great affections for the boy," she said calmly. "Selene has been sneaking out to meet with him for years before this, actually, Your Highness."

"What?"

"It is true," Yana reluctantly revealed. She had to let the king know for the safety of Her Highness. Her voice lowered as she added, "They have met somewhere for nearly every night since the boy had arrived here. It only makes sense that Selene would sneak out to see him again. The trip to Silverton, by transport vehicle, is relatively short."

He felt his face turn livid red at the thought of his sister hanging with that brat after hours. It was bad enough that the kid had gotten to watch over her for almost all the daylight hours, but to hear this was too much for Dorian. He shook his head sadly. "I don't know what's worse, that she was taken by kidnappers, or she left on her own," he said. He leaned back in his seat and sighed. "This is all my fault. What was I thinking, allowing her such freedom as I have given her?"

Yana took a precautious step towards him. "You have tried to bring her up accordingly, Your Majesty. I do not think that she meant to break your trust," she told him, her voice soft, holding no trace of condemnation. "You have merely tried to encourage her to do what she thought was best. I'm sure that she has a perfectly valid reason for why she simply had to go."

"She might not have even gone of her own free will, Yana," Dorian reminded her. Then he smirked. "Although chances are that is what happened. I will call up the hospital and have them check and see if she is there or not. If she is, a transport will be sent to pick her up. And if she's not, the city will not rest until I have Selene back here, safe in the palace, once more."

Yana nodded. Suddenly, she dropped to a prostrate position, her long abated tears at last let free. "I'm so sorry, Your Majesty," she whispered, her voice etching with sadness. "This is all my fault. You are not to blame. You wanted me to keep track of her, and I refused. But now, how I wish I had listened! How I wished that I had seen the situation more from your point of view! All of this trouble is a result of my impertinence!" she wailed.

At this, Dorian stood up, and walked over to her. He bent down and took hold of her shoulders. "Stop this, Yana," he said quietly. "You will not change the past by being sorry. But you will know better next time, right?" When she looked up at him and nodded, he gave her a slight smile. "Good. Then there is some good that came out of this mess."

"I am truly sorry," Yana sniffed.

The king took out a handkerchief and held it out to her. "I forgive you, but only if you forgive me. I should not have asked something of you that you felt was wrong. I at least could have worded the request better."

Yana nodded, and they both gave a nervous laugh. Dorian took her hands and helped her to her feet. "I will have somebody call the hospital," Dorian told her, allowing himself to keep her hands in his. "I promise."

"Thank you, Your Majesty," Yana replied, her eyes still moist, but sparkling now with a glimmer of resolve and gratitude.

Dorian squeezed her delicate hands affectionately. "Go now. All will be well." And letting her go, she turned and left Dorian and the throne room. Dorian couldn't help but grin at her retreating form. She really was a very pretty, very fascinating young lady, he thought. He kept getting lost in her eyes when she looked up at him. He kind of hoped that he would see her again soon.

***

Cyerra had slumped over and folded her hands together as she waited for her aunt to wake up from her unconsciousness. The first dim light of sunrise was peeking out from behind the skyline of the horizon. There were no clouds in the sky for now.

She looked over at Ronal, who had dozed off some time ago. He had been busy all day, she thought sympathetically. She was grateful for him, and it pained her to think that he would have to leave her soon to go on duty in the north.

Cyerra was thinking of tracking down a nurse to see if there was a way that she could possibly get to see her aunt, but then Kadrianne appeared out of nowhere, walking down the hall. There was a sense of urgency in her steps, and Cyerra wondered if something was wrong all of a sudden.

"Cyerra," Kadrianne called out to her. "Cyerra, I have to talk to you!" There was no mistaking the dread in Kadrianne's tone. Cyerra jumped up from her seat and hurried over.

"What is it, Kadrianne?" Cyerra asked. "Has something happened?"

"Yes … and it is not good, not good at all. The princess is nowhere to be found."

"Oh … I see."

"Is that all you can say at a time like this?" Kadrianne looked at her incredulously. "I can't believe it. I'm terrified of what the king will do, if we can't find her. I mean, she could be anywhere! She could've been captured by rebel forces, or whisked away to a secret holding place to be bartered back for land or other terms! She could have even been killed!"

"There is also the possibility that she could've run away as well," Cyerra said pointedly. "I mean, do you really think that an enemy of ours could slip past all of the security we have here?"

"It is unlikely," Kadrianne agreed. "But that means that … " Her voice trailed off and Kadrianne suddenly turned her gaze inquiringly up to study Cyerra's face. "What do you know of this, Cyerra? Something tells me that you know something that you don't want to say."

"Well –" Cyerra was about try and dodge Kadrianne's astute observation when a nurse aid came up to them and interrupted their conversation.

"Beg your pardon, Ladies, but I have come to inform Lady Cyerra that her aunt, Rou Saché, has awoken. She is doing fine now, but her external bruises may not heal very quickly."

Cyerra bowed her head in thanks. "I appreciate everything that you have done for her," she said gratefully. "Thank you so much."

"You are welcome," the nurse aid told her. "If you wish, you may see her now. She is asking for you."

"Thank you. I will go see her," Cyerra said, looking uncertainly at Kadrianne. Once the nurse aid was out of hearing range, Cyerra said, "Kadrianne, I cannot talk about this subject now. I am on leave from work today anyway. Please, go and ask Yana or Rosaria, or even Chevée about it. My aunt has awakened, and I must attend to her now."

After a moment, Kadrianne sighed. "Very well. Yana has gone to inform the king. I will wait for her outside of the throne room." She paused as she moved to turn around and head back, long enough to say, "I hope that your aunt is feeling much better now."

"Thank you," Cyerra said. "Good luck … " She watched as Kadrianne disappeared down the hall as quickly as she had come moments before. Cyerra let out a small sigh of relief. She had not wanted to lie, even for Selene's sake.

She started to head to her aunt's room, pausing only a moment as she walked by Ronal's sleeping form. She wondered if she should wake him, but she thought that it was better for him to get what rest he could for now.

Cyerra opened the door to her aunt's room and smiled, glad to see her aunt was sitting up, awake and alert as ever, as she rested against her fluffed hospital pillows. "Auntie!" she called out.

Her Aunt Rou looked at her, but didn't smile. Instead, an expression of graveness came across her middle-aged features. Her words managed to stop Cyerra in her tracks as she made her way to the side of the ward bed.

"Cyerra … He has come back. Aemon has come back to the city."

***

Selene opened her eyes to find herself in an eerily familiar white room. She unsteadily reached up and tried to wipe the remainder of sleep from her bleary eyes. When her eyes were completely adjusted to the light of the room, she noticed that she was not alone in the room.

"Dorian!" she exclaimed in a hoarse whisper. "What are you doing here?"

He glared at her. "I had the head of staff call up this place, to see if you were there. When your doctor told me that you were here indeed, rage and relief at the same time overcame me. When he told me that it looked like you had suffered a relapse into your former weak condition, I was floored with worry. So I came to see you myself."

431

He had been distraught with concern all day, as he had watched her sleep fitfully. He had never known his sister to have problems sleeping before this.

"How long have you been here?" Selene asked slowly. She wasn't sure that Dorian had forgiven her or not.

When he shot her a look of disappointment a moment later, she was pretty sure that he hadn't. He shook his head and said, "It does not matter. I wanted to get away from the palace a bit anyhow. Some disturbing news has come to our attention and the military personnel's deployment has changed and moved up. But I left it in the hands of those who know how to handle that kind of situation; I need to get a grasp on this one, this one between you and I." Selene gulped as his golden brown eyes flicked over to instill a sense of dread in her.

Dorian got up and began pacing in front of her bed. "What I want to know is why you decided that this little fieldtrip of yours would be all right by me. Am I too lenient with you, Selene? Is that why you feel so compelled to disobey me?"

"No! No, that is not true, Dorian," Selene objected. "I'm sorry, I am, that I worried you and caused you such grief –"

"You do not even have any idea of how much I have suffered!" Dorian interrupted her. "You could have been kidnapped by terrorists, rebels, you could have been killed! Don't you realize that you are the only hope for this world?"

Selene shook her head. "No, I am not," she rejected. "I cannot be. I am sick just as everyone else is."

"What are you talking about?" Dorian scowled at her. "Don't talk such nonsense to me. You mean so much to everyone, Selene. You are my only family, have you forgotten that much? Do you know how much I would blame myself if anything ever happened to you?"

"Dorian … " Selene felt a jolt of surprise and rush of guilt. "I'm sorry, I really am. But please understand, I am suffering much more than you know, too."

"I don't see how running away solves any of your suffering," Dorian huffed. "I have a transport waiting for us at the landing station. It will leave in an hour. Do not be late."

"Wait!" Selene called out to him. "I know that I don't deserve your forgiveness, Dorian. But I had to come, for Etoileon's sake." Her words seemed to hang in the air for a silent moment.

"Selene," Dorian said as he turned his head back to her, "I forgive you this time. But I will not be overlooking this. You will be punished when we all get back to Diamond City. However, I realize that you are under a lot of pressure and believe it or not, I understand. That is why I have asked that your protector, that silly boy, be moved to the palace medical ward, now that it is finished."

Selene felt her eyes widen in surprise. "What?"

"Yes. He will be coming with us today," Dorian said with spite lacing his words. "I cannot help that you care for him so, but I do not think that you should be tempted to go outside of the palace again … at least not until it is safe."

"Dorian," Selene breathed. "How can I thank you for this?"

"Stay where you are supposed to, Sister," he snorted as he left the room. "We leave in an hour."

Selene watched as the door to her room shut with a small bang, but she felt a smile start to form on her face. Dorian had granted her forgiveness, and he was willing to make her pain easier to bear by moving Etoileon to the palace, where she could see him every day if she wanted! It was almost too good to be true. She looked out of the window in her room, blinking at the bright light. "Thank you," she whispered as she stared wondrously into the sunshine.

****

King Dorian alighted from his transport glider, dressed for the Assembly of the Crown Forces. He was wearing his finest armor, which had been polished to a shine for the meeting that hour. He wore the traditional general's cape, and held onto the spear of war, a tradition that had been followed since ancient times. Dorian was quickly followed by his combat in arms. The men behind him were the most skilled marksmen of their time. They were all dressed in apparel and mood alike as well, for the assembly today was no ordinary assembly. There was one ordinary civilian with him, however—Josiah the Judge. The eager man had come to offer his support of the Council to the King. Dorian had gladly allowed the friendly judge to accompany him as they all headed for the outer keep.

"Your Majesty," Josiah spoke up quietly, "How do you think the people will take the news?"

THE MOONLGIHT PEGASUS

"I'm hoping that they will not riot at this point," Dorian couldn't help but smirk. "Excuse me, Josiah, for my bad timing of my sense of humor. I was not very calm when I first heard the news, myself. I cannot ask my men to change around all their plans at once, and if it were not such a dire situation, I would not. But this is turning into a costly war, and we must change, or face destruction."

Josiah nodded. "I agree, Your Highness, as sorrowful as it is," he said sympathetically. "Times of war are never easy, but giving up or slowing down just causes more problems. It is best that the situation is taken head on, not so the victor can begin exploiting the spoils, but so that people everywhere can be once again reassured of something that goods and money will never buy them—their peace. It is sad to think that people believe more and more that to have happiness, they need to have more things. They don't realize that having a lot of goods and resources means nothing if they will still die in the end. They put their trust in their treasures here, forgetting that there are some things money and power will never guarantee. Until something is lost, no one will ever fully realize the worth of the more eternal desires, such as peace, hope and love."

Dorian nodded. "You are a wise man, Josiah. I agree with you."

Josiah bowed his head respectfully. "I have always had faith in you, Dorian," he said, using the king's given name. "I have long considered you a friend of mine. I am glad to be here beside you. Your men will not abandon you this hour; if they have any respect or love for you at all, as I do, then I can say without any doubt that they will be, again, like myself, in

435

THE MOONLGIHT PEGASUS

that they will be honored and privileged to stand beside you, in this battle to end all battles."

Dorian felt his eyes mist over slightly. "Thank you, Josiah, my friend," he said, before he walked out onto his platform. It was time for him to speak at last.

***

Ronal watched as the king approached the pulpit and quieted down at once. He and several of the surrounding troops and leaders had been discussing what was going to happen to them. It had already reached the ears of the crowd that reassignments were in order for all of them. He watched as the king raised his hands, and his trumpets sounded, telling the crowd to cease making any noise at once.

Dorian looked more determined than Ronal had ever seen him. Maybe it was something about the armor, but the king had an air of strength about him that was not to be overlooked. Placing his hands on the sides of the platform, the king was silent for a moment as he looked around the crowded outer keep.

"Gentlemen, Fighters, Soldiers, Enforcement Members … Everyone. You are all here today because you have willingly chosen to fight against the rebels of this world. You are all here today, to answer the call that you have felt in your heart. All of you, for taking that first step alone, are heroes. No one deserves to be asked to take the life of another, especially when that one may be the life of his brother, his neighbor, his father, his son."

Everyone remained silent still as the king paused. They seemed to be waiting on edge for him to continue.

"I am proud to count you among my number," Dorian said. "Each of you has proven his worth to this nation in some way. And before this week is done, I know that each of you will again use your gifts for the good of our world." He looked away from the men, out into the distance. "Sapphira is a beautiful world, isn't it? I look every morning, and I cannot recall a time when I have seen the same sunrise twice. The seas and the wind almost sing their harmony throughout this world. The plants grown here in Diamond City flourish, as though to show off their beauty for the pleasure of others. The animals here are docile, each one kind distinguished from the other." Here he smirked. "It is only when I look at the people born of this world, do I begin to find the ugliness of nature. Many are not so, some cannot help it. I can say assuredly that there are people who are good, for the sake of goodness. But I have yet to find an individual who was bad for the sake of badness." He dropped his playfulness as he turned to the serious part of his message. "I believe in the goodness of man, and I choose to believe this. That is why I will mourn the loss of both rebel and friend. But I will not be one to condone the evil that they do, so in order to give justice to the world, I must kill. And so I will. There is a great battle ahead of us, in only a few short days. I have come to tell you that many of you who were to be sent away are now to be kept here. The rebel army, numbering close to a hundred legions, is camping out on the border of this great city, of this great world. I have come to ask you, Are you ready to fight?" With this, Dorian lifted up the Spear of War, in great exclamation. "Are you ready to fight?"

There was a great wave in the crowd as each man held up their own arms, mimicking Dorian's hold on the Spear.

Ronal was among those who raised up his arms in triumph. But even as he did, he wondered if he was watching his life with Cyerra fly away, out of his grasp forever.

***

Aemon felt a surge of pride fill up his chest as he watched his army assemble. He'd come to the outskirts of Diamond City to prepare for the final battle of this war. His advisor, his Uncle Emanon, had brought him to this special place in hopes of redeeming his dead brother's name.

Aemon had no such plan for restoring the honor of his father's name. As far as Aemon could tell, his father had been a selfish, narcissistic man, who had left his family to go and fight a war over another woman. But Uncle Emanon, his father's younger brother, was sure that Aemon would come to see the nobility of Ammos' actions. Aemon was skilled enough to know that disillusioning his uncle would only hinder his military efficiency and delay the arrival of the new world government.

The army numbered about a hundred legions, filled with young men from many islands and areas around the Continent. They were going to charge the city in a matter of days, once all the weapons had been distributed, the men counted and identified, and the final draft of the plans reviewed by all the soldiers. Aemon knew, looking at the sun set in the far west horizon, that all the preparations would be finished by noon on the third day. It would be then that he would call his army to attack.

His only regret was stopping by his former house. His Aunt Rou had been home, and he had surprised her. His Aunt Rou was Emanon's sister as well as Ammos', but her years of living near the house of the monarchs had dulled her sense of discontent with the government. She had, in recent years, blamed the poor island education system on her feelings of rebellion. At least, that was what he'd gathered from her before his commanding general had knocked her out cold. His two companions had torn the house apart on the inside while Aemon had run up to his room to grab his father's flag.

He'd kept it safe all these long years, as though he'd known from a very small age that he would fulfill the destiny that his father had tried and failed at. The azure hue of the flag had faded over the years, but the constellation of the Four-point prison in the center of it remained a resplendent white. There was a small rip running partially down the middle of the flag, and each year, it seemed to grow longer, no matter what Aemon did to it.

Now, he handed the flag to his uncle. "Here, Uncle Emanon," he said. "Put this on the tallest pole we have. I want this to be carried before the troops in battle, as a symbol of the fulfillment of time."

"Yes, I shall," His uncle responded with an amused look on his face. Emanon was a tall, muscular man in his late thirties. He looked like his nephew, with dark hair and gray eyes. On some days, Emanon found it entertaining that he took orders from his imbecile of a nephew, but his true master, Obsidian, had promised that Aemon would bring untold riches to Emanon for his diligent advising and his keen overlook on the matters they faced as the final battle approached.

Now holding the flag of his brother who had gone before them, he felt that Aemon had done something right on his own. His brother Ammos would be proud of Aemon for this. It was one thing to avenge the death of his family members, but it was another to restore their honor and triumph in their upheld beliefs. Emanon remembered all too well the day that he had lost his oldest nephew and his brother.

As he called for his servants to deliver the flag to the forward flag bearer, he felt a longing in his heart for his family. He missed them still, though it had been over eighteen years since they had been taken away from him. He suddenly wondered if he would ever see his twin sister again.

***

For the first time in weeks, Selene could not get to sleep. She stared down at her covers with almost a hateful look in her eye, as she was caught between self-pity and self-loathing.

There was no explaining her feelings. She felt weary, as though her heart had been burdened with a heavy weight. She felt sick, and could not stand the sight of food or drink. She would only sip water from time to time, and she found that it had turned bitter to the taste. She felt like she was empty, but she felt full of guilt; she felt tired but she could find no rest. She longed to talk with Pegasus, but she dreaded facing him.

"These days have been so hard on me," she thought out loud. "I have proven to be weak and undeserving more than ever in the eyes of Crystallon." Surely then, she reasoned, she could not feel any worse in facing Pegasus. But what if he would be nowhere to be found? She had strayed so far away from him in just a matter of hours. To think, she thought, that I had just talked with him two nights ago! Now I am lonely, and I can't feel his presence within me at all.

Selene glanced out the window and saw the millions of pathway lights glowing, as soldiers began to register for their deployment around the city limits.

Thanks to the credibility of Cyerra's Aunt Rou, and the agents of the Crown who backed her information up as correct, it was found that the rebel army was preparing for a great battle at Diamond City in a matter of days. Selene knew that she would be ordered to stay inside the palace as the fighting took place, but she wished that Dorian would send her away somewhere. She frowned as she recalled how she had seen Dorian take the news when he'd come back from picking her up at the hospital.

Her arrogant brother had practically grinned at the news; he had known along with Aemon that the winners of this battle would win the war. There were so many soldiers and Fighters on call for this battle that there would be no room for any new recruits for some years.

There was a sense of anticipation hanging in the air, even from what Selene could see down below in the courtyard. There was a great deal of teary-eyed and crying women down in the courtyards. They'd been allowed to wait for their loved ones to be assigned, as well as a short time to say their good-byes, before the battle started. Selene watched them, and suddenly wondered how Cyerra was doing. It couldn't be easy on her, Selene thought as she kept her eyes on the masses below. Selene knew that Cyerra would be heart-broken over it. She made a silent promise to herself to allow Cyerra to take it easy over the course of the next couple of days before the battle was rumored to start.

Selene slumped back down. There were rumors that told of the great number of troops that Aemon had rallied to go behind him, rumors that declared the monarchy to be at a strong disadvantage. The princess feared that her friends, her loyal people, and even the ones who aligned themselves with the enemy, would be killed or hurt as a result of all this. She wished that there was something she could do to stop it, but she knew, thinking of the overshadowing darkness that hid in her own soul, she was at a loss to even save the one person she ought to have been able to save—herself.

The rest of the night passed slowly for Selene as she tossed and turned, unable to find rest.

***

It was raining again.

The soft pitter-patter of the rain falling against the windows and walls of the palace could be heard clearly through the silent hallways. The castle was filled with an unspeakable sense of dread. The day for the troops to be sent out towards the rebel army camp had come. Even the skies seemed to know it, and many believed it was for that reason that the rains had come.

The princess had not found any rest in her light sleep; the thunder and lightning of the storm had caused her to jolt awake any time that she felt herself drifting off. But she was not the only one who had been kept awake during the long, black hours of the moonless night.

Cyerra made her way through the palace, her steps slow and her eyes glazed over. She had no particular destination in mind, as almost the entire staff had been allowed to sleep late. The king had seemed to know that his workers and servants would need some quiet time before they set about to do their work. Almost all of the employees had agreed with the king, and none had objected.

Though the battle had not yet begun, it seemed only right to mourn. The battle for the Continent would commence, and then all would be swept up in fervor, rejoicing with the victors, or mourning for the lost, or even both. There was not a soul in all of Diamond City that would not be affected in some way; time for mourning the loss of innocence and the loss of this tranquil and comforting ignorance was needed. With change always came sacrifice, and this sacrifice was one to be mourned.

Cyerra turned the corner and found herself out in one of the open courtyards of the palace. There was no roof over this courtyard, but the walkway surrounding it had a section of elegant roofing installed to shield her visitors from the persistent raindrops. Cyerra felt the splash of the falling rain on her shoes and her dress, but she did not move as she watched the view before her.

There was a small pavilion in the middle of this smaller courtyard that arched up just reaching past the surrounding walkway roof. The roof of the small pergola was shaped like a dome, and the columns that supported it were of the ancient fashion. For some reason, Cyerra suddenly felt the urge to take shelter under it.

She picked up her skirts and made her way down the path to the pavilion, her pace never changing from her solemn march, even as the rain soaked her skin and dampened her clothes. Her hair began to whip around her face, the wet strains sticking to her as the wind picked up. She did not really care; on some level, she gloried in it. There was something so alluring about breaking free of the comforts of the modern world, to find oneself caught up in nature's storm, she thought.

When she came in under the pavilion from the rain, she was shocked to see that someone else was there. She could hardly believe her eyes as she looked down at his crouching form. "Ronal?"

He looked up at her. He hadn't heard her arrive over the sound of the rainstorm. "Cyerra," he welcomed her, a smile slowly finding its way onto his face. "I was hoping that I would get to see you again today." He looked away as he added, "But I wasn't expecting to see you this early."

"I can leave, if you want to be alone," she offered softly. She knew what he was feeling, and that there was little chance that she would be able to help him.

"No, please. Stay," he swept out his hand, beckoning her to come and sit down next to him on the pavilion floor. "You always manage to cheer me up. That's one of the things I loved about you, even when I first met you."

Cyerra drew back slightly, catching the tone of his words. "Please, don't do that," she begged. "I don't think I can stand hearing all of the reasons why you love me. Not now, of all times."

"I suppose that it is rather poor timing," Ronal agreed. "But I have to, because I might not … get another chance to say what exactly is in my heart for you." When she remained silent, he continued. "Cyerra, I have nothing at this point in my life to offer you, only the promise that I will never forget you. Whether death should come between us or not, I will keep the memories of our days together close in my heart.

You have brightened my life in these last few months. Of all the things in this world, the one thing I'm most grateful for is meeting you."

Cyerra felt hot tears streaming down her face as she shakily nodded. "Ronal … please be careful. Please promise that you'll come back to me."

Ronal shook his head. "I cannot make a promise like that," he said. "I do not honestly know if I would be able to keep it. And I can't cause you to hate me for that, should I be gone." He shifted closer to her and wrapped his arm around her. "This world is changing so quickly, all of a sudden," he told her, whispering in her ear. "So many things that seemed important before, don't really seem so significant now. So many things are new and strange, and I'm not sure that any of them are good, either. But I do know that you will always have a place in my heart, and you will always be a good thing to me. Thank you for giving me a chance. Thank you for caring. And thank you for being you. I love you."

Cyerra nodded, too full of emotions to say the words back to him. For a long while he just held her, as the rains slowed and the sky began to lighten.

Selene had not meant to overhear Ronal's farewell to Cyerra; she had been passing by the open courtyard, and had heard the familiar voices as they were carried on the wind. She'd stopped and listened, the tender words drawing her in. She now turned and slumped against the cold granite walls of the palace, slowly sinking to the floor as she laid her head in her hands.

Was this war so eminent that it threatened to tear love apart? Would such pain be forgotten or rewarded? Would suffering ever really be gone? The questions filled her head, and there she stood, the princess of the torn-apart world, trained in all forms of study and learning, considered to be the sign of peace, and loved by so many, with no available answer.

She looked up from her lap and felt her heart ache for one she loved. "Etoileon," she murmured thoughtfully. I will go and see him, she thought. "I miss how you used to comfort me," she whispered softly. She recalled how another used to comfort her, too, and nearly cried again. Standing up, she brushed herself off and hurried to go and visit Etoileon, wishing that she knew of the place where she could see Pegasus once more as well.

****

There are some advantages to being a princess, Selene thought as she breezed right through the medical ward hallways. Normally, she would've had to go through several people and nurse stations, trying to answer all their questions as they decided whether or not to allow her in. But being a beloved member of the royalty, she merely had to show up and they all moved to please her.

The Diamond City Medical Ward was located adjacent and connecting to the palace. The building had been built into the slanting landscape, on the large hillside of the Table, but it had taken more than a few moments of walking for Selene to arrive at her destination.

Opening the door to his room, Selene felt her sadness for the war soften as she gazed upon the familiar features of her protector. The rain still hit the window in the hospital wardroom where Etoileon had been brought. He seemed to be much better off than the last time Selene had been with him. His color was good and his vital signs were all well. The resident doctor had informed her that there was no visible reason why he had not awakened yet; Etoileon's fever was down from before and he was receiving the best possible care for his present condition.

She moved over to sit by him and reached down to take his hand in hers, as she had done last time. "Hi Etoileon," she greeted him lovingly in a hushed voice. "I hope that you're doing better today. I know that you at least look peaceful." She tightened her hands around his and bowed her head low. "I wanted to tell you that Dorian did punish me for going to see you. I am not allowed out of the palace grounds, as usual, but I have a couple extra study sessions on proper etiquette and there are a few of the King's guards that stand watch over my room during the night." She paused here and drew back from him, letting go of his hand and moving to look out the window towards the outer keep.

How strange it was to know that there were soldiers and Fighters and the defenders of the Crown in that part of the palace. There were people who were going to die in the next day or two standing in that mob of people in the rain, listening to her brother the king, as he tried to encourage and comfort them.

She leaned against the windows and folded her arms to her chest. "The Great Battle is going to start soon, I hear," she said. "I am glad, if nothing else, that this coma has taken you out of the battle. Your friends are going to battle soon, including Ronal. I heard him telling his sweetheart Cyerra goodbye. She must be so troubled over his fate. I cannot imagine the feelings that she must be having right now." She looked back over at him. "I did not have to worry about you prior to the attack," she whispered. "I never had to say goodbye. I never got that chance."

She broke away from the window and came back to lean her head down on his still shoulder as she felt her face scrunch up. There were no tears left in her, but the pain was as sharp and as real as ever. "That is why I must apologize," she whispered against him. "I almost had you taken away from me, by my own decision. I had a chance to make you well, and I committed your memory of me to Obsidian for that chance. I willingly turned to the dark master in an effort to help you. I'm sorry. I believed that I was doing right; I believed that I had to do it almost, because of my feelings for you. I felt that I should do all that I could to help you, and because of that misguidance, I almost lost you. I am so sorry, so grieved, and so tormented over how I almost let you be changed forever. I can't believe how fortunate I am, that the Guardian did not allow Obsidian into your mind before he and his servant were dispelled."

She laid her head on his shoulder, feeling the warmth of his breath into her hair as she remained there. She was hoping that she had managed to shake him out of his slumber, but he didn't alter his conditions in the least. Her eyes lowered, and her heart couldn't take it anymore. She had apologized, but she still felt the guilt of her decision.

Maybe it's because I not only failed Etoileon, but Pegasus as well, she thought despairingly. Thinking of her other hurt friend, she shook her head. I'm so sorry, Pegasus. I know I am unworthy of you, and I can never make up for what I have done this time. How I wish that you could help me now, she silently called out to him.

She suddenly felt like screaming. Like crying and sobbing until she grew hoarse and weary of her calls. Selene sat up and sighed. Clutching his hand in hers once more, she tenderly brushed some of Etoileon's stray bangs away from his face. "I will see you soon," she promised, getting up and hurriedly leaving.

He had felt so dead to her in there, she thought as she started running. Nurses and aids dodged around her as she fled down the halls and around the corners. Trays upset, carts crashed, and people fell as Selene lost sight of them in her attempt to outrun the void that was haunting her. Etoileon had never felt so far away from her as he did in there. And Pegasus, she couldn't feel his presence at all. Why would he stay with someone who didn't obey him, didn't trust him, and couldn't find it in herself to have faith that he had kept his word that he would always be with her? She could think of nothing to answer that question. "Only a miracle," she replied cynically.

Selene finally stopped, bending over as she tried to catch her breath. She put her hands on her knees and leaned over, allowing her heart to slow down as her body took a rest. When she had taken several deep, calming breaths, she looked up and found herself in a familiar place. She'd stopped at the door to the staircase that led up to her High Tower.

"Huh?" Selene was dumbfounded. "How did I end up here?" she wondered. She had no memory of running so far, so quickly. The time that it had taken her to get there had been several more minutes than what it had seemed to her. She looked at the door carefully. "Should I go up there?" she asked aloud, and instantly there was a whisper in her heart that said yes.

There was a part of her that wanted to go up there. Up there were memories of happy times with Etoileon that made her almost feel alive again. Up there it was also closer to the realm of Crystallon, where Pegasus and the Guardian both resided. And it was far from the soil of Sapphira, where all her trouble came from. So with a braveness she had never known before, she started up the stairs to her High Tower room, wishing every step of the way that there would be peace for her at last.

***

To her disgust, there was nothing peaceful about being in the High Tower just then. The rainstorm poured down on the tower heavily, seeming to be just one stream outpouring from the clouds instead of millions of little drops. The lightning that laced through the skies seemed much too close for comfort, and the thunder boomed so loud that Selene thought that she would burst her eardrums if she remained there too long. Worst of all though, was that there was no light. The stars and moon were all blotched out by dark, black thunderclouds, and the city lights were hard to make clear from this high up. All around her, the darkness swirled and seemed to seep into her space, even her very skin, as she watched out of the Tower room's large windows.

Selene placed her hands on her ears to soften the sounds of the raging storm outside and tried to find a spot to sit down; in all of her times in the tower, it had been rare that she would be in the room. She loved to be on the balcony, looking down on the city at her feet.

"Why am I so scared all of a sudden?" Selene said to herself as she looked around. She decided that she had been foolish to come up there, what with the large storm outside

450

so intimidating. She started to head back to the stairwell entrance.

But it was just then that a lightning bolt crashed through the window, and thundered roared, causing Selene to shriek and fall to her knees on the ground. The storm scared her so badly, but she could not move. She curled up into a ball and felt like crying. For long moments with the endless storm echoing all around her, Selene just laid there on the floor, too scared to move, too afraid to do little more than whimper to herself.

The storm began to sound like it was being muffled. Selene felt the slight spray of rain on her face, and her eyelids grew heavy with weariness. In the midst of the storm, she was called to sleep.

***

She adjusted herself onto her knees, and was slightly surprised to feel, instead of a hard, cold, wet floor, a soft padding of sand. She looked up to feel the mist of a sea on her face instead of the rain of a thunderstorm, and to hear a familiar voice calling out to her instead of thunder.

"My precious, precious child," the voice called. "Are you there?"

Selene looked up to see her dream world start to change as she shook her head, too ashamed of herself to answer his call. The skies in her dream grew cloudy and dark, and the waves began to slosh all around. The wind picked up, almost like a whirlwind, causing her to wrap herself up in her own arms, trying as best as she could to protect herself.

451

Her face scrunched up as the sand blew in her face, but it wasn't long before Selene peeked out to watch the storm as it overwhelmed her. The sand whipped her face, and she suddenly let go of herself, too depressed to do anything any longer. She had no strength left in her, even to protect herself.

She stood up, her eyes catching sight of a glimmer on the horizon. Her heart leapt. Could that be Pegasus? she wondered. Her eyes filled with tears. No, it could not be, she thought, because I have gone away from him. She looked down the beach, and this time another sight in the sky caught her attention.

There was a scene from her life, a memory, flashing across the broad sky. Selene watched as it came more and more into focus, and then she was able to identify which event it was.

This one was the day the tenth anniversary of the death of her mother. Selene saw herself placing a bouquet of flowers on an ornate gravestone. She remembered that day; it had been a hard one to get through. She hadn't known her mother at all, and still she missed her.

Then the scene faded, as another one took its place. This one was her twelfth birthday celebration, and Dorian had arranged for a magnificent performance from one of the globe-touring circus and animal companies.

Soon another came, and another after that. Selene watched as happy times and sad times alike flashed across the gray clouds of her dreamland's sky. The day that Haiasi, her brother's dear companion and advisor, had been buried. The time that Selene had helped plant the courtyard flowers. The time that she had argued with her brother at the lunch table about starting her education. Graduating from Master Norio's training sessions as a full master of self-defense. Splashing around in the fountain near the Great Hall. Meeting with Etoileon. Dancing with Etoileon. Losing Etoileon.

Somewhere in the stream of vivid memories, Selene noticed that there were a set of footprints in the sand that came up with each passing memories. Some of the memories had two sets of footprints. Some of them only had one. Selene frowned at this, wondering what it could mean. She looked again and realized that it was during the sad times of her life, the painful trials, the agonizing hours, that there were only one set of footprints in the sand.

She thought about what Pegasus had said to her about never leaving her, about knowing her for years. If one set of those footprints is mine, she thought, then the other must be his. But why would he leave me when I am troubled? She examined the footprints closer and saw that one this slide, one of the two sets of feet looked like they belonged to a horse or some kind. That confirms it, she thought, he must have not been here with me. But she was still troubled at the thought of him leaving her, especially in the times of her life when she had been troubled. It didn't make any sense, she thought.

"Pegasus," she called out. "Pegasus, please! Tell me why you would leave me in the harder times of my life … tell me, why are there only one set of footprints in the sand when I am distressed?" She looked up to the sky, and her eyes filled with tears. The wind caught her hair and danced with it. No answer. Selene sank down to the sand, her one hand grabbing a hold of it and then letting it fly away.

Then all of a sudden came the bright shimmering light. Selene did not wake up from her dream as she covered her eyes from the blinding force. The winds stopped, the clouds dispersed, and all at once Selene felt the beauty of her dream being restored and strengthened. But the blessings did not end there.

He called out to her. "My precious, precious child, I am here with you."

Selene precariously opened one eye and looked around. The sight that she saw caused her gaze to open up completely, widening at wonder. Pegasus was there, right in front of her, waiting there for her to come to him! Never had he looked so pure, so white, so absolutely refreshing. Selene gasped as she looked around as everything glowed with a shimmering sparkle. She stumbled as she tried to get up, she was so astounded and completely amazed.

Then her eyes fell once more upon Pegasus and she started to him, tripping on her skirts. When she was only a couple of steps away, her doubts jumped into her mind once more. She halted. "Wait," she said slowly.

He said nothing, so she continued on, saying, "Pegasus … I saw the scenes from my life across the sky. And I saw the footprints, too." He nodded. Selene struggled to keep her thoughts straight. "Well … I was wondering why … why you left me when I was going through the sad times of my life. They are the only scenes that have only one set of footprints in the sand." She looked down. "I don't understand why you would leave me, right when I would need you the most, I think."

Pegasus waited until she looked back up at him before he said, "My precious child, I love you so much. I have been with you, walked with you since the day that you were born, and even long before that. I would never leave you. It is during those times of trial in your life, when you saw only one set of footprints in the sand, it was then that I carried you."

Selene felt her heart leap with untold elation at his clarifying words. She smiled, and even then she couldn't contain her joy. A hearty laugh escaped her, and she jumped up with a renewed spirit. She felt her hands encircle around her beloved dream guardian, and she continued to laugh joyfully as he held onto her.

"I have been waiting for you to turn your eyes upon me once more. There is something I want you to see," he whispered softly. "Please, will you come with me?"

Selene nodded her head, still holding onto him as her dream faded away.

***

"Wait!" Selene cried out as she found herself back in the human world. "No! I didn't get a chance to find out what it was that Pegasus wanted to show me!" She sat up and found that she was still holding her hands over her ears. She also realized that there was no sound coming from the outside anymore. She looked over and saw that the rain had stopped and the thunder and lightning had been rendered silent once more.

"Huh?" She got up and hurried out onto the balcony, and felt her heart soar at the familiar beauty of her city below. "Wow, everything looks beautiful," she whispered in awe.

"Yes, and this is just one city around this world."

Selene jerked around to find that Pegasus was flying right beside her balcony. "Pegasus! You're really here … am I still asleep?"

"No, you are awake in the human world once more," Pegasus assured her. "I am here in your world, as real to you in this one as I am in the realm of your dreams."

"Incredible!" Selene exclaimed happily. "I thought that you were sent only to the dream world."

Pegasus shook his head as he flew. "The time has come for the power of Crystallon to be opened up to those who are sick with the Dark Plague here on Sapphira. I am acting according to the perfect will. I have been given the strength to get through to this world."

Selene took a step closer to him. "I don't understand," she told him.

"Come with me," Pegasus invited her, flying down to the balcony in order that she could climb on him. "There is so much I wish to tell you, my precious one."

Selene hesitated for a moment. "Are you sure it's all right to sit on your back?" she asked. "And I won't fall off?"

"Trust me," Pegasus smiled at her. "I will not let you fall. I have carried you before."

Selene did not recall him ever carrying her, but she realized that it had been because she had been so distracted by looking at the trouble around her. Of course he had carried her before. It was only by his mercy that he was here now, wasn't it?

She took a hold of his mane and climbed on, nearly screaming as she slumped forward on him as he began to fly with her. Suddenly Selene looked down at her High Tower, and laughed as her chains were broken and she experienced that freedom that she had been longing for since she could dream. She could almost hear the snap of the chains as they were forced away from her, with the power of Pegasus pulling her away from the binding of her sorrows, her pains, and her sufferings. Under the wings of Pegasus, she felt no burden of her former life.

They soared up into the night, tumbling all around the clouds. Selene laughed and held tightly to him, and after a while it seemed that he would go into a twirling dive and plummet through the misty clouds just to hear her laugh, so he could laugh with her. Pegasus and Selene continued soaring high through the starry night, eventually seeing a trace of light on the horizon.

"This is so beautiful!" Selene shouted up to Pegasus as the wind played with her gown and blew across her face. Her hair was caught up in the excitement, twisting and turning with the currents of the wind. His mane fluttered about, his soft and perfectly white hair tickling against her skin every so often. She continued to hold onto him as she leaned forward, calling out, "Sapphira is so pretty! Is this how you see it all the time?"

Pegasus shook his head and glanced back at her. "No. I see so much more than the outer beauty. I will show you."

With that, his wings folded back and he plunged down into the atmosphere.

Selene saw the clouds briefly as they fell through, and then the waters of the Sapphiran seas came into view. She wondered if they were going to hit the water, they were going so fast, but at the last possible second, Pegasus turned up and he flew just above the water, making it appear to the onlooker that he was in fact running on the waves. Selene giggled as the spray bounced up and hit her.

Soon they came upon a land, and Pegasus slowed down. "The people here cannot see us," he told her as he gazed back. "Men have long convinced themselves that some things are for dreams, and not for their reality. Only with the faith of a child can a person see into a whole new world of possibilities."

Selene nodded, and then smiled sadly. "I bet even if they could see us they would think they were just hallucinating."

"You are right," Pegasus agreed. "That is why only the one who knows the hearts of men can judge properly."

They came up on the shore, and saw a great island wedding celebration was taking place. Selene felt her face turn into a soft smile as she watched the bride and the groom share their first dance with each other. All of their friends were gathered around, all saying congratulatory words and shouts of encouragement. Pegasus turned to her and there was a twinkle in his eye. Selene smiled back at him, for she knew that he approved of such a celebration of love. She couldn't help but wonder if she would ever get to have a wedding as lovely as this one.

After several moments watching the affections of the partygoers below, they headed off once more. The light of the sun became more and more visible as they traveled. Eventually, Selene spoke up. "I hope that those two have a wonderful life together," she said.

"They will, if they remain strong and true to one another," Pegasus told her. "That was Kani Island. It is a small place, but it is known for several of its achievements. We are coming up on several other islands, where I will show you more of both this world's beauty and ugliness, of its joy and its pain."

Selene saw on the one island another kind of celebration. This island celebrated the birth of a new, healthy child. Another island mourned the loss of its leader. Selene felt her eyes water as she listened to the eulogy of the man's wife, and she said, "Death is not very pretty, I suppose."

"It is necessary, I'm afraid," her friend told her. "The Dark Plague was given to man by a lie. Obsidian had told the people that they would not die if they turned away from the Pure Light. His lie has brought about all the suffering of this world and the pain of the one in Crystallon at the loss of his children. The Dark Plague offers only death and certain pain. The only goodness in this world is a result of the Guardian's deep love for every soul, even the bad ones, on all of Sapphira for all time."

"But how can the Dark Plague be healed?" Selene asked.

"Only the light of a pure soul can save that which was lost," Pegasus explained. "Think of it like this. A soul resembles a flame. If the Dark Plague gets hold of that flame, the light will fade, and the passing of a human life will occur.

However, a pure soul has the power to bring the light back to those who have the darkness in their hearts. But then the darkness could easily corrupt it again. So in order to simultaneously have the darkness expelled from a tainted soul and rekindle the human's soul, the light of a pure soul must be used."

"I understand, somewhat," Selene said. "But why? Can't the Guardian just overlook a person's evilness?"

"Not if there is anything as justice in all of creation," Pegasus shook his head.

"Pegasus … can I ask you something?" Selene asked.

"Yes, of course."

"Well … you said that there is a lot of darkness in this world, as a result of Obsidian's lie."

"Yes."

"Well … do you know my friend Etoileon?" Selene blushed. "I was wondering if he had been corrupted by the darkness in any way, since … since Obsidian was ready to use him in order to get to me, in order to get to you. I do not understand why he dislikes you enough to do anything so evil, but … " her voice trailed off, and her gaze turned away from him as she shook her head.

Pegasus looked at her thoughtfully. "My precious Selene, I think it is time that you know of the whole story. Knowing what you know now is not enough for you to appreciate to the fullest extent of what the Guardian and his Son have done, and will do, for you."

Selene looked up at him as she grasped more tightly onto his mane, leaning forward so she could hear his every word. They continued to fly through the skies of Sapphira as he began to tell her his tale.

***
Chapter 12
In the Beginning …
***

There were a flock of sea swallows that flew up and around Pegasus as his wings carried them beyond the clouds again. There was a faint light in the sky, from the oncoming dawn of another day.

Selene looked around below her, trying not to feel nervous as she waited for Pegasus to begin his story. She had been so eager to learn all she could about him, but she was beginning to think that maybe she wouldn't be able to handle the truth. All of her assumptions would be gone. She could no longer pretend that certain things were not wrong.

Pegasus glanced back at her, as though he knew her thoughts. He seemed to give her an encouraging, comforting look. "In the beginning, the Guardian dreamed of all this world. He made the wind and the seas, and then the land and the plants. He spoke, and his word was done. Long before the beginning of time, much longer than the ways of man can completely understand, the Guardian had designed this world for the enjoyment and peace of those he loved, and those who loved him. He gave them free will, even though he knew that there would come a time when they would make the wrong choice because of their attraction to the darkness."

When he paused here, Selene asked, "But why would he do that? Why wouldn't he just make us love him back, to keep us from falling ill?" She suddenly recalled that Pegasus had told her before why the Guardian would do such a thing. "All for the sake of true love?"

THE MOONLGIHT PEGASUS

"Yes," Pegasus nodded. "I tell you the truth, love is always choice, Selene. You can choose to be there, or you can run away from it. Either way, the choice is ultimately yours. Love is also practical. It is willing to work and to wait. It is willing to forgive. It is willing to endure to the end of all things. It always hopes for good, always tells the truth in the face of punishment, and it never fails, never has and never will fail. There is no greater way to show your love to someone to give your life for them, to live for them as well as to die for them."

Selene smiled as the warm words washed over her. He was right, she thought.

He continued on. "The Guardian has shown much love to this world, and soon you shall see his greatest demonstration of just how much he loves each person, how much he loves you."

"I can't wait," Selene said excitedly. "I don't really know so much about the Guardian, Pegasus, but I want to learn! What I do know of him, however, is enough to make me love what I do know, and want to know more."

Pegasus smiled. "The Guardian gave this world the free choice to love him," he repeated. "And with the creation of humans into his world, he rejoiced with them, taught them, and showed them the way to live in his world."

"Sapphiran scientific history says that man came out of the seas, millions and millions of years ago," Selene told Pegasus.

"People sometimes look for a way to exclude the possibility of a higher power," Pegasus explained. "There are people who will tell you lies, and show you miracles. But they are not of the Guardian's power."

"You mean like Melantha?"

He nodded. Selene looked away briefly. "I shouldn't have believed her."

Pegasus looked back at her. "Let me continue," he said. "When the Guardian had finished dreaming of this world, with no detail forgotten or left unfinished, he called upon the attendants of his home, Crystallon, to help him watch over it."

"He created Crystallon, too?"

"There are some things you will not understand for now," Pegasus reminded her, "But there is no one, no small thing, whether in Crystallon or locked behind the Four-point Celestial Prison, whether male or female, angel or demon, human or inhumane, nothing at all that will exist outside of the reach of the Father of Crystallon."

"The Guardian?"

"Yes."

"Then why is he called the Guardian and not the Father?" Selene asked.

"The human world has drifted away from him," Pegasus told her. "They prefer to give him a name that is less personal. Father implies that he loves them and looks after them like a father, while what the humans desire is maybe a

THE MOONLGIHT PEGASUS

creator, but not one who would interfere with their lives of sickness."

"Oh," Selene murmured. "I see. That is so sad to hear, if you ask me." She looked away. "I never really had a good father figure. Dorian, my brother, raised me. I would love to have a father, I think. Do you think that I could think of the Guardian as a father?"

He nodded. "He will give you the means by which you will become his eternal child," Pegasus promised.

"Is that his demonstration of love?" Selene asked.

When Pegasus looked at her with a twinkle in his eye, Selene had her answer. She smiled and he continued with his story. "After the humans were created and placed here on Sapphira to live, one of the guards loved the praise that he received from his fellow guards too much. He eventually decided that he deserved to be the only one who should watch over the universe of Sapphira."

"Obsidian?"

"Yes," Pegasus nodded. "Obsidian tried to steal away Sapphira and the rest of the Guardian's creation. He failed, and was banished from Crystallon because of all the damaging characteristics of his heart. He had been pure once, but one stray thought and too much praise had twisted his goodness into something that had never before happened; he sought after the love and attention of others, and by the time that Crystallon had regained peace, there was no repentance in Obsidian. He only wanted revenge."

"Just like Aemon," Selene whispered thoughtfully.

Pegasus paused a moment, before saying, "The son of the rebel has been influenced by his uncle into pursuing revenge. He has been burdened greatly, but his rebellion is still small compared to that of the Ultimate Rebel, Obsidian. That family has been the means by which Obsidian had hoped to corrupt the monarchy."

"Why is the monarchy so important? Is it because our leadership determines the law of the world?"

"Partially," Pegasus explained, "But it is always been one of the greatest wishes for Obsidian to poison the minds of the kings and queens. Some years after the introduction of the Dark Plague into the world of humans, the Guardian still held enough influence in this world to call out his followers. Out of them, he gave them a leader and set him apart, promising that until the end of Sapphira's time, they would hold onto the throne of the world."

"So if the monarchy is corrupt, then there is no hope for the future generations?"

Pegasus nodded. "That is the plan of the dark master," he agreed. "He has been attempting for so many years, that even in his suppressed prison, he has managed to do some damage. Your father was one of his first targets."

"I know my brother has drifted away as well," Selene told him. "I wish he would see what I do. I wish everyone could."

"There will come a day when the people will see, and still not believe," Pegasus told her, his voice heartrending and poignant.

"I think that has to be one of the most fearful things to think of," Selene murmured.

"You fear that when the Guardian's love is revealed, people will be unable to even recognize it, do you?" Pegasus looked back at her. "That is something to be concerned for, yes."

"Oh!" Selene realized. "I'm sorry, please go on with your story."

"Once Obsidian had managed to infect the world with the Dark Plague, the Guardian punished him, by sealing his form away in the Four-point Celestial Prison in the sky, each of the four points to be locked. But one point was left unsealed. It would be sealed by the four kinds of existence: the Guardian, the Spirit, the Rebel, and the Human. The Guardian sealed the one. The Spirit has shut the one. The rebel himself unknowingly sealed his fate with his betrayal; but humans have yet to seal it."

"How are we going to be able to do that?" Selene wondered. "None of us can fly up to the stars."

"You have yet to even begin to comprehend the mysteries of the world beyond this one," Pegasus told her. "But I say to you, Selene, you will live to see that day. The lock needs to be sealed with the blood of a pure soul, but now that Obsidian has escaped, the entire life of the pure one must be given. The darkness shall devour the Pure Light, but in turn the darkness shall be devoured. Both shall die, but one shall live again."

"What exactly do you mean?" Selene asked softly. She felt a tremor in her heart at his words.

"The Seal of Blood cannot be closed with a normal sacrifice, Selene," he looked at her kindly. "For there to be any love in this world, any hope of love at all, the Guardian has made it so that the Seal will be a calling of all people to know his love, for to capture and bind the evil away from this world, a perfect love is required. Perfect love casts out all shadows. The time is swiftly approaching, the time when you and all others will know just how far the Guardian will go in order to make you completely his."

Selene looked around and suddenly realized that he had flown her back to the palace. He leveled himself in the air as she climbed off of him and alighted back on the balcony of the High Tower. When she turned around and looked back at him, she felt a new terror arise within her.

"Pegasus … " she started to say, looking away from him. "I was wondering … am I going to see you again? I know I've asked so many questions tonight, but this is the one I want to know the answer to the most!" she admitted. She fell to her knees. "Obsidian told me once I had betrayed you, and that you could not live in my dreams anymore. I'm scared that I won't see you again, and that I have failed you." She slumped over. "I am not worthy of you."

"Selene, my precious one," Pegasus came down and stood next to her fallen form. "Do you believe in me?"

She looked up at him with a confused look on her face. "Of course I do. I know you have a power in you that I will never be able to have, a power that I will never earn on my own."

"Do you love me?"

"Yes. I love you so much for giving me hope and courage and being so patient with me," Selene confessed, smiling a bit. "I honestly don't know how you can put up with me, but in all the time I've known you, Pegasus, you have never been too busy or too distracted to talk with me, listen to me, and help me. I am so grateful for your loving kindness to me; I think perhaps that is the real reason I love you. I love you, because you love and accept me."

"Do you trust me?"

"I would trust you with all my life," Selene told him. "You have never broken a promise in all the time we've been together. How can I refuse such a wonder? How can I turn away from a trust that I desire so much to be real?" Her tears leaked out of her eyes as she looked down. "And the funny thing is, I'm not sure that I even know who exactly you are, but I have never felt such certainty when I say that you are the essence of dreams."

Pegasus spoke softly to her. "I am the Spirit of the Guardian himself, the Lord of Dreams and Sapphira and Crystallon, Creator of all. Before all, after all, I am. Your transgressions against me and against others have all been forgiven; your heart has repented. I cannot interfere with the consequences of what has passed, but I will be with you through all things."

Selene looked up to him. "But then why did you save Etoileon from Melantha's conditions?"

Pegasus shook his head. "I answered his call, Selene. He knows of me, and of Obsidian. Your friend had protection from the dark master because he trusted in the power of the

Light; and also because he had something from me, that I had given to you."

Selene thought hard and then it hit her. "No! My feather!" she exclaimed. "I gave it to him, but I thought I lost it. Where did it go?"

"It went into his heart, right in his own body," Pegasus told her. "And there it kept him alive from Obsidian's attack. But it would have been useless against the bargain, had Etoileon not have loved you as much as he did." He leaned closer to Selene and said, "Love is one of the greatest gifts that the Guardian has bestowed upon this world, Selene. While it is considered a weak emotion in this human world, it has the power to do the greatest things. Strength comes from the love that is in the heart." She looked away and felt a blush rise up on her cheeks.

She then looked up at Pegasus and gushed, "Thank you. I'm so glad that you are here."

He looked down at her gently. "There will come a time, Selene, that I will not seem so real to you. Please remember our time together, and what I have said to you. For though I will never leave you, I will not always be so physically present to you, even in your dreams."

"You will always be with me," Selene repeated. "But you won't be here?"

"I am as near as a whispered call, always. I live in you, now that you have been called to repentance. But you will not always see me or hear me. I told you this before; I have shown this to you. For even while you suffered, I was carrying you."

Selene nodded, finally realizing what he was telling her. She would always be with him, and he with her, but she would not realize just how much he really was present with her. He would guard her and guide her, and she would look to him for direction and growth.

Pegasus continued, "Like a cloudy veil the Dark Plague shields you from seeing the true glory of the Kingdom of Dreams, leaving you to gaze upon a shadow of a true reality. I tell you, Selene, this world that you know, it is not really real in some ways. It may feel real, but it is not important as far as eternal life goes. It is only in spirit that you leave this world for the afterlife, to Crystallon or to be locked away in the Four-point prison, and so it is in spirit you will hear me. It is the same with the rest of my followers."

"How much longer will you be able to stay with me?" Selene questioned him, a tremor of fear in her voice. She didn't want him to go away so soon.

"For a little while longer," he told her. "War between the Sapphiran loyalties has come, but few will realize that this is the Great Battle, between good and evil in the realm of the greater powers of good and evil, of the Guardian's Son and Obsidian. There has come a fulfillment of time in the world of man." He looked down at her with a sorrowful glance. "There will be many things that trouble you over the next few days," he told her, "But when you mourn for the lost, mourn with hope."

Selene nodded tearfully. She was still having trouble understanding what exactly he was telling her. She knew that he was going to stay with her and still reside in her. She realized that this kind of contradiction would only be true if she was in the presence of the Guardian. An incredulous realization suddenly surged through her, her blood quickening and her breath shortening. She had been in the presence of the Spirit of Crystallon, and he had treated her like a friend, when she deserved so much less. "Oh, Pegasus!" she cried, "I did not realize, I was so blind. You are truly the Spirit of Dreams, and I deserve to die … no, I deserve so much more than death. And yet you have been so kind to me. I have seen the Spirit of Greatness, and I did not know it until now!"

"Selene, my precious one," he said soothingly, "It is time that you learn my real name in this world." She still bowed her head low to the stone floor, her tears steadily flowing away from her eyes.

Suddenly, Selene looked up to see a great light shining as Pegasus began to light up the night, a glowing ball of light encased around him, as the transformation from Crystallon was complete. She shielded her eyes, nearly blinded by the great luminescence. When the light faded, she shook her head to clear her vision, and she saw him.

Dressed in simple white clothes, where her friend at been moments before, there now stood a young man. His hair was white, and his skin was bronzed. He looked to be only a few years older than Etoileon. But his eyes held the same crystal flame in them that she'd come to adore over the last weeks, and she knew it was him. "Pegasus?" she asked with a hint of trepidation in her voice.

He nodded. "This is my human form," he told her. "My father in Crystallon has called me here through the Spirit. We all are the same, but different. My name in this world is not Pegasus."

"Well ... what is your name then?" Selene asked tentatively. "Will you tell me?"

He smiled kindly at her, and she felt her breath rush out. Wow, she thought, he is breathtaking. There was power in him, coursing through his very blood. He took a step toward her and said, "My name is Adamas."

It was then that he reached out with his arms, his arms seeming as wide and as embracing as his wings had been, and he held onto her.

Selene felt the world around her dim as she was captured in his hug. When he let go, nothing seemed quite the same. But he winked at her, and then in the blink of an eye, he vanished in a bubble of light.

"Adamas," she breathed out as she gazed out into space, staring off into the night sky that they had flown through together.

***
Chapter 13
Evil Gathers
***

"Princess," a voice called out to her, as though it was coming from a long way off. She tried to tilt her head to listen more closely. "Princess!" The voice was much more angry and urgent this time. Selene frowned, confused. It was not the voice of Adamas, but someone else that she knew. But who could it be? She wondered. It was then that she noticed that she was still half-asleep.

She tentatively opened her eyes and saw that Aura had returned, and was now looking down on the princess with a mixture of concern and irritation. Seeing that her charge was awake at last, she gave a huff and said, "Well, it's about time! Master Omni will be waiting all day for you if you don't hurry!"

"I have a class today?" Selene asked sleepily, rubbing her eyes as she sat up in bed.

"Yes, His Majesty requested that Master Omni give you a smaller session today, as it looks like the rain will be holding up the battle once more," Aura explained as she, Rosaria, and Chevée were hurrying around to get the princess' clothes and hair supplies all together.

"It's raining?" Selene asked, surprised. "But it was all clear last night," she said. "I thought that the monsoons were about over. Isn't it time for blooming season yet?"

"Apparently not, Your Highness," Aura sniffed.

At her tone, Selene scrutinized her with a peculiar look. Why is Aura so short today? Selene wondered. Is it because I was angry with her before? Looking more closely at Aura's face, Selene would have to guess that not only was Selene the problem, but it had to do with the war, too. Selene sighed and looked away from Aura's face to the rain falling down outside her window. "Aura … I'm sorry for what I said," she apologized. "I have not been so really nice lately, have I? I am grateful for your service, and I do have to respect you for putting up with me sometimes."

Aura looked over and sighed. "I am sorry, too, Your Highness," she said softly. "I have never had a daughter before. I suspect that this is the type of argument we would have, though. Let's just try to put it behind us, okay?" Then she did something that she had never done before. She came over to Selene and gave her a hug.

Selene almost jumped at the surprise embrace, but she put her arms around Aura and said, "See? You did not burst into flames, breaking the traditions."

Aura laughed and let go. She was about to say something, but then her eyes caught sight of the water clock on the shelf by the princess' desk. "Master Omni expects you in fifteen minutes! Hurry!"

Selene nodded and sped up, trying to pull on her skirts as Chevée attempted to brush her wayward morning hair into a presentable fashion.

When Selene arrived in the schoolroom of the palace, out of breath and just barely on time, she saw that Kadrianne, Yana, and Cyerra were already waiting. She smiled at them as she hurriedly took her seat.

Master Omni had an expression of slight annoyance on his face as he looked up at her. "Well, thank you Your Highness, for finally joining us."

"I am not late," Selene insisted. "I am on time."

"A royal who comes in out of breath does not appear to be on time," Master Omni scolded her gently. "But since today's lesson has been insufficiently prepared due to a lack of proper preparation time, I will allow you to be late this once."

Selene looked away and felt like gritting her teeth in anger. Instead, she opened her book and tried to pay attention as Master Omni began to teach. Soon, losing the train of thought about mathematics and political studies, Selene found herself forgetting the trying times of the morning and thinking about Pegasus' new identity of Adamas.

Her eyes glazed over in wonder as she thought about his face. There hadn't been anything so particularly fascinating about it. His eyes had been captivating, it was true, but other than that he had looked like an ordinary man. The pristine white hair and the spotless clothing were a bit odd, but still. There was something so ordinary about him in the midst of all the extraordinary things about him.

She felt a smile grow on her face as she recalled flying with him through the skies of the world. Seeing all of Sapphira convinced her that there was beauty in this torn-apart world. Seeing it with Pegasus had convinced her that in order to see the beauty, all she had to do was look to him.

THE MOONLGIHT PEGASUS

Selene looked back at Master Omni as her classmates around her began to pull out their datasheets to take notes. She jumped out of her reverie and grabbed her own datasheet, grabbing the high-tech pen that went along with the note-taking program. She began to write down what Master Omni was saying, something about mathematical formulas, but then her thoughts wondered away again. She scribbled out a few words, not pertaining to the teacher's lesson at all. Soon, she pulled back from her work and read it over. She had written a poem, it looked like.

Wings of Light
Soar through the Night
The White Moon grins
The adventure begins
As Dreams take Flight.

Selene smiled, her thoughts remaining devoted to her dear friend, who had shown her so much, and had taught her much, that she could not shake him completely from her mind.

*****

There was much drunken laughter and senseless joking in the camp of Obsidian as the human soldiers entertained themselves. Having called his human minions to his side, Obsidian watched and reveled in the rainy celebrations of the rebels and the spirit warriors on his side. He had great cause for rejoicing, even when he was about to head into the greatest battle of all history. He leaned back under the altar that the humans had created to worship the powers of war, strength, and courage. Here he was sheltered from the rain at least; though he could not physically feel the elements of this world, he had to manipulate them so they would accommodate him and his comrades.

Obsidian watched as the men under his control cheerfully drink their ale and moonshine as they twirled around each other, swinging each other around and around. They were laughing too hard to maintain their grips on each other's arms. And the laughter only increased as someone, every so often, went flying straight into something, whether it was the ground, the tents, or another person.

It was as though they were celebrating their victory already, Obsidian thought. With the exception of the watch guards, and the Supreme Command Squad, there were hardly any sober soldiers in the camp that day as they all waited for the rains to disperse.

Soon, he thought, they would have to straighten up. It was a time to sharpen skills, prepare the weapons, and ready the forces.

Sulfas came up to Obsidian and gave him a wrinkled smile, his ghostly face contorted and twisted into a cheerfully frightening expression. "Master," he bowed low, "I see that you have taken your rightful place as you await the beginning of this battle."

"Ah, yes, I have," Obsidian agreed. "It is all so well to be here, Sulfas. I can't remember the last time I had so much fun. Probably the last time I was free of that dreadful prison. When Master of All, I shall lock up all of my enemies in that tiny prison and I will laugh in their faces as they try to break free. But unlike me, they will not manage so well."

"And what of the humans remaining?" Sulfas asked, grinning wickedly. Humans were pointless to his kind, so he was anxious to hear what Obsidian had in mind for them. They were really too much of a nuisance to do much with, other than for entertainment.

"I was thinking of just letting them all die painfully," Obsidian sneered, "but I had another thought first. I want to see them suffer, to see them squirm with pain and fear. Maybe I will allow the demonic beasts to have some fun with them first."

The demonic beasts were huge, scaly creatures with eight legs and a long body. They came in all sorts of monotone colors, but they all had faces that were scrunched together at one end of their bodies. Their snouts were big enough to breathe in an entire human in each nostril, and they had breath that rivaled the fiery burnings of Sapphira's inner core. They had long arms, and short, buzzing wings on their backs. No human could see them, but they frequently visited the bottom of a well or lurked in a forgotten tree stump. They had insatiable appetites for the darkness, and many of Obsidian's spirit followers were even scared of them.

"Oh, Master, truly you are a genius beyond all!" Sulfas exclaimed, shaking slightly with both fear and anticipation in his voice. "I cannot wait for this battle to be won."

Obsidian looked up at the lightning in the sky and closed his eyes. "I can almost see victory now," he said quietly, his mouth already watering for the taste of his foe's death.

"That human that is in charge of all this, Aemon? I think he should be one of the first to go," Sulfas said. "He was careless and caused all the city to hear of our coming."

"True," Obsidian agreed. "But not too soon. Let us save him for afterwards, when you and your friends are kings of this world, and I am its Master."

"Too bad, but I see your point, Master," Sulfas said. "What about that silly woman that you used to corrupt that princess? Can we dispose of her yet?" He looked pleadingly up to Obsidian's face, and said, "We should have a proper sacrifice for this celebration, don't you think? That Seer would make a fine prize our collected troops."

Obsidian thought carefully about Sulfas' suggestion. It was true that he could use a sacrifice, he thought. He waved his hand, and smiled. "Yes, but I think some entertainment with her before we kill her would prove much more gratifying. Let us bring her out here, so both human and demon can enjoy her great pain. I shall call out my servant, Emanon." He turned to Sulfas with a smirk on his face. "How ignorant and foolish some of these humans are, let me tell you. I barely used up any energy convincing some of these imbeciles to join us, even though they are walking into certain death."

"Yes, humans are so unassuming of just how much power we of the spirit world have over them!" Sulfas agreed. "All it takes is the right stream of thought, and we're in. It is so easy to get them thinking exactly what we want them to think. I cannot even count how many relationships, careers, and lives we've ruined since you came here to Sapphira, Obsidian."

"Well, it is somewhat surprising to see how inferior the human mind is," Obsidian agreed in a scathing tone. "Just

THE MOONLGIHT PEGASUS

watch this, as I control my slave, Emanon. He is as eager to have my attention as a silly child."

Emanon had not proved to be hard to control at all. Though he was strong in body, he was weak at heart and in his mind. He wanted revenge, and Obsidian could use that to the advantage of his purpose. And while he could do that with nearly any human, it was somewhat heartening to see someone willingly allow him such control over his thoughts and actions.

At Sulfas' command, the spirits began calling out for a sacrifice. The humans subconsciously began to hunger after blood as well, thanks to the power of the ghostly spirits. Their feelings easily wormed their way into the hearts of men.

Eventually, a soldier came forth. "I have found a traitor in our midst!" he cried out. He pulled out Melantha, pulling at her chair. He seemed to forget that she had been an honored guest at the campsite for the last few days.

"I am no traitor, you buffoon!" Melantha shouted, as the soldiers didn't seem to hear her. Some more of the soldiers came forth and bound and gagged her. With a few quick tugs, they had dragged her to the altar they had built earlier. Emanon, the general of the troops, came forward.

"Men!" he called out. "We have a found a traitor!"

There were several catcalls and shouting from the ranks of the men. Melantha's eyes were wide as she wildly looked around. She was trying desperately to bite away at the gag that had been shoved on her mouth.

Emanon held up his hand to silence the troops. "The great masters of war had always loved the taste of a traitor. They love to see their enemies butchered, until the ground runs red with the blood and the air stinks of killings."

"Yes! Yes!" cries from the soldiers all shouted in agreement. Their leader smirked and held up Melantha by the scruff of her neck, her frail form already squirming and kicking around in his grasp.

"And look!" Emanon shouted. "It is even better for the Masters today! A woman's blood has been very sweet to their lips, and the desire of them we worship desires and deserves nothing less!"

Melantha tried to shriek as the men all began to draw out their swords and began to wave them around.

Obsidian pulled the strings of his puppet decidedly, yet he could not help but feel the excitement of the crowd. They were bloodthirsty for death. He whispered out to Melantha, "You did not manage to corrupt the mind and capture the memories of that boy," he told her. "You might have done your job for me, but it was not good enough to keep you alive."

Melantha tried to reach out to him, as though she knew he was there, watching this scene. She managed to spit out the gag, and gasped out, "Why? Why did you do this to me, Obsidian? I thought we had a deal! It was not my fault that my power was blocked from that wretched boy!"

"We did have a deal, Melantha!" Obsidian cried out, his eyes gleaming in anticipation as the men came closer and closer to her, trying to slice open her body as Emanon hung her in mid-air. "You said that you wanted nothing less than to spend all eternity with me! You gave me your soul the instant that you decided not to kneel down to the one in Crystallon. Since then, your habits and your thoughts have been slowly transformed into the dark deeds I have willed to be done!" Then he laughed, and finally allowed his influenced humans to have their fun with her. His head threw back and laughed harder, as he watched Emanon toss Melantha's wrinkled body into the crowd, his cruel chuckle echoing into the emptiness of the night even as her blood spilt all over the ground and stained it red.

Sulfas beside laughed as well, and it was a long time before Obsidian's close ally wheezed out, "If this is just the death of one, imagine our victory tomorrow."

Obsidian nodded. He cleared his throat and said, "Yes, I do believe that tomorrow we shall see a victory like no other."

"I agree. Such a pity that some of our men will die though. Even if they are humans, they have been somewhat helpful in getting us this far."

Obsidian grinned. "Please tell me you are not serious," he said. "It will be all the better if these men die. We don't want any of the remnant to have the possibility of becoming Believers of Dreams. It is better that they die, and die suffering. So much more will they be prepared for the endless bloodbath that they will be welcomed with in the realm of the Demon Chasers."

"True. This is true."

Then Obsidian's facial expression huffed into almost an angry pout as he said, "I have been waiting for this battle since I had to flee into this world. At last I will have a victory over that hideous one, that … despicable, insufferable Guardian!"

***

It was dark inside his mind.

Etoileon could hear his heart beating softly in the distance, but he wasn't sure which direction it was coming from. He felt surrounded by it, but he didn't think that such a position was possible at this point.

He felt as though he were floating. There was nothing to touch him, and he felt cold. And yet he knew that he would not die. It was as though he was trapped between the world of the living and the world of the dead, and he could not really move in either direction. He was curled up in a ball, his head tucked down on his knees as he just floated there.

There was only a small amount of warmth, and it was coming from a small feather that he held carefully in his hands.

This is so strange, he thought as he allowed the feather to rest on his heart. What am I waiting for? Who am I waiting for? Will anyone save me from this?

Suddenly, there was a sparkle in the corner of his eye.

"Huh?" He opened his eyes and waited. There it was again, the sparkle! So he hadn't been imagining it. He turned his head and felt his mouth open in surprise. "What?"

Before him was a bright burst of sparkles, a small shadow that held no blackness in his mind. There was a stream of bubbling light pouring forth from it and Etoileon finally asked, "What is that?"

A voice called out to him. "Etoileon."

"Hold on!" Etoileon called out. "Who are you?" He thought about trying to move his arms out and almost swim out to meet the glow, but still, he knew he could not move. He was too concerned about losing his bit of warmth, the feather he held tightly to his chest.

"I have many names, young Etoileon. A dear friend of yours, a friend of mine as well, knows me as Pegasus."

"Pegasus?"

"Yes."

"Then you are the one who saved me from the clutches of Obsidian," Etoileon reasoned. "This is your feather."

He could have sworn that he saw a smile in the midst of the light. Was there an actual person there? Etoileon wondered. His eyes squinted and tried to get a clearer picture of the light source. It called out to respond to his observation. "Yes."

"Thank you. There is nothing I desire more in this world than to see the face of the one I love once again," Etoileon admitted.

"I know. But what of the next world?"

"I can't even think of it sometimes. I know about the Guardian," Etoileon said. "And I know of you, his Spirit."

"We watch out for you," Pegasus' voice told him. "We have watched out for you since before you were born, even before your father brought you to the Continent for his rebellion."

"So I am the Son of Ammos?" Etoileon asked. "Surely Obsidian was not serious."

"I tell you the truth. You are the eldest son of Ammos the Rebel, Etoileon, whether you like it or not," Pegasus told him gently. "But the evil of your father was not passed on to you. Hate is something humans learn, and become addicted to. We have called you for a higher purpose in this life than the purpose your father had in mind for you. The day that you arrived from Jewel Island, you were lost in a crowd at Gemstone Oasis. The eclipse of your mind had to take place as well; so with that solar eclipse by Shira, your mind was purified of the dark memories for a time. Obsidian had corrupted your mind even at a small age, but we looked on you with love, and left your memories of your former life behind." There was a softer characteristic in Pegasus' soothing voice as he said, "You have had a hard life, young Etoileon. But I have been there with you all this time, waiting for you to answer our call."

"I want to know you more," Etoileon admitted. He was trying not to cry; his voice remained stoic. "And I know that you must love me. I can trust you. I know that you can help me, and the entire world. I believe in your power, your abilities, and in your love ... I have so for many years, I suspect. But I didn't really see how much I needed it, how

THE MOONLGIHT PEGASUS

much I didn't deserve it, until you saved me from Obsidian's attack on my heart."

***

Selene felt the need to stifle a yawn as she headed down to the Great Hall for the evening meal. She knew that there would be no excusing herself tonight; it was whispered through the halls of the palace that this would be the last meal of the King. Selene couldn't help but feel that these people were too eager to believe such things. Of course, the maids and bellboys probably didn't know what Selene did— she had been guaranteed that the monarchy would hold its throne.

She had changed into a special gown for the occasion. For the dinner, she was resplendent in one of her signature white gowns, with a silver and gold embroidery trim. There was a gold and blue sash crossing over to her left side and pinned. It was a symbol of the Crown, and the members of the family wore it to only the most significant celebratory events. And Selene knew that the day before a Great Battle was considered to be among that list.

She and her handmaidens, all similarly dressed in an overcloak of white velvet and trimmed with golden threadwork, made their way down to the dining hall with an air of solemn acceptance. Though they tried to appear as though they were not troubled and everything was as normal as possible, they were all slightly on edge tonight.

Aura even showed up, her burgundy hair brushed back and piled up high. She was dressed in her own set of ceremonial robes, sewn with fabric colored a shining starlight blue.

Selene sat down in her usual seat, at Dorian's right hand; as the heir apparent, she would hold the throne if he failed to come back for dinner again. She knew from their curious expressions that more than one of the food servers was wondering if they were going to be serving another ruler in the next couple of days.

Dorian entered, dressed not in his ceremonial outfitting but in his wartime apparel. He gave a kingly smile as he entered and sat down, before he turned to Selene and acknowledged her. "Sister," he greeted her in a soft, warm tone. "I am glad that you are so eager to join us tonight."

"Us?"

"Yes, some of the army generals and a few of my troops are going to be coming," Dorian informed her as the water glasses were filled. He suddenly looked over at her and said, "Selene … don't let them see you falter."

"I am in control of myself," Selene assured him. "Just for you." She gave him one of her twinkling smiles and sat back in her chair.

"Good. I'm glad to hear it," Dorian replied. "I was walking around the palace today, overseeing the progress of the work. It has really come along, I must say. If all goes well, it should be completely finished by the time I return from this battle."

"Really? I thought they were close to getting done," Selene laughed. When he caught her eye, she wondered if he was going to scold her for her rather appalling joke. Instead, a moment later, he started to laugh along with her. Nearly everyone watching had to be surprised.

"If it is one thing I wish I could have understood sooner, Sister, that you have taught me, it is that I am too serious sometimes," he said after he had calmed down a bit. "As I was walking to come here, I tried to recall the memories of my youth, and I found that I had very little time for my own enjoyment."

"You are a good king, Dorian," Selene told him, her voice low. "But I would think that you would try to liven up your people as much as you try to improve their financial status conditions."

"Now that will never happen," Dorian joked lightly. "For I pay them too much already."

Soon they were joined by the other men from Dorian's lot of soldiers. Selene smiled at each of them, as they came by and took her hand in greeting. Some of them she could even remember from the days of her childhood. She would never forget Commander Kef, she thought with a small smile. Some of them even brought her small gifts. One gave her a rare coin with her picture on it, from the day of her birth. Another handed her a flower, picked from an area by the sea. Still another gave her a pure white handkerchief, with a tiny emblem of the royal insignia sewn into it. She thanked them and kept them close to her plate all throughout the main course.

The dinner was as lively to be expected; it was not the most joyous occasion to take place within the palace walls, but those that were present saw to keeping the smiles wide and as genuine as they could. Selene hated to hear about the war, but knew that she could not escape it forever. Still, as she listened to the polite talk of weapons and training, she couldn't help but feel helpless. How could she help these men? What could she possibly do for them, these men that were to fight at dawn's breaking? They were already going to lay down their lives for the way of life they had always known. Such a gift could hardly be earned, let alone appreciated to the full extent.

As the time went on, the warriors and the dinner atmosphere seemed to relax, and more and more natural laughter could be heard coming from the tables. Dorian and Selene both gave their share of comments and questions, as they told their stories and listened to others' tales.

It was a surprise then, when the doors to the main hallway burst open and a man dressed with the armor of a general commander, flanked by his troop of guards, came inside with haste.

The man bowed on one knee to Dorian and said, "Your Majesties," he nodded to Selene as well as Dorian, "I am Commander Rosemont, and I have come with grave news."

"Rise, Major General," Dorian gestured kindly. "Please, tell us of the news you have for us." Dorian was focused on Rosemont, but for a flicker of a second, Selene thought that he had looked over in her direction. She wondered if he was thinking of her safety, or if she would be concerned for his.

Rosemont rose. "I have been informed of the moving of the rebel forces outside of the city. Their rainy-day celebrations have stopped, though the rain has not yet let up entirely. But their drunkenness has gone all of a sudden. They are moving at the command of their General, a man named

THE MOONLGIHT PEGASUS

Emanon. Their leader, that detestable rebel, Aemon, is currently in their makeshift battle headquarters, ordering that all the weapons be cleaned and prepared, the swords sharpened and polished to a shine." Rosemont looked up at Dorian eagerly and said, "Just say the word, Majesty, and we could have a hundred missiles launched at their campsite, or anything else that you may want."

"No," Dorian spoke up. "No, we cannot bomb them. They are wise to have moved so close to the city; they know we cannot attack them without the possibility of killing any possible remaining civilians we may not know about. And anyway, it is too wet for the skyfighters to take off, it would be impossible to do any attack run at this point." He looked thoughtful. "This world is unaccustomed to war. We are a peaceful people, and war has never been so attractive that we would fight in the rain. But now, that has to change. I suppose that stepping up prep time now would be a good place to start."

Dorian stood up, and held up a hand to his guests. "We are to move quickly, men," he said. "The time has come to ready ourselves for battle. We fight at dawn, but I tell you the time to get ready and prepare ourselves is now, while the rain is falling. Our enemies are doing such in preparation for us. Let us move out! To the Camp of the Crown!" With this, his held out hand became a fist, and he thrust it out, as though to signify force and strength. The men all rose and began to cheer for the kindness in service and company that had been shown them in the last few hours.

Dorian had pushed past his chair and was heading for the door with his troops behind him when all of a sudden his arm was grabbed out from behind. He turned, surprised, to see his sister hanging onto his arm, trying to follow him. There was an anxious look on her face, as though she was both terrified and curious at the same time. He sighed and halted. "Selene," he started to say, but she cut him off.

"I want to go with you," she pleaded. "Dorian, please. I wish to be with you. I am scared for you. I would feel better if I was near you to watch over you."

He avoided looking into her beseeching eyes, which was probably why he managed to shake her off. "Please, Sister, it is no place for one as lovely as you. Stay in the palace, and wait for my return." For a moment he just stood there, until he saw that her eyes were cast down low. He silently groaned once more, as he was starting to get strange looks from his men. But then he looked down at his sister, who had meant so much to him even from the time when she had just been that little baby curled up in his arms, and he smiled gently. He drew her into a hug, and held her head against his arm as he patted her back. "I will return in a short matter of time," he promised. "Promise me that you will stay here."

"Oh, all right, I will, Dorian," Selene muttered reluctantly, a hint of disappointment in her voice. She waited until he had let her go and gone from the room before she headed off to the front balcony of the palace. She would wait in the palace, but nothing was going to stop her from seeing him off, she decided.

∗∗∗

The time had been quick in passing. The rains had been reduced to a heavy sprinkle by the time evening had given way into early morning.

Selene was exhausted, but she could find no rest. Even with the thought of Pegasus, she knew that there would be little or no sleep at all for her. As she watched Dorian lead the troops and the Fighters out of the palace, she did not wave, or even smile. Letting the rainfall on her stoic face, Selene could not find any words for this time.

She now sat down at her bureau, looking past the reflection in the mirror; she had lost herself to a world of thought. All the wetness had gone from her skin, but the feel of the cold breeze on her cheek had not disappeared. The memory of the icy winds and the drizzle of the rains on her face and her hair only caused a long sigh to escape from her.

So this was the last night of tranquil peace in her city, she thought as she grabbed a nearby cloak. She was restless, even as she looked around her bedchamber. She wanted to go somewhere, do something.

Having no other clear ideas, she decided at length to go and see Etoileon in the medical ward. Who knew if she would get the chance to see him over the next couple of days or not? She'd best go see him now, when she had the chance.

Having dismissed her handmaidens and her governess for the night, Selene made her way silently through the halls of the palace. The unnatural quietness of her home disturbed her, but she made no attempt to make herself feel more at ease; she knew that such attempts would be fruitless in the end.

The medical section of the palace was filled with people, and at the moment, was the only area that was still working hard. Doctors, and nurses could not stop for anything, least of all a war. As she walked down the narrowing hallways,

THE MOONLGIHT PEGASUS

Selene saw many aids running around, preparing rooms for those that were no doubt to be injured in the Great Battle. She gave each of them a small smile as she sauntered on by, but they were so distracted and preoccupied that many of them did not smile or wave back. Several overlooked her presence entirely.

Finding her way to Etoileon's bedside, she gave her first genuine smile since leaving the dinner table. Her unconscious friend was still not awake yet, but they had given him the medications to help with his external wounds. There were only a couple of scratches on his body that had yet to heal completely. His broken bones had been set weeks ago, and were growing once more quite nicely. Recalling how lifeless and beaten he'd looked when she'd first burst into his hospital room in Silverton after the attack, Selene could tell that he would be well enough to begin training once again in only a matter of a few short weeks, if he would only wake up.

"Hi, Etoileon," Selene whispered as she touched his shoulder. "The charts are looking good. It looks like you're almost all better. When we were at Silverton together, you even woke up for a moment. I was so happy about that." She delicately brushed his cheek with her hand. "You don't have a fever anymore, it looks like. You know, the doctors said that they don't really know why you're not awake yet. I have a feeling that only one person I know could tell me, but he can't tell me everything."

She got up and walked to the door, peeking out of the nearby window there. She saw the campfires of Dorian's troops burning, the trail of smoke winding its way up to meet the sky and then dissolve into nothingness. She turned back to Etoileon and sat down once more.

"Dorian's been called off to war," she murmured, not really understanding why she was still talking to him. "I'll bet that you would want to be out there, fighting with him. I know you don't really like him that much, but I do know that you respect him and you would fight to protect me. I know a lot of the soldiers and Fighters are out there. Ronal's out there, too. I wonder if he's thinking of you or Cyerra? I know that he is your best friend since you'd come here … " She gazed at his face, and she suddenly recollected how much Aemon had looked like him.

It was as though she was seeing things clearly for the first time. It was easy to recognize Aemon as Etoileon's younger brother. Selene suddenly wondered if Cyerra was the older or the younger twin. Thinking about the night when she had first met him, Selene found it odd that she did not take to Aemon as much as she had to his other siblings … he was closer to her age than Etoileon was. He and his brother, and even Cyerra when she thought about it, all shared similar features—the same dark hair, the same determination.

Looking down at her friend once more, she took his hand and said, "I found out that your father was Ammos, the rebel of the past, Etoileon. I do want you to know that my feelings are not altered in the slightest for this, because I believe in all the good I've seen come from this. It's hard to be grateful at a time like this, but I am so thankful for you, and that you were given to me. I also know war almost seems to strengthen the instincts in us, the ones that tell us what we believe and why we believe in certain things. And that's good, right? We all need to remember what we believe in a world like this, more than once, probably every day. Even love, we need to remember. If we can't remember it, we could lose it. Sometimes I wish I could remember the good without the bad, but then there is no way to see past both the good and bad, to see the power in the hands of the one who controls it all."

She watched as Etoileon continued to breath in and out. The sight of him at that moment filled Selene with an overwhelming sense of tenderness. There was something about Etoileon, she thought. Something in him, Selene also knew was present in herself; it was the capacity to dream, to hope for a better tomorrow.

She remained there by his side for some hours, talking to him off and on, as though he would awake if he listened to her long enough. She eventually dozed off, slumping over in her chair, still keeping his hand warm in hers.

***

It was hours later when Dorian was finally all prepared for battle. Well, almost prepared.

The storm was over. Dorian looked over his shoulder at the faint tint of morning's arrival on the horizon. He'd spent the night awake, listening to the silence of the approach of death.

There was no hope of seeing this day through without the shedding of blood, he thought as he turned around to face the light fully. He had been unable to rest, because he had been at the mercy of one of his greatest emotions. Relentlessly, he had been bombarded with his fears all night long.

Looking over at the gray sunlight, he had to almost smile. But his smile was stolen away by the cold shiver that had haunted him long before the war had begun. He looked down, away from the sunrise, and slumped down against the window seat of his private chamber. Sighing heavily, he put his head in his hands.

For a while, he let the silence surround him, as he tried to reach out and snatch up some peace, as though he could look up and grasp it in his hands. It did not come to him.

"What will I do, if I can't win today?" he whispered to himself. "What if I am killed? Is Selene ready to be Queen? What if something happens to her? What will I do?" He looked up and sighed again, a stream of seemingly endless questions still echoing in his head. He could find no solution in his mind, or in all of his knowledge. And the only answer that would come into his thoughts was the one that Dorian least wanted to hear. At last he gave in, and allowed that thought to take over his thinking.

Dorian knew that he could no longer deny what he had been denying since Haiasi had died when he was little; there was a higher power in this world. He looked back up to the window and knew that there was somebody working all of this out for the good. There had to be. There was no other way that any of anything could have made any sense. He realized with a stunning clarity that having no purpose in such a meaningless existence, no one would have even thought that there would be a purpose in life if there really weren't. There would be no searching for light if all they had known was darkness.

Dorian fell forward on his hands and knees, and said in a soft voice, "Guardian, I don't really ever talk to you at all. I know that I've been reluctant to believe in you because Haiasi died just when the kingdom needed his help, and I had grown to view him as a father. Losing him meant losing my faith in you. But I do know that you are there. And I know you are here. Please let everything turn out for the good of my kingdom. If you help my forces win today, I will see to becoming more of a devout follower and believer in you. I promise."

With that, Dorian stood up and brushed himself off, and felt a little better already. True, he shouldn't offer an ultimatum to the Guardian, but Dorian was a proud man. He didn't want to fall down on his knees quite so fast. He was still uncertain about many things, and even though he had no control over any of it anymore, he didn't want do anything too drastic. He still doubted whether or not there was a Guardian, but he was bound to find out the truth one way or another. There was hope in that at least, Dorian thought.

As he walked out of the room, the sun could be seen coming up in the sky from behind the horizon. It was unusually bright for a typical sunrise.

***

It was just after the rising of the sun when the armies of the Crown and the Rebels found themselves staring at each other. Dorian and Aemon both held their troops at the ready, their gazes fixed on each other as they waited for the opportune moment to send their troops forward, guns blazing, swords flashing, and fists punching.

The skyfighters were being freshly fueled and towed out of the hanger. There were armored cars and many equipped vehicles at both ends that prepared to be sent into battle.

The troops of the Crown had assembled and waiting a good ways away from the edge of the city, while the army of darkness was spread out among the desert hills. There was an eerie silence that descended on the plains as they waited.

Then Dorian waved his hand, and Aemon pointed forward. The time had come at last. The battle was to begin.

THE MOONLGIHT PEGASUS

***

Chapter 14
The Seal of Blood
***

The day of destiny had arrived at last. The battle that would put all others behind it was underway. Since the Rebels had arrived in the city limits days before, everyone had known this fight would come.

The troops seemed to rush forward together, running at each other, swords blazing, spears thrusting out, and shields held up high. Mostly among the men were the foot soldiers, but there were also a couple of landrovers and other transports on both sides that were advancing. When the warriors collided, the rebels with the soldiers of the Crown, it was almost as if a stampede had run directly into another stampede. A cloud of dust from the desert rose up as the warriors rammed into each other and unleashed the full force of their attacks.

All pilots were ready in the palace hangar, waiting for the signal to be launched. A few were watching the battlefield on the viewscreens by the palace cameras. A small television had also been hooked up, in order for the crew workers to be given the signal to help the pilots get off the launch pad. The television news reporter was a pretty lady in her forties, who was giving the news from a special flight vehicle called a cloudskimmer.

Down on the ground, mines exploded, bombs were thrown and received equally on both sides; the battlefield was soon covered in debris and fallen soldiers. By mid-morning, there were several hundred men in the hospital transports headed to the palace.

Over the explosions and roar of land vehicles, Dorian's voice was heard, directing his troops. High-tech communication systems had allowed him to call out his orders to all of his generals, who would redirect the information to the right parties. Dorian was not fighting with his troops; that would only be called for as a last line of defense. For now, he and his Second Chief Executive Officer Commander Rosemont, who had been a Major General in the time of Dorian's father, King Lukiahs, were stationed at a temporary compound that had been set up in the earliest morning hours by some of his loyal supporters.

Dorian looked at the Computer readout charts and sighed. "Commander, what do you make of this?"

"Tell the northern hook to hold steady, and the western front that they are clear to charge," the Commander advised, studying the telecast satellite readouts. "See, if you do that, you'll have a chance at surrounding the main flagship legions, and attacking from the middle. Once their forces are divided, there'll be an easier battle for us all to fight."

"I see your point," Dorian agreed. He had chosen Commander Rosemont for his knowledge of rebel warfare, and he was glad that the Commander was proving himself and his talents to be most rewarding. Picking up the small microphone that allowed his commands to be broadcasted to all available Crown forces, he commenced the message: "Attention all Generals. Advance the western front, and hold steady the northern hook. Cut through the Rebels at midpoint!"

He was saluted over the radio waves with a "Yes, Sire!" from several of the generals.

THE MOONLGIHT PEGASUS

Dorian relaxed for a moment, waiting for time to tell if he had made the right call on his battlefield positioning. Turning his attention to the live broadcast, he could see many of his men fall along with Aemon's as they shot each other, fought each other with any weapons they could find. It was almost too tragic for him to watch, but he knew that they were all dying for him, and he could not look away.

***

Emanon studied the schematics of the battlefield and looked around at his notes. As he fiddled around with the papers and tried to think of the plan of dealing with the force of the King's army, Obsidian leaned his hand on Emanon's shoulder. Emanon, or anyone else for that matter, could not see Obsidian but he was there to ensure his victory over the Crown and the Guardian, once and for all.

He grinned and whispered softly into Emanon ear, his persistent voice full of passion and well-chosen words. "Go straight on through the troops, and loop around to surround and destroy the parties effectively," Obsidian urged.

Emanon still was looking at his notes, busy looking at figures, numbers, and diagrams. Obsidian sighed and muttered to himself, "Wait for it, wait for it, come on … "

A moment later, he was gratified when Emanon snapped his fingers and looked up to Aemon, who was resting uncomfortable on a chair near the corner of the Headquarters' Tent. "Sire Aemon!" Emanon cried out joyfully, "I have come up with a brilliant plan to counterattack the Crown forces."

"Really? How wonderful," Aemon scoffed. "Tell the generals to go for it, whatever it is."

Emanon studied his nephew with a curious look. "Aren't you feeling well?" he asked. "You do look a bit pale."

Aemon's hands were gripping the chair arms and his whole body seemed to be shaky. "Either I am having second thoughts," he admitted, "Or else I am just getting sick from the putrid smell of blood that's hanging in the air."

"There's no way to tell," Emanon rustled his head affectionately, "But I do agree with you about the blood. Nasty, if you ask me."

"Go get the generals informed," Aemon scowled. "You're wasting time."

"Oh, right. Well, I'll be off then."

***

Selene was not dreaming as she lay there in the hospital room with Etoileon. She was sorely slumped over in her chair with her head propped up on his pillow when she was jostled out of her sleep.

"Huh?" She jumped up, almost falling out of her chair as she looked around to see what had caused her to get up. She was so preoccupied with determining what had awakened her that for the first couple of minutes, she did not notice just how much pain she was in. Selene looked down at Etoileon to see that he had turned around in his bed. Being a bit curious, she studied him a bit closer to see that he was

503

sweating and red in the face. Reaching out, Selene realized that he had a fever all of a sudden.

She frowned, and that was when she came upon her own pain. Her hand flew up to her forehead as she felt a twinge of her nerves. Her head ached, and so did her stomach. Was it like this for Etoileon as well? Selene wondered. She figured that as warm as her head was to the touch, there was little doubt that she had a fever too.

Her hand left her head to lay itself over her heart; it was perhaps in the most pain of all her symptoms. She braced her elbows on her knees and leaned over, crying softly in pain. What had happened to her all of a sudden?

She felt dizzy and suddenly found herself on the floor, on her hands and knees. She sat back on her legs and held her head as her heart began to beat faster. She wept and her hand reached out for the nightstand, in an effort to get herself off the floor. But instead of grabbing onto a secure ledge, Selene felt a hand take hold of hers.

"What?" She gasped, as she looked up to see Adamas standing over her, a kind smile on his face as he knelt down and let her rest her head against him. "What are you doing here?" she whispered.

"I have come to do what needs to be done," he told her gently. "I am going to fulfill the prophecy now. Look at me, Selene."

She gazed up into his eyes with heavy lids. He leaned forward and said, "There is a reason you feel so sick right now," he told her. "It is because there is a part of you that is fighting to take a hold of you; the evil that rests in you is trying to kill you."

"What?" She was tired. "There is an evil power in me, trying to kill me?"

"Yes. To fulfill the prophecy of the Guardian, some part of you must die," Adamas told her. "I want to ask you this. Selene … do you believe in me? Do you believe that I have the power of the Guardian in me, to do what he commands?"

Selene nodded blankly. "Yes," she whispered. "I believe."

"Then you will feel better soon," he promised her, as he picked her up and put her back on her chair. "I must go now. The time has come for the people of this world to see me, to hear my voice."

"Okay," Selene murmured listlessly. She was not feeling well at all. Beside her, in the bed, Etoileon was tossing and turning restlessly in his deep sleep.

***

There was a calling on the wind.

It came suddenly, almost too quietly. But Obsidian heard it. One moment he was triumphing in glory at filtering out Emanon's decisions and polluting his mind with evil schemes, and the next the hair on the back of his neck was tingling, and the air all around him had changed from smelling like blood to rose petals.

There was no other explanation for it. He had arrived. The one that Obsidian despised and hated the most, he had

505

come. He forgot his purpose in Aemon's tent and hurried outside, in order to get his troops ready for the first great battle of eternity.

As Obsidian came outside, the sunlight seemed to dull almost. There was a great shining light coming from the entrance to the palace that was shimmering with an amount of light that made the sun look dark in comparison. Of course, Obsidian knew that the silly humans could not see the light as he could, but there was only one way to kill the light. He had to get his ghostly crew together to contaminate the minds of the soldiers, to convince them to kill.

Obsidian watched detestably as his greatest foe descended down the steps of the palace, walked down the hills of the Table, and headed for the battlefield. He was clothed in a pristine white outfit, which Obsidian longed to see covered in blood. Eyeing this, his mouth seemed to grow even hungrier for his victory.

"All right, spirits of war!" he yelled, his voice calling out to all the ghostly spirits of his demonic army. "Come to me, for the moment has arrived, where the Son of Crystallon shall die!"

***

As Selene felt her head start to clear up just a bit, a nurse came rushing in. "Oh, Princess!" she bowed as Selene looked up at her. "I'm so sorry to disturb you, I wasn't aware that you were in here."

"What's wrong?" Selene asked in a hushed voice.

"I just saw the warning light go off in the doctor's lounge," the nurse explained. "Our patient is not doing very well, is he?"

"Etoileon? No," Selene shook her head weakly. "I'm not feeling so well either. Adamas … " she trailed off, letting her sentence go as she slumped over. "Where is Adamas?" she asked.

"What? Who? Who are you talking about, Your Highness?"

"Adamas! Where did he go?"

"I'm sorry, Your Highness, I do not know who you mean," the nurse explained patiently as she started to gather up Etoileon's medication. "I'm only in charge of this young man for now. I'll try to look up your friend in a moment or two when I'm finished here, all right?"

Before Selene could shake her head and try to explain to this nurse just who it was that she wanted to see, the doors to Etoileon's room burst open and Cyerra came bustling in. "Your Highness!" she said, her voice clearly telling anyone who heard her that she was quite relieved to see Selene alive. "There you are! We have been looking everywhere for you! The battle has turned bad, you must come and watch!" Cyerra took hold of Selene's wrist and pulled on her gently. "Come quickly!"

Selene was still in half of a daze as she allowed herself to be escorted out of the room. "Is Etoileon going to be alright?" she asked the nurse on her way through the door.

The nurse gave her a reassuring look and said, "I'm doing my best," she said. "I'm sure that we can take care of him."

"Etoileon!" Selene called out as Cyerra hurried her along. Selene felt sick as she was led down the hallway. Ahead of her, Cyerra was talking about the battle and how Dorian had to lead his reserves into the fight now, that it was that bad. Selene could not concentrate on what her friend was saying; the words of Adamas kept coming back to her, his promises of the monarchy being maintained, and that he would be with her no matter what.

She was just going to tell Cyerra that she was not feeling so well when they arrived at the front balcony; Selene was practically pushed through the doors and shuffled away to the edge, in order that she is able to get the best look at the scene many yards away, down below the edge of the Table.

All of a sudden, her eyes caught sight of a speck of light. Her eyes widened. Any thought she might've had before was gone as she gasped.

***

Etoileon continued tossing and turning in his bed, as his heart was racing, his fever causing him to sweat. The nurses and doctors of the palace were all confused as to why it was happening, exactly, because it had just started up so suddenly. They began to grow scared; it was rumored how much the princess cared for her darling protector. Their story was practically legend. Soon, the medical staff had run out of options, until one of them suggested calling Dr. Hamersley.

A few moments later, a viewscreen was connected and Dr. Hamersley careworn face was on the receiving end.

"So you say that he is experiencing unusual symptoms?" he asked. Taking a handkerchief out of his pocket, he thought carefully as the doctors responded to his questions and provided him with the necessary and available information.

After a moment of thought, the old doctor smiled gently. "I think that he will be fine," he said. His gaze drifted off to the ceiling as he considered it all. "But I wonder what it means … "

The Diamond City medical staff thanked him for his time as the viewscreen went blank. Back at Silverton, Dr. Hamersley nodded. "I wonder what the Guardian is up to, with that young man being so torn apart … hmmm. I will check in on him later, I suppose."

Back in his room, Etoileon continued to get worse.

***

The rebels attacked fiercely, driving hard into the soldiers of the Crown. The monarchy's forces were driven back, back, and back, until they were all at the area near the Gemstone Oasis. Dorian had grown restless, and left his command center to begin leading the troops himself. He figured that his warriors would be cheered to see their leader be among those who were fighting.

Stepping out onto the field, the rebels were shuffling off the legions of the Crown and separating them.

Among those who were surrounded by rebels, Ronal fought with his weapons as skillfully as he could. As he watched another rebel soldier go down by his hand, he almost had to give a grimy smile; he envied Etoileon. War was not fun, as it had been in class. Here, if he lost, he lost his life.

Ronal recalled his training techniques as he gradually becomes more and more surrounded. Keep balanced. Remain focused. Change direction. Surprise them. Watch all sides. Don't waste necessary energy. As he concentrated on surviving and just getting this day over with, Ronal remained determined to see this day through until the end, even if that meant his end.

Finally, he managed to get away from all of his enemies. As the final one in his area was cut down by his sword, Ronal looked over the top of the small hill he found himself on. He was near the palace. He could almost make out the tiny figures standing on the front balcony from here.

He turned and wiped the small trickle of blood off of his face, and was about to head for a more rebel-congested area when he noticed a man in the crowd. "What?" he squinted at the far-off figure.

There was a man, dressed in plain white clothes, with bright white hair and eyes that could be seen sparkling all the way over to where Ronal was standing. He was not holding a weapon, nor was he fighting at all. On the contrary, he was kneeling down and comforting the people he was talking to. It looked like he was a healer of some sort, but what caught Ronal's attention and held it for a long moment was that this strange man was healing both the rebels and the Crown's forces.

"What's he doing?" Ronal whispered out loud. He felt like maybe he should go over and see what he was up to. If there were a traitor who was helping out the rebels, the Crown would see to it that they would deal with him.

***

"Adamas!" Selene gasped, half in horror, half in relief. She had found him, yes, but he was walking through the middle of the battlefield as mildly as walking through a clear, green meadow. Selene was shocked and felt her jaw drop open as she saw that he was stopping every now and then to the fallen soldiers crying out in pain and torment.

"What is it, Selene?" Cyerra asked. Around her, the other handmaidens gathered and began to look at the princess with strange, unreadable expressions on their faces. They were no doubt taking in her flushed cheeks and shaking hands, wondering if she was getting sick by all this violence.

"Do you need help, Your Highness?" Aura asked, as she too turned away from the battle to study Selene's unhealthy features.

Selene shook her head and said with a weary voice, "Please, no." She then dropped down the ground, clutching her heart. Her eyes went blurry, and she dropped her gaze down to the ground as she tried to stay focused.

When she looked up, she saw that all of her attendants had come close, some kneeling beside her and trying to support her as she sat there. Selene looked past them all, through the bars of the balcony fence, to catch sight of her beloved Adamas as he continued walking through the crowds of soldiers. "Adamas," she whispered softly. She looked up to Kadrianne, Cyerra, and her other companions. "Adamas is the Light," she said, as though she was realizing this for the first time. Suddenly, all the memories and words of what Pegasus had said to her were making sense. "Adamas is the Light," she repeated.

The words caused strength, little as it was, to set fire to the desire of her heart. "I need to go to him!" she announced. Immediately, she struggled to get to her feet once more.

"Selene, you can't go down there!" Cyerra objected, grabbing Selene's wrist, trying to stop her. "There's a battle going on! You could be killed!"

"No! I won't be," Selene told her. "I must go to Adamas. He has taught me so much, Cyerra. And I believe in him. He can save us all, I know it. He won't let me fall." With that, she tugged free of Cyerra's hold and, still feeling a bit dizzy, headed for the palace exit.

Reaching the outside of the palace, as she had done several years ago for the Islanders' Reception, Selene began to run unsteadily, in order to catch up with Adamas. She had much trouble, though, due to the uneven ground; however, what her biggest obstacle were her eyes. They were blinded with tears.

***

The battle parted as Adamas made his way through the many soldiers. Some glanced at him and paid him no mind as other more dangerous enemies came up. Others just ignored him, letting him pass through. He was ordinarily extraordinary, and when it came down to it, he did not appear to be harmful. So for a while they just let him pass through.

Trouble started brewing, however, the moment Adamas began to tend to the wounded, talking with them. Those he sat with and saved watched him walk away with a new glimmer in their tearful, grateful eyes. Those he passed grew more and more annoyed, but still they let him pass.

Selene was breathing hard as she ran to catch up to him. She could not see him as well as she had been able to from the palace, but the healed warriors were kind enough to point her along the way. The forces of the Crown and the rebel warriors alike, who had talked with Adamas, friend and foe, all of those that had experienced the gracious healing of the kind man had experienced a love that transformed them. And the princess could see it, written on their faces, shining in their eyes.

Selene doubled over as her stomach cramped. She tried to catch her breath. She had been trying too hard too soon, she thought. She did not think it was wise for her to be about running around outside, let alone on a day of war, with her kind of ill symptoms. But she could not defer herself. There was a desperation sinking in, a hunger that would captivate her completely. She longed to be with Adamas; she should be with Adamas. There was a voice in her heart that would not be quelled, telling her to hurry to him.

He was almost to the middle of the battlefield when Selene looked up. She had glanced over at Adamas' spotless figure, just in time to see a man, middle-aged, with slightly graying black hair and fierce blue-green eyes start to head towards Adamas with a demonic look in his eye.

***

513

THE MOONLGIHT PEGASUS

"At last! At last!" Obsidian delighted, his hands rubbing together eagerly. "So, the Light has made himself visible to the humans, has he? This is excellent, very, very good for us!"

With Emanon in tow, Obsidian and his followers started to corrupt the thinking of the fighting men. While the soldiers parted at Adamas' approach still, they were hateful and despised him in their hearts. Poisoned against him, they glared at him with hard, degusted looks.

Selene started to walk toward him still, her steps halted by the raging crowds. As Adamas continued to show his kindness on the people around him, even in the face of their resentment, she threaded her way through the crowds, trying to get closer to him.

Cyerra and Kadrianne were following the princess, looking for her familiar form in the crowds of fighting.

Cyerra was just about to give up when she spotted Selene's dark blonde hair. "Look! Over there!" She cried out happily. "Let's go, Kadrianne! We have to help her!"

"I agree," Kadrianne nodded, flinching as a warrior almost knocked into her. "I can't see why the princess would insist upon coming out here, to this dreadful place."

"Maybe she wanted to say something to that Adamas person," Cyerra shrugged. "It has to be pretty important, anyway. I can't see why she has to be with him now, of all times."

They continued to struggle within the crowds as they slowly made their way to the princess.

***

Adamas halted in his footsteps, stopping in his tracks. By this time, there were people all around who were calling out to him, shouting names and obscene phrases at him. Calling him a demon, a traitor, and much, much worse, he simply looked at them and gave a knowing, sad look.

Then he held out his arms, opening them wide. He held out his arms, making his body resemble a fork in the road. He called out, despite all the angry yelling and incessant cruelty by the people, both monarch supporters and rebellion members, "For so loved is this world, and so despised is the darkness, that I have come. I have come to release the Pure Light!" His voice would not have carried very far, had he been just a human. But his voice seemed to whisper his words of love into the very hearts of every person on the planet, echoing out into the far reaches of space and time, never ceasing to be said even as he himself was silent.

Emanon was within easy reach of Adamas by this time. Now ceasing his chance to be a hero in the eyes of his friends and soldiers, he took out his sword. There was a small reflection of sunlight that gleamed from the sharp edge.

Selene had been hurrying towards Adamas, until he had called out his words. They had caused her to falter, to pause in her determination. Now as she watched, with wide, staring eyes, she saw the powerful warrior of the rebels prepare the deathblow to Adamas' body.

And there stood her friend, her beloved Adamas, telling his would-be killer of love. Selene could not seem to turn her head away from what was happening before her. She began to scream and she doubled over, as she felt the nausea start to

THE MOONLGIHT PEGASUS

take over her. She weakly looked up once more, to see that her beloved friend was on the ground, Emanon's sword waved high, covered in a thick red color of blood. For a moment, she tried to see if Adamas had escaped Emanon's blow; for a flicker of a second, his eyes caught hers. Then Selene felt dizzier than ever, and she fainted.

***

As Selene fell into a deep sleep, across the distance and inside the palace, Etoileon suddenly jolted out of his coma. He looked around the room and tried to recall where he had been before he'd blacked out.

When he came up with nothing, he looked around. Looking at a chart on the nightstand table beside his bed, Etoileon discovered that he was in the Diamond City Medical Ward, and he had been in a coma since the aerial attack on Diamond City a couple of months ago.

"A couple of months!" Etoileon read and reread the date on the chart again and again, trying to remain calm. "How could this have happened?" he looked out his small window in the room and saw a small section of the battlefield. "What is happening?"

Then he remembered his dreams, and the Pegasus. "I wonder what he meant, telling me all that," Etoileon murmured thoughtfully. He tried to get up out of bed and managed, not without some struggle. The floor felt cold on his feet, and he almost had to lie down again as he grew dizzy.

His door opened up and a nurse came in, one who had a large, charming smile. She looked down at Etoileon and said,

THE MOONLGIHT PEGASUS

"Oh, this is wonderful news! The princess will be so glad to hear that you're awake."

"Selene?"

"Yes, Her Highness. Now, if you would be so kind to just relax here and lie down again, I will go inform them at the desk –"

"Where is she?"

The nurse pursed her lips in a slightly annoyed manner. "Beg pardon?" she asked.

"Where is Selene?" he asked again. "I need to see her, now."

"I'm sorry, Sir, but she had to leave about an hour ago," the nurse replied. "But I'm sure she'll be back as soon as she can, she's almost always in here."

"Where did she go?"

"I do believe that she was called away to watch the battle on the front balcony," the nurse said flippantly as she gathered up his chart and tried to straighten up his bed somewhat. She gestured to him to get back on the bed and lie down, but he didn't budge. "I need to go to her."

"No, you're not well enough," the nurse protested, but it was too late. With the will of a Fighter, Etoileon yanked out the food tube and medicine bag from his skin, grimacing a bit at the pain, and got up. "Stop it!" the nurse was desperate.

"I'm sorry, but I have to go," Etoileon told her, walking unsteadily out of the door. He headed in the direction of the palace's main entrance, leaving an irked nurse behind. "I have to go to Selene."

He'd been watching over her for years. He knew when she needed him. And she needed him now.

***

Adamas fell to the ground, bleeding severely. The blood went everywhere on the ground, splattering even those far away as others followed the suit of the rebel leader and began to puncture Adamas' once-spotless body. Selene was even speckled with his blood, as Adamas continued to live, wounded countless time, on the ground. Each new injury he received was celebrated, both by rebel and Crown fighter alike.

Cyerra and Kadrianne both watched the scene with tears in their eyes, Kadrianne with her hand held over her mouth in shock. They hurried towards where their princess laid, unconscious and blissfully unaware of the gory bloodbath that was taking place. Kadrianne took hold of Selene's knees, and Cyerra clasped onto the princess' shoulders. They started to head back to the palace, trying fiercely not to cry.

***

Etoileon went out to meet them, his legs sore and his body weak. He could barely walk straight and he felt lightheaded. But he could not shake this feeling that he was needed. So he continued on, drudging his feet in the muddy, blood-soaked ground. His eyes widened in shock as he looked around and found that his home had been turned upside down while he'd been asleep.

He had gone to find Selene on the front balcony, or at least in the general area, only to discover Aura was weeping uncontrollably. Once she had seen him, she blurted out the whole story as to where Selene had gone.

"And we couldn't stop her!" Aura had cried, grabbing onto his shoulders and nearly shaking him, as her eyes were wide and full of tears. He shuddered as he recalled how she had nearly bowled him over, racing to him to cry on his shoulder. Aura had barely noticed that he had awakened.

Now, as he walked down the path of war, in search of his princess, he looked around to see that there was a bit of a riot going on some yards away. Hurrying over as fast as he could without losing his ability to stand up, Etoileon was paying too much attention to his destination to see what was right in front of his path.

He tripped over a person and landed in the mud. Etoileon groaned as he pushed himself out of the dirty mush, and spit out some mud that had flown into his mouth. Brushing himself off, he turned to apologize to the one he had tripped over. Only to see his brother's face staring back at him. Pegasus had told Etoileon that he was Ammos' son. That meant that Etoileon and Aemon were brothers.

"Aemon!" Etoileon shouted, half in surprise, half in controlled disgust.

"You!" Aemon was struggling to get untangled from Etoileon's legs. "You mind moving?" he shoved at Etoileon unsuccessfully.

"I'm sorry," Etoileon apologized. He quickly got up and reached his hand down. "Let me help you, brother."

Aemon grabbed his hand and stood up. "What do you mean, 'brother'?" he spat. "You are my enemy. Let me go." For by now Etoileon had taken a hold of Aemon's wrist.

"Listen to me," Etoileon said. "I am a son of the rebel Ammos. He is my father. I was here with him before, during the first rebellion nearly two decades ago. I got separated from the soldiers."

"You're lying," Aemon scoffed. "What evidence could you have anyway?"

"Well, we look somewhat alike," Etoileon muttered. "And I have the word of the Truth. That's all I can give you now." There it was again. The call that Selene was in danger. He had to go. "Look, we'll catch up on family history later, but I would not lie about such a thing. I have to find someone."

As Etoileon went away, Aemon felt a deep chasm open up in his heart. There was something familiar about him, Aemon thought. But was he really his brother? Would he want such a person for a brother? He could not answer these questions just yet. But somewhere deep inside him, he knew that Etoileon was telling the truth, despite all his logic and reasoning, and hopes, he had to be telling the truth.

Etoileon walked at a somewhat faster pace as he neared the midline of the battlefield. Everyone appeared to be a standstill, as it was just a bunch of guys in the middle, huddled in a circle. Looking closely, a smile jumped to his face as he spotted two handmaidens heading toward the palace together.

"Cyerra," he called out, for the moment forgetting that she was a sibling of his as well, and hurried over. He was just about to ask them if they had found Selene when he saw that they were carrying her limp body in their hands. His throat dried up and he had a hard time finding his voice as he managed to ask, "Is she … ?"

Cyerra shook her head. "No, she's just fainted," she explained. "We're headed back to the palace," she told him, much to his relief.

"Good. Let's get her to the hospital," he suggested.

All of a sudden, it happened. A great Light soared up from the middle of the battlefield, as at last Adamas is proclaimed dead by the close-up witnesses.

Etoileon and the group and all people stepped back as the Light blasted out from Adamas, casting a glow on everything.

The dark spirits tried to flee, but they found that they could not move. Adamas' body glowed, and his blood shone luminously, almost seeming to dazzle throughout the entire world, making every human radiate a white glow.

Then the darkness overtook the sun; an eclipse completely blocked the bright sunlight that had pierced the morning and noontime sky. The stars twinkled one last time and then faded into the black night.

Etoileon hurried Cyerra and Kadrianne along, leading them through the world of shadows as they all headed for the palace once more.

***

Everyone screamed as the world was suddenly encompassed by a darkness that they had never known before. Children could be heard whimpering, and even adults were nervous and shaking unsteadily.

The skies went dark, darker than ever before. Not a single star was seen in the atmosphere as the land was eclipsed. Lightning and thunder laced through the sky; the world saw little but shadows. There was only one light remaining. Everyone, human and spirit alike, was still.

The darkness gathered around where Adamas' body lay. Even as he laid on the ground, covered in his own blood, and torn apart by the human's treatment, The Pure Light, as it died, shone brighter than ever. The Light seemed to reach up forever, as though it were going straight up into Crystallon. Some would say later that it almost appeared that the Light was pouring down from Crystallon, rather than bursting out from Sapphira.

All of sudden Obsidian and the evil spirits felt as though they were being swept up in a great whirlwind. "No! No! What is going on?!" Obsidian yelled as he tried to grab a hold of something that would keep him anchored to Sapphira. "No! Curse you, Adamas!" he cried out into the eternal darkness, screaming out painfully as he was tossed about in the wind of the great force pulling him. He slipped away into a pile of demons and evil spirits, and the Dark Plague remnants, as their dark luminance began to dissolve into the

Pure Light and disappear into the only place where there were no shadows to be found.

When all the darkness had been absorbed, it was quiet. The Light remained, glowing softer and softer. Adamas' body suddenly began to disappear. And just like that, he was gone.

Then all at once, the Light departed from the humans and faded into the night sky, leaving the humans on Sapphira to look up at the sky in reverence, speechless and amazed.

THE MOONLGIHT PEGASUS

***

Chapter 15
The Pure Light Rekindled, Love Revealed!
***

It was three days later.

The world was still consumed by darkness, as all of humanity watched with wide eyes and fear for some kind of sign. For long hours, there had been no light at all in any part of the world. The people of Sapphira had lived the few last days in nothing but the shadows of black and blue hues, and the few bonfires that had been lit.

The people could see only shapes, but they could not make out the distinct characteristics of people more than a couple of feet away, and even then they had to study the features most carefully. The whole world was possessed by a frightening overcast.

Those who were on the battlefield mostly stood around or sat down, remaining where they were. A few panicked and tried to find someone that could help them. They could not find within themselves the power to move or to say much of anything. Some were weeping; some were shocked. Others were rendered speechless as they continued to stare at the black sky. Only a small percentage was running around in fear, shouting and calling out for light and for help. They all seemed to be waiting, but for what, no one was quite certain.

Those who were inside the palace never left the sight of a window, all of their attention turning up to the sky every so often. They were waiting too.

Etoileon remained by Selene's side, as she lay on one of the makeshift cots. He kept a watch on the room's television, which was running a report on the battlefield zone and the affect it was having on the rest of the world. Far as he could tell, no one had been able to do much other than wait for whatever it was they were waiting for. He understood how they felt. He was feeling restless himself. Looking down at the sleeping princess, he almost envied how she had fallen unconscious during this time; there would be no sense of discontent and impatience for her. He wondered if she was waiting in her dreams the way that the rest of the world was.

His gaze turned to focus once more one the black overcast outside. Still nothing, he observed disappointedly.

Others remained with him in the room, but there was complete silence. Not one of them spoke a word, even to ask how Selene was, or what was going to happen. Aura had curled up in a corner, hugging her knees her chest as she slowly rocked back and forth against the wall. There was a haunting look on her face that clearly told observers that she was thinking deep thoughts, mulling over her life. Cyerra would pace around every so often, her eyes darting from the battlefield, to the sky, to the others in the room. Kadrianne just sat in a chair, a hand over her mouth and her eyes focused on the scene outside the castle keep. Every so often, tears for no apparent reason would stream out of her eyes. But still, no one said anything at all.

The world seemed to be at a standstill, no one really knowing what to do. They were all just waiting, waiting to see if the sun would shine again.

Etoileon looked down at Selene, and then up to the sky. He had to wonder if these were the days that night was

THE MOONLGIHT PEGASUS

allowed to reign over, and if the light of day would ever break free once more.

***

Dorian felt his knees shake as he collapsed to the ground, too amazed and weary to have any strength to stand anymore. When the night had blanketed over them, just at high noon a few days ago, he'd stumbled around, his eyes unable to see anything, and unable to look away from the sky. He'd been there for so long, he didn't really know how much time had passed since the light had disappeared. He slumped over onto his hands and knees, and felt as though his eyes were still glued to the sky, where the light had been.

All around him, his troops had slowly started to get up and walk around tentatively. It had been about three days, he knew. Surely by now, the men were starting to believe that the sun had been extinguished. There were fires that were burning low light, but it did little to enlighten the battlefield area. Soldiers everywhere gathered around the small circles of light, starting to talk in hushed whispers.

Dorian felt a hand on his shoulder and he jumped. "What is it? Who's there?" he asked, squinting to see if he could make out the features of the man before him. No luck.

"Sorry, I can't see," the other one explained. "I'm having trouble moving around."

"Oh. Well, there is not enough light to clearly see anywhere," Dorian reasoned lightly. "It's okay."

"Thanks. Mind if I stay here a while? I'm trying to find some of my legions, but I don't seem to be having any luck, unfortunately."

Dorian suddenly wondered if he knew this person he was talking to. His voice was that of a younger man, but not too much younger. It sounded familiar. Before Dorian could inquire as to just exactly who it was that he was talking to, the man started to break down.

"What am I saying?" he muttered spitefully, as his voice cracked. "This battle is no longer important. Striving to win this battle means nothing anymore. Survival is the main thing now, along with making sure that family is okay. What was I thinking?"

"It's okay," Dorian said, trying to scoot over. He was still turning his attention every now and then to the sky, but he tried to reach out to his fellow warrior in the darkness. It was almost comforting to him, to try and help this young soldier. "You're right about family. I have to let my sister know I'm alright, now that you mention it."

"I saw my brother just a while ago," the man told him, his voice still sad. "I thought he was dead! But he was alive, and he'd been here, all this time. But now, to see him, and the sun burning out … it's … it's just too much. All of my energy seems to be gone, and I can no longer stand the thought of fighting. I just want to go home and live in peace."

"Maybe the light being gone for now is a good thing, in that way," Dorian whispered softly. "Maybe it was meant to teach us to value such … such a resource. We've gotten so used to it being there, we don't stop to remember it as much as we should. Just like … world cooperation, I imagine. Does that make sense to you?”

“Yeah, it does,” the young man said, his voice clearing up a bit. Dorian heard him clear his throat and sniffle. After a long moment of silence, the man spoke up again. “I wish the world could live in peace, and be prosperous.”

“We can,” Dorian assured him. “We just have to work together. Maybe if the light comes back, or we can figure out a way to talk with the rebels, this battle won’t be necessary anymore.”

“The rebels? You want to talk with the rebels?”

“Yeah. Why? What’s wrong?”

“I thought we were the rebels,” the young man explained.

“I’m fighting for the Crown,” Dorian smiled. “Are you a rebel?”

“Yes … you wouldn’t happen to be King Dorian, would you?” there was small chuckle in the man’s throat as he asked the question.

Dorian cocked his eyebrow, a little suspicious. “Yes, as a matter of fact, I am.” His tone was uneven and clearly wary.

The man laughed softly, the first laughter to be heard since the days of night had begun. “I thought I recognized your voice,” he said. “It’s Aemon.”

Dorian started to laugh as well now. “How ironic.”

They both laughed harder, Dorian reaching out and wrapping his arm around Aemon's shoulders like a brother. "What do you say that we organize some peace talks, Sir Aemon. I know that you want peace, and I long for it too. I cannot fix you up with Selene though, just warning you."

Aemon smiled. "That's too bad," he said. "But I understand now. I can see things more the way that they are and the way that they were meant to be. It is too coincidental that I can see nothing at all."

Dorian looked back up at the sky and nodded, understanding. "I can't see anything either," he told Aemon, "But for some reason, I can see more than I could before."

"You as well? I keep watching to see if the light will come back."

"I have a feeling it will," Dorian told him. "We have just got to keep looking, I guess. That's all."

"Well, even if it doesn't, let's get those peace talks arranged soon," Aemon said. "I am beginning to worry about my family."

"Me too," Dorian told him. "Me too." After a moment, he noticed that another campfire had been lit just a few yards away. Clapping his hand on Aemon's shoulder once more, he looked over to the firelight and said, "Let's go sit over there. It's time that we talked some more about peace. We've held it off for this long."

"I agree," Aemon admitted. "But you may not like some of our terms."

"You will not like some of ours."

"Well … "

"It's worth it though, right?" Dorian asked.

"Yeah, it sure is. All right, Let's go," Aemon said, standing up and reaching down to help Dorian pick himself up off the ground.

***

A little while later, Aemon listened to the other soldiers talk quietly as he sat by the king. He was not feeling like himself at all, he realized. Normally, he was filled with irritation or anger, but now … now all he felt was more relaxed and confused.

He had met his brother, his older brother. His older brother who had supposedly been dead all these years had come back to life almost. What was Aemon supposed to feel? How could he even begin to talk about what he wasn't sure of? He looked up at the sky, hoping that Cyerra was doing okay. He wanted to tell her later that their brother was alive, that Etoileon was their brother. Aemon frowned as he recalled the first time that he met with Etoileon before, at the Islanders' Reception. He looked down with embarrassment and shame as he remembered his heavy-handed tactics and how he used his unearned superiority to push people around. It had been effective, yes, but could he really be proud of himself now?

He also felt sad that he had been deprived of his brother when their father Ammos had died. Etoileon had only been about three or four years old, but Aemon suddenly wondered

530

THE MOONLGIHT PEGASUS

if it would have been Etoileon who would have taken the burden of responsibility of him and Cyerra, rather than Aemon.

Aemon decided that when the peace talks were over, he would conduct some more talks of a similar nature with Etoileon and Cyerra. He felt no desire for war now. Being alone in the dark of the unending night had made him want to have his friends and family more than he wanted world domination and power. Power might put him over everyone else, but it would also set him apart from anyone else as well. Being caught up in obscurity of the shadowed world made him realize that he did not want that at all.

He had wanted to make the world befriend him, to be ruled by him. Now he wanted to befriend the world, to live in harmony. If he ruled the world, the problems he would burden would wear him down. But if he had friends, he would be much happier sharing his burdens with them and helping them carrying theirs. Individually, he was not strong enough to carry the world. But with others, they could all share and share in the joyous times together while they did.

He was just starting to smile a bit when he felt someone shift beside him. Aemon looked over at him, and saw that all the men in the circle were staring up at the sky. When he looked up, he noticed that there was a stream of lightning flickering. Thunder came with it, and the wind began to blow harder.

The fires went out, and the lighting grew brighter and brighter, the thunder boomed and the wind raged. The soldiers could be more and more clearly seen as the light began to flash out an intense power.

"What's going on?" he murmured in wonder, as he found himself once more spellbound. He and the rest of the soldiers stood up, and held their hands to block the wind from their faces as they just stood there, watching and waiting to see if this is what they had been waiting for.

***

Etoileon remained calm as the lightning and thunder broke through the blackness. Gradually, the stars were coming back into view, some of them twinkling brighter than ever it seemed. He looked up just in time to see the traces of lightning in the sky, and he almost had to smile as the others in the room, save for Selene, jumped and flinched at the sudden activity.

He looked down at Selene briefly, wanting to pay as much attention to the storm outside as he could. He saw that Selene had no change in her conditions at all. Relieved, he allowed himself to watch the scene before him.

At this point, he thought, I know everything's going to be okay. He had witnessed the power of the Guardian before in his dreams. That being stated, he had no doubt that these past three days of darkness would bring about some desired circumstance. His gray eyes absorbed the scene before him, his mind puzzled by how even though he knew that everything was under control, he was too amazed; he was too astounded for words.

As he watched, all of a sudden, a small bubble of light appeared from the high clouds. The light shone with a brilliant and stunning power; all around, it was almost as though music of deliverance could be heard.

"Hallelujah," he whispered, smiling. He was about to get up and go over to the window for as close of a look as possible when his hand was squeezed. Looking down, he saw that Selene was beginning to stir slightly. Thank goodness, he thought, relieved. *Everything's okay going to be okay now. I'm sure of it.*

***

The Light poured out from the sky, the small bubble growing larger and larger. The sky's lights began to glow brightly again, as though someone had flipped the switch on the circuit breaker of the stars. The clouds broke apart, and daylight arrived, the sun shimmering a brilliant golden yellow; all of the gray sunrises would be no more, as a renewed light gave a chance at life back to the people of Sapphira.

As the bubble of light came closer to the ground, it was apparent to everyone that someone was inside of it. When the man in the bubble finally touched down on the sandy surface, there was no sound to be heard.

Adamas had come back. The Seal of Blood had been given, and Obsidian, along with his forces, had been taken away from Sapphira to be securely locked in the Celestial Prison. The four points in the sky burned with a scorching blaze, as they had been rekindled as well by the surge of fresh hope.

Dorian and Aemon stared at Adamas, unable to speak.

Ronal dropped his sword and fell to his knees, weeping for joy as the sun rose and the light shone.

THE MOONLGIHT PEGASUS

Cyerra and Kadrianne hugged each other tightly and danced in a circle as they praised the return of the Light.

Aura got up from her crouched position and fell against the window glass, unexplainably drawn to the scene outside. She felt her cheeks grow wet as she gazed upon the beauty of the enlightened world.

All around the battlefield, soldiers and warriors everywhere started to remove their helmets out of respect. Some fell to their knees, crying at their unworthiness and shame. They had been the ones that had killed this man, after all! Surely he had been the greatest man who ever lived, who would ever live.

The news reporter didn't seem to notice that her camera had been broken, as she stared at the man who had come from the sky.

Etoileon leaned forward to gaze out the window, smiling and laughing as tears come to his eyes. Everything felt so wonderful, so perfect, he thought. It was as if the world had been gifted with another chance for living.

For that small moment in time, it was as if the whole world was watching this take place before them, all of them united in a new way with each other.

"My beloved Adamas … he's come back."

"Huh?" Etoileon looked down to see Selene, just as her eyes opened up slowly. She gave a small sigh, and then a tiny smile came to her face.

Etoileon squeezed her hand in his, nodding. "Yes, he did! Look!" he agreed with her as he pointed out the window at the great center of light. The Pure Light had been set aflame once more, all darkness was banished to the other side of the Celestial Prison. And it was all to be believed, thanks to the man who had brought back the light.

"Hope has been reborn, the cure has been delivered," Selene whispered softly, as she turned her head to look out the window at the golden sunshine of dawn. Etoileon nodded again. She smiled brightly, staring at the battlefield for a long moment before she turned her attention away from it.

She realized for the first time that it was Etoileon who held her hand. Her eyes widened and then filled more happy tears. "Etoileon," she whispered in awe. "Is it really you?" He nodded and her face lit up. "I can't believe that you're here! I'm so glad that you're awake at last." A few of her tears trickled down her cheek as she tried to sit up the whole way.

Kadrianne caught Cyerra's attention and they sneaked out of the room, Aura in tow. The governess was about to object, but Kadrianne interrupted her arguments. "Lady Aura," Kadrianne urged, "Please come. These two need their privacy. It is a special moment."

"But I want to stay, in case something should happen," Aura argued. "What if something bad should occur?"

"We'll take our chances," Cyerra promised. "Besides, I want to leave anyway. I want to go and see if Ronal is all right on the battlefield. It might take me awhile to locate him, and I want to get started. I worry for him."

The handmaidens soon managed to assure Aura that all would be well; Aura half-heartedly agreed, and left Etoileon and Selene alone to themselves in the wardroom.

Etoileon waited until the others were out of the room before he spoke again. He smiled kindly down at Selene before he spoke. He started to help her straighten up in her bed as he went on. "I've been here with you, in this room, for the past three days," he told her. "I woke up when the darkness was finally taken away from me." He told her of how the Guardian must have protected him all through his coma, and how Pegasus had even talked to him.

Selene nodded. The smile went away from her face as she said, "Etoileon, I found out who your parents were."

"I know now, too, who they are," he nodded solemnly. He drew back a bit from her and said, "I guess this means that we … " He couldn't bring himself to say it.

"We what?" Selene asked. "I don't have any problem with it, Etoileon. It makes no difference to me who your parents were. I wanted you to know that." She looked away for a moment, wondering if she should tell him now how she felt about him. Before she could say anything, he came closer to her and began to speak.

"Selene," he whispered softly, "There is something I want to tell you." He brought her hand to his cheek and said the words that Selene had wanted to hear from him since they'd met. "I love you … I'm in love with you." His face turned a dark red as he looked away, too flustered to look at her. He glanced back up at her almost shyly and added, "I've wanted to tell you that for a long time."

Selene felt her heart nearly burst with happiness. "Oh, Etoileon … " she pulled herself up and placed her cheek on his. "I love you, too, and I think I have since we met, all those years ago. I know what real love is now, thanks to Adamas, and I know that I love you so much. There are many that I love and many ways that I love. But the love I feel for you, I have never felt for another." Tears blurred over her vision at this point, as he wrapped his arms around her tightly and held her.

For a long time the two of them remained that way, as they watched the renewed light of the sunrise course its way across the skies.

Selene rested comfortably against Etoileon, and wondered all of sudden if she would get to see Adamas again. She knew he was back, but she did not know when or if he was going to come and see her again. She hoped that he would, and that he would come soon.

***

Dorian sighed as he leaned against the doorpost outside of Selene's hospital room. He listened as she told Etoileon of her love for him at last. He sighed softly. No one else was really around, but he did not want to alert either Selene or her protector to his presence outside of the room. It was a tender moment for the two of them, and it was only proper that it remain private between the two of them.

He'd said good-bye for now to Aemon when the light had come. Dawn had broken, and Dorian had thought of his family first. After all, Selene was all he had. He had to be concerned for her. Before Aemon had gone, as he had wanted to check up on his uncle Emanon and start heading

537

for home, they had made arrangements for Aemon to come back to the city for peace talks in the next week or so. There would have to be several repairs done on Diamond City before he arrived again, Dorian realized. If peace was to come at last, then it was only proper that the only previous known requirement for it be done with splendor beyond all previous celebrations—his sister's wedding.

Now as Dorian stood with his weight against the doorpost, he watched as Etoileon embraced his sister. He sighed, knowing that the time has come to allow Selene to get married to the one that she really wanted.

He silently turned and walked away with his gaze down on the floor, his resolution solid, his heart knowing that he had known that the day would come when he would have had to face this. From the first glance, he recalled disgustedly, the love between his sister and the boy had been evident. Still, it was remorseful for him—this boy, of all of them. The son of the rebel Ammos, who grew up poor and struggled for survival on the streets ... this was the one she chose? Out of all the representatives, and all of their sons, this was the one? He supposed that Selene had always been unique.

"Your Majesty?" a tentative voice called out to him from down the hallway. Dorian looked up and brightened immediately, to find his sister's handmaiden, Yana, hurrying toward him.

"Yana," he smiled.

She came up to him with tears in her eyes and wrapped her arms around him in a fleeting hug. "Your Majesty, did you see it? Wasn't the sunrise just miraculously glorious today?"

"Are you all right?" he asked as she smiled up at him while she was crying.

"Yes, I am just … I am just so happy! Look at what the light has brought—what could be better?"

"I can't think of a lot of things, that's for sure," he remarked, smiling happily along with her. "Would you like to walk with me for a while?"

Yana blushed. "Okay. Where're you going?"

"I don't know yet," he admitted with a grin. "But it might take a while."

***

Chapter 16
The Hardest Challenge Yet
***

It was some time later when Adamas arrived back at the Palace, still in his human form. He walked through the open doors and started to head towards the main courtyard. Once he got there, he smiled, finding Selene there. All throughout the courtyard, other people, whether members of the High Court, or lowly maids or footmen, adult or mere child, all of them were strewn about that evening. They were enjoying the luxury of the prolonged daylight, playing and relaxing all around the courtyard. But when Adamas came inside, they all stopped what they were doing and looked up, as though they were aware that they were so close to a miracle.

Selene felt her breath catch in her throat as she saw Adamas coming toward her. She was so distracted; she didn't even notice that all in the courtyard ceased their activity. The children were the only exception; they scurried over to Adamas, trying to get his attention. Adamas grinned and knelt down, eager to play and talk with them. Selene watched the heart-warming scene as Adamas stood and placed his hand on the head of each child, whispering something she could not hear to each one of them. When the children had all nodded and hurried off to continue their game, Adamas looked up and smiled at her.

For a moment she almost thought she was dreaming again, but she had known that he would come to her in time. Selene had desired to see him once more, and as the happiness began to overflow in her heart, she ran for him, his arms opening up wide as she approached him.

He caught her up in his embrace and picked her up, as though she were a child. She laughed, and he laughed with her. For a long moment Selene looked into his face and smiled. But as he set her down, she could see that there were scars all over his body, even a few on the contours of his face.

"Are you all right?" she asked him quietly.

He nodded. "I am fine. All that has needed to be done for now, has been done," he smiled at her. "The Plague can no longer harm you. You have been given the cure, and the rest of the world has been given the cure as well." He looked past her, as though he knew there were other eyes watching him beyond the palace doors. Then he said in a low voice, "I have come to say good-bye. My time here has come to a close. It is time for me to leave this world."

"Are you going back to Crystallon?" Selene asked quietly, her voice quivering slightly. She was full of sadness at his leaving.

"Yes." He nodded. "I am being called back home."

She peeked a look up at him as she asked, "Will I ever see you again?"

He smiled. "The cure," he told her, "has also opened up the way to Crystallon, to those who would believe in his work and realize their need for it. I know that you are sad, but you know that I have a great work to do there." When she looked up at him questioningly, as though she wasn't entirely sure as to what he was talking about, he nodded and said, "I am going to Crystallon to make sure that your home there is all ready for you when you come."

"Are there a lot of homes that you have to make ready?" He nodded happily at her to answer her question. Then he looked back over at the palace entrance to the courtyard, to see a familiar face looking at him with wonderment.

Etoileon came up to stand beside Selene. "Adamas," he bowed deeply. His eyes were slightly glistening as he said in a wavering voice, "Thank you." He'd choked the words out awkwardly; he had meant to say farewell, but Etoileon was having trouble talking at all. He hoped that Adamas knew what was in his heart and in his mind. Looking into the twinkling eyes of the man before him, Etoileon gave a small smile. So he did know, Etoileon thought.

"My children," Adamas smiled at them. "It is good for you to love one another. Be kind to each other, and always remember to forgive each other. Life is too short here on Sapphira for it to be caught up in anger and resentment." At his words, he placed a hand on each of their heads gently, and said, "I would like to congratulate you on your wedding," he said, his eyes twinkling. "I pray that you both would enjoy a life of meaning before the eyes of this world. I ask that you both be blessed in the Guardian's name."

Selene and Etoileon both blushed. They had yet to tell the others about their engagement. They had decided to wait to tell anyone else, for there would have to be time to begin making the terms of peace with the rebels.

"Adamas," Etoileon asked all of a sudden, with renewed energy and curiosity. "There was something I was wondering about."

"What is it?" Adamas asked, although from the look in his crystal eyes, Etoileon knew that Adamas already knew what his question would be.

"I wanted to know what happened to Obsidian," Etoileon confessed.

"Ah, yes," Adamas shook his head. "Sadly, the fate of Obsidian and his followers is not a happy one. Obsidian has been sent to the Four-point Celestial Prison once more. He and his followers are trapped there, never to break free into this world again. His time will come for judgment, and then his fate, shall be sealed. He power here has been broken, but it will be some time before he is completely forgotten. With the passing of his shadow and all the memories of his trouble, the days of Eternal Sunrise can begin at last."

As he finished saying this, another person came up from behind the courtyard entrance to talk with Adamas. It was Dorian. Selene was surprised to see Yana was only a few steps behind him as he approached them.

Dorian came up to Adamas, surprising everyone by embracing the man who had shown such goodness to him and his world. He whispered something into Adamas' ear, and Adamas nodded at Dorian.

Dorian let him go and dropped to his knees in reverence. "I would like to confess both my faith and my blindness, Sir. I have failed to see the true light of this world, until I saw it in your heart. I know now that I can trust you, but I do not know if I shall always do so. Please, help me with my unbelief!" Dorian looked up at the man before him with a pained expression. Selene could hardly believe that this was her brother, so incredible was this joy in her.

"Haiasi is in good hands, young king," Adamas told him softly. "He had not been lying to you when he told you of my Power. I should like very much to see you and him together one day, beyond the gates of Crystallon." Adamas reached down and touched his shoulder. "Have faith. Haiasi is not the only one in good hands, my child. You have begun the peace talks with Aemon already, I know. My heart rejoices, seeing this world once again begin to rebuild." Dorian looked up at him, transfixed. He was about to ask Adamas how he'd known about the encounter with Aemon, but he could not find his voice.

Adamas seemed to know his question and squeezed his shoulder affectionately, reassuringly. He paused for a moment, and then added, "These sorrowful days of war have shattered the peace, and broken it. However, you have begun to realize, because it has been broken, how precious and glorious it is." Dorian nodded, and then stepped back as Adamas switched his attention on Selene once more.

He turned to Selene and pulled her close to his heart as he knelt down, enfolded her in his arms. "My precious one," he whispered as he held her close, "You must continue to dream beautiful dreams. Let your dreams, and your love, shine in this world, so that I may shine with them, and that others will see me through you."

"This is the hardest thing that I have had to do, Adamas," Selene whispered, clutching his shirt with her fingers. "I don't want to say good-bye to you. I still want to see you … I love you."

"Selene … I will never leave you," he whispered back. "Look at this world around you, and you will see the wonders that have been made by the power in me." He put his cheek against hers as he told her, "Listen carefully to me. I will be with you always. When the wind whistles through the air, know it is I, calling out to you. When the trees bloom, know it is I, showing you the beauty of this life … and when the flowers blossom, and the rains fall, I am. When the moon glimmers and the sun shines, I am. Even as the shadows wait, and danger lurks, I am. Through all seasons, I will not change; I will not falter in keeping you and this world in my hands. Before all things and after all things, I am. You shall see me again, at the end of this age, and for all infinite times beyond. I love you so much, my precious, precious child." At his parting words, he let her go. Before he pulled completely away, he passed her a familiar book.

Selene stared. It was the little silver book she'd borrowed from Dorian's library. She precariously held it in her hands, letting it fall open to the last pages of it. She felt a gasp of surprise escape her as she saw that the entire book had been magically filled with new chapters of text. Looking back up at Adamas' face, he winked at her, letting her silently know that he wanted her to keep reading and pass his message along to others.

Selene nodded and cried silently as she felt him step back from her, clutching the book to her chest. She wished that he could stay with her on Sapphira. She wanted to tell him that, but it was then that he started glowing, surrounding by a blazing white light. All of a sudden, the clouds opened up, a great light shining through, creating a halo effect. And then Adamas looked up, and he began to smile. A moment later, in a whisper of feathered wings, he was soaring into the sky, into the clouds. Selene watched him disappear as the clouds once more came together and the light faded away.

THE MOONLGIHT PEGASUS

As she turned back from watching Adamas' ascent into the clouds, Etoileon patted her shoulder, trying to comfort her. "Are you all right?" he asked. "We all love him, Selene. He and his works and his love will not be forgotten. I can't even really begin to thank him for what he's done for me."

Selene looked up with him with a small smile. "I mourn his loss here on Sapphira knowing that I will see him again," she told him. "But until I do see him, I have him in my heart, not as a memory, but as a living, speaking presence." She glanced over at Etoileon shyly. "And I am glad to that you are here with me … my love." Then he wrapped his arm around her shoulders and they headed inside together. All the courtyard remained speechless and unmoving, many of them still watching the skyline to see the small glimmer that sparkled brightly on the horizon, before it faded away into the sunset.

***

Adamas looked down below at Sapphira and smiled warmly. "There had been a time in the world of humans when all dreams had been beautiful, but the darkness began to corrupt them. Now justice has been done. Our promise to the humans of Sapphira has been kept. Now that the darkness has been crushed, and the cure for the plague has been delivered, the dreams of the world will become even more beautiful." And as he watched, so it was.

ABOUT THE AUTHOR

C. S. Johnson, formerly C. A. Sabol, is the author of several young adult novels, including *The Starlight Chronicles* series and the *Once Upon a Princess* saga. With a gift of sarcasm and an apologetic heart, she currently lives in Atlanta with her family.

Please read on for a sample chapter of her next work, *Slumbering,* Book 1 of *The Starlight Chronicles,* an epic fantasy adventure of Hamilton Dinger, a fallen star who, until a meteorite comes crashing into his city, lives a typical, charmed teenage life.

☼<u>Prologue</u>☼

Wingdinger

The winter winds were cold and harsh, laced with particles of hail and snow. The air was dry, the sun was hidden, and just from looking at it, I could tell Lake Erie was in the freezing temperatures. Apollo City, along with the rest of northern Ohio, was covered in a blanket of gray-white snow/slush, but city inhabitants were still trying to go about their humdrum lives with as little interruption as possible.

I had to say, the *eela*–shadow monster–rampaging all around the city wasn't helping. Not in the least, if you can imagine it.

As he hovered in midair, today's choice of monster giggled as he began attacking another crowd of people. He'd shown up a few times this past week, but this was the first time I'd gotten close to killing him without breaking curfew or skipping class.

Not that I minded those things, of course; I just minded getting in trouble for them.

This sinister-ling is Daikan. He "specializes" in cruel humor, but not the kind I liked or agreed with; some of his material was *really* lame. He'd been nicknamed "The Jester" by the local press–anything to get sales up without infringing on Batman's legal rights.

While he certainly reminded me of some kind of ex-con carny, there was a villainous twinkle in his eye all too reminiscent of his many demon predecessors and his fearless Sinister leaders. Not to mention there was the same cringeworthy delusion laced in his laughter.

"Ha-ha, I told you I would have you rolling with delight sooner or later," he cried out mockingly, as indeed, the crowds rolled over, though in pain. "Daikan always has a trick up his sleeve!"

Who knew who he thought he was talking to? Some people were snapping photos, while others were running away screaming. All of this chaos was happening, of course, while I was attempting to destroy him.

Unfortunately, this was nothing out of the ordinary. It was just a typical day in the life of the superhero known as "Wingdinger." Me.

My fingers gave an icy snap as I clenched my fists. "No one's laughing down here," I retorted angrily.

Just so you know, I had a right to be angry. Daikan had largely ignored me that day, and only paid attention long enough to laugh at me. And the third-person referencing was getting old.

THE MOONLGIHT PEGASUS

"Watch your back, kid," Elysian, my 'pet' changeling dragon, thundered at me. He swooped down and curled protectively around me just as Daikan slashed out his attack.

Spindles of power trickled through the sky, swiping over us as Elysian ducked and I dodged. There was a sudden break as a nearby tree fell and I heard something—probably one of the old city park buildings—crumbling behind us.

"Let's go," Elysian muttered, ignoring the glare I gave him as he leaned down to let me up on his back. But I, reluctantly, climbed on.

I wanted nothing more than to fly on my own two, irritatingly useless, wings.

As Elysian took flight, the wind bit at my face, matching the bite in my tone. "Look who's laughing now!" I taunted, tackling the laughing trickster right out of the air. Something puffy and squishy gooped through my gloves as I no doubt punched through a lung, knocking the wind (along with other substances) out of his body.

"Ugh . . . Gross." If only this were some kind of video game, I thought ruefully. *Me and the guys would be all over it.*

A split second later, I was thrust back into the fight. Several events blurred through my mind as the end of the battle became eminent.

THE MOONLGIHT PEGASUS

Flinging the pus off of my fist . . .

Elysian's brief approving sneer . . .

Falling from the sky, tangled up with the demon body . . .

Ah, the welcoming rush of adrenaline. I'd become quite the junkie since this started.

I grinned to myself; I liked this trick. After several months of fighting off these monsters, I no longer had any fear of falling.

Instead of freaking out like I used to, I clawed my way on top of the evil *eela,* forcing my enemy down even more as we slammed into the ground.

Jolted but still standing, I victoriously wiped a spray of dirt off my face. "Ha. Got you!"

Elysian scuttled over. "Good work, kid. I think we did great today."

We? I rolled my eyes.

Elysian had spoken too soon. Or maybe he jinxed me, because the next moment, Daikan propelled himself upright with more power than I'd thought possible, sending me flying back through the air as he roared angrily.

"Ugh." Of all the places to land, it had to be in a pile of frozen dog poo. "Gross." *Why did I always have to land in something completely revolting!?*

I looked up just in time to see Elysian unleash an attack of his own. My dragon's bright celestial fire hit its mark as I stood up and hurriedly tried to clean myself up. Being a superhero is not as important as looking like one, in my opinion.

"Augh!" Daikan cried, the dragon fire slowly eating away at his colorful clothes and sizzling into his wrinkly skin. Even though I love my barbeque, it was a gruesome sight to watch him flap and burn. It probably would have been more enjoyable if he was dead. And plucked.

"Finish him!" Elysian called out.

"No one defeats me," I murmured, letting myself smile. *For once, we are going to get along all right without—*

A hot, blazing arrow of light suddenly soared out of nowhere. It struck the demonic creature in the head, unleashing a small bright explosion and bombing out brain residue. I jumped back and shielded my face. When I peeked over seconds later, Daikan was gone.

I groaned. I'd thought too soon. *She's here.*

Following the trajectory of the arrow, I looked up. And there she was.

Starry Knight, skillfully perched in the trees, was looking down on me, both literally and figuratively. "I told you to stay away from this business," she called out in a disdainful greeting, as was her per usual.

"Oh, just go away," I stomped my way over to my supposed counterpart. "I was doing just fine until you showed up. *And* I was here earlier than you."

"You are just getting in the way." She glared back, tightening her lips, obviously irritated. "It's clear you still don't know much about them, do you, *Wingdinger?*"

Since I was pretty sure she was making fun of me in addition to insulting me, I bit my bottom lip angrily, raging for blood. That was just like her, to disregard all the effort I'd espoused trying to learn more about the different demons suddenly plaguing our city. Believe me, between the *eelas,* the *tenwaleisks,* and the *bakreels,* I'd had more than enough outer dimensional demon instruction.

But even so, who really cared if I didn't know that much yet? All I really knew for sure was that I had to fight them. That had to count for a lot of it—over half of it, really. And the other stuff, well, I'd figure it out later, when I had the time and/or the inkling to care.

Starry Knight jumped down from the heights of the tree. "Since you appeared, I've had to save you more than I've had to defeat these monsters."

"Hey! I got some of them, too," I protested. *At least two or three, anyway…out of ten or twenty or….Who's really counting here anyway?* "I would've had this one, too, if you hadn't stolen my chance!"

"I'm sure you wouldn't have been able to do it," Starry Knight replied, waving me off. "You haven't gotten any stronger in the last weeks. Just give up and leave this to me. Oh, and I'd make sure to get some stain remover on your clothes." She flipped her long hair over her shoulder as she flew off, her stark white wings beating gracefully.

The embarrassment and anger burned, steaming hot. I thrust my fingers into my "wingdings" at the sides of my head, for which I was named, and tried not to scream. The pain of tearing at my feather-crown didn't help.

And neither did Elysian, of course. (He never does, trust me.)

"Don't worry about it, kid," Elysian told me. "You'll get the next one."

"What if I don't?" I asked sharply. "What then?"

"Don't do this to yourself. She's not worth it." Elysian transformed. As a changeling dragon, he had the ability to transform into any reptile, but he often just pushed back his wings, sucked in his big dragon belly, and shrunk down to the size of a small lizard or chameleon. It was handy for travel purposes, I had to admit, but more often than not it meant he was nearby. And I didn't really like that.

"Maybe she's got a point. *She* seems to be getting more powerful." I doubted Elysian had noticed the increasingly intensity of Starry Knight's arrows in the past few weeks. I also doubted he'd be able to refrain from making some irritating comment about it if I brought it up.

"Don't forget, we don't know much about her," Elysian said, honestly and exasperatedly. "If you really think she's getting more powerful, it could be a problem."

"You think?" I snorted distastefully. *Of course she is a problem! She'd been a problem since day one.* "How do you think she does it? How do you think I can get strong enough to beat her?"

"You're supposed to be concerned with the demons, so forget about her."

"You know what I mean."

"Frankly, I agree with Starry Knight; it's your own fault you're not getting more powerful."

"What!?" My gaze blazed into Elysian's, and he (wisely) shuffled back a few feet. "How can you say that? You're the one who's supposed to be 'mentoring me' or however you put it."

"I cannot teach a know-it-all!" Elysian glared at me. "Look, you've accepted the task of defending the world from the Sinisters, but you're still as arrogant and self-centered as you always were. And it's worse since you've been given the powers. You still rely mostly on your guesswork to get the job done."

I motioned to my uniform, my transformed self. "Selfish? How can you say that? Do you know what I'd rather be doing while I'm fighting off the forces supposedly bent on destroying the world? I could be on a date!"

"Ugh! You make this so hard!" Elysian sighed. "You might have accepted the truth of your destiny, but there's more to believing than just accepting the truth. There's more to power than strength."

I muttered out a string of curses, probably a bit too loudly for Elysian's taste, because he chastised me a moment later. "You could get a lot more powerful if you just had some self-control."

"What do you mean by that?"

"I mean you can't even control your language, or your anger, or your actions. No wonder the demons laugh at you! You'll bring about your own destruction soon enough with that kind of attitude."

Before I could respond, the large clock tower in the city chimed, and I had another reason to hate my life. "Aw, great! It's after my curfew! Cheryl and Mark are going to be upset. Can tonight get any worse?"

Almost as soon as the words were out of my mouth, Elysian piped up with a half-smug, "Here comes the press."

And right on cue, a desperate-looking journalist hopped out of some nearby bushes, followed by several more of his camera-wielding posse. "Excuse me, Mr. Wingdinger, sir, can we get a couple of questions?"

I immediately ran for cover.

"Stop! We need to talk to you!"

"Come back, we want to make a deal! You'll be rich!"

"Where's Starry Knight?"

Anyone could tell you I was not usually shy in front of the camera. But the last thing I wanted was to do was to take financial responsibility for all the buildings and vehicles and other stuff that had been damaged in the previous months, and the blame for all of the people I hadn't saved. These were the major reasons I ran away from the press and cringed at the thought of interviews.

"Come on, Elysian," I said quietly. "Fly us away from these soul-suckers."

Elysian cocked an eyebrow at the irony and smothered a laugh, transforming once more. Moments later, we were safe and out of reach.

How did this all happen? How did I manage to get drafted into humanity's last defense in an interdimensional war?

Truth be told, I wasn't exactly sure how it all began. All I really know was the day this mess exploded into my life, I'd been thinking about much more important matters. Much, much more important matters…

560

THE MOONLGIHT PEGASUS

Thank you for reading! Please leave a review and check out

more of my books!

THE MOONLGIHT PEGASUS